The
TOWN
That
FORGOT
How to
BREATHE

The
TOWN
That
FORGOT
How to
BREATHE

A NOVEL BY
KENNETH J. HARVEY

Secker & Warburg
LONDON

Published by Secker & Warburg 2004

First published in Canada in 2003 by Raincoast Books

2 4 6 8 10 9 7 5 3 1

Copyright © Island Horse Productions Ltd. 2003

Kenneth J. Harvey has asserted his right under the Copyright, Designs
and Patents Act 1988 to be identified as the author of this work

First published in Great Britain in 2004 by
Secker & Warburg
Random House, 20 Vauxhall Bridge Road,
London SW1V 2SA

Random House Australia (Pty) Limited
20 Alfred Street, Milsons Point, Sydney,
New South Wales 2061, Australia

Random House New Zealand Limited
18 Poland Road, Glenfield,
Auckland 10, New Zealand

Random House (Pty) Limited
Endulini, 5A Jubilee Road, Parktown 2193, South Africa

The Random House Group Limited Reg. No. 954009
www.randomhouse.co.uk

A CIP catalogue record for this book
is available from the British Library

ISBN 0 436 20638 2

Papers used by Random House are natural,
recyclable products made from wood grown in sustainable forests;
the manufacturing processes conform to the environmental
regulations of the country of origin

Printed and bound in Great Britain by Clays Ltd, St Ives Plc

For Emma Sarah, Katherine Alexandra and Jordan Rowe

"... Thy way is in the sea,
and thy path in the great waters,
and thy footsteps are not known."

— *77th Psalm*

CONTENTS

THURSDAY

Miss Eileen Laracy shuffled up the higher road in search of lilacs to lay atop her white chenille bedspread. With the summer sun fierce above her, detailing each line in the wrinkled mapwork of her face, she sang lamentfully:

"Bury me not in da deep deep sea,
where da cold dark waves will swallow me,
where nar light shalt break t'roo da darkenin' waves,
'n nar sunbeam find me silent grave."

Smacking her toothless gums together as if savouring the splendour of the afternoon air, she paused to fish an embroidered handkerchief from the sleeve of her green and white striped dress. The bandana that covered her head and was tied beneath her chin was green with a multitude of tiny blue polka dots. She blew her bulbous nose vigorously, then wiped at it several times before shoving the handkerchief back up her sleeve.

"A girl on shore many tear will shed,
fer 'im who lies on da ocean bed,
where above 'is heart da whale will hiss,
'n 'is pallid lips da fish will kiss."

A lone fly buzzed close to her ear, interrupting her mournful dirge. "G'way fly, ya bloody nuisance," she griped, raising her tiny hand to swat it away. "Lest ye be a lilac fairy in disguise." She chuckled, then, humming, continued on her search.

With their brief lives and breathtaking fragrance, lilacs were considered a favourite of the spirits. Miss Laracy welcomed visitors from the afterlife, unlike those who feared them as navigators assigned to carry off kindred souls. She devoted an inordinate amount of time to attempting to lure them into her home, offering sanctuary through her faithful presence.

From the time she was a little girl, up until middle age, she had been spoken to from beyond the grave. But shortly after her forty-fourth birthday, on a brisk fall night, the spirits no longer came to simply sit and stare while she lay in bed, or pass plain comment back and forth. Their serene fellowship had been a comfort. Miss Laracy had spoken with them of infants and of generations passed on, for they were filled with the blaze of their ancestors, lineage that trailed after them like a stream of unbroken dusty amber. This was the endowment when a mortal passed on — the melding of energy of familial souls linking the chain of spirits, augmenting their command of the absolute.

Through years of births and deaths, Miss Laracy had grown accustomed to endings and beginnings. Yet she had never stopped missing the spirits. Even the mysterious presence of an unheld candle gleam travelling up the stairs was a hopeful sign she longed to witness once more. Eileen Laracy sighed as she proceeded up the higher road, her doll-size feet disrupting pebbles. A child screamed shrilly at play and a lawnmower droned down by Codger's Lane. She glanced north, to her left, the land sloping toward the old square houses arced around glistening Bareneed cove. It was a fine day, yet she felt out of sorts. A hollow spot had ached in her heart since that night the spirits abandoned her.

A couple of crows cawed back and forth, announcing her advance. Gazing up at the sharp blue sky, she searched for the black birds. She listened, counting the crows by their caws. One for sorrow, two for mirth.

In her pocket, she clutched a piece of thick oval-shaped hardtack, sailor's bread so hard you could snap a tooth off trying to bite through it. As a rule, she kept a piece in the front pocket of her dress when near the woods. It was a gift for the fairies should the tiny creatures appear fluttering before her. When settlers ventured forth from England and Ireland, crossing the Atlantic to ply the fishing grounds around Newfoundland in the 1500s, hardtack was one of their staple foods. It was a natural choice to offer the fairies, to prevent them from transporting a person off to their underground abodes. As a child, Miss Laracy had seen the fairies twice and had given them the bread, careful to keep her eyes averted. A child didn't want to be carted off by the little people. What happened to babies and children who were taken by fairies was common knowledge. They would be returned not as themselves, but of a different shape and size. It had happened to Tommy Quilty from down the road. He had been changed; he had also been given 'the sight.'

Miss Laracy stopped to regard a house with a steeply-sloped glass roof, which was set far back from the road, a dark purple aura shrouding it. The twisted branches of two small lilac trees grew close to the house, a good distance down the lane. "'Tis where dat artist hides away," she informed herself. "Da one who lost 'er daughter. All dat unrest," she tutted, her heart going out to the woman for her troubles. "Shockin' stuff."

Shuffling on, she glanced probingly at the bushes along the side of the road, vainly searching for evidence of blueberries. A brown butterfly with black-tipped wings fluttered around. She paused to watch it, caressing a memory of how she and her playmates used to catch butterflies when she was a child and tuck them under a rock. The next day, when they returned and tipped up the rock, there'd be money in place of the hidden butterfly.

Looking up, she realized she was in front of the old Critch house. There was a small blue car in the driveway, the lid of its trunk open. New folks moving in for the summer. The lower branches of a lilac tree extended close to the side of the road, their scent intoxicating. Miss Laracy understood wholeheartedly why the smell attracted the spirits. It was right beautiful. She raised her wrinkled fingers to fondle the delicate flowers, rubbing lavender dust between her fingertips. Her eyes flicked toward the half-open front door. A man appeared there, his eyes on the grass as he stepped out; he faltered at the sight of her.

Miss Laracy waved her arm high. "How's she goin', me ducky?" she called.

"Pretty good," said the man, squinting to try and make her out.

"I was wunderin' if I could borrow a few o' yer lilacs?"

"Sure." The man stepped nearer. "Yes, be my guest."

"Me name's Eileen Laracy." Miss Laracy grinned and winked while she bent a thin lilac branch back and forth before yanking it off, making the once-connected branches shudder. "Wha's yer name?"

"Joseph Blackwood." The man extended his hand. Miss Laracy shook it attentively and gave him the once-over. He was neither too tall nor too short, with solid limbs and warm, capable hands. His manner of dress indicated a townie: scarlet shirt, jeans and new summer shoes, no baseball cap stuck on his head like most other men these days. An almost handsome face with sandy-blond bangs thinning atop a high forehead. Blue, clear eyes that could look right into you, without a trace of ill intention. The smile he gave her was natural, not put on, and he used it freely in the face of a stranger. Miss Laracy suspected he would guard himself more with those he loved. But, most importantly, the gauze-like vapour that floated around him was pale blue with deepening edges. A transition between ease and unrest.

"Dere's a Blackwood lives in Bareneed. Doug Blackwood. 'E be kin ta ye?"

"My uncle."

"I never knew 'im ta 'av any relations."

"We're from St. John's."

"Awww," Miss Laracy said with a wary intake of breath. "Townies."

"I guess so." Joseph chuckled disparagingly. "I'm an evil townie. You should do away with me now and get it over with."

"Naw, 'tis not me lot ta save ye frum yer sufferin'." Eileen Laracy grinned, warming toward him. "'Av ye got a pencil 'n a bit o' paper?" A small girl came out of the doorway, her sneakers pausing on the threshold as if suddenly glued there. The girl's curly blonde hair was clipped shoulder-length, and her eyes were great and expressive. She had a comely face with a sprinkle of freckles high on her nose and cheeks. No more than seven or eight by the looks of her. In one of her hands there was a notepad and in the other a pen. Miss Laracy's curious attention lingered on the girl before she felt compelled to glance at the neighbouring house, her eyes leading her there. *A connection brewin'*, she told herself.

"Hello, me love," she finally said to the child.

The girl gave no reply.

"Say hello," prompted Joseph.

"Hello," the girl quietly offered.

"This is Robin," Joseph explained.

"'Tis a beauteous day, Robin. Look at it all 'round ye." Miss Laracy gestured with a grand sweep of her arm.

"Sure is." Joseph stood with his hands on his hips, watching her nimbly plucking lilacs off the tree. "Can I get you scissors for that? Oh, you wanted a pencil."

"Naw, no use fer scissors." Pluck, pluck, pluck. Soon, her wizened face was practically concealed by the mass of mauve flowers. "But a bit o' paper would be right grand."

"I've got some in the car." Joseph stepped to the passenger side and leaned through the open window, rummaging in the glove compartment.

Miss Laracy nodded hopefully at Robin. Their eyes were locked in uncertain yet thoughtful recognition, until Joseph returned and offered a pencil and a scrap of white paper torn from a pharmacy bag. He had one of those itty-bitty black wireless phones in one hand and was pushing buttons and listening intently but not responding before he tossed it in through the car window.

"Can't stand cellphones," he said.

"Den why ye got one fer?" Miss Laracy stepped toward Robin and, noticing a figure on the notepad, asked the girl what she had drawn.

Robin slid the pen behind her ear. With both hands she held up the pad for Miss Laracy, who saw that the figure was a fine rendering of the neighbouring house, only her version had the house made entirely of glass. All around it there were amber swirls.

"Ye've a fine talent fer art."

"Thank you," said Robin in a quaint yet somewhat strained voice.

"Do us a favour 'n hold dese fer me, sweet one."

Robin set down her pad on the front step and opened her arms while Miss Laracy daintily transferred the bunch of lilacs, practically burying the girl.

"'Av a good whiff o' dem," she said, then accepted the paper and pencil from Joseph. She began writing, squinting and scrawling in a painstakingly slow thick script that involved the concentration of her entire body. Done, checked and seemingly pleased with her work, she returned the paper and pencil to Joseph.

"Dat be me name 'n phone number," she said, nodding at Joseph's hand. "Come down 'n see me. 'Av a chat, a cup of tea 'n a raisin bun."

While whispering fondly to the lilacs, Miss Laracy used both hands to affectionately gather the bulk from Robin. She then abruptly turned toward the tree and plucked a few others. It was charitable of them to allow her this favour. With thanks, she winked at Joseph. "Finest kind," she said, noticing Robin staring at the ocean, sparks of silver reflecting in her ocean-blue eyes.

"Ye see da shimmerin'?" Miss Laracy gasped, anxiously peering toward the water while bending near the child.

"Shimmering?" Joseph raised a hand, shading his eyes, searching.

"Yays, 'tis sumtin' ta see."

"What is?" Joseph asked, scanning the harbour, trying to discern the focus of their attention.

"Wouldn't be made plain ta da likes of ye," she said, straightening in indignation to her full diminutive height. "If ye be a fisheries officer."

"How'd you know I was a fisheries officer?" he asked with a smile.

The old woman jabbed a finger at his car. "Parkin' sticker on yer windshield, buddy."

"Oh."

"Secrets fer fisher folk 'n da blessed, not da likes of ye." With a huff, she commenced shuffling away, but soon paused to peek down at the lilacs in her arms, the sight of them gorging her heart with adoration and reverence. Coquettishly, she glanced back at Joseph. "T'anks fer da flowers, me ducky." Regarding Robin, Miss Laracy couldn't help but return with a piece of much-needed advice.

"If ye journeys in da woods make sure ta take a bit o' 'ard tack."

Robin nodded, her lips parted in wonder while she watched Miss Laracy shift the mass of lilacs into the crook of her arm and reach deep into her dress pocket to extract an oval lump. Miss Laracy offered it to

Robin, who merely stared at the smooth-edged curve of bread, then at the fingers of the veined wrinkled hand holding it upright, pointed toward the sky.

"Ye be da blessed," she whispered secretively. "All form o' protection be known ta ye."

"That's okay," Joseph interjected with bridled amusement, hands casually in the pockets of his jeans. "We can pick some up if we need it."

Miss Laracy shoved the hardtack back into her pocket. Grumbling, she gave Joseph a scalding grimace and was about to leave when she caught sight of the silver once again shimmering in Robin's bewildered eyes. She leaned her lips near the girl's ear, and whispered ardently, "Ye see da shimmerin'."

Robin nodded uncertainly.

"It be da fish tryin' ta fly, me love."

EIGHT DAYS AGO

Murky despair pervaded Donna Drover's mood as she hesitantly approached the step of her son Muss' square fisherman's house. The dark roots of her blonde hair showed plainly in the sunlight. She hadn't bothered having her hair done that month, a routine she usually diligently adhered to. The perm had grown out completely. Her hair's want of style emphasized the rough chunkiness of her face, and the brown bags under her eyes were made more apparent by her recent paleness. She coughed a smoker's cough.

With the nauseating heat from the sun beating down on her, she stood facing Muss' door, noticing, toward the bottom, a brown yellow-speckled lichen clinging to the weather-worn wood. In time, this would creep upward and cover the entire surface, making it impossible to paint the door. Donna tried scraping it off with the tip of her sneaker, but her effort left no mark. She stopped, not wanting to alert Muss to her presence. She knew what awaited her behind that door: Muss would be seated in the parlour, a frightening violence eclipsing his eyes whenever he dragged his stare away from the television to regard her. His anger seemed to have compounded each time Donna visited. Ten days ago, when she suggested they take a shot up to the Caribou Lounge for a beer and a bit of video lottery, Muss had refused to leave his home, claiming there was nothing left for him out in the world.

Donna glanced down at the plastic bag in her hand — groceries for Muss. She had taken it upon herself to bring food, yet her son merely observed the deliveries with disdain. On her previous visit, Donna had noticed the other bags she had dropped off still resting on the table beneath the kitchen window. Not even the carton of milk had made it into the refrigerator. That fact disturbed her more than anything, the souring milk within the container insinuating a thickening dread.

Donna had forced herself to visit, pulled herself away from her favourite soap operas and talk shows. Lately, when watching television, she suspected that she was no better than some of those crazy women on the programs. Muss was her son and she was ignoring him, even scared of him. Didn't he need her? She checked over her shoulder, her eyes scanning the harbour directly across the road; the surface of the water was calm, unbroken by a single sea creature. How many times had she sailed out from Bareneed harbour to fish the waters? And how many times had she listened to the stories of what lurked beneath? The tales of giant fish and survival against all odds. The legends. Fish in the water. Fish in the sea. All meaningless in her deadened heart now.

A black car rumbled along the road, heading deeper into the community. She wondered who it might be, but lost interest at once. Taking a step backward, Donna then checked the parlour window, the lace curtains drawn. She had made those curtains years ago and hung them herself. Muss had even helped. He had been such a sweet boy, a kind gentle boy, helpful and always trying to relieve the tension between her and Muss' father, Francis, with a joke and a smile. Without further thought, she turned and trod toward her pickup truck, climbed aboard, laid the bag of groceries on the passenger seat and watched it for a moment before starting the engine. She checked the rearview, waited for a power company repair truck to pass, then backed out.

Two days ago, Muss had gruffly declined Donna's offers to make him supper. He refused to look at her when she spoke, simply stared at the television, his gloomy eyes two shallow pools that lacked recognizable depth, his dishevelled black hair tangled, as if blown by a steady wind, and raven hair coarse on his face. He wore the same black jeans and blue denim shirt he'd been wearing for weeks. Occasionally, he'd grumble viciously, then sigh apologetically, as if he meant nothing by it. Startled, he'd gasp in a panicky way.

Pulling out of Muss' driveway and onto the lower road, Donna thought: He'll kill me if I go in there again. She passed alongside the L-shaped concrete wharf. Crab pots, like rusted metal frames of huge lampshades, with green or orange netting woven around them, lay stacked in need of repair.

Two crab boats were tied up at the wharf where three children cast lines out into the calm water, trying to catch their deaths. No, not their deaths, but fish. Why had she thought such a thing, she wondered. Why? The children were catching tomcods, flatfish or sculpins. But what were they really catching, what unheard-of forms lay secreted away beneath the fish scales? Why did the children catch the fish at all? Didn't they just let them go again, throw them back? Pure futility. And why the desire in the first place to snag and pull living things from the sea?

Farther out, fins of the albino sharks stirred circles in the gleaming blue water. Nearer shore, a turquoise tail reared up and slapped down with a resounding splash. Tentacles of a giant squid languidly curled and uncurled six feet above the surface. Although she could somehow see it, she ignored it all the same. It was stupid. Foolish. She fought against a growing urge to claw out her own eyes.

Donna continued east, the Atlantic Ocean to her left, adjacent to the lower road, houses and barns at her right. Sunset colours hung in the sky. The hues had struck the water and were melding as her pickup rolled along, yellow and orange turning pink and purple like an ugly bruise.

Donna blandly regarded the colours. They were less vibrant than she remembered, losing their essence, fading toward grey. Another sunset. A feeling of uselessness curled in the pit of her stomach like a slab of indigestible food. She used to love going for walks around this time, her gaze fixed on the massive ocean, her mind filled with awe. The weight of the sea.

It was all too real to her now. Her evening walks were a thing of the past, as was her love of this place. She had nothing. Nothing. A sick son who hated her. No job. Bareneed, once a lively and warm place, now stank of drabness and heartbreak.

A mercurial flash thumped the bonnet of her pickup, then bounced to the left as Donna slammed on the brakes, bucking ahead. "Christ!" Recoiling in her seat, she immediately checked her rearview. A seagull swooped down to retrieve a small fish, a sleek caplin by the looks of it. The caplin must be rolling in on the beaches to spawn. They would bring the whales with them to feed on the millions of fish that struggled ashore to lay eggs each summer.

Donna cursed violently under her breath as she drove on, reaching the end of the lower road, the pavement turning to gravel and veering sharply left, up the steep incline of Codger's Lane. In her rearview, she glimpsed the ocean and a series of small houses in the community of Port de Grave far across the inlet. A sequence of silver flickers hung above the water, like fireworks popping in succession. The flashings floated higher, hung for a moment, then descended, plunging into the ocean.

Halfway up Codger's Lane, Donna veered the pickup into her driveway. The tail end slid as the tires skidded on gravel, and Donna realized how fast she had actually been travelling. If she had continued up Codger's Lane she would have arrived at the abandoned church and graveyard, where the asphalt resumed and the higher road cut sharply west, back toward the community, offering an extensive view of the square houses, the protected bay and the massive rock-etched headland that towered above the three white buildings of the fish plant across the harbour.

Fuming about her careless driving and the litany of misdeeds regarding her son, Donna twisted off the engine key and stormed out of her pickup, slamming the door. The old barn behind her house grabbed her attention. It was absent of colour, black and white, with the evergreens behind it and the green grass to either side. She thought she saw someone out of the corner of her eye — a child in the doorway, a girl aged seven or eight with sleek rust-coloured hair and a soaked dress plastered to her frail shivering body. Her face was pearly and mottled green and her buried-blue lips grimaced in a misshapen, bloated way.

The vision sent a shuddering chill through Donna. The girl resembled the daughter of the artist who lived by herself up on the higher road in the house people said was heated by the sun. The daughter, Jessica, had disappeared with her father some time ago. She knew the girl's name because she had contacted the police when the child had first appeared in her barn more than ten days ago. A policeman who wasn't from around here had come. He looked different, with dark skin, brown eyes, like he was Native. Sergeant what? Who? A car thing. A police pursuit. A chase. Yes, Sergeant Chase had come. A search party had scoured the woods. Not a sign of the girl. Donna felt horrible shame for giving false hope to everyone, particularly the child's mother.

On the second sighting Donna made another call to the police, but once again their efforts proved futile. The girl was not found after the third reluctant call either. Finally, Donna had stopped using the telephone. She wouldn't even answer it when it rang. The voices at the other end were unrecognizable. She could not see their faces. She did not know them. Threatened by the loss of her faculties, she would hang up and guiltily wonder what she had done wrong.

The air had grown startlingly quiet. Donna strained to listen. Only the silence became amplified. The door to the barn was open. No girl there now. Donna would burn the barn to the ground if she had a match. It was cluttered with old things, things she would never use, things that reminded her of her past life, her husband, long gone, her job, long gone, her life … No, burning the barn was insane. What was she thinking? She would hack it to bits with an axe, splintering the wood, her heart quickening with release as each quaking blow found its savage mark. The axe blade biting into wood. Sticking. Stuck. Lodged.

A scant breeze rose, delivering the unsettling quiet of a child's hushed words: "Fish in the sea."

The sound of chopping in her ears. Then deafness.

Donna was not breathing. Panic gripped her heart. It raced frantically, kicking percussively in her breast. *This is it*, she wearily informed herself. *I'm dying. I'm finally dying. This is death.* Dizziness wavered behind her eyes. She shut them and braced herself for the blackness that had been threatening for weeks. It was suddenly complete yet impenetrable. She had to snatch a breath, hold the oxygen in her powerless lungs.

No pressure to exhale.

No urgency to draw another breath.

It was as if she were already dead.

She made a conscious effort to exhale. Then, without the slightest prompting from her lungs, she drew another deeper breath, held it in until, lacking momentum, she knew it was time to exhale.

"Sweet Jesus!" she gasped as another chill coursed through her flesh. Sweat soaked her hands and brow, trailed along her cheeks. She feared a heart attack. But there were no chest pains. No pain anywhere. She was light-headed, disoriented. She thought she might faint as she reminded herself to pull in another breath.

Exhaling through her wide-open mouth, she moved forward, but stumbled, white fear draining strength from her knees and ankles. She slapped one hand against the beige vinyl siding. Gazing at the sky, she saw the grey, hubcap-size satellite dish affixed to the front of her house and, beyond that, the empty blue sky.

She heard the girl's icy voice: "Myyyyyy fawww-ther went to sea-sea-sea to see what he could see-see-see, and all that he could see-see-see was the bottom of the deep blue sea-sea-sea."

The soaked girl stood in the barn doorway, an iridescent sea trout in her hands, the V-shaped tail quivering. Donna fixed her eyes there, then bowed her head. Bone-weary, heart hammering, buzzing in her ears, she felt no greater need than to lie down. She rationalized: *If I'm inside, I'll never get out.* She braced her other sweaty palm against the siding, and her knees gradually gave way until she found herself kneeling on the grass, dampness seeping through her track pants. She lay back with a despondent groan.

All was still in the world, all confined and still and draining colour. Donna stared at the pointless eternity of blue sky as it diminished to grey, the sun burning a blackened silver. She lay paralyzed on the grass, trembling in fits and starts, unable to move as she witnessed three white seagulls, no, not gulls but grey-winged fish, circle above her, high in the slate-grey sky.

THURSDAY AFTERNOON AND NIGHT

Doctor George Thompson, a portly man of sixty-one with a boyish, good-natured face and a thick mop of grey-and-white hair, paced anxiously out to the front desk to escort Lloyd Fowler and his wife into the examination room. Thompson was puzzled to see Lloyd Fowler in his office. Complaints of breathing difficulties should have seen Lloyd sped to emergency and yet, according to the information hurriedly imparted by Lloyd's wife, Barb, Lloyd had refused to visit the hospital but had agreed, with much cajoling, to visit Dr. Thompson. He had been rushed in ahead of those in the half-filled waiting area.

"Let's have a look, Mr. Fowler," Thompson said. The white paper on the examination table crinkled as the patient settled in place. The doctor studied Lloyd's ruddy face in a way that obviously unsettled the man: grey eyes that seemed a touch too far apart, white nose hairs and eyebrows in desperate need of trimming. He knew that Lloyd was in excellent shape for a man his age. In fact, he was in fitter health than the doctor himself.

"You don't smoke, do you, Lloyd?" Thompson warmed the stethoscope in the palm of his hand, a service he usually reserved for women, but thought appropriate considering his patient's unease.

Mr. Fowler shook his solid head, his eyes scanning the carpet.

"Unbutton your shirt, please. Any history of heart disease in your family?"

"No, sir," he said bluntly, unfastening the second and then third button. Mr. Fowler was not one to make a fuss, being the sort who would visit a doctor only if his arm was hanging by a thread and then dismiss the injury as a trifle, nothing serious, just another means of testing his God-given abilities to conquer the mere mortal in himself. "I can make due with one arm, no problem there," he might staunchly profess, then go about labouring twice as hard, heaving and grunting to menace the expectations of disbelievers.

Lloyd Fowler's wife had dragged him in to see the doctor. Barb was a slight woman with black curly hair and masculine features made more severe by the black down above her top lip. She and Lloyd had just left Muss Drover's funeral. Muss, Donna Drover's son, had died of causes unknown to Thompson or any of the other doctors who had examined him. They had suspected depression, even speculated that Muss had taken his own life. There had been rumours, but an autopsy had ruled out suicide. And now Donna was presently on a respirator in the Port de Grave hospital. Donna had experienced breathing difficulties, much like Lloyd Fowler, even though no cause had been determined after a battery of tests. It was an unusual case, like nothing Thompson had experienced in his thirty-eight years as an MD. The doctors at the hospital believed there might be a link between Muss' death and Donna Drover's condition, but no correlation could be verified. The balm of scientific explanation, which usually offered some sort of soothing relief in the face of death, could not apply itself to Muss' demise. The man, although young and in seemingly excellent health, had simply quit living his life.

"Take a deep breath," Dr. Thompson requested, sliding the head of the stethoscope over the thick white tangle of hair on Mr. Fowler's chest.

Mr. Fowler drew in a fierce breath through his nostrils, frowning all the while.

"Okay, out." The doctor listened intently. "Another one." He glanced at Mrs. Fowler, who stood close by, clutching her purse, ready to do whatever the doctor might suggest. "Take another deep one and hold it." Dr. Thompson, straining to listen, held his own breath. Nothing out of the ordinary. Fowler's lungs were clear, his heartbeat regular. "Okay, breathe."

He shifted the stems of the stethoscope from his ears and stared into his patient's eyes. Mr. Fowler sat straight on the examination table, his white-haired hands gripping the edge of the black vinyl, his eyes fixed on a diagram of a skeleton posted on the wall.

"Any pain in your chest?"

"No, sir.

"Pain in your arms or legs?"

"No, sir."

"Any burning in your lungs, when you breathe?"

"No, sir."

"Heartburn?"

"No, sir, nothing like —"

"Trouble sleeping?"

Mr. Fowler steadfastly shook his head, tightened his lips.

"Ever wake up sweating, heartbeat pounding, feeling like you're not really there?"

"Christ Almighty, no!" He glared at Thompson as if the doctor were stark raving mad.

"He was just walking and got dizzy," Barb Fowler butted in, inclining her body forward. "It was like he couldn't breathe. It happened before, too."

Mr. Fowler shot a hostile glance at his wife. "Be still, woman!"

"How long ago?"

"I don't know," Mr. Fowler hotly responded, his cheeks flushed. "I first noticed of a Sunday, last week."

"It's Thursday now," Thompson noted. "Get down from there, if you like."

Mr. Fowler nodded and diverted his glance toward the cream-coloured venetian blinds as if mortified to be in the doctor's presence. "It's nothing," he muttered, sliding off the table and buttoning his shirt. There was a short space of silence, in which Thompson watched his patient through the corner of his eye, and then Lloyd Fowler caught his breath.

"Allergic to anything?" Thompson asked, returning to his desk and carefully sitting, trying to repress a groan, but mumbling "Cripes." His knees were bothering him more than usual today, aching from arthritis. The extra pounds he had packed on over the winter months were exacerbating his condition. He would have to ease up on his late-night addiction to jelly doughnuts and milk. Rich cream sauces and imported beers, sweet liqueurs and slabs of brie and havarti with dill were practically a daily indulgence.

"He's not allergic to anything, Doctor."

Thompson opened Lloyd's file and sifted through its contents. Nothing to indicate a history that might precipitate breathing difficulties. No signs of asthma, although he should be sent for tests. But shortness of breath was shortness of breath. A warning sign, a portent of greater complications.

"Plenty of pollen in the air. It's a bastard for causing inflammation. This time of the year especially. Your eyes water at all?"

"No, sir," said Lloyd. He now stood by the wall with his hands at his sides. Like a big child called into the principal's office, Thompson mused.

"Your heart sounds perfect, your lungs are clear. Could be allergies, a touch of asthma, or it could be nothing." Thompson scribbled on his prescription pad. "This is for routine blood work. We haven't had any blood out of you in years. We'll have a look. Might be an infection. A virus. If there was chest pain, I'd book you for a stress test. Maybe I'll do that anyway, just to be on the safe side." He tore off the top sheet and laid it aside. "This one's for allergy and asthma tests. I'll have an appointment made at the hospital in St. John's." On ripping off the second sheet, he handed both orders to Mrs. Fowler. Her husband glanced at the small white sheets while trying his utmost to ignore them.

"How about exercise?"

"He likes his television a bit too much these days," Mrs. Fowler chided, then whispered to the doctor, "since young Bobby's passing away." Mr. Fowler darted another piercing glance at his wife. This seemed to be the breaking point, the moment of ultimate humiliation that heaved him toward the door.

"So," Mr. Fowler barked. "I'm not goin' ta drop dead?"

Dr. Thompson chuckled agreeably, feeling his chin double. He leaned back in his chair and twiddled his pen. "I don't know, Mr. Fowler. Any of us could go at any minute."

"I s'pose so," said Lloyd Fowler, yanking open the door and striding off.

Mrs. Fowler watched her husband leave. Then, hesitating a moment, as if agonizing over the substance of her next disclosure, she leaned toward the door through which her husband had just fled, peeking out.

"Something else?"

Convinced the coast was clear, she faced the doctor and confessed, "He's got a real temper lately."

"How so?"

"Angry a lot."

"Irritable?"

"Yes, doctor. Only worse."

"You mentioned Bobby's passing away." Thompson paused a moment, out of respect. He set his elbows on his desk to further punctuate his shift in tone. "The breathing problem could be panic-related, depression. Has his routine changed much? Does he still enjoy doing the things he used to?"

"No, not at all. He's different."

"Sounds depression-related. I could give him a low-dose antidepressant. I'll need a thyroid test."

"Lloyd wouldn't touch anything like that."

Thompson scribbled on his pad, tore off the sheet and stood, handing the scrip to Mrs. Fowler. "Maybe you could convince him to try a few of these anti-anxiety drugs first. See if they make him feel better."

Mrs. Fowler placed the prescription atop the others in her hand and, with a burdensome sigh, neatly folded them, opening her purse to secrete them away.

Thompson escorted Mrs. Fowler to the hallway. "Bring him back if things don't improve." In a lower voice he said, "Keep an eye on him," and winked, in hopes of lifting her spirits.

"Yes, doctor. Thank you." Mrs. Fowler gave a fleeting, vanishing smile, then passed ahead of Thompson and through the waiting area as the doctor accepted the next patient's file from his receptionist. He frowned to himself at the sight of the name, then called out: "Aggie Slade." He bit his tongue, preventing himself from adding: the community's most renowned hypochondriac. "Welcome, Aggie. Welcome. What form of pestilence have you got today?"

꙰

Lloyd Fowler turned furtively as his wife hurried out the clinic door to join him on the wooden landing. He remained still with his jaw clenched, his eyes squinting at the late-afternoon brightness reflecting off cars in the gravel lot.

"Those people," he grumbled. Having spoken, he was made aware of his need to breathe. His face flushed redder and he snorted hotly. Irked, he snatched a breath, steadfast in his refusal to regard Barb. "Those people in that waitin' room thinkin' me a sick man. I'm no sick man."

"No, Lloyd," Mrs. Fowler reassured him, reaching for his shoulder. "It's probably nothing."

At the touch of his fretful wife, he stomped down the three stairs, cursing his need to grasp after another breath. A deep one. How he hated where he lived, the land and the sea with all its unremarkable creatures that cavorted foolishly. How he dreaded the sensations that he was losing his mind, losing his breath, losing what he was. A plague of pointlessness tormented his bones. How he despised his average wife and his average house. When was it that the world had lost its character, he asked himself, and sunk to a level of such unendurable plainness?

~❦~

"Don't go in there by yourself," Joseph called.

The two-storey square barn was painted rust-red; several small panes were missing from its white-trimmed windows. A sheet of plastic had been positioned behind the openings where someone had masked the holes in hopes of keeping the elements at bay. Not a breeze stirred. An insect buzzed behind Robin, a bumblebee by the sounds of it, hovering low to the ground where it drifted from delicate wildflower to wildflower. A bird twittered from high off in a tree or passing through the blue sky. The narrow barn door was ajar. It, too, was rust-red. At its centre, a white heart was evenly painted. With notepad clutched to her chest, Robin stepped up on the worn threshold, one hand reaching to rest on the outer wall where paint was peeling from the clapboard. Blindly, she picked at a flake, felt it beneath her fingernail.

"Why not?" Robin complained back at her father.

"I haven't checked it out yet. Could be nails on the floor. Come on, now, help me bring in the rest of the stuff."

Robin faced the barn's dimness, her eyes adjusting to discern indistinct shapes. She thought she made out an old mattress and a piece of tall furniture.

There were four tires closer to the door; she could see them quite clearly. She held her breath, listening for movement, straining to catch the scamper of mice or stray cats. She heard a dripping, like water pattering on the floor, from upstairs. Then buzzing. Not the sound of a single fly. More like the hum from a mass of flying insects. With her eyes tipped toward the sounds, she wondered, *Flies or hornets?* At the thought of hornets, she stepped back and caught the movements of a young girl, deep in the barn, raising her hand to her face as if to shield herself from the light. Flinching, Robin dropped her notepad. Immediately she crouched and gathered it up, her eyes fixed on the space where she had seen the girl. No one. But as she stood, the girl came back into view and so Robin suspected the girl to be only her own reflection in a dusty full-length mirror toward the back. She leaned to one side and the reflection did exactly the same. She scrunched up her nose then scratched it. What did they say about an itchy nose? Going to have a visitor, or a fright.

"Robin, come on and help," her father called, grunting under the weight of some load he was carrying. "Don't be a slouch."

The sound of the dripping slowed, then disappeared. The drone of flies faded. A smell of rotting fish wafted over her, the odour so disgusting that she twirled away and made a small noise. In the stillness that followed she waited for her body's reaction, only to feel her stomach and throat constricting. She retched, wanting to spit out the taste. She scraped her top teeth against her tongue. "Daddy, what's that horrible smell?"

Joseph, bent over the trunk, straightened with a pillow tucked under each arm, and sniffed the air. "I don't smell anything. Lilacs, maybe."

"No, it's stinky."

Her father shrugged and shook his head. "I don't know." He awkwardly gripped the handles of a black travel bag, clenched the pillows tighter beneath his arms, and headed toward the house. "I can't handle this heat," he muttered. "Gimme snow instead."

Robin noticed how the car was parked on the grass because the driveway was overgrown. She liked the idea of everything growing wild. There were small red flowers in the grass and the lilac trees alongside the road were in full bloom. The smell of lavender mingled with the scent of grass warmed by the sun, and overpowered the smell of fish. In the distance, down over the sloping landscape of scattered evergreens and tall wild grass, and beyond the old square houses, the ocean glistened blue in the intense summer sun. The sun made her itchy. She scratched the back of her head, feeling the dampness in her hair, and watched for the silver flashings the little old lady had pointed out. The fish trying to fly. She remembered drawing flying fish a few weeks ago and flipped open her notepad, thumbing through the sheets only to discover that the drawings were in an older notepad. The old woman, Miss Laracy, seemed happy to know that Robin drew pictures. She had called Robin's drawings "art." Robin liked the old lady a lot.

Her father blew out a breath as he stepped from the house. His forehead glistened as he poked around in the trunk, squinting, then pawing sweat from his eyes. "Grab that bag," he said, nodding toward a plastic bag of food. "I'm taking a break." He sighed and sat on the lip of the trunk.

"You got Crunkies. My favourite."

Joseph laughed and mussed up Robin's hair. "What d'you think of the house?" he asked, tipping his head toward it. "Neat, or what?"

"It's great. I love it." Robin whisked the pen from behind her ear and began drawing the house.

"It belonged to a fisherman, years ago. They moved it from another community farther up the coast."

"Moved it?"

"Yeah, they moved all the houses back then. You know how?"

"Why'd they move them?"

"The government said so. They wanted everyone closer together, so they could put down roads and connect everyone. A lot of people took their houses instead of building new ones. You know how they moved them?"

"With big trucks?"

Her father laughed. "No. Not like now."

"Horses?"

"No. One more guess."

"A hundred men?"

"Uhn-uhn, they floated them, on the water." Joseph stood and turned to regard the harbour. "Floated them in there, to shore, then up over the land."

"They didn't. Houses don't float." Regardless, Robin drew water under the house. Waves with pointed peaks.

"Yes, they do. People built big rafts with barrels under them, and towed the houses along the water with their boats." Joseph lifted a cardboard box of plates and pots from the trunk. They rattled while he secured his grip. "They took their houses with them. Ocean nomads. Pretty neat, huh?"

"Yeah." Robin was busy creating a raft under the house, hurriedly positioning barrels in place. "What're nomads?" she asked, hoping it was a word that could be translated into a picture, defining her floating houses.

"People who move from one place to another. That's how important their homes were. Now, break's over, get to work."

"I'm drawing."

"Put that away for once."

With a despondent sigh, Robin folded shut the notepad cover, but hurriedly flipped it open again to add seven fish flying over the roof of the house.

"Put that away, I said."

Briskly, she did as instructed, frowned playfully at her father, made a move to open the notepad again, teasing him, but catching the unfriendly look in his eyes she relented. "Can I have some Crunkies? I'm starving."

"You look like you're starving," Joseph said in a kinder tone. "Poor child."

"Can I?"

"It's vacation. You can eat whatever you like."

"Yay! You're the best dad ever."

Her father grinned and winked before turning toward the house. Robin glanced up at the top floor, its windows fitted with small square panes that she counted with a studious eye. Eight little squares to a window. Everything felt so old out here, so different from her home back in the city. Even the air was different. Her mom would love it. Spirits sinking, Robin tucked her notepad under her arm and grabbed the plastic bag. "This is too heavy," she groaned as her father stepped into the house.

"Tough," he called back, the dishes and pots rattling as the box shifted in his arms. "You're out around the bay now, maid. You've got to be strong and hardy."

Robin paused to peek at the woods behind the barn, then at the barn's upper windows, the glass intact. She knew it was an unsafe place by the muted grey glow that wavered from it, the colour she had associated — from the time she was a baby — with a fluttering danger that tingled in her tummy like hunger. A pulse of grey and a low secretive whisper, a young girl's voice: "Robin." With a freezing-cold shiver and a quick prickling sweep of gooseflesh, Robin took one step back. The slow drip of water and the drone of flies filled her ears. The smell of rotting fish snatched away her appetite. "Yuck." She made a sour face as the grey around the barn deepened against the pretty blue sky. "Daddy?" she called uncertainly. "There's that stink again."

⟋⟍

Eileen Laracy carefully cradled the warm partridgeberry loaf in the flat of both palms. It was neatly wrapped in wax paper, the folded ends secured with evenly cut lengths of masking tape. *A right lovely li'l package,* she thought, admiring her handiwork. The road was empty and Tommy Quilty's house was three ahead, just beyond the community hall. Miss Laracy took a deep breath of the fresh, invigorating evening air and fancied young lovers off somewhere in the grass on such a night. Kissing and hugging and making sweet promises. She grinned to herself. "Oh, yays," she said, smacking her gums together, then winking at the mischievous grandeur of the thought.

When she passed the hall, her ears pricked up at the sound of some commotion within. The noise of men's muffled voices and then a squelching sound like the radio from a taxi. Maybe a meeting of the volunteer fire brigade. The metal door was shut so she was prevented from having a peek inside. Wandering on, she noticed a green van parked in the shadows beside the two wooden bins, one for garbage, the other for recycling, at the side of the hall. On the occasional Tuesday, when she missed the garbage truck, she would drag her bags over there and toss them in herself. A bit of exercise never bothered her. She was still as fit as a fiddle. She squinted at the van and, in the light of a nearby streetlight, made out the insignia of the army on its back doors. What was the army doing in the hall, she wondered. Maybe planning a game of bingo to raise money for a new rocket launcher or a grander helicopter.

Again, she heard a man's voice, but this time it arose at her left, issuing from Edyth Pottle's house on the corner of Pottle's Lane. Miss Laracy was positive the voice belonged to Darry Pottle. He was shouting, a peculiar thing as he was usually such a quiet young fellow. Never said two words to anyone. It was only Darry and his mother living in the house. Both of them once had jobs, splitting and gutting at the fish plant, until the cod fishery shut down. Miss Laracy craned her neck, trying to hear more clearly. A light flicked off in one of the rooms and there was silence; the house appeared devoutly black. A car raced down the road, headlights blaring on high beam right into her eyes, music thumping within, as it roared past. "Da livin' drift," Miss Laracy said with a disheartened intake of breath while she turned and watched the car's red tail lights shrink and disappear.

Miffed, she stared down at the loaf in her hands. Its bottom was warm like a baby's. What she wouldn't do for the gift of a grandchild. Impossible, considering she herself was childless and barren as a desert now. She headed on, aware of the flow of the brook running alongside Tommy Quilty's house. It washed under the road and continued on to empty in the ocean. Tommy declared you could still catch a mud trout in that brook if you had a barrel of patience and a big fat worm. Nothing like the sound of a brook running in the night, the pebbles rattling under the meek effervescence of water. It was a comfort. Yet she knew better than to linger there. Standing alone at a brook by night was sure to invite the worst sort of luck.

A light was on in Tommy Quilty's parlour window. Miss Laracy shuffled down the dirt driveway beside Tommy's rusty brown van and approached the back door. The yard was illuminated by a powerful spotlight that lit up the clutter as in daylight. There was an array of metals and a few rundown yellow buses, without wheels, parked farther in. A stray white and grey cat strolled along the grass, disappearing under one of the buses. Another bus, the one that Tommy used to gather people for bingo and card games, was parked nearer the house. Tommy was a collector. Things that people no longer had use for, Tommy was happy to haul away, strip down, and use in parts to fashion an entirely different notion. Being as he was, he lived in a state of expectation, seeing into the future long before it arrived.

The wooden screen door was hooked open. Miss Laracy knocked on the inner door, but Tommy was already standing in wait, opening it for her and nodding a welcome, grinning a wide grin with the corners of his mouth pointed directly up. A few of his crooked teeth were black-edged and the tuft of hair at the top of his head was a clot of brown curls that hadn't seen the rake of a comb in many a year. He wore creased brown trousers and a cream-coloured shirt with the buttons done up tight to his throat. Miss Laracy could not help but notice the red tinge of illumination hugging his body; his aura itself was reassuringly yellow with waves of blue. By the red tinge, she knew that Tommy had been drawing. It was the passion, the flush, compelling the blood nearer the surface of the skin.

"I brung ye a patridgeburry loaf." Miss Laracy raised it close to Tommy's nostrils as she stepped up with a soft grunt and moved past him, requiring no invitation to enter. "Fresh frum da oven, me old trout."

"Right nice of ye," Tommy said, nodding twice, as Miss Laracy laid the loaf on the old kitchen table and then turned to regard Tommy's beaming smile of appreciation. He was a lovable man, a wondrous man with a heart of pure gold.

"Wha' sort o' mischief are ye up ta?" she asked, rubbing her palms together. "Let us in on yer mystery."

⟞⟦

Joseph reclined on the narrow parlour couch, watching Robin sleep in the wingback armchair across from him. His daughter always appeared much younger in sleep, her features adopting infantile qualities. Observing her in this manner gave Joseph a thrill of adoration, but also a twinge of paternal fear that Robin could come to harm. She appeared exceedingly vulnerable. He wondered if he would ever lose that acute need to protect her.

Robin had been reading a book about wildflowers, how to identify the various species and what significance they held in the lore of days gone by. Joseph had ordered her to leave her notepad, which now rested on the rug, having fallen there when Robin dropped into sleep. The notepad was open on a page featuring sketches of multiple sea creatures rising out of the water. Joseph wondered where his daughter had acquired her talent for art. There weren't any artists on his side of the family, none that he knew of. He didn't think there were any in Kim's family tree either. Robin's teachers had often commented on her artistic inclinations; she was miles ahead of the other children.

After being forced to give up on her drawings, Robin had found the book on flowers in a glass cabinet in the corner of the parlour. She loved flowers of any sort. She had already picked a bundle of lilacs and wildflowers from the backyard and arranged them in an old blue glass on the kitchen table. One of the first things that needed doing, according to her. She had told him the names of a few of her favourites, but Joseph did not possess the concentration required to commit the names to memory. He had a book as well. He had packed it in his travel bag, brought it along from his apartment. A collection of Newfoundland sea legends as related by sailors and fishermen. Kim had given it to him years ago. He had hoped that the stories would set the mood for their summer adventure. If he could only focus on reading them. He was not one for reading. He would rather be doing something, up on his feet and wandering around. Kim was the one who could not get enough of books. At every free moment, she had a book in her hands, usually an old literary title, a novel from a bygone time where the female character suffered grimly through her subjugated status and was mastered by a dark, violent man. Joseph had no time for those sorts of books and he could not fathom why Kim was so interested in reading about tragic lives. It was as though she romanticized existing under such harsh conditions.

For whatever reason, probably because he felt out of place and agitated, he found himself reading the same sentences over and over again. The words would not sink in. He was trying not to think of Kim, how much she would adore this place. In fact, he knew for certain that she would value the place more than he actually did. Her sensibilities had become his. He had changed. He had been changed by Kim. The nuances of this sort of house would have meant nothing to him prior to their relationship.

Watching his daughter's tender face, Joseph recalled the way Kim often commented on how adorable Robin was in sleep. Kim had looked gorgeous when Joseph had picked Robin up that morning. He had a perfect memory of her stepping out the front door, dressed in rust-coloured, loose-fitting cotton pants and matching blouse, carrying Robin's bag. A pair of binoculars hung around her neck. Her short brown hair had just been washed, and gleamed silkily. She was wearing his favourite deep-brown lipstick, the shade that brought out the colour of her eyes. He had studied her face, newly intrigued by it since their months apart. The high cheekbones that lent the appearance of freshness, of undiminished youth; the perky nose. His eyes had lingered on the scar on her chin from a bike accident when she was twelve, another wide scar on her right wrist. There was something about her scars that made her human, fallible.

Nine years ago, when Joseph first laid eyes on Kim in a downtown pub, he had assumed she was the frivolous type, fashion-conscious and full of empty talk, but nothing had been further from the truth. She had just received her master's degree in marine biology. She had a winning smile, but was an exceptionally private person, chose her words carefully, and drank extra-proof beer instead of fizzy wine. She was a beautiful contradiction. He had fallen in love with her as she spoke of the multifarious behaviours of crustaceans and other bottom dwellers that existed silently beneath countless tons of seawater. The ideas she cautiously committed to words were alight with poetry.

What had become of those days, those conversations? Now their relationship was all about money, politics, who was right and who was wrong. The right and wrong way to spend money. The right and wrong way to raise Robin. The right and wrong way to open a tin of corn, cut a slice of bread, stack the magazines, position the chairs, fold the clothes … Who was the busiest? Who slaved the hardest? Who did the most work and who did the most work around the house? Who had suffered the greatest martyrdom, as Kim used to say with sarcasm. What had changed Kim? Had he changed her, as Kim had claimed? And, more importantly, what had changed him? He was no longer what he thought himself to be, but a man divided within himself, parts of who he once was anesthetized and detached.

An inner wavering, a sense of being at sea for days and then abruptly put up on land, came fully over him. Alarm surged through his body. He broke out in a sweat as his heartbeat lurched to rise out of him. It was an effort to swallow, his throat a shut muscle. He sat up straighter and gripped the rough upholstery of the couch. Eventually, after four laboured attempts, he managed to swallow.

The first time this had happened, only two weeks ago, Joseph was convinced he was dying, felt as if his mind was slipping from his skull, his heart pounding in his neck and temples. He had difficulty drawing breath, and was stricken with tumultuous panic. He had stood in front of the bathroom mirror, to ensure he was still in the world, and watched his reflection swell and shrink away from itself, his shuddering knees banging uncontrollably against the cupboard door beneath the sink. He was about to call an ambulance when the clutch of the onslaught slackened. "Panic attack," his doctor had matter-of-factly pronounced, while scribbling out a prescription for Ativan. "Nervous system overload. Probably from stress due to the separation. It's amazing how common they are." Joseph had wondered if the doctor was referring to separations or panic attacks as being common. His doctor was always speaking quickly, in a hurry, double-booked. He tore the small sheet from the pad and leaned across his desk, handed it to Joseph between two fingers. "One or two of these under the tongue when needed. They work fast." The doctor nodded. A done deal. Pills would fix him. Science would stabilize him. As simple as that.

As Joseph rose from the parlour couch, a piece of paper crinkled in the top pocket of his shirt. He fished it out. It was Eileen Laracy's name and number. A strange old woman. He did not want to think of her; she was almost creepy. He laid the bit of paper on the side table and went into the hallway, steering his mind away from the removed feel of the house. It would only dislocate him further. His eyes felt strained as he sighted his travel bag at the head of the stairs. He carried it to the second storey and turned toward the front of the house where his bedroom overlooked the community and harbour. He plopped the bag onto the soft-springed bed and unzipped it, dug around for the bottle of pills beneath his clothes. Toothbrush, disposable razor, pills. His sweaty hand trembled as he uncapped the bottle. Flinching, he almost dropped the two tiny pills, but managed to place them under his tongue. He shut his eyes and stood perfectly still, drawing deep breaths and exhaling in a measured rhythm, counting to five, waiting, sensing the slackening gradually melt through him, a soul-unburdening warmth that loosened his centre.

Joseph opened his eyes and started at the reflection of a man in the window. A bulky man with a beard. Joseph spun around to face an empty room. A stark bed, perfectly made. A wooden rocking chair with a hand-embroidered cushion. A boarded-over fireplace. No one there. He checked the window. The man was gone. Joseph shook his head, dumbfounded. His hand came up to rub his cheek. Stubble, but no beard.

Striding downstairs, he considered waking Robin, but that would be selfish. Instead, he stepped outside for a dose of much-needed fresh air; the sweet summer night often soothed him with memories of childhood. The lights of the houses down toward the water were pristine, everything honed and exact. He tipped up his chin and gazed at the multitude of stars. A dog bayed in the distance as if challenging Joseph's entry into the outside. Somewhere between him and the water, a car horn honked once and a cow commenced mooing. He turned toward the solar house. An agile shadow drifted over the grass and then the front door opened, light from inside giving definition to a woman with strawberry-blonde hair, wearing a loose white dress. She checked over her shoulder, both hands on the edge of the door as she guardedly shut it. Intrigued by the sight of this woman, Joseph watched the door for a while longer, but it did not reopen. He checked the windows, yet the woman's image made no appearance. He was about to turn away when another shadow, lower to the ground, swept over the grass. A big shaggy black dog approached the solar house and sat on the front step without making a sound, staring patiently ahead, still as a statue, stern as a keeper.

-◊-

I am living with the dead. In sleep and in waking, I am living with the dead. Even my dreams are blighted and impossible to abide. Night after night, I continue to witness Reg's grim countenance. Jessica has informed me, in her newly grown-up manner, that because I continue to love Reg I must face him when I sleep, yet he cannot manifest himself in waking hours. The love is not strong enough. It is poisoned with hate. And hate him I do for leaving me in such a state of constant indecision and convulsion of the spirit. Reg insists that I must kill whoever was responsible for making him commit such fatal deeds against himself and Jessica. His livid voice has been droning in my head for months now, claiming that a man is coming, a man with a daughter. The living goading the dead. Each night, in my dream, Reg gives over the handle of a slim-bladed knife. Time elapses without focus. I am sleeping. I have awakened. When I gaze down at my hand, I see that my dress is stained red, the stain seeping until I am absolutely scarlet, every inch of my dress and skin. My stomach muscles flinch and I awake again, cramping and holding my belly, a sob like a blade itself caught in my throat. Jessica.

Claudia Kyle laid down her fountain pen and shut her journal against the polished oak table. Three candles flickered in holders before her. Regarding the journal's cover, which featured a cherub surrounded by giant white and scarlet flowers, she considered which master had painted the scene. Rembrandt, she suspected. She thoughtfully slid her hand over the surface, noticing two specks of ink on the sleeve of her white satin nightdress. What might be done about it? Ink on cloth. She could not help herself. Grasping the fountain pen, she pressed the tip against her sleeve and wrote in large flowing letters: *My gown is parchment. I wear it like a skin that tells my story by design.*

Claudia gazed up and focused on the black glass of the window, which made plain the reflection of her haloed face. The powdery whiteness of her skin held pink highlights and her copper hair, hanging to her waist, was brushed back over her forehead, held in place by a white band. She had once thought of herself as graceful and people had often commented on her poise. Now, with each passing day, spans of time in which she ate less, refused to allow even a drop of water to pass between her lips, and stared through eyes that seemed not often hers, she merely considered herself frail. How much distance between frailness and grace, she wondered, her pink eyelids fluttering.

Urging her dazed concentration beyond her reflection, she dismissed herself. Her reflection was now a blur. The dark landscape sloped away, dense evergreens distinguishable by streetlight in the foreground, the uppermost treetops declining toward the lower road and the lights from clusters of square fishermen's houses positioned around the harbour. The lights reflected in the dark water in a way that mirrored memories of Christmas. On sunny days, the ocean was a distinct saturated blue. So expressly pretty and blameless. Across the harbour a rugged headland towered massively above the water, a blackness blacker than the sky stuck in the gentle vista, as though the headland were cut from charcoal cardboard, a vacant hole abandoned there to spellbind the senses.

This panoramic view of Bareneed, from the house's large upper window, placed Claudia high above it all. Visiting friends or journalists, standing in Claudia's studio, were astonished by the sprawling, picture-perfect scene. It did not seem so long ago when journalists, a different sort from the arts reporters who had occasionally visited, were at her door proposing questions about the disappearance of her husband and daughter. Occurring near Christmas, the disappearance had been just the sort of tragedy the media hungered for; their own special holiday-season feast. It had been eighteen months ago, the Christmas before last, and still not a single word or sign from her loved ones. She would not believe her dreams. Abstraction fashioned them. This she repeated to herself, fearing that she was losing her mind. To believe that Reg hadn't done something unthinkable to Jessica would be a remedy of sorts. Yet she also knew that his violence, a violence that had churned out of nowhere, had perverted him, made him "evil." There was no other word for it. He had become evil, his most savage will unguarded.

When Claudia and Reg were first together, Reg had been kind-hearted. He had wept with joy at Jessica's birth, bawled like a baby himself as he cautiously held his infant daughter for the first time. He was the perfect father, always on hand to play a game of cards or hide-and-seek, or to tell a wonderfully magical story about his father, mother or grandparents. He was a devoted husband, mindful of Claudia's needs and her delicate disposition, always a quiet yet strong presence, until his job was taken away from him. That was the turning point. After, he had started neglecting his family, keeping to himself, uttering a bare minimum of words. A few weeks later, he was watching Claudia and Jessica with a menacing scowl. He made them afraid, went so far as to curse at Jessica for something so insignificant as accidentally smearing peanut butter on the television's remote control. He had even snatched hold of her, grabbed her small arms and shaken her until she screamed, her shrill voice a wobbly rattle. Claudia grew nervous and terrified of him, was considering plans to take Jessica and leave, when Reg had disappeared. And Jessica with him. It was the grey dawn of a blustery winter's day. Harsh wind and frozen snow had stung Claudia's face as she stood out in the elements, calling for Jessica, screaming her name into the blinding white uproar. Two days after Christmas. Five days before New Year's Day. Eighteen months ago. The police had kept the file open. They were still searching for Reginald Kyle. Reg and Jessica.

The higher road in front of Claudia's house was paved but rarely used. Earlier that day, a car had passed with a young girl who had regarded Claudia from the passenger seat. The car had pulled into the driveway of the Critch house next door.

The thought of a child so near disturbed Claudia. She would be concerned for the girl's safety, with the woods close. The woods and the water. But she was worried for herself as well, worried at the thought of a girl skipping by, so full of life. So painfully full of life.

She heard the barely perceptible spill and rush, within the walls, of the water that was heated by the solar panels and pumped through the skeleton of the house.

"Mommy?" a young girl called from a chamber somewhere behind Claudia's back.

Claudia remained facing the window, her eyes staring beyond the room, out over the shadowed landscape.

"Mommy?" cried the voice. "Did you see the girl? The one you were just thinking of."

Claudia refocused on her pale reflection, her wet eyes shining, the coal-black ocean beyond. Two tears broke loose, crept along her cheeks toward the corners of her mouth, then farther down, the droplets hanging from her chin, before Claudia finally dabbed them away with her fingertip.

She brought the liquid to her lips and smeared it there, yet would not allow herself to taste.

Why am I still capable of tears, she wondered. Where is the water coming from? Her thirst had reached a new level of intrigue. Although her heartbeat now fluctuated even when it was not taxed by physical movement, although she experienced spells of dizziness, she could move as she wished, pacing briskly up the stairs, and she would not so much as shed a single drop of sweat. She was still capable of tears, yet her body could not produce sweat.

A shadow shifted over by the Critch house. The vague outline of a man, faced toward the barn. There had not been a woman in the car. Where was the woman, the wife, the mother?

"Mommy?"

Claudia turned and stared toward the doorway, through which she could glimpse two indistinct hardwood stairs descending to the lower storey.

She heard singing: "Myyyy fawww-ther went to sea-sea-sea to see what he could see-see-see, and all that he could see-see-see was the bottom of the deep blue sea-sea-sea."

Claudia's fingers stirred as if to divine the hidden texture of the words. Her eyes watched the jitter of her fingers; objects shifting independently of her will. The sleeve of her gown covered her arm with the words: *I wear it like a skin that tells my story by design.*

"Mommy? Did you know the girl is here?"

Claudia remained silent, still. She would not ask "who?" yet the girl's voice answered as though in turn: "She has a name like a bird, and she can see between dreams and waking, so we'll be able to play together. We'll be friends."

⌒

Rather than put Robin in her own bed, Joseph had tucked her in next to him for security and then switched off the bedside light. Presently, he lay beside her, wide awake, his thoughts illuminated.

Earlier in the day, Joseph and Robin had been out exploring fields and wide-open spaces, houses and barns with huge country yards separating them, old lanes barely wide enough to drive a car through. All of it sweet-smelling and vivid under summer sun. Joseph felt like a kid again. Free. He had wondered where his Uncle Doug's house might be located. It was possible that they had passed right in front of it without knowing.

Bareneed was everything he had expected, full of charm and character — a perfect place for a summer vacation. When he had first discovered the advertisement in the *St. John's Telegram* stating that the old two-storey fisherman's house was for rent in Bareneed, a nostalgic smile had visited his lips. At once, Joseph had thought of his late father, Peter, and then of the black and white photographs of his Uncle Doug who still lived in Bareneed. Doug was a stern proud-looking young man in the pictures. He would be in his late sixties by now. Joseph hoped he would get to see his father's homestead, where he assumed Doug still resided. He hadn't mentioned Doug to Robin yet, for he was uncertain how his uncle would react to the news of their visit, considering the rocky history between his father and Doug. But, in all fairness, that shouldn't stand in the way of Robin getting the chance to know her great-uncle.

As a fisheries officer, Joseph had patrolled the waters around most places in Newfoundland, but he still marvelled at the eccentric names. Bareneed. He recalled its position on the map, an hour and a half southwest of St. John's in Conception Bay. Other communities in the area had equally colourful names: Cupids, Port de Grave, Shearstown, Cutland Junction, and Burnt Head. What better place for a child? A historic house, a rustic barn, the bountiful ocean. During their three-week stay, Robin would get a heaping taste of the outport way of life. A bit of family history. A link to the past.

Uncle Doug, a hardy fisherman like his father and grandfather before him, had disowned Joseph's father when Peter resolved to pack up his family and head to the city. Joseph had been an infant at the time. Peter had declared he was through with fishing, didn't care for the lifestyle, wanted better for his family. *Better.* That was the word that had exacted the damage. A life on land. Joseph's mother had said that Uncle Doug accused Peter of going after the easy life, turning soft, becoming a townie. A nasty racket had ensued and the two men never spoke to each other again. Uncle Doug had, however, attended Peter's wake, standing in the corner of the funeral parlour, all alone in his one good suit of clothes, then leaving after a respectful amount of time had elapsed. At the open grave, with the polished casket about to descend, Joseph had searched around for Doug but had not located him.

God only knew what Doug thought of Joseph becoming a fisheries officer. No doubt the old-timer assumed the whole lot of them had turned traitor.

Uncle Doug was Peter's only brother and the last living member of that family, and so Joseph felt a need and obligation to get to know him before he was gone, taking his stories and family folklore with him to the grave. Joseph had already heard a few stories from his father, who had told them while staring off through the window and speaking in a faithful tone of reminiscence and honour.

There was the tale about how Uncle Doug had been in his fishing boat during a violent storm and how the top half of his thumb had been torn off in a winch. The thumb had plunged soundlessly overboard in the gale, and Doug had sewn up the bleeding stump with a needle and fishing line while standing intently in his rocky boat, the sea swelling and rearing around him, sloshing over the edges, threatening to capsize his vessel, spraying salty mist into his eyes.

Another yarn told of the time when he and Peter were teenagers out in their boat on a beautiful summer's day. They had heard a sound in the distance and gazed skyward to spot a biplane flying toward them from the horizon, sinking lower and lower, heading straight for Mr. Hawco's house up on the ridge which it soon struck, tearing the second storey off before swerving wildly and humming shrilly directly down at Peter and Doug. Miraculously, the plane missed them, plummeting into the water, no more than thirty feet from their boat. Doug leaped from the dory and swam toward the smoking plane, in a fit to rescue the pilot. But as he neared he could see no pilot, no sight of him in the cockpit. After climbing up on the wing, Doug discovered that the pilot had been decapitated in the crash, and the head was nowhere to be found.

If all the stories were true, Uncle Doug was nothing less than indestructible.

Joseph's parents had both passed away, his father first, of brain cancer thought to have been caused by toxins in the building where he worked for thirty years as a government clerk in the tourism department. His mother had died six months later. Natural causes, the doctor had said. A smothered heart, Joseph assumed. She had been retired from her position as a nurse for only four years. His parents were intelligent hardworking people with a robust sense of humour. Of everything, he missed their humour most, the evenings spent gathered in the living room swapping stories of past stupidities and adventures gone wrong that left them in fits of laughter, gasping for breath and swiping tears from their eyes. Joseph regretted that Robin had barely known them. They had died three years ago, when Robin was only five.

Joseph recalled how this afternoon, as soon as the car had pulled into the Critch's grassy driveway, Robin had leaped out to investigate the possibility of other children in the area. There was the solar house directly west of them, and to the east, farther up the higher road, an abandoned church. No children there. A group of people had been lingering around a fresh grave in the adjacent graveyard as Joseph and Robin strolled by. No doubt, the body from the funeral they had passed on arriving in the community. Joseph had thought of his Uncle Doug. It might be him in the casket. Wearing the expressions of the deeply grieved, the mourners had merely looked up to regard Joseph and Robin, making no motion nor acknowledgment.

Joseph stared at the ceiling, the old wooden slats painted white, the ancient brass light fixture with its bevelled orb. Who was the woman in the solar house? He tried clamping onto her image, yet his thoughts kept drifting to the graveyard, the sullen people who had watched them pass. Morose faces gradually recast by anger.

-◦)

Tommy grinned at Miss Laracy and tilted his head toward the narrow hallway that led to the front of the house. "I were drawing."

"Da fish?" asked Miss Laracy, fondly patting the warm partridgeberry loaf where it sat on the wooden kitchen table. She felt stirrings of hunger and could do with a slice and a mug of tea, but she was set on seeing

Tommy's drawings first as they were always of great interest and of such spectacular craftsmanship.

"No, not fish, udder stuff." Turning abruptly, Tommy headed down the hallway, the walls to both sides cluttered with dozens of framed biblical quotes done up in fancy writing, and framed black and white portraits of families unrelated to Tommy. Miss Laracy's favourite biblical quote was "By Grace Are Ye Saved." There was lovely truth in that sentiment, yet she also liked to joke about it with Tommy, pausing to tap the frame glass and say, "By Grace are ye shaved."

Tommy gave a generous sweep of his arm for her to follow.

"Rayna's over fer a visit," he said.

"Ye got fresh butter fer dat loaf?" asked Miss Laracy, keenly on Tommy's trail.

"Yays. I'll put da kettle on if ye desires a cup."

"Love one," piped Miss Laracy, stepping into the parlour and giving Tommy a wink. "Finest kind." The parlour was crowded with furniture of assorted styles and ages. Miss Laracy nodded at Rayna, who was seated in a state of terminal relaxation on one of the low-back couches, a drink in her hand, an uncapped and half-filled bottle of amber rum on the coffee table beside her. The glow from her aura was dangerously dim and mould-green, which signified she had been drinking for quite some time. Her liver was out of sorts, her bodily humours tainting the inner light. "Evenin'," said Miss Laracy.

"What're ya at," Rayna blurted out, her head wobbling slightly while she licked her puffy lips. She was wearing a pale blue T-shirt and navy stretch pants that weren't the slightest bit complimentary considering her figure. A woman her age should look after her figure, Miss Laracy said to herself. Although men these days went after anything, so there was hardly any point in keeping up appearances. They weren't fussy about what they settled for. Just look at the mess of her mop of hair, like a birch broom in the fits. Such a sad state of affairs. Rayna had let herself go since losing her husband. No major loss there; her husband was no real catch, a worthless scum-of-the-earth sort who drank the grocery money away. Miss Laracy noticed that Rayna's feet were bare. A shocking display. She had kicked off her sneakers and peeled off her socks. The utter trollop.

"Care for a swally?" Rayna asked, sloppily raising the bottle.

"Naw. Narry a part o' dat foolishness."

Tommy stood stiffly by the mahogany dining table, where his drawings were laid out. The table, with massive carved legs, had been salvaged when someone threw it into the yard to make room for a shiny new chrome one. Next to the table, a blue-washed sideboard with two deep drawers displayed a cluttered arrangement of yellowing, patterned plates that featured tiny roses. A curiosity shop, with nothing for sale.

Tommy touched one of his drawings with his finger, giving it a slight nudge away from himself, then briskly shoved his hands in his pockets. The drawing directly in front of his burgundy brass-studded leather chair detailed three large insects hovering over a mountain. It was drawn in black charcoal, a fact made evident by the black streaks along the front of Tommy's shirt. He rubbed his fingers there, slowly up and down while he watched Miss Laracy, modestly awaiting her treasured opinion. He nodded sheepishly and grinned, encouraging her.

"Tommy's great drawer," Rayna hollered. "N'ver saw no one's good 's him."

"Wha's dat?" asked Miss Laracy, ignoring Rayna and shuffling nearer to squint down at the picture.

"Hel'copters," Tommy announced, his eyes widening in warning. He pointed toward his lace-curtained front window. "Over da headland."

Miss Laracy picked up the drawing and held it secure to her eyes. "When dey comin'?" she asked, the paper brushing the tip of her nose as she meticulously considered each square inch.

Like a timid schoolboy, Tommy shrugged his shoulders, shifted on his feet. "Cup of tea or what?" he asked in a fit of nerves.

Without fail, this happened each time Tommy presented his artwork to Miss Laracy. It was obvious that he harboured a longing to show off his artistry, but, after doing so, he wasn't fussy about discussing what he had created. It was as if the omens he sketched were injurious and — when they ultimately arrived — somehow became his responsibility.

"Cup of tea," Rayna muttered sleepily. "Not 'xactly." She chuckled once and blew out through vibrating lips. A sound like a horse. She laughed shrilly, unevenly raised her arm and let it drop, slap against the side of her leg.

Miss Laracy glanced back at Rayna, who had drawn her feet up on the couch and stretched out on her side. Her eyes slipped shut and the glass in her hand tipped at a precarious angle above the scarlet oriental rug. Fortunately, she had drained the glass. While she breathed in sleep, her aura appeared fortified, made stronger now that her physical nature was at rest. The glass dropped from her fingers and thudded against the rug.

"She's not feeling da best kind," Tommy apologized, affectionately. "Out of sorts, she is. Poor soul."

"Imagine so."

"I'm watching out fer her."

"Yer a Godsend, Tommy, me son."

"So, I'll put on da kettle."

"Yays," said Miss Laracy, setting down Tommy's drawing with a ponderous expression. In a heartening tone, she felt obliged to add, "A cup o' tea would be right nice." She saw that Tommy was watching where she had laid the drawing. He was staring at what he had invented and she could have sworn she saw movement reflected in his pupils, the helicopters shifting, or perhaps it was just where tears had begun to gleam in his eyes, despite the fact that he was trying so hard to hold steady his smile. Miss Laracy reached out to comfort his hand in both her own.

"Dun't ye worry yerself 'bout da t'ings ta come, Tommy, me love." A doting, toothless grin was advanced as comfort. Miss Laracy patted his hand devotedly. "Dun't ye worry none 'bout wha's ta come before us. Dese t'ings always pass. Dey always pass and never do us no real harm in da long run."

-∽⦿∽-

Joseph wished that he could simply shut his brain down, flick a switch to face an insensible black void. Even though he was lying still and removed from his actions of the day, swift images kept revisiting him of their own accord. Presently, his mind was replaying his and Robin's drive out from St. John's. Robin had been excited for the first half-hour on the highway; she sang along with the latest tunes on the radio, invented her own lyrics for the bits she was uncertain of, and smiled at Joseph in that extraordinary daughterly way. For a while, she even forgot about her drawing, an obsession that was beginning to worry Joseph. It was a pleasure to hear Robin's voice. But then Joseph, tiring of the sugary triumphant pop music sung breathlessly from the pinnacles of mountaintops, pushed in a tape of opera music.

The momentum of the car and the serenity of the orchestration lulled Robin into silence. Without a word, she reached down into the bag at her feet, took out her notepad and pen, commenced drawing. The music, none of which Joseph could readily identify, sustained the majesty of the highway landscape: the blond, green and burgundy barrens scattered with massive grey boulders tossed here and there by the calamitous withdrawal of the ice sheets, the lines of evergreens densely tangled together in the far distance, and the small ponds scattered haphazardly.

Occasionally, Joseph would glance at Robin, her unblemished face, the childish integrity of her mannerisms. Brimming with love and pride, he would brush her hair back from her cheek or take hold of her hand, the one not holding the pen, and marvel at the size of her fingers. They held hands for most of the way out.

When they finally arrived at the turnoff for Shearstown Line, a sign indicated that Bareneed was twenty-three kilometres away. Rolling fields opened up around them. Sheep grazed and hay lay harvested and bundled in lush green pastures. Joseph and Robin inspected the land; the opera music came to a crescendo and receded, infusing them with grace.

"Isn't this beautiful?" Joseph commented.

"Yeah," Robin quietly agreed. At first, she merely glimpsed at the landscape, in between strokes of her pen, but soon her attention was drawn fully to the land and she leaned forward with her arms on the dashboard.

A sign indicated the turnoff for Bareneed.

"There it is," Robin said.

Joseph eased up on the accelerator and took the turn. Far ahead, a rocky headland loomed over the harbour. Generous parcels of land separated the square narrow-clapboard houses, but as Joseph and Robin moved deeper into the community the land at either side of the houses diminished. The houses were still attached to large parcels of land, but the land stretched out at the rear, backyards inclining toward the craggy grey hills that protectively framed the north and south sides of the community.

Joseph checked Robin's expression to see what she thought of the place. "This is it."

"It's pretty. There's water, right?"

"See the harbour up there?"

Robin stretched higher in her seat. "Oh, yeah. Wow! Cool!"

"Nice old houses, hey? Maybe we can go fishing later."

Robin grinned mischievously and curled her fingers up close to her face, while quickly raising and lowering her eyebrows. "Really? Right away."

"We have to get settled first."

They passed the post office, across the road from the red one-storey community centre and fire hall. Within moments, they had the ocean directly at their left. Robin looked toward Joseph's window, craning her neck.

"Look at all the boats!"

"Practically everyone in the community owns one."

"The water sure is beautiful, isn't it, Daddy?"

"It sure is, sweetie." Joseph gave her a closed-lip smile, then glanced at the steady dark blue surface that he had sailed on for more than twelve years. Mostly smooth times, only the occasional altercation with local or foreign fishermen engaged in illegal harvest. The worst had occurred a few weeks ago: as he boarded a vessel, a bucket of rotting fish had been dumped on him. Even after two long showers, the smell was still there, either on his body or plugged in his nostrils.

The water was magnetic. Watching it, Joseph experienced a rush of satisfaction at his daughter's ability to distinguish the beauty in the sea, to mirror exactly how he felt.

Up ahead, there was a gathering of cars along both sides of the road, the afternoon sun glinting off windows and chrome. People, outfitted in old-fashioned dresses and suits that reminded Joseph of his high school graduation, meandered toward a church. An ache of nostalgia. He eased up on the accelerator as Robin took an interest in the activity. As they neared the church's steps, Joseph spotted the black hearse.

"Is that a funeral, Daddy?" Robin asked.

"Yeah, I think so." He slowed the car to a crawl, as a sign of respect for the deceased, but also to avoid running over anyone.

"Who died?" Robin whispered in an achingly sad tone that was so sorrowful it was practically moist with tears.

"I don't know, sweetie."

An elderly man and woman, arm in arm, were strolling down the road. The black-haired woman wore a shapeless white and black striped dress and a plain black hat. The old man wore a blue suit that was buttoned tight across his belly. He paused and was rigid, seemingly taking deep breaths, one hand to his chest. The old woman was openly concerned. Joseph watched them in the rearview as the car rolled on, the woman gripping the old man's arm and cautiously leading him ahead. Should he have stopped to offer assistance? There were plenty of people around, people from the community who knew each other. Why should he have stopped?

Presently, Joseph refocused on the dark bedroom, letting his memories drift. The house seemed so still as he settled from his recollections. The watery wavering afflicted his body again and he was forced to think back, to anchor himself to memory.

Before picking up Robin earlier that day, he had loaded the car with pillows, blankets, books, dishes, pots, food and — most importantly — the fishing rods. He had been looking forward to this trip for months. He adored his daughter and was pained by the separation that limited his access to her. At night, lying on the couch in his apartment, he would imagine playing crazy eights or backgammon with Robin or watching a movie together, a big bowl of popcorn with chocolate melted over the top resting between them. Robin loved popcorn and chocolate, even more than the movie itself, which she didn't seem to care too deeply for. Movies could never hold her interest for long. Several times Robin had even turned her nose up at rented movies to continue playing some elaborate imaginary game. When asked why she didn't want to watch, she had told her father: "Too much of it's there." "Too much of what?" Joseph had asked. "All of it. You know, like the story and people. They show you everything." Joseph had not pressed her further but assumed that she was referring to how nothing was left to the imagination. Robin much preferred going outdoors and playing on the swings in the park, Joseph chasing her up the slide and growling like a dog while she yipped with delight. With these memories in his head, Joseph would get up and wander to the spare bedroom, Robin's room, and stare at the empty bed, the bed she would always make herself. He would glance over her toys, her stuffed animals, and her drawings tacked to the walls, and feel so alone and haunted. He'd have to leave the apartment and go for a walk to ease the melancholy that solidified in his limbs like lead.

Again, he drew his thoughts back to the bedroom of the Critch house with its faded rosebud wallpaper. Not a sound, save for Robin's soft breathing. He studied his daughter, kissed her cheek, studied her some more, then kissed her forehead.

On climbing out of bed, he ventured down to the dim kitchen. Leaving the light off, he stood by the counter, his hands on the cool rim of the sink while he gazed out the window. He had a view of the solar house, stars reflecting in its sloping roof. He waited, content to simply stand there, watching for signs of life in his neighbour's house. A faint gleam arose in the darkness behind an upstairs window, the orange hue swaying brighter and duplicating itself in another corner. A progression of candles being lit. A pale figure appeared in the window. The copper-haired woman in a scarlet nightgown with a half-collar that was buttoned at her throat. She raised her hands and pressed them imploringly against the glass, her eyes fixed on Joseph's kitchen window.

~♏~

The television flickered across Lloyd Fowler's face. He was seated in his darkened living room, watching a documentary on the Second World War, black and white images of naked wasted bodies stacked in inflexible mounds. Grey rib cages. Grey faces. Grey emaciated legs. While fighting in WWII, Lloyd had had no idea of the inhuman crimes being carried out by the Nazis. There had been rumours, but he and his fellow soldiers in the Royal Newfoundland Field Regiment had never anticipated the atrocities. It made what he had been through seem trivial. Regardless, he had once felt pride knowing he'd played a part, however minor, in shutting down those bastard Germans. He had once thought it honourable. Now, he couldn't care less. Whatever horrors people committed against one another were none of his concern.

He took a deep breath, heard a sound from the kitchen: Barb keeping an eye on him. She had wanted him to take pills that the doctor prescribed. "For what?" he had shouted back at her, slamming his fists into the arm-rests of his chair. "What? What?" A rage smouldered in his chest, a barely containable urge to spring from his seat and pound the living daylights out of his wife.

"You want something, Lloyd?" came her whispered voice from the cool kitchen dimness.

He waited a moment, drew a breath, shut his eyes and gazed into the inky blackness. He would kill her, then kill himself. Kill her with his stony fists.

"Lloyd?"

He opened his eyes, checked himself against his murderous intentions and tried to summon what he might want, but he felt no need that he could justify with words. "Nothing."

"You sure?"

He gave no reply, simply breathed, his eyes stinging with hatred. *Why the trouble with my breathing?* he demanded. Was this the way an old man died? He flashed on an indistinct memory of his son, Bobby. Virtually a stranger. Dead. Hepatitis, Barb had told Lloyd, but when he heard there was Plexiglas over the open casket at the funeral home, all his suspicions were confirmed. AIDS. Did Barb think he was stupid? He couldn't care what it was. It didn't matter to him. He hadn't spoken with his son in fifteen years and he refused to attend the funeral. Bobby had been buried on the main-land, in Montreal, next to his dead boyfriend. Barb had wanted Bobby brought home to be buried in the family plot, but Lloyd would have no part of it, leaving Barb to fly to Montreal alone. Lloyd was glad that his son was dead, truth be told. He was glad and mortally satisfied.

"You okay?" Barb's concerned voice.

Again, Lloyd Fowler shut his eyes. He felt the pitch-black swell of the sea, rising, the death that the sea held for them all. His hands pulling on the latticework of a net, his weather-beaten hands dragging in the empty weight, black water running from the net holes.

"I'm going back up. Why don't you come to bed?"

His eyelids raised of their own accord. He filled his lungs with a deep breath, the silence all around him suffocating. His fists tightened, rock-hard, on the worn armrests. Sleep was of no use to him. It offered neither relief nor rejuvenation. Not a dream in months, only this sombre vision of the sea. The stairs creaked as Barb ascended. Lloyd caught a final glimpse of her — slippers, calves and nightgown — then averted his gaze back to the TV. The black and white bombers were flying through the black and white sky. He exhaled, waited. No urge to pull in another breath. How long could he last without breathing? The flat needlessness seemed infinite. Bedsprings protested above him, taking Barb's weight. If he stood, he could climb the stairs two at a time, rush into Barb's room and beat the blood out of her. Beat her until she screamed and shrieked and died, his head buzzing with hysterical fear and excitement, his life somehow newly returned to him.

He refused to draw another breath. Outright refused. Never again. His skin prickled. On the small screen, black and white bombs fell through bland grey clouds as Lloyd Fowler shut his eyes, his grey leathery fingers working the net from the black water, the tendons and veins in his hands taut, the pores breathing, the net rising with a snagged rubber boot, water gushing from the opening, running over a patch of grey flesh practically aglow as it was lifted out of the water, the wet sheening leg, and then the thick oilcloth of decades-old trousers. A man, his hair swaying in the water like seaweed, his collarless shirt of grey and white pinstripes, his forsaken eyes fixed on the ebony sky high above the boat.

Lloyd Fowler's hands pulled harder; the body rose fully out of the water and dropped into his boat. Then came another body, trapped in the meshing, the small head of a child, wet white hair, eyes open, battle-grey bloated lips smiling in welcome, then parting to say: "You've found me. Keep fishing, you'll catch my father."

Where are the fish? he wanted to ask the girl. *Why are there human bodies now? Is this my new trade, fishing the dead from the sea?* These questions came in fragmented images more than words. He had lost his command of language.

His lungs empty and without need, Lloyd Fowler stared at the television screen to see deep inside himself. Airplanes. Bombs. Memories. Gradually he grew more and more light-headed, his swimming thoughts merging with the flashing pictures before him. His head weakly slumped forward, chin resting on his chest. Not another breath to trouble him.

FRIDEY

"Hey, slow down," Joseph called as Robin ran giggling from the front yard, out toward the higher road. "Yeah, you. I'm talking to you, lazybones. Look at me. I'm the one carrying all the gear." He was trying to act as jovial and foolhardy as possible. Summer usually made him feel that way. Vacation. Cut free from the hundreds of tiny hooks that work snagged in his thoughts. It was a blazingly hot morning. Not a whiff of a breeze. The parching sun was already tightening his skin. Maybe he should wear a cap. Since his hair had started thinning a few years ago, he had become concerned about sunburning his scalp, his brain boiling, but he just couldn't bring himself to wear a hat. He wasn't a hat man. He checked over his shoulder to make certain the door was shut, then waved the two fishing rods in the air. "Hey!" He raised the hand carrying the orange tackle box. "What'm I, your beast of burden?"

"Yeah," Robin called cheerily, skipping ahead in her yellow T-shirt and pink shorts that prominently featured white pussycat faces. Her sandals flopped against the asphalt as she ran on. Joseph appraised the bobbing braid he had worked into her hair, a lopsided but fairly competent job.

"Come on, slow down." He caught sight of tiny blue wildflowers growing in the tall grass beside the evergreens and maple trees on either side of the road. It was wonderful to see flowers in such a casual way. Checking ahead, he found Robin at a standstill in front of the solar house. She then stared back at him, her expression gloomy.

A few birds tittered in the trees as he neared his daughter. In the summer stillness, he heard the faint squeaking of a clothesline being pulled, someone taking in or hanging out their wash.

"Nice house. Lots of glass," Joseph observed. He particularly admired the second-storey balcony. What a great place to sit and watch out over the community. "It's a solar house. You know what that is?"

Robin said nothing.

"Big windows. Natural light." Turning to determine what might be viewed from the windows and balcony, he gazed out over the community and harbour. A stunning scene. "Do you know about solar houses?"

Robin shook her head.

"The panels trap sunlight and heat water that's piped through the walls. The water keeps the house warm."

With the sun on their faces, they both studied the house in silence.

"You can see everything up there," Robin said with a confidence that surprised Joseph.

"How would you know, shrimp?"

"I can see, too, you know," she insisted, squinting toward the sloping road.

Thirty feet away, a woman was approaching, her head bowed as if immersed in thought, her arms folded against the bosom of her long cream-colored cotton dress, the pleated length grazing her sandalled feet. Her copper hair was combed away from her forehead, held back by a cream-coloured band. The striking pallor of her skin insinuated the appearance of old-world daintiness and contemplative restraint.

"Robin," Joseph whispered. "Stop staring." He gently nudged his daughter's shoulder with the tackle box. "Come on." He ambled ahead, his cheeks flushed hot. Without doubt this was the woman from last night, the woman who stood in her window as if beckoning to him.

Continuing down the quiet road, he tried to lure his eyes away, to pretend interest in the landscape, but they fidgeted back to his enigmatic neighbour. Less than ten feet from them, the woman looked up, not even slightly startled, to regard Joseph and Robin.

"Afternoon," Joseph said as Robin edged near him, pressing into his leg. He tried not to imagine the woman in the window, her hands pressed against the glass, her fingertips turning white, but the harder he tried the more his eyes insisted on exploring those ringless fingers and hands.

Observing her this near, Joseph was struck by the strange contours of her body, the slender and sensual shape of her arms and legs juxtaposed against the ampleness of her breasts and broad hips. A figure out of place, dispro-portionate to herself, yet this disparity only worked to heighten her allure.

"Afternoon," the woman finally replied, without offering a hint of smile. Her voice was raspy, parched. She tried clearing her throat while glancing at Robin for a shaky moment. She licked her full lips and blinked, her eye-lids blossom-pink. Her face was heart-shaped, her nose remarkably small, and her green eyes dipped at the ends, insinuating a melancholy that appeared to characterize her nature. "You must be in the Critch house." Vacantly, she observed Joseph. Had she even seen him at all last night, or had she been watching for someone else? If so, then whom? Who could possibly have his eyes fixed on her, besides him? There was only his house and the woods surrounding it. Had she been staring into the woods?

"Just got here," Joseph blurted out, at once feeling like a fool.

"That's my place." The woman loosely gestured toward the solar house, her eyes flitting down at the road, then in the direction of the harbour as if preoccupied with the water.

"We're out to catch some fish." He raised the fishing rods. "I guess that's obvious."

The woman gave no reply. She studied Joseph's hands with interest, mindful of the fishing gear.

"Great view," Joseph said.

"It is."

"I'm Joseph." He moved to extend his hand, the one gripping the tackle box. Awkwardly, he laid the box on the cracked asphalt and offered his hand.

The woman touched his hand hesitantly, holding only the tips of his fingers for a brief moment. "I'm Claudia."

"And this is Robin."

"Hi," said Claudia, proposing a courteous but weary smile. Without wait-ing for a reply, she wrapped her arms around herself, gave a shiver, and strolled toward her house, oblivious of the two she had just been speaking with.

"Hello," Robin finally said.

Joseph placed his hand on Robin's hair and drew her head to his hip. "I guess we'll be seeing you," he called after Claudia. "We're here for a few weeks." He bent to pick up the tackle box.

"Okay," Claudia said, already halfway along her grassy driveway. Again, she stared toward the water, shading her eyes from the gleam of the sun.

"Thanks," Joseph called in return, an inappropriate politeness that might have been mistaken for derision. But Claudia was too absorbed in her own thoughts to take any notice.

Feeling slighted, Joseph continued on in silence. A moment later, he glanced back to see Claudia stepping in her front door, shutting it. He recalled the black dog from last night and searched the front yard. No sign of it. He wondered why Claudia had acted so distant. He was convinced she had been staring directly at him last night for well over ten minutes, all the while his heart going out to her, feeling for her desolation, before she had drifted into the candlelit depths of her bedroom.

With a sigh, he chided himself for behaving like a schoolboy. He was here with his daughter. A flirtation would be unfair to Robin. Regardless, he steadied his heart, tightened it, assured himself that it was over with Kim. It pained him, but he had to be realistic. They simply did not belong together any more. Their interests had shifted and they had ceased caring about one another. Joseph knew every little detail about Kim. She had revealed each thought, each aggravation, each of her likes and dislikes, each trivial and complex consideration. She had embraced the age of openness, and the age of openness had obliterated any whiff of mystery in her. The politics of marriage debasing marriage itself.

Robin had been the only thing keeping them together, but even she — sadly — was not enough to reinvent their love.

Now, Claudia possessed a Victorian beauty, a seemingly placid femininity, that gouged at Joseph's heart. She was what he believed, in his idealist and unrepentant male core, to be the consummate woman. And it was summertime, which further exhilarated matters, linked as the season was to the promise of romance, whimsy and flights of fancy. Dazed by amorous thoughts, he glanced back at the solar house. Robin was already watching there. She raised her arm and waved.

"Who's that?" Joseph asked.

"A girl."

"Where?"

"In the top window."

Joseph checked but saw only the reflection of one of the big fluffy white clouds hanging in the blue sky. "I can't see anything but clouds."

"She's behind the clouds, Daddy," Robin said, obviously frustrated with him for his stupid blindness. She waved again, her arm sweeping gracefully through the air. "See, she's waving."

~◊

New procedure dictated that Sergeant Brian Chase cruise through Bareneed four times over the course of his shift. Two weeks back, he had rarely visited the small community, which was off his main run — Shearstown Line. The RCMP had stepped up its patrol of the area, to make its presence obvious, let people know the police were available to lend a hand if required.

Bareneed was usually a peaceful town, no different from any other outport community — the occasional youth mischief, assault, a car in a ditch, impaired driving or domestic disturbance. Recently, however, there had been an undercurrent of unease and violence. Nothing like the trouble Chase had experienced in the Native communities in Saskatchewan. Eight years of his early career had been devoted to investigating some of the worst things he'd ever seen, until there had been a worsening in the signs of depression that his wife, Theresa, had been exhibiting. His talk of rapes, child abuse, suicides and murders had seemed to actually wound her. Theresa was unable to buffer herself against the grimness the way Chase had learned to. Even after he vowed not to talk about crime of any sort, it appeared as if Theresa was still absorbing the bleakness that Chase's body had faced and somehow retained. In her sluggish, medicated tone, Theresa had said: "I can feel it coming off you, Brian. The terrible end of things." Not only the words but the manner in which she had spoken them made him angry with himself. The way she regarded him made him feel like an outsider in his own home, and he was already experiencing plenty of that in his work. Being half-Native, he was viewed with animosity by many Natives. It didn't help matters that he had chosen to be an RCMP officer, to walk in the shoes of the white man, to inflict white man's laws upon the people of the First Nations. Regardless, he was still reluctant to move away. He had made a life for himself in Saskatchewan, his roots were there; his mother had returned to life on the Red Lake reserve after his white father's death. A boating accident. Alcohol was involved.

Chase had learned to bear the manifestations of Theresa's illness: the eradication of intimacy of any sort between them, her utter disregard for his accomplishments, her constant dwelling on past difficulties. He had accepted these symptoms, helping out around the house, doing his own cooking, washing, ironing, and in his free time burrowing into a very different life on the internet. The crime sites were what fascinated him. He had countless sites bookmarked where he read about old cases and studied crime-scene photographs which he downloaded onto his hard-drive. He had amassed quite a comprehensive collection and even knew the details associated with each photograph, the engrossing calculations of each death. His particular area of fascination was with drowning victims: people who had drowned accidentally or had taken their own lives, and murder victims who had been dumped in lakes. Why did people feel the need to put themselves in water? Why did killers assume that a body should go in water, as if returning to its rightful place?

In his emotional seclusion, Chase had even begun visiting chat rooms and having conversations with new friends of all sorts, establishing relationships through the wires while Theresa dozed on the couch in the living room. He believed he had found a way to deal with his brutal loneliness, but when Theresa's doctor proposed that her depression might be largely situational, living as they were on the edge of the reserve, there was no other choice. Chase felt compelled to seek a transfer to a detachment with a low crime rate, in a region rural and remote.

Theresa had taken to country living. She had weaned herself off her medication and no longer lay on the couch alone all night, mindlessly ingesting whatever happened to be on television. She bought country magazines from the local drugstore and made plans to remodel the old house they had bought for a song in Port de Grave. Property rates were so low it was ridiculous. Their house hung on the edge of the water, the ocean literally in their backyard, and the hospital a few hundred yards up the road, just in case. As much as he wanted to, Chase couldn't put much faith in Theresa's bursts of clarity and energy. He had experienced them before. She would become almost manically interested in a project, put herself completely into it, until she burned out and then withdrew into herself again.

A few days ago, a new bottle of antidepressants had appeared in the bathroom cabinet after Theresa had started complaining of bad dreams, dreams that always worsened and portrayed such repugnant acts of horror that she would not even repeat them to Chase. The pills stopped the dreams. They also killed her passion.

When Chase wasn't on duty, he was up to his eyeballs in gyprock, plaster and pine. When he could steal a few minutes of free time, he was on the internet. He had upgraded his computer before leaving Saskatchewan, figuring he'd need it to keep in touch with the guys.

Arriving on the scene of a disruption in Bareneed, Chase still marvelled at the ease with which it could be contained. All over before anything began. The domestic disputes were the only violations that posed a genuine threat. You never knew with a domestic dispute. But he hadn't come across any crazies with shotguns threatening to wipe out the world. Not yet anyway.

The worst thing he had faced was a man who had committed suicide in his front yard. The man had used a shotgun. Chase and one of his fellow officers were required to pick up globs of the man's brain to put in Baggies. The fire department had to be called in to hose down the front of the man's house where it was sprayed with blood.

Sitting in his cruiser after stabilizing a situation, Chase would assure himself, "This is nothing," while his mind reeled through the dead he had witnessed both on his computer and back in Saskatchewan.

The tranquility of country life was oddly distracting after the gritty chaos of the Red Lake reserve. He'd often have the urge to trade stories with his fellow officers at the Port de Grave detachment. The guys would swap their tales and Chase would start picturing what was left of the murder victims, the barbaric rapes, the mutilations, the frightened beaten children. He'd glance at the floor and see a body spread out there, a stiff arm with grimy fingernails poking out from beneath his desk, slimy green pond reeds wrapped around its wrist. He'd open the trunk of his cruiser to reveal an unfitting array of butchered limbs. He'd see a deserted cardboard box on the side of the road and suspect there was a blue baby inside. Plenty of stories to tell. Regardless, he chose not to say a word, had no idea how to pick the right words. Speaking about such tragedies would seem like empty-headed bravado. And it was anything but. It was human anguish and human sorrow: nothing to be made light of.

Chase had started to catch the nip of violence in the air in Bareneed. The recent shutdown of the cod fishery had left half the town unemployed. The seasonal crab and shrimp fisheries still carried on, but not nearly as many men and women were employed in those sectors. Chase had learned all about Bareneed's plight over his seven months stationed in Port de Grave. Job loss created idleness and all that went with it: shifts in morals, alcohol becoming solace, abuses born of frustration and powerlessness, and suffering turning so severe it manifests itself as rage.

Chase passed the community wharf that arced around the head of the bay, noted the small boats and dories tied up in a given order. The ocean made him nervous. He had seen enough drowning victims, suicides in bathtubs, children in lakes, to have developed a healthy fear of water. Beyond the dock, a breakwater held the water calm around the wharf.

Cruising on, Chase arrived at the large L-shaped concrete pier owned by the Atkinsons, a family of wealthy merchants. A man and a young girl were fishing off the end of the wharf. They weren't familiar; probably tourists. Chase wondered if they knew about the ban on removing cod from the waters. Even though it wasn't his duty, he decided to educate them about the restricted fishery as both a means of introducing himself and to quell his curiosity about the newcomers. In any event, they would at least have been warned if a fisheries patrol officer turned up and caused them trouble.

He steered the cruiser onto the gravel strip bordering the dock and clicked the gearshift up to park. He chose to leave his hat off, be casual. He gave the same consideration to his sunglasses, but decided to leave them on. Otherwise he would be squinting like a fool. Leaning out of the car, he immediately regretted quitting the air-conditioned vehicle. Not very often was he pressed to switch on the air conditioner, considering Newfoundland's maritime climate, but today the humidity was appalling. He checked the hasp on his revolver and hesitated before the lip of the wharf; the abrasive smell of creosote, saltwater and rotted fish hung in the summer air. The wharf seemed stable enough. He glanced in the water and thought he saw a body floating face down close to shore where the caplin were spawning. The mass of slim fish swarmed around the body, striping it black. Chase dismissed the vision; it must be only a recollection of a photograph or of a case from his past. Nothing more substantial than that. If he looked away, the body would be gone and, sure enough, when he did, it was.

꧁

Joseph was crouched beside Robin, instructing her on how to reel in her line. At the sound of footsteps, he swiftly turned to see a mountainous RCMP officer treading toward them, his boot leather gleaming in the sun, his hands on his hips as he scanned the poles and rigging on one of the shrimp boats. The officer was vaguely Native, dark-haired and dark-skinned. His attention shifted to the rocky beach where a number of seagulls were picking through the swarms of tiny eggs and caplin, dead or alive, washed and washing ashore. Two gulls, facing each other, flapped their wings and screeched in combat.

Nearing Joseph, the officer smiled and said, "Afternoon."

"Afternoon." Joseph gazed up with an expression of conditional friendliness. He felt unrested, his nerves raw. Last night, he had been troubled by dreams of sinking in water, a thick water like quicksand that had steadily dragged him under. He awoke, then fell asleep again, only to be immediately drawn back to the dream of sinking.

"Great weather."

"Sure is." Joseph studied the officer for a moment, guessing at his height and weight — must be at least six-foot-six and two-hundred-and-fifty pounds. He said to Robin, "Just leave the line there, sweetheart." He straightened, feeling the strain give way to weakness in his knees and legs.

"Don't lean too far," he cautioned as Robin carefully inclined forward to check over the edge of the dock where her red and white spinner dangled in the water. Six fish, large and small, were gathered around Robin's bait, facing it. The water was tinted green but clear, the shapes of rocks plainly visible on the bottom.

"I can see fish, Daddy."

"They're down there, all right."

The officer chuckled and shook his head. He removed his sunglasses and poked one ear stem into his top pocket. "Kids love to fish."

"That's for sure," Joseph took in the peaceful community, bathing in its amiable yet rugged terrain. "You must be a busy man," he remarked with an ironic smile.

"Not really. Just here for the holiday. My wife needed a rest."

Joseph searched the officer's large brown eyes, his soft yet hawk-like features, but could not determine if the man was being serious. If it was humour, then it was exceptionally dry.

"Catch anything?" the officer asked.

"Just got here."

The officer considered Robin as she bobbed her line in the water. "Plenty of caplin around. You could reach into the water over there and scoop up bagfuls."

Joseph tested the air with a deep breath. "No problem to tell."

"Yeah, there's a certain appealing aroma."

Two seagulls flew low overhead in a straight line, one after the other.

"Feast time for the gulls," the officer announced, gazing up. "Hey, come back with my supper." He waved a fist toward the sky then glanced at Robin, who was smiling at him. Her eyes moved to his gun holster, hanging from his wide leather belt.

"I don't have any children," said the officer to Joseph. "Wish I did. And I haven't fished either. Not once. What does that make me, I wonder?"

Joseph had no idea how to respond.

"Usually only slimy cunners around. I know that much. The locals call them connors. The occasional sea trout, but they're hard to come by, as they say. Tomcods every now and then, but you probably know about tomcods. They're as rare as mermaids."

"Can't keep them."

"You do know."

"I'm a fisheries officer from St. John's, so there's no worries there."

"Aw, a man with teeming pools of oceanic knowledge. Still waters run deep, I guess."

"I guess," Joseph agreed with a chuckle, then thought, *What does that mean?*

"I got one," Robin shrieked, jiggling her legs. "Daddy, Daddy. I caught a fish."

The tip of the blue rod bent in an arc. Robin clutched the rod with two desperate hands and leaned back. "Daddy!" she squealed with both fear and delight.

"Reel it in, sweetie." Joseph gazed over the dock, the magnetic imbalance of being too near the edge straining the muscles in his eyes. A wide-mouthed ugly fish with dark-green mottled skin was hooked a few feet beneath the surface. The density of water distorted its exact size, but it was unquestionably a sculpin.

"It's heavy," Robin whined, frantically hauling up and grinding her teeth. "I can't turn it."

Joseph recalled how Robin, four or five at the time, used to adamantly profess "I can stir it in myself" whenever Joseph tried to help her reel in the line. It was one of those incidents he hadn't thought of in years. He reached to grab the line, wound it around his fist, and lifted the fish out of the water, surprised to see red markings flash on its side.

"Wow," exclaimed the officer, no doubt for Robin's benefit, although he seemed curious about the odd markings. "That's a big sculpin. I don't think I've ever seen one that big. Made for the record books."

Joseph let the fish flop onto the concrete dock. Only its gills moved, opening to expose its blood-red innards and then shutting: an exile's desperation.

"I caught a fish." The glee in Robin's voice faltered as she leaned closer to stare. "Can we keep it?"

"Watch its horns," Joseph warned. "They can cut."

"Yuck."

"Never saw one with red marks before," the officer commented.

Joseph delicately set the toe of his sneaker against the sculpin's head and crouched to work the hook from its rubbery lip. It certainly was an exceptionally ugly fish. Brownish-green, golden and off-white, with red stripes. Knobby, tough and spiny. Big round black eyes pulsing, patchy skin and horns barbed by its gills. The sculpin's red markings appeared to leak along its sides as Joseph twisted the hook to disengage it.

"It's bleeding," Robin cried. "Eee-yuck."

"No," Joseph corrected, paying close attention to the peculiar advance of the red streaks. "It's just the colour."

The sculpin thrust up and down, not in a flopping rhythm but in spasms, as if being electrocuted. It slipped from under Joseph's sneaker and jerked up off the concrete, then wetly slapped down. Using the line, Joseph dragged the fish back toward him. It made a sticky gurgling noise as a deep rumble nudged the dock.

The officer checked toward the massive headland across the water. "They must be blasting somewhere," he proposed. "Maybe road work."

"Maybe terrorists," Joseph joked, but the officer didn't seem to get it. Feeling his fingers turn warm while he tried to disengage the hook, Joseph whisked them away. Flesh-coloured fluid seeped from the sculpin's wide mouth. A solid object began edging out as he wiped his fingers on his pants — a flesh-coloured sculpted orb, topped with something that resembled hair, matted in mucousy clumps.

"What the hell's that?" Joseph asked, standing farther away to get a better view.

Fluid pooled around the orb as it slid out of the sculpin's mouth, fully revealing itself: a small doll's head, the chipped lids shifting open, black eyes staring up at them in surprise. Painted porcelain lips cracked in a harrowing smile.

A seagull screeched overhead, dropping the caplin that had been pinched in its beak. The sleek fish plunked onto the dock beside Robin, whose fingertips had been reaching for the doll's head.

"Don't touch that." Joseph snatched hold of her wrist.

Alarmed, Robin gave him a pained look. Was his grip too tight? He loosened it, let go, as if he had been struck.

The sculpin was now utterly still; even its gills no longer throbbed. From rubbery lip to spiny tail, it was entirely red, as though it had been dipped in paint or dye. Another faint rumble shuddered through the dock.

"Weirdest thing I ever saw," said the officer. "You really know how to catch them." He mussed up Robin's hair. "I'd say that's a keeper."

FRIDAY NIGHT

The pages of the photo album were so worn it seemed as if one more turn might break them loose from their beloved sequence. For decades, they had typified the exquisite fragility with which Miss Laracy cradled her captured memories. Presently she sat with the album on her lap, the black and white photographs secured by silver corners. She studied them, as she always did, with a soul-reposing smile. She was seated on her comfortable purplish-grey couch. Her small parlour was cluttered with knicknacks from her life, and her parents' and grandparents' lives before hers, each item an integral link in the chain that once led the spirits to her. The particles of love in these objects. The scents of love. The calm-handed love of the departed absorbed through touch and breath.

The furniture was solid and wooden, the cushions of the couch worn with knitted coverings tossed over the armrests. There were ancient leather-bound books in a glass cabinet and a bookcase filled with 78-speed records tucked away in sleeves beneath the gramophone. On the coffee table before her, a cranberry-glass candy dish sat beside a cigarette lighter embedded in the head of a carved polar bear. It had sat there for decades even though no one in the house smoked. Beside the couch stood a black wrought-iron lamp, its frosted orchid-shaped orb softly aglow, casting light upon the photo album that rested on Miss Laracy's lap. The pages were made of black matte paper, the black and white photos bordered in white.

Miss Laracy examined the face of her fiancé, Uriah Slaney. He was outfitted in his officer's uniform from the Second World War. He had sent her the photo with his writing on the back. "Here I am in France. Nothing like Newfoundland. Love, Uriah." She ran her fingers over his smiling face, the Eiffel Tower in the background. Uriah had survived the war. He had survived the loss of one leg — a small price to pay to have him back home. Safe, alive. The loss of the leg had wounded him beyond the physical. But Miss Laracy had done her best to nurse him, to assure him that it was of no matter. It was not the leg that she loved, but him, his boyish kindness and lackadaisical charm. "I loves ye," she whispered, her adoring gaze alighting on another photograph. It was of two young lovers seated on a blanket. It had been taken during a traditional boil-up in the fall. They had been picking blueberries with their parents down beyond the old church where the berries grew in abundance. There were mostly blueberries but also the occasional hidden patch of partridgeberries, polished red and growing in moss low to the ground. Miss Laracy's father had taken the photograph of her and Uriah. They were both smiling yet positioned in an uncertain fashion, kneeling and sitting back on their haunches. A pot and kettle rested on a metal grate over a fire behind them. Boil-up. How long had it been since she had had corned beef and cabbage boil-up while picking blueberries? It had been one of her favourite outings.

Her smile was imbued with the same warm sentiment expressed in the photograph, as though her father were capturing the memory once again. So long ago. How many lifetimes? The camera was a brand new contrivance to them, just like the automobiles that were beginning to replace the clip-clop of horse hooves travelling up and down the lower road.

That day had lingered in her mind as one of those flawless afternoons. Not too hot, not too chilly. A comfortable sun in an autumn-blue sky, and a gentle fall breeze. After her father had snapped the photograph, he had left the young lovers alone. A while later, while their parents were off farther in the bushes searching out secret places where plump unpicked blueberries grew, Uriah laid back on the blanket and Eileen rested her head on his chest. He had caressed her hair. Presently she shut her eyes, recalling the cool fall air and the heat of the sun, the comfortable and intoxicating time, the flying bugs turned sluggish by the coming cold. Uriah's fingers in her hair, making her moan with delight for the very first time.

"Yays," she whispered, nodding quietly. "Yays, he had." She turned a page and studied the final photograph of Uriah, sitting in the dory wearing his salt and pepper cap, the beak shadowing his eyes but not his broad smile. The woollen sweater she had knitted for him made him so dapper, so rouguishly handsome. It was knitted from ocean-blue wool that she had bought at Garfield Ralph's in Cutland Junction. It was fine soft wool, of a lovely blue that made Uriah's blue eyes beam brighter. Edward Pottle was sitting beside him. They fished together. Uriah had gotten over the loss of his leg, was using a wooden one in its place. It never slowed him down. Never sullied his character. Never made him less of a man in the end.

Miss Laracy studied the photograph of the two of them about to venture out in their boat, out on the open sea to net their catch. Without a gust of warning, chaos had blustered in on the wind, boiling the sea black in an unsteady count of minutes. The dark sky closing down on waves rising like black hills fifty feet high. The sky descending, the ocean rising to become one and eclipse the two human specks in the speck of a boat that had dared to venture forth.

They had been missing for two days when Miss Laracy baked the three-bun loaf of bread that was meant to aid in the recovery of her loved one. A calm night was required and it was just that. With the loaf fresh from the oven, she removed a long holy candle from the box that had been blessed by the priest. She inserted the end of the candle soundly in the soft centre bun and made certain that it was straight. Waiting until her mother and father were doubtlessly asleep, she then swept on her shawl and carried the warm loaf down to the edge of the water, the surface of which was glassy-still in the night. Not a breath of air. She set the loaf onto the beach-pebbled shore and lit the candle wick with a match from the front pocket of her dress. Taking the bread in both hands, she approached the water, bent and set the loaf afloat. It bobbed evenly but remained near her. She gave it an encouraging push and the bread, with the single candle flame atop it, drifted out to continue on its course. The loaf of bread, baked by her hands, kneaded and shaped and baked by the hands of the lover of the man who had been lost at sea, was known to be the sole means capable of finding that man.

Crouched on the shore, Miss Laracy had watched the bread continue out, as though directed by her will, toward the mouth of the harbour.

She had stood there and drawn her shawl tighter around herself as the night was beginning to chill. *Bring 'im back ta me 'n I will make certain no 'arm comes ta 'im again,* she had pledged. *Bring 'im back ta da love he deserves.* She had watched the flame become smaller and smaller, until it was no longer in sight. Faithfully, she waited, expecting the flame to soon become bigger and bigger, returning to her with her lost lover in his boat, her conviction guiding Uriah back to her.

The chill, compounded with the pre-dawn damp, became more miserable. Regardless, she continued her vigil. As the hours passed, her legs grew weary and she sat on the shore, shifting to get comfortable atop the round and oval rocks. Positioned so, beneath the moonlight, she would not take her eyes from the horizon.

In time, her head began to slacken drowsily, yet she caught herself and forced alertness back into her body. If only she might lie down for a few moments. Nearby, within reach, she noticed a piece of driftwood, a hollow smoothed in the centre by the perpetual lap of waves. It was not so big that she could not pull it toward her with one hand. She extended her arm and took hold of the driftwood, dragged it nearer and then reclined, fitting her head into the hollow, the slope of the depression not so deep as to block her view.

She continued watching, her eyelids shutting occasionally, but only for instants before she was attentive again. As she came back to herself from one such lapse, she sensed a glimmer on the horizon that she suspected was the candle flame and the loaf of bread returning. Her heart began to gladden with expectation. It was there, no doubt, the flickering, the lightening. Anxiously she sat up, then rose to her feet. The darkness itself appeared to be withdrawing to ease her desperation. She had done it. She had actually done it. But then the flickering broadened, spilling along the horizon, and the entire world before her — not merely her own small world — began to brighten before her eyes.

It was only the dawn. The dawn once more without Uriah.

Uriah Slaney and Edward Pottle had never been heard from again.

Miss Laracy set her unsteady fingertips to the photograph, and traced the outline of her fiancé's face.

"Uriah," she whispered adoringly. "Ye still be me one true love. 'Tis da gospel trute."

⁓⟲

Joseph stood in the dark yard at the side of the Critch house, his attention directed toward his neighbour's lighted window. Crickets sounded from the front lawn and electrical wires hummed faintly. Down toward the lower road, a cat cried persistently as though wanting to be let in. The same shaggy black dog from last night was seated on Claudia's front step, watching the road, paying not the slightest heed to Joseph. He wondered if he should dump out the supper scraps for the dog. There was a leftover hamburger and fair-size helping of french fries. He made an involuntary sound toward the dog, a kissing noise, but the beast ignored him. Robin would love to play with that dog, if only it would show itself in daylight.

After supper, he and Robin had played tag in the yard and then, drained of energy, Joseph had suggested going inside to listen to the radio. Robin had reluctantly agreed, after clinging to his legs for several minutes and pleading to stay out. The radio could pick up sound from one of the television channels. A sitcom was on. They listened and pictured the characters talking, wondering what actions went with the words. Joseph had proposed that one of the women had taken out her eyeballs while saying: "Is this what you've been looking for?" The canned laughter had roared and they had laughed extravagantly. In another scenario, a man had said: "This is all I get?" Robin had insisted that the man was cradling a giant zillion-pound globe on his shoulders. Smart girl, Joseph had thought.

At bedtime, he had hurriedly read three books to Robin, anxious for her to fall asleep. He was exhausted and yet his thoughts kept leaping ahead to the moment when he might steal a glimpse of Claudia.

The glow from the solar house's front window consoled him. Two people alone, in separate houses, much the same as him and Kim. But was Claudia really alone? So far, there had been no evidence of a man. Joseph gazed up at the sky. Bright stars and then dimmer stars and the dust of stars so far away that he felt chilled. He had not anticipated these feelings of loneliness and longing, but was strangely afflicted by them since coming face to face with Claudia.

Back in St. John's, he always busied himself with research on his computer, keeping abreast of the latest news on ocean management, or poring through magazines and journals. When he grew bored of work, he would set out for a walk downtown, have a slow beer while watching people around him, speculating about the uniqueness of their lives. Then he'd pick up a video on his way back to his apartment. Plenty of distractions. Out here was a different story. The stillness made him ponder life in its most unadorned form.

He shifted his attention back to the house. Immediately after Robin had explained about seeing the girl in Claudia's window, Joseph had wondered if the child had been left alone in the house, or if there was a man present. A father. He hoped not. Claudia's striking despondency must be rooted in harsh or cruel deeds. Hopefully, her daughter provided her with the same sort of joy that Robin gave Joseph. That was always the bottom line. Children. Everything went back to children. Everything was done for children, and in turn the most precious and endearing reassurances were received from them.

There was no vehicle in Claudia's overgrown driveway. He felt sure there would be a vehicle if there was a man. Most likely a pickup truck. Perhaps the man was away. At sea. But the driveway was completely overgrown. Joseph considered wandering down the road and having a peek in the windows, to glean the truth of who might be living there.

Standing in the outdoors at night, watching Claudia's window and sensing the cool summer air against his skin, he felt the prickle of arousal rise up. Thoughts of a closer look further titillated him. He recalled the binoculars that Kim had given him back in St. John's. Heart already racing with excitement, he turned for the back door, checking the dimly lit ground, careful not to trip over clumps in the grass.

In the kitchen, he paused and stared at the binoculars where he had left them hooked over the back of a chair. What good would any of this do? When he was still living with Kim, he had used the binoculars to watch sparrows, finches and blue jays in his feeders. Yesterday morning Kim had lifted them from around her neck and looped them around his, saying, "For whales." He had accepted the binoculars, never anticipating the way they might be used. Raising them, he caught a whiff of Kim's heart-engaging perfume, no doubt from the black casing, the heat from her body transferring the scent. Whales. "What animal would you be if you could be anything?" Robin often asked her mother. And Kim's reply was consistently the same, "A whale."

Despite his hesitations, Joseph went outside and cautiously raised the binoculars, focusing on the solar house's large side window in the second storey.

As Claudia walked into view and paused behind the glass, Joseph's heart kicked up its pace. He fidgeted, yet held the focus steady. Claudia was wearing the same crimson nightdress, buttoned tight to her throat, that she had worn the previous night. She gazed down at an open book in one hand. Her other hand held something, perhaps a pen. She was writing. A large painting was hung on the wall behind her, above a bed, it seemed. A painting of waves crashing against a brown and grey cliff, the white spray arcing and foaming into the air.

Engrossed in her writing, Claudia approached the painting and then sat, her head and shoulders in view, her back against the wall. There was no gesture toward another person who might be sharing the bed. This magnified vision of Claudia, engaged in the simple act of reading over words she had written, of unconsciously turning the pages of a journal, was gorgeously erotic. It had been almost a year since Joseph had experienced sexual comfort.

Headlights swept across the grass and spilled over Joseph, casting him in faint light. A car was climbing the hill of the higher road. He let the binoculars drop, jolting his neck, and stumbled back into the shadows.

The car paused in front of Claudia's house. The shaggy black dog watched it, tipped its snout in the air and sniffed. Furtively raising the binoculars again, Joseph saw that Claudia was still in bed, reading. She glanced up and toward her window, conscious of a sound. Joseph's palms turned sweaty. The taboo of spying, the sense of betraying Kim, the notion of being caught, all these set his hands trembling and seared a flush in his cheeks. Regardless, he continued watching for a moment longer, not caring if he was found out, before lowering the binoculars to consider the vehicle slowly rolling through the darkness. He moistened his lips, listening intently. The purr of the engine implied that it was a large machine. As it advanced, Joseph learned that it was a jeep.

Pass, he winced to himself. *Pass. Pass. Keep going.* It stopped at the end of his driveway. Joseph backed deeper into the shadows; his spine struck the edge of clapboards and he cursed under his breath, considered inching toward the back door, rushing inside to hide. His heart pounded, the rhythm of his breath turning shallow and tight as a light flicked on inside the jeep. A man in a green army jacket and beret was studying a map. The driver, outfitted in the same garb, pointed to a spot on the map and the passenger wrote something there. The light was switched off and the jeep continued up the road, toward the graveyard and abandoned church.

"Daddy," pleaded a young girl's voice from the direction of the barn.

The hairs on the back of Joseph's neck rose at the sound. Every pore of his body broke out in a sickly sweat as he stole a look toward the barn's shadowed doorway. Was it Robin? Was she trying to scare the hell out of him? No one was there. His ears strained to catch another sound as he scanned the top floor of the barn, his vision snagging on an image in the left window: a bearded man's pale-green face illuminated by faint moonlight. Two ashen hands held up what appeared to be a fish as the man stretched open his mouth to an inconceivable width. Turning his head in profile, he slid the head of the fish between his lips, vigorously ramming it down his throat with the butt of his palm. The impression was gradually dispelled as the moon was shrouded by drifting clouds.

Joseph raised his shaky binoculars to focus on the window, but saw only cloud movement reflected in glass. No man. He directed the binoculars to Claudia's house. The candlelight had been extinguished. A cool breeze rose, chilling his sweat-soaked clothes as he lowered the binoculars.

⁓🜊

"What's your name?" Robin asked the orange-haired girl she knew only as Claudia's daughter. They were standing absolutely still, one across from the other, in the loft of a dilapidated barn. Layers of weighty nets, hung above them to dry, cast a mesmerizing cobweb of light over their faces and the accumulation of mouldering fishing gear. Water dripped on the girl, but not on Robin. The girl simply stared and held up her hands, palms facing Robin, seemingly unaware that she was soaking wet, soaked to the bone.

"What's your name?" Robin repeated.

"Hold up your hands," the girl instructed. When Robin did so, the girl clapped her own hands together once, then rhythmically patted Robin's palms against hers, the girl's right hand to Robin's right, then her right to Robin's left, crisscrossing after each clap, singing: "Myyyy fawww-ther went to sea-sea-sea, to see what he could see-see-see, and all that he could see-see-see was the bottom of the deep blue sea-sea-sea."

Robin couldn't help but laugh, as if the idea was funny. She wanted to play the game some more, even though the girl's hands were icy cold and wrinkly, as though she had been in the bathtub too long.

"Your turn," said the girl.

Robin patted the girl's palms in the same crisscross pattern: "Myyy fawww-ther went to sea-sea-sea, to see what he could see-see-see, and all that he could see-see-see was the bottom of the deep blue sea-sea-sea." She watched the girl's sad eyes and felt a desire to hug her, until the black smear inside the girl's mouth crept out, showing around the edges of her lips.

"What's your name?" Robin asked again, feeling scared and alone, wondering how far away she was from her parents, and which one of them might be the nearest because they were in separate places now.

The girl gave no reply.

Robin kept asking. It became like a knock-knock joke with no answer. Funnier and funnier. Robin began laughing hysterically. And the black oily smear leaked thickly from the corners of the girl's mouth, the festering laughter she was holding inside finally seeping free.

The girl sat down on the water-rotted floor and wiped at her chin. A number of building blocks in the shape of barns were arranged in front of her. Candle gleams shone within them, illuminating the tiny windows. Robin sat in front of the girl and the two children switched the blocks back and forth.

"I like living in these," the girl said with a sigh of resignation. She stared down at the blocks, pinpoints of lights reflecting in her eyes. Red and green and yellow, like Christmas-tree lights. "I live in the things my mother makes."

"You do?"

"Yes."

"How?"

"There's so much love in them, they keep me here, near her. The wires, you know, they cut through everything. They make us blind, whip us to pieces. They send us screaming."

"What wires?"

"The ones that connect the world for all the wrong reasons." The girl stacked one barn atop another, the candle gleams flickering. The top barn sank into the one beneath it, transforming into a single barn with the characteristics of both blocks.

"Hey, let me try." Robin stacked two blocks yet they refused to meld.

"What did you get for Christmas?" the girl asked, the colourful dots in her eyes lingering even after she gazed up.

"It's not Christmas," Robin protested. "Is it?"

"My father ended us. The wires make him go higher, farther. But sometimes he comes down because my mother still loves him, a part of her does. If my mother lets go of me …"

"What?"

"She'll only see me in dreams."

"Oh." Robin smelled grass and flowers. She looked around. They were in a field with circus animals: elephants, tigers and dogs were grouped around the far edges, while the trees were filled with parrots and multi-coloured birds of fanciful shapes and descriptions. "Cool!"

"This is a place where you can only imagine," the girl said, unimpressed. "Imagine, imagine, imagine. That's all there is to do when you're dead."

"Are you dead?"

The girl nodded. "Dreams make us real, you know? We come to life then. They're the only things that can do it now."

⁓◎

Two tiny white Ativan rested in Joseph's palm while he diligently studied the prescription label for the maximum dosage he could safely ingest.

Finding no such amount, he popped the pills, careful to keep his tongue steady over them while they dissolved to paste.

I'm seeing ghosts now, he repeated in his head while he changed his sweat-soaked clothes for clean ones from his suitcase. He stood, wide awake, in the brightness of the bedroom. Seeing ghosts. A foreign room in a foreign house. A room from bygone times with cream-coloured rosebud wallpaper and hand-carved ceiling trims and baseboards. All of his movements were hyper-real, his breathing amplified in his ears, every shape and colour an assault on his overwrought senses. A ghost. A man. What was Joseph doing here? Why wasn't he home with his preferred distractions that prevented him from staring too deep inside himself? His computer, his television, his twenty-four hour mini-marts. Home with his street lights and hospitals within driving distance. Hospitals with pill-wielding doctors and nice placid nurses to lay him down on a sterile white bed and give him drugs to float him happily out of his mind.

He tried to focus on one untroubling preoccupation, such as counting the drips of a leaky faucet. Monotonous order that would make him plain to himself. Rapidly searching his thoughts for a safe haven, he stumbled on Kim. Was she alone at home or out with her rubber-boot-wearing colleagues at the Ship Inn, sipping her standard pint of Guinness, licking froth from her top lip, smiling generously at a man seated beside her. A shiver rattled Joseph.

He stepped to the bedroom window and stared toward the harbour, where lights from houses reflected long trails on the black ocean. A sequence of silver shimmerings flashed out of the water, soaring then descending. But a few flickerings continued drifting higher, their graceful looping progression like the flappings of wings, ascending toward the massive headland and then plunging behind it.

Joseph shut his eyes and took a deep breath, counting to five on the intake, then to five again as he exhaled. Behind his lids, he saw the red sculpin and doll's head sliding from its mouth. He had kicked the fish back into the ocean after commenting that it might be full of toxins. Instantly, he regretted having done so.

The officer had laughed the comment off, then said, "You never know, though. They dump everything in the ocean these days. And everything's poison now, right? Kill you just like that." He had snapped his fingers and then, as if on cue, a man had stomped out onto the deck of the *Atlantic Charm* and hurled a white Styrofoam container into the ocean before ducking back in the ship's cabin. The officer said to leave the doll's head where it was and Joseph wondered if it might be evidence of some sort. Striding to his vehicle, the officer returned with a Baggie and an oversized set of tweezers. He methodically put the doll's head in the Baggie. "Souvenir," he said. "The guys won't believe this."

Joseph felt compelled to open his eyes, intuiting danger. A red sculpin. There was no proof of the existence of such a thing. Of course, there had been stories. Red dragon sculpins. But they were merely stories. Fishermen's lore. A myth passed on through generations. A portend of approaching calamity. He could call Kim to confirm the non-existence of the creature, to confirm that he was not mad. The entire episode with the sculpin seemed like a dream, far away and yet undeniably familiar and faithful to itself. The sculpin story would give him an excuse to call Kim. She mightn't know for certain, but she did have a friend who specialized in genetic deviation in marine life. What was the man's name? Arrogant guy, sweater-wearing vegetarian with a beard and big lips. Tobin. Luke Tobin.

Joseph was rooting himself in familiar thoughts, and the crest of tension dissipated. His heartbeat steadied and he felt a serene lagging in his veins. The pills were working. It was not so difficult to think now. Smooth effort. Smooth. He continued regulating his breath, pulling in air through his nostrils and counting to himself, "One ... two ... three ... four ... five," exhaling through his mouth for an exact count. *How far away is a hospital?* he wondered, spooking himself again with abusive, alienating thoughts. A sinking feeling clasping hold of his ankles and dragging him down to his self-fulfilling depths.

"It's okay," he heard his daughter mumble from the other room. He shot a look that way, expecting to see the ghost-man standing in his doorway. No one there. A blank. A frame. Robin must be dreaming. Joseph searched around for something to snatch up. An old cane in the corner. He rushed to it, gripped it in his hand and cautiously peeked out into the hallway. Not a soul to be seen. Holding the cane at ready, expecting someone or something to leap for him at any moment, he crept toward Robin's room and tilted his head through her door frame. She was sleeping soundly. He lowered the cane, set it down by her bed, then watched her quiet face, so peaceful. He placed his hand on her cheek. Warm. Was her chest rising? He stared there. Hard to tell if the bedsheets were lifting. He bent to pinch her nostrils and she stirred. He kissed her and smelled her hair, his eyes noticing the open notepad beside her. A drawing of three insects hovering over a huge rock or a mountain. As usual, Robin had drawn herself to sleep. Joseph removed her plastic container of crayons and her notepad, placed them on the uncluttered top of the dresser, then turned back to study his daughter once again. She was so beautiful and cherished. He would be devastated if anything ever happened to her. There was already such distance between them.

SATURDAY

Doctor Thompson was roused from a dream of a museum visit. The glass cabinets had displayed garments from people feared drowned in shipwrecks, items salvaged from trunks that had found their way to beaches, awaiting owners who would never arrive to claim what was rightfully theirs. Other glass cases protected chunks of wood recovered from vessels sunk in collisions with rocky cliffs or icebergs. Brass plates fastened to cabinet fronts detailed the history of each artifact. Thompson paused by a life-size exhibit of people outfitted in the fashions of various periods. The words inscribed on the brass plate read: DEATH BY DROWNING. He thought he saw one of the figures blink just as the bell for closing time rang, awakening him. He sat up in bed, remaining tucked under the stifling covers, aware of a chainsaw revving in the distance. Someone cutting wood for the winter already.

The telephone rang. *Has it been ringing?* he wondered. *What's the day? Saturday. It's Saturday and the weekend clinic is where? In Burnt Head?* He assumed it was anyway, but the persistent ringing of the telephone made him suspect that he had confused the days and overslept.

When Dr. Thompson picked up the receiver from his bedside table, Will Peters, the pathologist at Port de Grave Hospital, informed him that Lloyd Fowler had been brought in. DOA.

"What cause?" Thompson asked bluntly. He had a long history of disliking Peters' distinct air of superiority. Why so superior? After all, the man was keeping company with dead people. Maybe that was the key. Peters didn't have to suffer the courtesies of the living.

"Not certain," Peters remarked in a flat tone. "Not quite finished the autopsy."

"Heart attack?" asked Thompson, already irked enough to be experiencing the onset of a mild headache at his temples. He squeezed there, shut his eyes and squeezed.

"No heart attack. Heart's fine. No damage there."

Thompson breathed a quiet sigh of relief. He had examined Lloyd Fowler just two days ago, on Thursday, and if the man had died of a heart attack then the doctor would feel some measure of guilt. *Did I actually miss something? Am I senile? And if I am senile, would I have the slightest idea that I'm batty?* He heard the soft thumping of paws ascending the stairs. An inquisitive meow. Agatha, his cat, must have heard him speaking.

"His wife said he was having trouble breathing. Lungs are clear, though."

Thompson thought of Donna Drover, Muss' mother. Muss had died of "natural causes," but now things weren't seeming all that natural. Donna Drover was still on a respirator on the sixth floor of the Port de Grave Hospital, her condition unchanged. Lungs functioning at capacity. No inflammation or obstructions in the respiratory passages. Was it really depression as a few doctors had speculated? Could depression shut down a person's ability to breathe?

"Doctor?"

Agatha leaped up onto the bed, making a sound that was half-purr and half-meow, then leaned into him, rubbing her black fur against his cheek and purring with majestic affection. Only in the morning was she so emotional. "Sorry, I'm just a little stunned." He unconsciously rubbed the cat, sliding his hand down her back and loosely gripping her tail.

"Natural causes. There's toxicology tests yet, of course. But I don't see anything that would indicate poisons. No alcohol."

"Another 'natural causes.'"

"It happens. Rumour of more bodies, too. How 'natural' their deaths are is anyone's guess. I'd say drowning."

"What bodies?"

"From the harbour in Bareneed."

"Bodies? How many?"

"Not certain. Two, probably."

Agatha pushed her face against Thompson's so that he had to turn away. Peters was always a bit of an alarmist, a fan of conspiracy theories. An avid reader of books trumpeting the authenticity of UFOs. He occupied his own bizarre world. "What do you mean 'rumours'?"

"I haven't seen the bodies. Supposedly there's two. They're *not* for us to see. It's the army or navy that's taken control of them. Their own forensic team is involved."

Thompson was at a loss for words. He felt a sneeze coming on, pressure gripping at the back of his nostrils. Agatha. He was mildly allergic to felines. He glanced at the night table for his allergy medication, but there was only the mystery novel he had been reading the previous night, the cover featuring an illustration of a body floating face down in water. The sneeze clutched him, holding him in a fit of torment, unwilling to arrive. Finally it retracted, without delivering its payload, and his eyes watered madly. He felt tingly and faint while he wiggled his nose and sniffed up.

"Out of our depth," Peters said with a snicker.

"Right." Thompson dabbed at his eyes and mulled over Peters' words. He didn't care to stay on the phone any longer. "See you Monday." He hung up without waiting for a "goodbye" or offering one. He was scheduled to do rounds at the hospital on Monday morning, but Lloyd would be gone by then.

"How's my little pussycat doing this morning?"

Agatha meowed as Dr. Thompson picked her up and lovingly rubbed his face in her fur, despite his allergies. *Damn the allergies*, Thompson told himself, already sensing the bone-slicing ache in his knees. *And damn this useless body of mine.* He carefully stood and, with his free hand, tugged up the waist of his sagging boxer shorts. No sense lying in bed with his eyes wide open. "Wonder how our flowers are doing, hey?" He picked up his mystery book to read while on the toilet, trod barefoot downstairs to the kitchen, mindfully laid Agatha on the floor, his paperback on the table, and yanked opened the refrigerator door. Yawning, he scratched his chest, then rubbed his extended belly. *Two eggs*, he thought. *Two deaths.* He shut the door and decided on cereal.

While pouring the flakes into his favourite cobalt-blue pottery bowl, he glanced down at Agatha pushing and winding between his legs. The occasional "natural causes" death was to be expected, but Thompson, a life-long fan of a good mystery, was convinced that something was genuinely amiss. It wasn't just his fascination with puzzles, but rather a gut instinct. And what was all this foolishness about bodies in Bareneed harbour?

He poured cream over his cereal and sprinkled on a full teaspoon of sugar. He was supposed to be using low-fat milk, because his cholesterol was high, but low-fat milk lost its chill too fast and made his flakes soggy. Low-fat milk was disgusting. Low-fat anything was an outright pox on the creamy white epidermis of pleasure. If a man wasn't permitted to enjoy life at his age, then what was the point? It was fine to hand out advice, but following it was a different matter entirely. On the counter, three pill bottles were lined up beside his wineglass from last night. There was still a mouthful of Wolf Blass Red Label at the bottom. A shame to waste even a drop. He opened the pill bottles and shook out one pill from each. Novo-atenol for high blood pressure, Ranitidine for reflux, and Isoptin for his arrhythmic heart. He washed them down with the remnants of the wineglass, thinking: *Good for the heart.*

"What's the world up to today?" Thompson asked Agatha. "Death is what it's up to," he answered. He carried the bowl out onto the sunny back patio where he sat on the Adirondack recliner in his boxer shorts and ate in luxurious peace. The patio was edged with flower boxes on three sides. Thompson did a visual inspection: clusters of teeny purple lobelia, yellow marigolds, the little faces of light-blue and white pansies staring up at him, red petunias not fully bloomed even in June, but they'd last into the fall, as would the pink impatiens. They were strong — unlike the pansies, delicate creatures. He mustn't forget to poke some food pellets into the soil. A few sparrows chirped in the far-off woods and Agatha stared in their direction, chattering with trancelike desire. The chainsaw had stopped, thank the Lord. Chewing a spoonful of flakes, he sensed a rumbling reverberating through the wood in his chair.

"What're they blasting now?" he asked the cat. "Hey, Agatha. They're always blasting something. Have to get through it, by God. Punch a hole through rock. Forge ahead." A wasp appeared out of nowhere and lingered over his bowl. He swatted it away, but undeterred it flew at him with greater determination. Again he swatted it, shifting in his chair as the wasp became more agitated. He swatted it frantically as it hovered around his ducking head. Grunting, he laboriously shoved himself to his feet and overturned his bowl on the patio, the pottery smashing in four large pieces, the cream spilling against his bare toes. He gazed down at his feet. Agatha had come over to investigate, sniffing, then nonchalantly lapping up the cream while keeping her eyes on her master. She seemed to be hoping that he might not notice her tongue darting in and out, or, at the very least, forgive her indiscretion.

Two more wasps, attracted by the cream, were hovering in a hazy manner. One of them rose toward Thompson's knee. The other flew away, then back again, nearer, coming directly for his lips. He let out a blunt shout and skipped and leaped toward the doorway, bolting inside and slamming shut the door. He checked himself for wasps and, finding none pronged in his skin, peered out the small window. His favourite bowl broken to bits on the patio. Agatha serenely licking up the milk.

"Blood-of-bitch wasps," he muttered, opening the door a crack. "Come on, Agatha. Save yourself, girl." The cat regarded him with contemptible disinterest, then continued lapping. "Stubborn beast." Why weren't the wasps bothering Agatha? They were probably in it together, conspiring to rob him of his cream. He let the door shut, giving up on the outdoors and stepping into the kitchen, spotting the dish on the table that had held his late-night slice of pizza warmed in the microwave. There was sauce around the edge. He slid his finger in the sauce and brought it to his lips. Tangy and spicy. He had stayed up late last night, indulged a little more than normal, with the understanding that he could sleep in this morning. No such luck. He felt hazy around the edges, woolly in the brain.

He had planned a visit to the museum in St. John's, taking Agatha with him, smuggling her in in his doctor's bag as he had done twice before. Years ago, he had started carrying his bag around with him as a means of transporting his various pets into functions. He had taken his dearly departed chihuahua, Peppy, to movies in such a manner. Peppy would sit quietly in the opened black bag, intently staring at the big screen while Thompson fed him popcorn and cola that the little dog lapped from the doctor's cupped palm. Agatha, on the other hand, didn't care for movies. Her fascination lay with the Beothuk bone displays of the indigenous Newfoundland Indians that the islanders had massacred. Museums were her bag, so to speak. Today was a perfect day to enjoy a leisurely stroll through the museum. Yet a nagging curiosity urged him to visit the hospital and examine Lloyd Fowler. Personal procedure dictated that he call Mrs. Fowler and offer his condolences. He hoped she was not taking it too badly. What words of reassurance could he possibly put forth to quell the flow of tears?

⁓🍂

A siren wailed in the distance. Joseph checked his watch — 7:45 a.m. — and leaped out of bed, rushed to the window. *It's coming for me?* he distraughtly informed himself, half-asleep and paranoid from a vivid dream and fitful sleeping. He thought he might need to flee, but soon, gathering consciousness, he fixed his bearings.

An ambulance was travelling west on the lower road, heading out of the community. Joseph had finally fallen asleep at dawn, after tossing and turning for hours in the sultry room. An opened window with an old-fashioned sliding screen fitted in the gap had made no difference. There was not a breath of fresh air.

Joseph's gaze followed the ambulance. Sickness on wheels. He was sweating horribly and a grimy odour wafted from his skin. Why, he wondered. Was it caused by the heat or the strain on his ill-rested body? Such a brief sleep. Where was Kim? Upon first waking, he had believed that she was in the room, that she had left the room for only a moment. To go where? To take Robin from him. Take her home? No, he had actually *dreamed* of Kim. She had been in the company of another man, the man with the beard, while Joseph crouched in the corner of this very bedroom, secreted away. Only Kim knew of Joseph's presence. There was a teasing look in her eyes, mingled with a despondency. This was the burly exciting man Joseph always assumed Kim wanted, the man full of tall-tale adventures, the mountain climber, the scuba diver, the half-frozen, half-eaten, record-breaking explorer made animate from the books she often read. Kim had once thought that Joseph was such a man. A man of the sea, a man of rugged fisherman stock. When they were first dating he had proudly detailed his lineage. Kim had expected outlandish stories from him, but beyond the tales he had been told of his Uncle Doug, Joseph could offer nothing more, seemingly stripped of historical significance in his move from outport to city. And, as it turned out, Kim was not entirely what she seemed either. Joseph soon discovered her taste for the extravagant, the refined, the superficial. "Good quality," she called it. "You pay for what you get."

In the midst of coming to terms with the previously unknown displeasures of each other's personalities, Kim had brought home a pregnancy test kit, and both of them had stood over it, staring as the colour faded in. The results were positive, their own emotions mixed. Six months on, after leaking amniotic fluid for a month and being confined to a hospital bed, Kim had been sitting on the toilet when the baby simply slid out. "She was perfect," Kim later told Joseph. "I wish you had seen her." But he had not wanted to see her. It would be too painful to forever embrace that memory. He had picked up the baby's body from the morgue in the hospital's basement. The business-as-usual attendant wrapped her in a cloth that Joseph had brought along, a special fabric that was to be made into a bed covering for the baby. And Joseph had carried her out to the car, tears welling in his eyes from the weight in his hands, the weight he had never thought possible for something so small. He was terrified, broken hearted and deeply angered by the fact that, without formality, he was able to leave the hospital with his dead baby in his hands.

They had buried the baby in a too-small hole cut in the earth. No priest, only the gravedigger standing respectfully in wait to cover over the petite box that Joseph's father had crafted. No words were spoken. Language would have choked them.

For too long Joseph had felt that he was not what he was supposed to be, and the loss of his first child confirmed his suspicions. Joseph had tried to be strong for Kim, to let her grieve, but the baby's death had driven an emotional wedge between them. Yet they had remained together, clinging to one another in the acute incapacitation brought on by loss, until Kim had become pregnant for the second time. Sixteen months after the still-birth, their second baby was born. They had called her Robin, the name they had chosen for their first child.

These memories were intrusive, almost punishing, as if Joseph's mind was working to smother recollections of his recent explicit dream. What had disturbed Joseph most about the dream was that he wasn't even slightly angered by Kim's carnal extravaganza. Rather, he had watched it unfold with a detached fascination, the bodies entangled in a fevered, sweat-coated manner, Kim enjoying the sex wholeheartedly, moaning lavishly and tightly wrapping her legs around the man, greedily urging him to thrust meanly into her. Would the man make her pregnant? Is that what she wanted? A child from brawny stock. Kim was not like that in bed, not in real life, not with him. This vision of a sluttish Kim, a Kim born of his own fears and desires, made him long desperately for her. Suddenly he felt an overwhelming need to return to St. John's.

He watched the ambulance continue west, rolling along the ten-kilo-metre stretch of lower road that eventually connected to Shearstown Line. Joseph wondered who was sick. Immediately, the funeral from yesterday came to mind, the town gathered to bid farewell. Was his Uncle Doug among the crowd? Everyone knew when someone died out here. And, no doubt, the entire community turned up as a show of respect.

Should I call Uncle Doug? What would I say? I'm just here for the day. We rented a house but I think we're going to head home because I saw a ghost in the barn. Would his uncle chuckle at the comment, or take it as an omen to further fortify the lush cumulative density of yore? No doubt Uncle Doug would soon hear word of Joseph's presence in town, if he hadn't already.

The ambulance was practically out of sight. The siren could no longer be heard. Perhaps it had been switched off. Something dead inside, like his heart. The sirens off. He frowned and yawned and turned his thoughts to Claudia. Too bad he wouldn't get to know her better. In the past few minutes he had decided for certain to head back to St. John's. His emotions were raw. Anything could happen. He could talk ceaselessly for an hour, sink into a brooding pestilent silence, or burst into tears. Another night in this house would do God-knows-what to him. He wanted Kim.

He wanted his home, not his apartment. His home, the one he had painted and helped furnish and pay for. His bedroom that he and Kim had decorated as a lesson in compromise. A familiar female body sleeping beside him, to snuggle into, to sleep like a baby.

The ambulance was now completely out of sight. Joseph shifted his attention to the ocean. In a boat, two people in black shiny suits and scuba gear were fishing an object from the water. They hooked it with a silver pole and leaned to pull it aboard. Heavy by the looks of it. The size and weight of a body.

Has someone drowned? He heard sounds from Robin's room, his daughter moving in the sheets and groaning a protest to waking.

"Daddy?" her sleepy voice called.

"In my room, sweetie." How would Robin take the news of leaving? They hadn't even met his Uncle Doug yet. Hadn't located the old homestead, leafed through musty photo albums, or sat transfixed while spirited tales of his ancestors were spun. He heard Robin stretching and yawning. She would definitely be disappointed, but that would pass. They could go camping. No, the woods were too eerie an alternative. Night noises would scare the bejesus out of him. They could go away, on a plane, to Toronto. There was a big theme park there. They could go on rides and be terrorized in a fun way. Terror that had a tangible beginning and end. Terror that you bought and controlled. That was *his* kind of terror. It would cost a few dollars, but it'd be worth it to get away. They'd stay in a hotel. Robin would like that. Room service and lying in bed watching TV. The little bars of soap and little bottles of shampoo. A child's paradise. But then the thought of being isolated in a hotel room in a distant city made Joseph feel even more anxious and despondent.

The sound of two drowsy feet trod toward him. "Morning, Daddy."

Joseph turned from his view of the boat to see Robin standing in the doorway, dressed in her fairy princess nightdress. Adorable. "Morning, beautiful."

"I'm hungry," she said, frowning, perfect little hands dangling by her sides. "My throat's sore." She came lazily over, hugged him and held on, pretending to fall asleep on her feet, her body going limp.

"Let's get some breakfast." He took another glance out the window. The ocean was calm and a deeper, richer blue than the sky, the day already hot beyond the glass. He thought he saw another bundle floating just behind the boat, toward the headland, a bag of garbage or a marker of some sort. He picked up his daughter and she cuddled into him, let her warm, sleepy head rest on his shoulder. *Nothing more perfect*, he thought, cradling one hand against her hair. *Paternal bliss!*

"I love this place, Daddy," Robin said, raising her head.

"You do?" He smoothed her hair while she ran a hand over his cheek.

"You need a shave. It hurts."

"I don't know if I have a razor." He shuddered at the word "razor," knowing he had one in his suitcase. He did not want to touch it. "I've got the shiverys."

Robin laughed into his shoulder. "Can we stay more than three weeks?"

"I don't know." Approaching the stairs, he then commenced his careful descent, hugging Robin close, her legs wrapped around his waist. "You're getting way too heavy."

The old stairs creaked beneath the white and burgundy runner. The hallway was bright in daylight. Nothing frightening about the day. Everything plainly before his eyes. No dead people doing dead-people things.

"What're we gonna do after breakfast?"

"Oh, I don't know. Maybe we should head —"

"Can we go see Claudia and her daughter?"

"I don't —"

"Pllllease, Daddy." She bounced in his arms as he negotiated the final step.

"Whoa. Get down now," he declared, leaning forward. But Robin clung on, straining his lower back.

"Please, please, please." Robin wore a big cartoon frown. She batted her blonde eyelashes, a trick she had learned from Kim. "Please."

"Get down, Robin," Joseph snapped, the pain in his back radiating into his hips and shooting down his legs. "You're hurting my back."

She let go at once and stood there, eyes glassy, arms folded across her chest. A real pout this time.

The damage was done. Joseph couldn't help but try to make amends. Robin deserved a vacation. They deserved to be together, even if it meant him overdosing to keep his nerves in check. He'd give it one more day, give Bareneed another chance to calm instead of incite him.

"Okay," he said, sighing dramatically. "All right, okay, okay." He crouched down, face to face with Robin. Her eyes turned glassier. She wiped away a tear with her nightdress sleeve. "I'm sorry," he said, making a sad face. "Forgive me?" Maybe things *would* be okay. *It's just the act of settling that's toying with my imagination,* he reasoned. He couldn't be completely out of his mind. Or was he? Maybe he was nuttier than two fruitcakes, as his mother used to say.

"I forgive you, Daddy."

"Ah, ain't you sweet."

They hugged.

"I love the smell of you, Daddy," she said, holding on. "I still have your pillow from home. When you're not there, I smell it. It smells just like you."

His heart gave a pang and he clenched her tighter, kissed her neck. *What sort of emotional wreckage must I sort through and abide,* he asked himself, *in order to return us to before?*

⁓◐

The air in Miss Laracy's kitchen was filled with the smell of toasted bread. She had cut the slice so thick that it barely fitted into the toaster. The thicker the better to sop up her tea when she dipped it in her mug. She found the bread to be not as good as hers, but it would have to do. Just last year she had abandoned her ritual of baking bread every Thursday, as she had for the past sixty years. The kneading was too difficult. It drained the life right out of her. Now she was reduced to buying her bread from the supermarket. It wasn't nearly as dense as the buns she used to make, it never held the heat as long and was lighter as though made of one-part sawdust, but it would have to do. These were the perils of getting old and having to purchase the lesser-quality baked goods from a supermarket. *What could be more disheartening?* she asked herself.

Miss Laracy had been awoken by the sound of a siren, an uncommon occurrence in Bareneed. She knew right away that the siren belonged to an ambulance. The fire trucks had long, drawn-out, wailing sirens. Police sirens were more bubbly, like warped ovals running after each other. The ambulance sirens were sharper, shriller and to the point, prickly as a cushion full of pins. Who was took ill now, she wondered. She gave a cranky shake of her head while smearing plenty of butter on her toast until the shades of brown were glistening and smelling lovely.

She then turned with her plate and mug of tea. Her eyes caught sight of a large drawing on her table. It was one of Tommy's by the looks of it. She hadn't remembered putting it there. Tommy hadn't gifted her with anything to take home with her last night as he sometimes did. Perhaps Tommy had been by in the early morning and dropped it off. He often did that, anxious to show Miss Laracy what he was up to. He didn't seem to ever catch a wink of sleep, but was constantly prowling around, drawing and visiting and checking on people to make certain they were okay. Anyone ill at ease was sure to have their spirits lifted by Tommy, for he had a way of bringing a smile to a worried face.

The drawing was of two little girls who stood side by side behind what seemed to be a waterfall. One of the little girls looked just like the blonde one she had met at the Critches' house up on the higher road. Miss Laracy set her plate and mug on the table and studied the drawing. The other girl she did not recognize.

A sound beyond her kitchen caught her attention. She stared toward the hallway as a door creaked. At once, Miss Laracy thought of spirits; but it was daylight, so she feared that probability was far off.

"Who be dere?" she called out, just as Tommy stepped into the doorway. He was scratching his head, his fingers in his mussed-up hair, and watching her sheepishly.

"I were by last eve after putting Rayna ta bed." He pointed back the way he had come. "I sat fer a spell in yer parlour 'n passed right inta slumber." He laughed outright, his bottom jaw coming forward, his chin jutting ahead. Laughter bucked in his chest as though it were the funniest thing he had ever heard. "Imagine dat? Me dozing off just like a babe."

Miss Laracy laughed too and raised her hand to him. "Yer a real card, Tommy, me love. Come 'av a cup 'o tea."

Tommy approached the table and stood watching his drawing while Miss Laracy poured him a mug. Leaning over the table, he gave the sketch consideration.

When Miss Laracy turned with the mug, she saw that Tommy had drawn a series of girls, all the same as the one from the Critch house. He had outlined shadows of the girl tilting at an angle until she fell over and lay on the ground. Then he began on the impression of a man, a big man with a rough beard who was standing over the girl.

"Dat be da girl frum up da Critch house," said Miss Laracy.

"You were widt her. I knows." Tommy kept sketching, his fingers moving urgently as though he must finish capturing the vision before it was snatched away from him. "I been drawing pictures of da long deceased," Tommy muttered. "Dose pictures on da walls of me hallway, dose families."

Miss Laracy placed a hand against Tommy's back while he scribbled wildly.

"All da families dat were gone, dey're coming back soon," Tommy admitted.

"In what way?"

"Dey be coming back," said Tommy. "Dey be dead but dey be coming back." He turned over the sheet and commenced drawing on the other side, lines of bodies stepping from the water, heads and shoulders and chests emerging from beneath the surface. And then creatures wafting all around them, drifting like mist from the bodies themselves, taking shape from the movements of the once dead.

⁓◐⁓

Claudia stood on the threshold of her daughter's bedroom and gazed numbly at Jessica, who sat facing the wall atop the unmade bed. The child was trembling, her long hair matted in wet strands. Claudia had been watching the stagnant image of her daughter for a puzzling stretch of time. "Jessica?"

The child furnished no reply.

"Why don't you put on some dry clothes? You have plenty of nice outfits."

Not a word from Jessica. Not the slightest motion other than shivers. She was as static as a photograph suspended before Claudia's eyes. How is it possible to remain so inert, Claudia wondered. "You don't need to stay like that, do you?"

Silence amplified by immobility.

"Jessica?"

A young girl's playful laughter. Claudia twisted toward the sound. The laughter came from near the walls. When Claudia looked back, Jessica had budged a foot or so, yet the child remained breathlessly still.

"I'm going downstairs," she said, more to herself than anyone else. She shifted her eyes from the collage of photographs pinned to her studio wall above her desk, the series that captured Jessica sitting on her bed, facing the wall, having just come in from a walk in the rain and sulking over some minor misdeed. Claudia gazed down at the journal on her desk, picked up a pen and wrote the words: *I held her small hand. I held her small hand. I held her small hand. I held her small hand. I held her small hand …*

Again, the laughter of a child. Claudia stood and backed away from her work table beneath the wall of photographs. She turned and approached the wide stairs leading down from the second storey; the gradual slope was a pleasure to descend. Eight summers ago, Reg, after studying information about solar houses for months, had built the house with a few of his buddies. Claudia had been pregnant with Jessica. Her husband had constructed the house using plans ordered from a television program. The huge panels of glass were delivered on a flatbed truck, raised and set in place by a crane. Claudia had been outraged by the cost of the windows, but when she objected Reg had insisted that the price was worth it. "You're the sort who needs all the light you can get," he said, with a wink. "For your work, I mean." Reg had been so supportive and proud of her pottery. Yet he expressed these feelings to her alone, not wanting to alienate his friends and family by holding his wife's art on a pedestal. This was Reg, through and through. Always treating everyone as an equal. They had been living in Reg's parents' house, an old square dwelling on the lower road adjacent to the harbour. Reg's mother had passed away and left the house to her only son. Although Claudia tried to work there, she soon became frustrated by the lack of space and inadequate shelving. The rooms had been built small and practical, to be proficiently heated in the days of wood and coal stoves when the southwesterly winds off the winter ocean pounded the house. As Claudia began exporting her wares, another kiln was required to keep up with the orders. She had hardly had room enough to turn around in her cluttered space, and it was hindering beyond belief.

When the new house was completed in late August of that summer, Claudia and Reg had moved to their position overlooking the harbour, a post that Claudia adored. The roomy front half of the upstairs was her studio, while the back section contained two large bedrooms.

Presently, the living room opened up at Claudia's right as she descended the final steps. The enlivening blond pine walls of the high-ceilinged room encouraged an impression of possibility and release. Bright morning light illuminated the expansive area, glinting off the framed artwork on the walls. Ocean scenes. Calm waters and violent seas. The ocean, Claudia meditated. So much like the currents that move us inside.

At the bottom stair, she was stopped in her tracks by the sight of a young girl beyond the front door.

"Jessica?" Claudia muttered. How could Jessica have made it outside so quickly?

The girl was smiling, her hands cupped around the glass running vertically down the centre of the door. It was the girl who had come to live in the Critch house. Live there for how long? A bulky figure stood behind her, a hand on the girl's shoulder, drawing her back. The girl's father? The man and the girl she had met on the road yesterday. She couldn't recall their names. A nerve-sudden disruption — knocking. Claudia's hand shot to her chest. Yet she continued to the door, stealing a glance over her shoulder, at the incline of stairs.

Shutting her eyes, she paused a moment to steady herself. She could hear the girl's voice and movements muffled behind glass. Why couldn't she stay still, silent? Claudia gripped the knob and took a deep breath before slowly easing open the door.

"Good morning," the man said, his open enthusiasm swiftly tempered. He glanced at his watch. "Did we get you up?"

"No, not at all." Claudia tried a smile, a pleasant one, hoping to suspend the man's hesitations. Squinting, she hooked a strand of hair behind her ear and recalled that she hadn't brushed it this morning. What time was it, she wondered. Breakfast time? She hadn't brushed her teeth either and caught a whiff of her foul breath. *No water must pass my lips. Not a drop of it.* She hoped that she was drying up inside, erasing every stain of moisture. The glare of the outdoors was too bright for her. She felt unsightly, brittle in the presence of others. The too-bright ocean lay in the distance, the harbour that provided safety from the violence of waters farther to the east, farther out of sight where the true nature of the sea commanded itself.

"Robin was anxious to meet your daughter." The man glanced at the girl with an expression demonstrative of his conspicuous love of her. He placed a palm on the top of her head. "It'd be great for them to get together. Beautiful morning."

"My daughter?" Claudia's unsteady smile tremored, then wilted from her lips. The dusty pink high in her angular cheeks drained. She could not prevent her dazed, sunken eyes from becoming fixed on Robin. "You know about my daughter?"

"Yes," the girl said, her voice a peep.

"How?" Her skin tightened. She felt her face grow more unbecoming by the moment. Words were making her uglier.

"Is this a bad time?" the man asked.

Claudia darted a perturbed look at him, the colour returning to her cheeks, outrage scalding the delicate flesh within her mouth. "Yes, it is a bad time."

The girl gazed up at her father, who simply said, "Oh."

"I mean, no." Claudia touched her lips and glanced worriedly up the stairs. "It's just …"

"She's asleep?" the man suggested, his eyes noticing Claudia's sleeve, the words she had written there in elaborate strokes of calligraphy.

"Yes," Claudia quietly agreed, accepting the plain solution. "Yes." She lowered her arm, newly engrossed by the girl's stillness, her inactivity.

She could not help but bend down, face to face with the child to watch more closely. Adopting a pleasant yet overwrought disposition, she asked: "Where did you see Jessica?"

The girl hesitantly pointed skyward. "In the window."

Claudia's eyes tipped up. "My studio!"

The man's brow creased with what appeared to be confusion, then trepidation.

"We'll come back another time," he said.

"In the window of my studio?" Tingling whiteness permeated Claudia's vision. In her ears, a needle-sharp buzzing mounted. She meant to grip the girl's arms, discover if she was actually flesh and blood, and, if so, hold on for dear life. However, reaching ahead, she lost her balance and swiftly braced a hand against the hardwood floor behind her. "Jessica," she muttered helplessly, as the keen snowy whiteness sparkled to shroud the image of the young girl. She sat back on the floor with a thud, her hands wrapped around her knees, her head pressed between them, her arms and scalp sweating while she breathed into her dress. "Go away," she said, words smothered in fabric while her blood throbbed in her temples and at the base of her neck, "Please … take her … and go."

~⦿~

The hospital was a home away from home for Dr. Thompson. Where some might experience fear or trepidation, he felt at peace in the bright sterility. There was an orderliness — forms, routines, procedures — that patterned his thoughts, a cleanliness he was not obliged to keep dusted. In his occupation, it was necessary to focus on the bright spots as opposed to dwelling on the infirmity. How else was it possible to survive? There was hope on most of the floors. Absolute hope or vague hope, but hope nonetheless.

The morgue, however, was a different matter entirely. Even he experienced the bleak pull of oppression taking the elevator to the basement; he caught a whiff of formaldehyde as the elevator reopened, the odour intensifying as he advanced toward the morgue doors.

Inside, the attendant, Glen Delaney, in his standard white lab coat, was seated on a stool adjacent to the metal counter. He was scrutinizing his finger, probing it with what appeared to be a set of tweezers. Thompson assumed that Delaney was attempting to remove a splinter. The attendant raised his head for only a moment, to glance at Dr. Thompson, before refocusing on his object of concern.

Ignorant bastard, Thompson cursed under his breath. What was it with these morgue people? He searched for the pathologist, but he was nowhere to be seen.

"Is Dr. Peters in?"

Delaney shrugged. Shrugged! If Thompson were a younger man, in his thirties like the attendant, he would blurt out a scalding remark about manners, but — with age — he had embraced the virtues of restraint. After all, what was the point? Delaney would never change. He was a particular sort of character, and only severe emotional or physical trauma could possibly draw him out of his self-absorption.

Thompson pulled himself away from his cruel thoughts to study Mr. Fowler, who was still laid out on the table, not yet stuffed away in one of the drawers. He took a step nearer Fowler's body to study the pathologist's incisions that always appeared so sadistic, somehow disrespectful. The first thought that never failed to present itself whenever he found himself in this unfortunate situation was: *The man is dead, no doubt about it. Look at him. They are taking him apart, disassembling, slicing bits of him away to determine what brought on his demise. Tough hardy man standing in my office two days ago. Slab of dissected meat today.* But where was the true Mr. Fowler? The essence of the being.

Thompson glanced around for a chair; his knees were aching. He shifted his weight from one foot to the other. He wanted to say something to Delaney, who continued prodding his finger, to simply bring a bit of humanity into the room. He might ask about Mr. Fowler's death, but he had already learned the details from his telephone call to Mrs. Fowler. She had found her husband in his chair. Dead. As though he were sleeping, except for the colour. The colour of the skin was all wrong. Grey. "Like boiled cabbage," she had gasped on the intake of a sob.

"How's business?" Thompson asked Delaney, expecting the standard response: "Dead."

"This is no business," the attendant answered, poking more furiously at his finger. "This is a hospital."

Thompson frowned. Delaney's attention to his finger was further grating on Thompson's nerves. What was he doing anyway? The doctor was about to break his rules of restraint and say, You stupid fool, but his attention was diverted by the morgue doors opening behind him. A tall dark-skinned police officer, who must have been at least six-foot-six, set one foot into the room and came to a standstill, as if anticipating censure.

"Is this the morgue?" he finally asked.

Christ! thought Thompson, *What do you think this is? A Sunday picnic?* He bit his tongue. After all, the police officer's inquiry was fair enough. "I believe so," said Thompson dryly. He heard Delaney snicker and, immediately, felt sympathy toward the police officer and more animosity, if that was possible, toward the attendant.

The officer stepped in, leaning forward to avoid the top of the doorway even though his head could clear it. He stood beside Dr. Thompson and stared at Mr. Fowler's body, his eyes scanning the six wide stitches of nylon that had sewn up the body. He removed his cap, tucked it under his arm, then smoothed his neatly trimmed black hair, seemingly out of respect, every strand in place. "That's a dead body there," he said. "Right?"

Thompson considered the body, wondering what exactly the police officer's question might mean.

"Yes," was all Thompson could come up with.

"Sometimes I wonder."

"Well, if they're in here they're most probably dead."

"Guess so."

Delaney turned to get a good look at the police officer. After registering an expression of incredulity, he returned to his finger obsession.

"Aren't morgues terrible?" the officer said sorrowfully, as if addressing Mr. Fowler.

Despite the gravity of the circumstance, Thompson thought he might bust out laughing at the officer's melodramatic tone.

"He's dead," said the officer, regarding the doctor. "That's Lloyd Fowler, right?"

"Yes," Thompson replied.

The officer stared searchingly into Thompson's eyes while extending his hand. "I'm Sergeant Chase."

"Dr. Thompson."

"Great," said Chase, shaking Thompson's hand, pressing his lips together and firmly nodding. "Nice to meet you. Straight enough death?"

"Mr. Fowler?"

"Yes."

"How do you mean?"

"Foul play?"

"We're waiting on toxicology reports, but it seems a natural death."

"Okay." Chase turned toward Delaney, watching the man on his stool poking at his finger. The officer appeared more and more puzzled by the attendant's behaviour.

"What sort of splinter would you get in here?" Chase called out. "With all the steel."

Thompson noticed beads of sweat collecting along Chase's hairline.

"Bone," said the attendant.

The police officer grimaced. "You should open a window in here," he suggested, as if this might be the solution to the attendant's problem. He searched around but there were no windows. "Scrubbing death clean," he muttered, a little green around the gills. He stuck a finger in the collar of his shirt. "Hot in here?"

"Not really." Thompson could practically see his breath misting in the frigid air.

"Can I speak outside?" Chase asked, swallowing hard.

"Outside of what?" the doctor mused, playing the devil's advocate.

"No, right." He gave a weak smile and licked his lips. "I know I can speak outside. I mean, will you speak outside with me?"

"Yes, of course."

Chase raised a hand to the attendant. "Nice talking with you. Good luck with your bone graft." Again, he ducked his head on the way out. "Less life in that attendant than in poor Lloyd Fowler," Chase commented, then was silent for a moment, drawing breath.

"You need to sit down, I think," said Thompson.

"I thought I was." Chase leaned sideways, gripping a strip of wooden trim that ran horizontally and midway down the walls. A short piece that bridged two longer pieces broke loose in his hand. Chase slipped, an awkward scrambling of long limbs, before he caught himself and straightened alertly in an attempt to appear nonchalant. He gazed at his fist and noticed the piece of wooden trim there, two finishing nails sticking out the back. He had dropped his hat and bent to retrieve it. Neatly setting it on his head, he remained crouched.

"When I was in training," he said, attempting to fit the piece of wood back in place, "we had to go to an autopsy. The way they cut people up is worse than any moose butchering I've ever seen. They made us hold the heart." He hammered the wood with the side of his fist. Wincing, he examined his hand. "Yee-ouch! I think I need a doctor." Chase smiled up at Thompson, the white-toothed smile charismatic, generous, the colour returning to his face. A blush evident beneath his brown skin. "Hospitals ghoul me out. I don't mind crime scenes any more than the next guy, but hospitals cram my head with whiteness."

"Don't stand too quickly. You're too big a man for me to catch."

"No, I'm fine now." Chase nodded thoughtfully, gradually straightening from his crouch.

"You investigating Mr. Fowler's death?"

"Don't know yet. When we have a number of deaths in a community, CIIDS, our main computer system, alerts us. Automatically, just for safety's sake. We investigate to determine if there's an actual link or risk. New policies."

"Computers."

"Where's the escape hatch?" asked Chase, scanning the corridor. "I'm lost."

"The elevator's just up there."

On the main floor, Thompson checked with the head nurse in Emerg. There had been two patients treated for shortness of breath within the past two days. The first was an elderly woman from Port de Grave with a heart condition who had been admitted and held for observation.

Nothing out of the ordinary there. The second patient had been treated and sent home. A seventeen-year-old male from Bareneed, Andrew Slade. Thompson knew the Slades. He was their family physician. Andrew was overweight and had become a bit of a bully lately. He lived with his brother and sister-in-law, his parents having perished in a car accident. Driving drunk. Mrs. Slade, Andrew's sister-in-law, was the most spectacular hypochondriac of all Thompson's patients. She had been in to see him just a few days ago. What was that for? He could not recall, might have been for anything in the book. When Andrew had visited Emerg, the doctor on duty had diagnosed the boy as suffering from allergies and sent him home with a script for Allergan. The doctor's eyes searched the ground at his feet. Something was trying to reveal itself to him. He thought of Donna Drover. Muss Drover. Lloyd Fowler. Shortness of breath. Andrew Slade. If something happened to Andrew Slade then the coincidence factor would surely be negated.

Sergeant Chase was still lingering around the waiting area when the doctor stepped from the admissions booth.

"You want to tell me something?" queried Chase.

"It's just allergy season," the doctor said, not wanting to be an alarmist.

Chase poked through his shirt pocket and extracted a small piece of paper with a few words scrawled on it. "What about Muss Drover?"

"Natural causes. His mother's upstairs."

"What for?"

"Respiratory complications. She's stable. No sign of virus. That's what had us concerned." Thompson glanced toward a five- or six-year-old boy who had begun crying in the waiting area. The boy's mother, seated beside him, was glaring at her son with narrowed eyes as if she might strike him at any moment. "No respiratory virus," he muttered, distracted. The child's mother yanked the boy by the arm and then swatted him soundly in the face and cursed him. The child wailed louder.

Chase, also witnessing the spectacle, immediately approached the mother. Thompson had twitched to make a move but held himself in check, allowing Chase to go about his duty. He heard the officer ask the woman for a piece of identification.

A young girl with blonde hair and a gauze bandage wrapped around her left wrist sat on the other side of the woman, and beside the girl sat a man, perhaps the girl's father. He was staring menacingly at Thompson.

Again, Thompson gazed at the floor, distracted. He recalled what Mrs. Fowler had told him about Mr. Fowler being unusually agitated. She had gone into greater detail over the phone, after her husband's death. She had explained that he had become violent to the point where she considered packing up and leaving him. "Truth be told," she had said, tearily, "I was frightened for my life, Doctor."

Thompson looked up as Chase approached. The officer flipped shut his pocket notebook and patted it with his fingertips. He glanced back at the woman then said confidentially to the doctor: "I took the info for social services to pay her a visit. Plus I'll write it up. Name and address. That's abuse. You're a witness, right?" He slid his notebook into the top pocket of his khaki shirt and took another glance at the woman, who would not regard them.

"I most certainly am." Thompson watched the woman take hold of her son's hand and squeeze it, bow her head, shut her eyes tightly and tremble. The girl with the bandaged wrist had an imploring aspect to her eyes, as though pleading for help. The man at the girl's side continued staring directly at Thompson.

"Well, anything else on your mind?" Chase asked.

"No, nothing."

"I'll see you then."

"Guess so."

Chase extended his hand. Thompson shook it, then watched the officer leave by the sliding double doors.

After a few moments spent glancing at the varied faces in the waiting area, Thompson left the hospital. He climbed into his four-wheel drive and headed out of Port de Grave. He would connect with Shearstown Line, and then make his way to the turnoff for Bareneed. Andrew Slade. Thompson knew where the Slades lived, in a suburban bungalow on Slade's Lane, not far from the harbour. He decided he'd drive by and have a look. If Andrew appeared to be at home, then Thompson would stop and ask a few questions, check his breathing.

Thompson noticed his own breathing — the intake, the exhale. He became conscious of it to the point where he thought he might actually spook himself. As a distraction, he switched on the radio and listened to the music. Gordon Lightfoot singing: "If you could read my mind, love. What a tale my thoughts could tell." Thompson sang along, trying to convince himself that all of this was nothing at all. Yet he could not shake the suspicion that he was missing something fundamental in his analysis of the situation, that Bareneed was about to be gripped by the outbreak of a powerful virus previously unknown to anyone.

~∞)

Joseph required no more convincing. *We're leaving*, he told himself. *Packing up and leaving now.* This summer rental idea was a major mistake. A nightmare. There were the creepy visions of the man in the barn last night, plus the young girl's voice calling "Daddy," and now Claudia's news that her daughter and husband had disappeared eighteen months earlier.

"We're leaving," he told Robin while he popped open the car trunk. "Get your stuff. No argument. No discussion." It was an unhealthy place for a young girl. The country. Far too much imagination for her own good.

"Can we have just one walk?"

"Did you hear me?"

"Yes."

"Did you hear what Claudia said? Her daughter, the one you saw in the window, is missing."

"No, she's not."

"Missing." He pointed toward the house. "Go."

"Please, Daddy." She clamped her hands together, begging. "One walk."

"No." Joseph noticed that she had drawn symbols on the backs of her hands with red and black markers. Lines, arcs and full circles.

Tears. The pout.

"Robin, look." He bent down and touched her shoulders, more to brace himself than reassure her. "This place is too strange. I don't want to stay here. Don't you want to leave?"

Robin shook her head. Two tears broke and ran in trails toward her lips.

Joseph stole a look toward the water. Sunny picturesque town. Was it just him? Was this whole thing simply a manifestation of his imbalance? It was morning. Daylight. Safe. No ghosts in daylight. If they didn't leave this exact moment, then what would be the harm? They could leave after lunch. Plenty of time before dark. He was feeling guilty enough as it was, denying Robin the vacation she had anticipated for months.

"I'm not crazy, am I?" he asked Robin gently. "Am I crazy?"

She gave him a little smile and Joseph wiped her tears away with his thumbs.

"Okay. One walk."

Robin grinned, hugged him briskly. "Thanks, Daddy."

"But we're leaving right after."

"Can we go to the water?"

"Sure. Let's go." Joseph shut the trunk and gripped his daughter's hand. They headed down the higher road toward the community wharf. Joseph thought ahead to Kim. How would he explain? Kim would suspect that he had a screw loose if he went on about ghosts. She was a biologist, a scientist. Grounded. How would all of this affect his rights to see Robin? What if he was, in fact, going crazy? Would Kim seek a restraining order against him?

A cool breeze was picking up. He checked toward the east and saw, far out along the watery horizon, banks of thick grey clouds looming. Rain on the way. If they packed up within the next few hours, they would avoid it. He didn't want to drive in the rain, but he definitely would if he had to. He'd drive at two kilometres an hour in thunder and lightning, sleet, hail, raining toads, if that's what it took to get him out of here. He drew a deep breath. He needed oxygen to ease the startling sense of panic that rose through his body. His pills were back at the house. The house was within view. He saw that Robin was staring back, her eyes fixed on Claudia's house, her attention focused on the top window.

"There she is, Daddy," Robin said, pointing.

"Who?" Joseph said, his eyes already on the window, an even shade of blue reflecting from the sky. No girl.

"See her?" Robin waved and yanked free of Joseph's grip, hurried back up the road.

"Robin," Joseph demanded, lurching after her. "Come back here."

"She's gone," Robin huffed, her feet faltering. "You scared her away."

"Scared *her*!" He reached for and grasped hold of his daughter's hand. "Come on. Let's go to the wharf and then we're heading home before dark. That's it. We can go somewhere else. Camping or on a trip. How about Toronto? Hawaii? Madagascar?"

"I'd rather stay here. It's more fun."

"Fun?" Joseph snatched a look at Robin's face. "Fun?"

"We didn't even see Uncle Doug."

"We can do that another time. It's not that far from St. John's. We'll come back. Hey, how'd you know about Uncle Doug?"

"Mom told me. What about Jessica?"

Joseph took a deep breath. "She'll get by without us." He wanted to add: She's dead, a ghost, for God's sake. She'll be fine. It's we, the living, who are in desperate need of protecting.

"It was Jessica I dreamed about last night. She's the one I saw in the barn."

Joseph skidded to a halt. "The barn? Our barn?"

Robin's face gave nothing away.

"When?"

"It was only me in an old mirror," Robin said, crinkling her nose and shaking her head, trying to make it sound less important. "It wasn't her. No. Nothing. Forget it."

"When was this?"

"I don't know. Yesterday."

"Let's stop talking. Come on, let's just walk. Talking's bad. Walking's good for the body. Walk faster." They stepped quickly down the road, the sound of their footsteps brushing against gravel and asphalt. Then came the percussive sound of distant hammering. Two crows were cawing off to their left, in the woods. A bird swooped overhead, casting a brief sweeping shadow before a fish hit the road ten feet in front of them. Joseph looked up, saw the crow sailing off.

It should be silver, Joseph thought, regarding the fish as they neared it, but it was entirely black and the black was stirring. The fish was covered in a mass of black flies, eating, spewing, and laying eggs.

Joseph gaped down. He squinted and forced his eyelids shut, opened them again. The fish seemed to be grey now. Not black at all. Grey flies crawling over each other in frenzy. Grey flies like he had never seen before

Robin watched the fish, then shifted her eyes to meet his. He was about to ask her if she saw grey when she proposed a question of her own:

"What's it like to die, Daddy?"

Oh, shit, Joseph thought.

-⟋❀⟍-

Andrew Slade squeezed the piece of homemade bread into a wad in his sweaty palm. There was something nice and sickening about the feel of the bread. Something about it he could not completely remember. He caught a flickering image of his Nan's face. An old woman there and then gone, barely recognizable, a whiff of homemade bread rising from his pudgy hands. He looked up at the sky, the sun bleaching the soft white rounds of his face whiter, his unkempt, greasy black hair sheening. His green eyes glistened like the sparklings in the water. Three white dots reflected there, as three gulls hovered high out over the harbour, drifting, squawking needily. Andrew opened his fist, studied the bread, the imprint of the lines of his palm dented into it like roots. He grinned spitefully and rolled the wad between his palms until it formed a round ball the size of a high-bouncer. His fishing rod was already outfitted with a big number-ten hook. He bent down and felt the pressure in his face, his eyeballs almost bulging; his jeans were too tight again. He was growing out of everything he owned. Rasping a breath, he raised the hook between his pudgy thumb and index finger, shoved the ball of bread over the curved tip. When it was snagged firmly in place, he stood and raised the rod, and cast far out into the harbour. He was hoping one of the stupid creatures beneath the surface wouldn't eat the bait. He stared sullenly toward the sky.

"C'mon," he muttered. "Wha's da matter, ya want it toasted?"

One of the gulls broke away from the others and sailed toward the water, aiming for the surface and skimming it, rising toward the sky as Andrew's reel whirred and the coils of his fishing line tautly spun out.

Grin darkening, Andrew gripped the reel's handle and held it steady. The tip of his rod wavered as the line jammed. The seagull spun around in the sky, like a car twirling on black ice. It frantically flapped its wings to right itself and then hovered there, caught, squawking. The sky was blue. The gull swam against it, pulling back, flapping its wings, trying to remain adrift.

"Yes," Andrew spat through his teeth. "Gotcha." He diligently turned the handle of his reel and the gull, struggling to pull away, gradually sank toward him. The gull would soon be in his belly. Someone had told him it tasted like chicken, only greasier and not as much meat. Seagull and french fries, with gravy. Or maybe he couldn't even wait that long, maybe he would eat it raw, chomp through the feathers while it was still warm. He dragged a bare arm across his lips, then glanced toward his right at a movement that had caught his attention. There was a man and a girl he did not know over on the community wharf. They were down by the dories, snooping around. Stupid arsehole tourists by the looks of them. Townies. Outsiders.

Andrew stared up at the sky, his seagull like a kite, straining the line and drifting sideways. He returned his gaze to the man and girl. From his pocket he took a knife; folding it open he cut the seagull free. He tossed down his fishing rod and watched his grey sneakers step away. Rocks on the side of the road. He could use the rocks to drive the townies off. They'd just ruin things, coming in here and changing everything. He'd like to pelt them with rocks and shout at them: Stupid arsehole tourists.

Bending down, he picked up a good-size rock. It was warm in his hand. A proper weight to do damage. He squeezed it and fear clutched in his chest. He noticed he wasn't breathing. It was as though the air had been sucked out of his lungs. He caught a fright and began sweating even worse than he already was. Pulling in a harsh breath, he heard his older brother's voice in his head, "Everything's ruined by people comin' into Bareneed, ruined by foreigners takin' all our fish in their giant factory boats offshore, stealin' from us, takin' all the jobs. Ruinin' everythin', ruinin' our lives. I'd murder the whole lot of 'em if I could."

Another raspy breath. Andrew shut his eyes against the sting from sweat. He saw nothing in his head as he swiped his slippery arm across his face, just an inky blackness that scared him worse than night. Opening his eyes, he hurried his pace along the road that arced around the harbour, as if to outrun the shallow blackness that he not only saw inside his head but felt too. The hard solid edges of the rock still in his hand. He thought the bread had hardened. He stared down, remembered nothing. The bread had turned into a rock. He took a deep breath, then saw the man and girl. Friggin' arsehole tourists. Friggin' arsehole tourists …

Andrew Slade ran faster, right toward the man and girl, wobbling because of his weight. When he was close enough for a clear shot, he hurled the rock, arm over head as if lobbing a grenade. He had meant to scare them with it, hit the wood of the wharf, but when it struck the girl in the back of the head he immediately ran toward Slade's Lane, ran all out, his breath tripping up in itself. He had no idea how to pull it together. What did he have to do to breathe? How did it work? It was like he had a plastic model of the body that needed to be glued together, one piece stuck to another. He hurried faster, his sneakers skidding on the turn. He dropped, soundly banging his shoulder, his face scraping against the asphalt, tearing the skin and embedding it with sand, gravel and a scattering of tiny grey rocks.

⚘

"Ouch!" Robin cried out, her hand shooting to the back of her head.

"What?" Joseph spun to guard his daughter and saw her face seize with pain. As he shifted quickly to comfort Robin, his foot stumbled over a coil of rough discarded rope and he lost his balance in an irretrievable way. He made to grasp for his daughter, who was now bent forward on one knee and clutching at her head with both hands, but the gesture was of no use. He was tipping, his arms making desperate circular motions, the toes of his shoes lifting off the wharf, his features pulling back in anticipation of descent. He caught a glimpse of a boy, far ahead of him, sprawled on the road; a blue four-wheel drive that had just turned up Slade's Lane, screeching to a halt, its front tire no more than two feet from crushing the boy's head. Tilting, Joseph kicked out, his ankle panging as it struck a board along the lip of the wharf. His limbs fought frantically to remain upright as he twisted sideways and plummeted into the frigid water, smacking the surface.

Joseph's breath seized behind his ribs. The water's biting chill drew his testicles into his body as if sucked up by a vacuum. He sank, cheeks rounded, hands out to protest his descent. When he no longer seemed to be sinking, he opened his eyes. He was suspended without the slightest upward strain. There was a rush of air bubbles like a multitude of transparent eggs before his eyes and, beyond that, no more than three feet away, a man plainly watching him in the glassy green water, a man with white wrinkled skin who was wearing a long heavy coat and thick knitted sweater. Joseph swept his arms down through the constraining water in an effort to rise. The man made no motion to halt Joseph's escape. Sluggishly revolving, Joseph faced another body in the murky distance. A woman wearing a white cotton nightdress with wide lace trim at each sleeve and along the collar. She, too, was gaping at him, motionless, except for the strands of her hair, which gently floated.

Joseph swirled in cumbersome circles, kicking upward, fearing the bony snatch of hands at his ankles. Yet none of the bodies beneath him, floating upright at the silty bottom, made a gesture to follow. Not a bubble escaped their lips as they stared at him, their inquisitive eyes patiently following the trail of his ascent toward the surface.

SATURDAY NIGHT

On her way up to bed, Kim retrieved one of Robin's blonde-haired dolls from the stairs, then, up another stair, she bent to grab a white T-shirt and a fairy-tale book. She was reminded of how that morning, when she had turned on the television, the channels had been filled with Saturday cartoons. They reminded Kim of her own childhood and thus of Robin. Not that Robin even liked cartoons, or television for that matter, although she did seem to enjoy documentaries on animals. Kim was so used to having Robin around that her daughter's absence created a palpable void. Time to herself was much appreciated, but how long could that go on before she actually started feeling lonely? Was it possible to go almost an entire month without seeing Robin? The idea pained her physically, her stomach and heart contracting in a lovesick knot.

"She's only been gone three days," Kim scolded herself.

At the top of the stairs, she turned left, into Robin's room. The wall toward the window was covered in sheets of drawings, mostly of monsters and creatures of Robin's own invention. Kim tossed the book and doll on her daughter's bed, noting how the peach-coloured bedspread was wrinkle-free. Robin made her bed each morning without needing to be reminded. She was responsible. Maybe a touch too responsible. She was a worrier and often had whimpering dreams of being lost or drowning, or of a friend getting struck by a car.

She's just like me when I was her age, Kim thought while she stepped toward her own bedroom to undress. She recalled the nights in her own childhood bed, dwelling on the possibility of her parents' death, worrying about dying herself. What would happen to her? Who would care for her if her parents disappeared from the face of the Earth? Best not to think of past insecurities. Best to think of what required doing in the present. She contemplated the academic paper, a study of the effects of sonar on marine life, that she was working on for *BioJournal*. It was due in two weeks; the date was circled in black marker on the Girl Guides calendar in her downstairs office. The paper was far from completion, and even further from the required seven or eight rewrites.

She slipped off her blouse and unclipped her bra, caught her reflection in the full-length mirror by the door and ignored it. She felt a general displeasure with herself and her situation. Her separation from Joseph was no longer something that suited her. It had made perfect sense at the time; their relationship had turned wretched and they desperately needed to be apart. Every conversation culminated in an argument. Over the course of the separation, at nights when Robin was in bed, Kim had had time to do a lot of thinking. One of her realizations was that perhaps what she was actually fighting against was not Joseph at all but the confinement of her changed life, of not being a free child herself any more.

She pulled down her jeans, removed her panties, and kicked them away from her feet. She had started sleeping nude a few months ago, something Joseph had always wanted her to do. She had denied him the pleasure, for some reason. Why? It made no sense to her now, this spiteful withholding. She had never expected to miss Joseph so much. Her friends assured her that the pain would eventually ease, but it had not. Not even slightly. In fact, it had grown worse.

The sheets were chilly as she climbed into bed. She made a shivering sound and pulled up the blankets while she considered coming up with some excuse to visit Robin and Joseph out in Bareneed. She saw them fishing off a wharf, going for walks on country roads, extending greetings to elderly neighbours, and spending time with Joseph's Uncle Doug. Thinking of Joseph and Robin together, she smiled and reached for her novel on the nightstand. She opened the book to her mark, took up reading where she had left off: the Victorian lady, of a once-spirited and artistic inclination, was seated in dreary repose in her bedchamber. Her eyes had lost their gleam; the two pools of blackness that now stared out at the static scene before her gave her countenance a look of Nature itself corrupted. Summoning the strength, she stood and raised the candlestick to assume her post as sentinel in the window. For well over a fortnight she had been awaiting the return of her husband and daughter. No word had come before them. Not a solitary sign to cheer her. The husband and daughter had vanished.

Kim shut the book with a sigh. Rather than fortifying her, she found the situation in the novel added a bleakness to her heart. Father and daughter together. It was a good thing, wasn't it? The house was quiet. Peaceful. She could read whenever she wanted. Eat whatever and whenever she wanted. It was okay. Separation was necessary for the senses to settle. In time, the excitement of longing would bury the excitement of confrontation.

Each time Kim imagined Joseph, recalled the good times they had spent together, the holiday in Spain, the wild laughter they often shared, the little things he did for her, the more she missed him and craved him there beside her. Gestures as simple as a slow caring massage or preparing a good cup of coffee became monuments to Joseph's generosity. He made the best cup of coffee she had ever tasted.

Of course, she knew there were obstacles that required sorting out. When Kim and Joseph had lived together, they had each had separate offices in the house, each with their own computer. They worked whenever they could steal a free moment. Robin was often left to draw or watch a wildlife video by herself. Not that she was neglected — they did plenty of fun stuff together — it just seemed that computers were gradually nudging the fun time out of the picture. Kim almost felt relieved when she didn't have to do anything with Robin, when she could turn on her computer and do a little shopping on the internet or rewrite one of her papers. And now, with Robin not here, she realized the actual amount of time she did spend working. It made her miss Robin even more.

As for the separation from Joseph, she felt that it had been mostly her fault. She had pushed Joseph too hard. She had tried to control him, keep him from his friends. Her jealousy had forced her to withhold her love, bit by bit, until it was virtually non-existent. Yet she knew the love was still there, smothered under years of monotony.

Working long hours was only part of the problem. Kim was a realist. She wouldn't kid herself. They had different views on how to raise their daughter. Kim believed that Joseph was far too easy on Robin, letting her get away with everything. Robin had Joseph wrapped around her little finger — not that she was spoiled, but she was a real daddy's girl. Joseph treated her like a baby. Kim wanted Joseph to be more practical in his instructions to her. What should he do, Kim argued with herself, enlist Robin in a boot camp?

Turning her head to Joseph's side of the bed, her expression of amusement wasted away. She stared down at her book, remembering how Joseph used to read to her in bed. The deep rhythmic sound of his voice lulling her to sleep.

Unable to focus on her reading, she looked toward the dark opened window. Raindrops spotted the black glass. A cool breeze reached her, saturating her with relief. Kim glanced at the nightstand. The telephone. She took a deep breath and was about to reach for it, to call Joseph and see how Robin was doing, when it rang. She flinched. Baffled, she stared at the phone, deciding whether or not to answer it. She waited for another ring and even thought of not answering at all. If it was Joseph then he would assume she was out having a great time. But then again, something might have happened in Bareneed. An accident. If it rang four times, her voice mail would kick in. On the third ring, she snatched it up, trying to sound cheery.

"Hello?"

"Hi, it's me." It was Joseph, his tone clipped, tense, as it often was these days over the telephone.

"Hi." She listened for his reply. Silence. "How's Bareneed?"

"Fine. Listen, Robin had a little accident today."

Kim sat up straight in bed. "What?" Gooseflesh prickled over her body, fright coursing up the back of her neck. Instantly, her palm was sweaty against the receiver's moulded plastic.

"Someone threw a rock and it hit her head."

"Her head! Did you go to the hospital?"

"Yes, it's okay. They said she was fine, but she has a fever now. We were on Shearstown Line, heading back to St. John's —"

"How high?"

"High?"

"The fever."

"Hundred and four."

"Christ, Joe. That's too high. Do you have any pills?"

"No. We were on Shearstown Line, heading back to St. John's, and I noticed she was hot and glassy-eyed and I didn't have any pills in the car. There's no drugstore. I didn't want to risk the drive. I came back, back to here —"

"Didn't they give you something at the hospital for her?" asked Kim.

"No, she was fine."

"Get a damp cloth and a pan of cold water and soak the cloth, put it on her body —"

"I'm doing that. I called the doctor. There was a doctor there today when it happened. He almost ran over the guy who threw the rock."

"Guy? What guy?"

"The guy who threw the rock."

"The guy?" She shifted her legs over the edge of the bed. "A man?"

"No." Joseph sounded genuinely rattled. "A teenager."

"Why'd he throw a rock? Was it an accident?"

"I don't know." There was a pause and Kim heard Joseph say, away from the receiver, "It's Mommy." Then Robin's low voice, "Can I talk?"

"Robin?" Kim called out.

"Hi, Mommy." Her sweet little voice was so weak, with the trace of a quaver.

"Hi, sweetheart. How you feeling?"

"Cccold."

"You want me to come out? I can come out. Right away."

"No, Mom. It's raining out. You might have an accident."

Kim's mouth was dry, her body tingling with a fear that now made her tremble. Regardless, she smiled at Robin's concern for her safety. "If your temperature doesn't go down soon, I'm coming right out. Okay? I don't care about the rain."

"Okay, Mom. Bye. Love you."

"Love you, too." The receiver made a ruffling noise.

Joseph was there again: "The doctor's bringing over children's acetaminaphen."

"If it's not down soon," she said strictly, pulling the blankets closer to her chest, "take her back to the hospital. It's very important. She could have a concussion."

"I know that. I'll call in half an hour."

"Don't take any chances, Joe. Get the cloth."

"I have a cloth. I'm doing —"

"That temperature has to come down or there could be brain damage. A hundred and four is too high."

"Okay." His voice was less steady now. "Okay. I'll call later. I'm here."

"Are you okay?"

"No, I'm not." He hung up.

"Joe?" The receiver was slippery in her hand. She nibbled at her lip, worried, then angry. What was Joseph doing out there? How could he allow someone to throw a rock at Robin? Why would anyone throw a rock at a little girl. "What sort of bastard?" she muttered, fuming as she slammed down the receiver. Tossing back the covers, she felt the sweat chilling on her body, the shock of fright dissolving her hold over herself. She stood and grabbed her dressing gown, fit her arms into it, tied the cord and hugged herself to get warm.

The rain began to gush, hammering the roof, but still she stood in a fit of inaction. She had been given her excuse to visit Bareneed. Robin, her baby, her only baby, had a dangerously high temperature. She felt blame well up inside her. She felt guilty as hell.

‑◀◎

At the sound of knocking, Joseph ran down over the stairs and threw open the front door. Dr. Thompson, wearing a yellow slicker with the hood pulled up, mindfully stepped in over the threshold of the Critch house. The rain was pouring down steadily. There was the roar of waves, either from the wind in the tops of the evergreens or from the distant beach.

"Thanks, doctor, for coming." A chill, drifting in from the open door, compelled Joseph to shiver spasmodically. He hadn't been able to get warm since falling into the ocean earlier that day, his bones seeming galvanized by a resilient compound of anxiety and ice. Dead fingers latched to his bones. Dead faces suspended and watching him. Beneath the water was something entirely different. He was safe here on land. In a house. Walls. Windows. Yet the rain was a concern in itself. The rain was like the ocean cascading down on them in a pattern. What was it trying to tell him? What shape was it taking?

"Not a problem," Thompson said in a sleep-groggy voice. He flicked down his wet hood and shook the rain from his black bag.

"Let me take that."

Thompson nodded and sighed as he pulled his arms from his slicker. Joseph could tell that the doctor was tired by the purplish bags under his eyes and his sluggish distracted movements.

"Thanks," Thompson said, coughing once as Joseph hung the slicker on a peg beside the door. "Upstairs?"

"Yes." Joseph led the way. "I've been putting cold water on Robin with a face cloth."

"Good."

Joseph reached the top of the stairs before Thompson, who was taking his time.

"Shoddy knees," Thompson said as he arrived beside Joseph. "You're lucky to still have yours."

Joseph glanced wonderingly down at his knees, then led the doctor to Robin's bedroom. A light with a pink plastic shade was illuminated on her night table.

Although Robin's eyes were shut, she muttered a few words, as if in greeting: "It's not Christmas yet."

The doctor, who smelled of wine and garlic, raised his woolly eyebrows and stepped into the room. He took notice of the silver pan of water on the carpet, the blue face cloth floating in it. Again he sighed, as he laid his bag on the edge of the bed and unfastened the closure.

Robin said: "But I didn't get you a present."

"A present?" The doctor grunted as he sat on the edge of the bed, "Christly knees," he cursed. "Frigging knees." Then, soothingly to the child, "Hi, Robin." He rummaged around in his bag on his lap. "I'm Dr. Thompson and I'm going to take your temperature. Okay?"

Robin, eyes still shut, said cutely: "That's for the turkey."

The doctor chuckled, "I guess you're the turkey tonight. You're hot enough. Can you look at me, please?" He shook the thermometer and tried reading it. "I can't see a god-bloody thing." He handed it up to Joseph who checked that the mercury was beneath the required number.

"Fine," he said, handing it back.

Robin opened her eyes. Her hair was matted to her forehead.

"Open your mouth, honey, please."

Robin sluggishly opened her mouth and the doctor inserted the thermometer. He then stood, with a louder groan, one hand on his lower back, and turned to Joseph, "As I've already said, I don't think the bump on her head was severe enough to cause this. She might just have a virus, an infection, something that her body's fighting. How's her breathing?"

"Her breathing?"

"Yeah, in and out." He pointed to his own mouth.

"Fine."

"Good."

"Should I take her back to the hospital?"

"I don't know. That's up to you. The X-rays were clear enough. The rock hit her here." He touched the back of his own head with two fingertips. "That's a tough spot. If it'd been in the front, temples, anywhere near there, then we'd have real cause for concern. And she had a nice bump which is a good sign." The doctor squinted, taking notice of Joseph. He lifted a pair of glasses from his shirt pocket and put them on, low on his nose. "You're shivering."

"It's nothing. Damp. How long can she be like this?"

"Not much longer. I'll give her something. If that doesn't bring the fever down, then you should dunk her in a tub of icy cold water." He turned toward Robin and provided a consoling smile. "Not much fun having that thing stuck in your mouth, eh?"

Robin mutely shook her head.

"Could you take that out for me?" he asked Joseph. "Back and knees are shot. Physician heal thyself. Some chance."

Joseph bent and slid the thermometer from between Robin's lips.

He resisted the urge to read it as he handed it to the doctor. Thompson studied the mercurial line, his expression remaining level. He then shook the thermometer, slid it away and extracted a bottle of pills from his bag.

"Cherry-flavoured," he said, smiling at Robin. "I have to resist eating them all myself, they're so tasty." He handed two to Joseph, who bent to Robin.

"Eat these, sweetheart."

Robin opened her mouth and languidly chewed the pills, moving her tongue around, pausing occasionally, her eyes shutting, then chewing again, stopping. "Can I have some water, please?"

Joseph lifted the glass from the night table, cautiously raised Robin's head and tilted the rim to her lips. She took a careful sip. A gust of wind hurled rain against the window and there was a lashing sound from toward the front of the house. Wires banging against the clapboard.

"Okay?" he asked her.

Robin nodded.

"How about yourself?" Thompson inquired in a low voice once Joseph stood to face the doctor again. "How are you feeling?"

"Can't get the chill out of me." He noticed the glass still in his hand and laid it aside.

"This is all upsetting. That fall in the water didn't help much." The doctor stared at Joseph's eyes as if expecting further disclosure. A silence settled between them before a gust of wind pattered rain against the window. Thompson turned to observe the dark glass. "Miserable old night," he offered, glancing at Robin before regarding Joseph again. "She should be fine. Don't worry too much."

Joseph shifted his attention to Robin, who seemed to be sleeping, her breath rising and falling evenly.

"Well …" said Thompson.

"Yes." Joseph watched Thompson raise his bag.

"Call me if —"

"Tell him about the bodies, Daddy."

Thompson and Joseph both shifted their attention to Robin, but it was as if she hadn't moved a muscle. The tone of the voice had been bright and healthy.

A shiver violently jerked Joseph's shoulders. He made a noise with his lips. "God," he said, involuntarily.

"She must be dreaming," said Thompson. "Fever dreams. You ever have them?"

"I guess so," said Joseph, his words clipped between tight lips.

"I always liked them myself," the doctor admitted. "The best ones always came just before the fever broke."

In the solar house, two dark figures, a woman and a ghost-child, stood in the top window regarding the four-wheel drive pull away from where it had been parked in front of the adjacent house. The vehicle passed beneath a streetlamp, which illuminated the sheets of rain and, for a moment, the form of the doctor. The vehicle then drifted down the higher road toward the clustered lights of the community.

"Poor child," the woman whispered, envisioning the calamity in her neighbour's house. The man dealing with a sick child in the middle of the night. Such worries. A sick child. Her heart went out to him. She gave consideration to venturing over to lend a hand, to test the girl's forehead for fever, to lay her fingers upon the girl's cheek and see that she was well, that the girl would be fine, survive beyond the trials of the night. But would the man accept the woman, allow her in without invitation?

The ghost-child stared back into the dark room, the light from the outside travelling only so far. She contained her breath, warily listened to the distant rustlings downstairs that soon became slow clumsy footsteps moving toward the stairway. A resonant exhale, troubled air gushing through a man's nostrils.

"He's here," gasped the ghost-child.

The woman remained still, her face submerged in darkness save for a thin wedge of yellow light along her cheek and jawline cast from the street lamp across the yard. There was no sound within the walls. And beyond the walls, only rain pounding the rooftop.

"He's coming up the stairs," announced the ghost-child, her voice thick and bubbly as though intermittently trapped beneath water, shoved under the surface. A struggle of words: "You have to ..." submerged, held under, then resurfacing, spitting out: "... stop loving him."

The woman sobbed once. She clamped shut her eyes, touched her brows with her fingertips, and shook her head fearfully.

"Stop, Mommy," the ghost-child shouted. "Stop loving him." Her voice rose to a shrill scream: "Stop it. Stop loving him. Stop loving him."

The woman sobbed louder, as the ghost-child drifted back from the window, hiding in the corner, cowering, shivering, dripping wet. Droplets of water monotonously dotted the carpet as if from a leak in the roof, the rain knowing no boundaries. The woman fixed her eyes on the ceiling and there were beads of water, vaguely silver, that hung pulsing, waiting to drop.

"You see him," a voice roared behind her. The drops on the ceiling burst all at once to soak her through and through. "That man who's come."

The woman shook her head, buried her face in her drenched hands, sobbing.

"You harlot. Just because I'm dead you think … you think …"

"I don't love you," she mumbled. "I don't love you, I don't …"

"You do. Look at me, I'm here."

There was no sound, only stillness. The woman suspected that everything she had imagined thus far might just be that — her imagination — until, yanked back by her hair, away from the window, into the stark darkness, she shrieked with pain and fright. A bulky shadow was upon her, lashing out, as she raised her feeble hands to protect herself from further harm.

Claudia weakly laid her pen in the centre crease of her journal. The tendons in her hand were taut, aching. She watched out the window. In the glass, in its reflection of pervasive darkness and finite light, she saw Jessica standing directly behind her.

"Are you dreaming, Mommy?" Jessica asked.

"I don't know, sweetheart. Am I?"

"Sometimes, I can't tell, Mommy. Do you think it matters?"

"Does what matter?"

"How real I am, Mommy? I don't know how real I am."

—◈—

Steadily, the rain beat the ocean's black water. The surface appeared like liquid charcoal sparked by a million points of dim, muted light. A pair of sentries stood on the large L-shaped concrete wharf where two shrimp boats were tied up, the wood creaking in the swell of the water. Both men wore dark-green slickers and were scanning the water, each with a set of binoculars.

"You can't see a thing," one of them said loudly, above the drone of rain. The other gave no reply.

A hundred feet from the wharf, almost halfway toward the massive black headland, an orange object broke the surface, bobbed and floated, the pouring rain making it glisten subtly beneath the moonless sky.

The first sentry pointed. The other immediately shifted his binoculars toward the area of attention.

"It's a dead fish. Orange dead fish. Big one."

The other nodded and remained focused, watching, witnessing a gush of mist or fog rising from the water to hover and linger over the object. Then it was suddenly washed aside by the advent of a body surfacing and bobbing thickly.

The two sentries, having already lowered their binoculars, climbed down the side of the wharf where their small craft awaited boarding. The first sentry engaged the engine and steered toward the body while the other stood at the rocky bow of the craft with his binoculars raised.

Once alongside the body, the sentries were puzzled to discover that the corpse appeared dressed in the fashion of a sixteenth-century explorer with breaches, vest and leather shoes. It floated on its back, its gaze unperturbed by the rain, its moist eyes staring patiently toward the grey-black sky.

─◌─

Miss Laracy could not sleep when the rain was pounding her house. "When rain blow frum da east," she whispered to herself, "'tis neither good fer man nar beast." The downpour disturbed all in existence: the sky was disturbed, the air was disturbed, the ocean and earth were disturbed. Every single thing was changing outside her place of shelter. The wood of her house grew wetter and the bugs nibbled at the rot and multiplied in numbers. She saw and felt all of this in her bones as she slid the black long-spouted kettle onto the damper of her wood stove. The rain was filling up hollows in the earth, speeding the rivers, adding weight to the sea.

A gust of wind pelted the kitchen window with rain. Miss Laracy watched the divide in the lace sheers and detected movement against the dark glass, rivulets of water distorting her view of the outside.

From the time she was a child, she had loved the sadness of the rain. The weeping quality, the great outdoors saturated and going soft. On nights like these, she would eagerly anticipate being tucked in her bed, already warmed by two heated beach rocks from the top of the stove, and gaze up at her father, who would tell her stories or sing songs while the rain roused memory itself. He would tell her about his voyages to Labrador, the Eskimaw and their strange behaviours, the way the women strapped their babies to their backs and first chewed food for the babies before passing it into their little mouths. He would explain about Dog Island where the savage dogs that pulled the Eskimaw sleighs in winter were abandoned to run wild in summer. The dogs would be brought there in boats after the thaw and left to fend for themselves. "When ye were close enough, a mile or so off da shore, ye could catch da sound travellin' in da air, a mournful sound so beauteous dat it drew tears right ta yer eyes." Her father would sit at her bedside, swirling a finger in his thick whiskers, while he spoke in a low grave tone. "Da dogs howlin' frum dere miserable station. Dey would trot down ta shore when we sailed by. Dey would be barkin' 'n howlin' like mad wicked beasts, bitin' at each udder. Hungry. One or two would try ta swim out ta us, dere eyes fixed so steady on yer face, but den dey'd turn 'n struggle back, paddlin' hard widt dere paws, runin' outta life. Too far in da water. Too long a stretch fer dem ta cross." Her father would go on to tell tales about the men he had sailed with, men from distant outports who believed in incredible superstitions. These beliefs never failed to intrigue and inspire Miss Laracy. They seemed so true, so rooted in childlike reason. Superstitions were magical. At such times, there would come a pause in her father's storytelling and then he would commence singing, in a high, velvety boyish voice, a voice so unlike the one he used for speaking. And while he sung to her, the room would seem to gently rock, up and down to the sway of the verse, as though she were in a boat out at sea and her father's voice was the abiding waves that could carry her through anything. Her father would sing her favourite song, the one that told of the death of her father's father on an ice pan while hunting harp seals in 1897:

Da spring o' 'ninety-seven boys
Fer if ye never knew
Da hardship o' da frozen pan,
We suffered widt dem too.

We struck da seals off Cabot Isle
Five days out from da port,
We t'ought ta have no long delay,
'N loadin' would be sport.

Eleven t'ousand prime young harps
We put on board dat day,
'N sixteen t'ousand more dat night,
We safely stowed away.

That was the happy part, the part about work and success, but Miss Laracy always waited for the tingle of tragedy, her heart quickening at the sound of her father's words turning sweeter, sadder as he glanced toward the window, at the pouring rain or blustery snow that spurred him on.

Next day a storm broke off da ice,
Which ript t'rough our port bow,
Ta save a life t'was just enough,
Fer each man ta look how.

We suffered awful hardship den,
When often cold 'n wet,
'N all da dangers o' da spring,
We never will forget.

Here her father would pause to stare warily into her eyes, as though to caution her, wondering if she might be ready for the worst of the lot:

'Twas bad enough till deat' it came,
Made our condition worse,
Fer one o' our brave harbour men,
Died on da twenty-first.

When doin' duty like a man,
Our comrade stopped ta fall;
From which he suffered much too dear,
Til deat' did give a call.

Den shipmate Thomas Laracy
Such hardship could nar stand,
'N on da twenty-ninth he sighed,
Passed on ta better land.

Tears would bubble up in Miss Laracy's eyes as she heard the name of her great-grandfather spoken along with the ruinous details of his death. This, coupled with the sheer beauty of her father's voice, would make the tears stream down over her face, wetting her hair at her temples, for she could not help but imagine her grandfather laid out on the eternally white ice, the wind howling around him like those abandoned beasts on Dog Island. He was dressed in plain woollen pants, a sweater and a moth-eaten coat. His clothes were caked with clumps of snow and he lay on his side while the other men stood around him, their heads inclined to protect themselves from the stinging bite of the wind. They watched over him, incapable of doing another single thing for their noble friend as the snow banked up around him.

He bravely fought ta keep up fit,
Ta see his friends once more,
But never will his footsteps tread
Upon da Southern Shore.

Oh Newfoundland, in north and south,
Around in every bay,
Take pity of our poor countrymen,
Caught up in dis dismal way.

Dey bravely died in duty's path,
'N God will mercy shed,
Dose men who toiled so hard on earth,
Ta earn a crust o' bread.

Plummeting tragedy, so heartbreaking and yet comforting in its affirmation of the inherent grimness in human nature. Miss Laracy would never fail to weep, and her father, done with his recitation, would then lean to comfort her, shushing her sorrows away.

Presently she watched the rain fall beyond her kitchen window, the rain that would, in months to come, transform to snow. She recalled how, after narrating his story or song, and after kissing her on the forehead and running his strong hands over the edges of the covers to make certain she was secure, her father would quietly step from her childhood bedroom as if retreating from a shrine. His lingering presence, the glow that outlined his body, that remained from the telling of the story, would distill as the ghost of Thomas Laracy, who would stand at the foot of her bed, not frozen and horribly bent out of shape, but warm and smiling and tipping his hat with a charming wink. He would then shut his eyes and sway as though hearing the tune that had summoned him, and cherishing it.

Thomas Laracy, a man Miss Laracy loved and knew only through verse. A dead man gone all these years, yet alive in her thoughts with a clarity that somehow mended her heart. And Uriah Slaney, her sweetheart, a man she knew as well as herself, a man kindred in belief and in the particles of his soul. If only she could see him again, in spirit, see him past his grave as she used to.

If only the spirits would be released from wherever they were secluded. "Show yerself ta me," she muttered under her breath. "Provide me widt da consolation o' yer peace." Miss Laracy turned away from the window and stared toward the stove. The water in the kettle was boiling. Steam rose above the stove, hanging near the ceiling as Miss Laracy grinned in conspiracy with herself. "Take shape," she said, chuckling, squinting to make out a figure from the steam. "Frum boilin' water ye once took shape in dis very kitchen." She waited, hesitating in earnest expectation, only to have her hopes grow more remiss. "Narry again," she finally said, stomping toward the kettle and snatching it from the damper. "Narry no more. 'Tis now me cross ta bear."

~☽

Joseph ran the cool cloth along Robin's belly, then smoothly up over her chest and across her face. He dabbed gently while his daughter steadily shivered. Robin pulled at the blanket to cover herself, but Joseph patiently eased the blanket from her.

"I'm sorry, sweetie," he whispered, "but I have to get your fever down. You'll just get warmer with the blankets."

Trembling, Robin nodded bravely. "Okay."

Joseph dipped the cloth back in the pan of cool water and rung it out. He feared the fever would never ease. He feared heart-imploding tragedy. It was an effort to pretend that harm would not prevail. Why did I bring her here? How was I to know? It was a vacation. How was I to know? Memories menaced him: Claudia sitting on the floor of her house with her head between her knees while Joseph wrapped his arm around Robin's shoulder and turned her from the sight; the reflection of the bearded man in the window; the underwater dead with their uncertain yet expectant eyes.

It was half past midnight. An hour of punishing and suspect images had tormented Joseph until, finally, the mercury line climbed to one-hundred-and-one centigrade and stopped. Pulling away from the noise and calamity of his thoughts, he noticed the stillness in and beyond the house. The rain had stopped. He checked Robin. She was lying calm in her bed, no longer trembling. She was breathing evenly, sweating profusely. The fever had broken.

Joseph stood from where he was kneeling beside the bed. He felt safety, touched by an enlivening spell of joy. The dreadful possibility of losing Robin had been cancelled and with it the claustrophobia of the events of the past few days. The relief leaned toward fellowship. He should call Kim. He should call her at once. He eyed the telephone beside Robin's bed. Call her now. Or leave her to suffer. Suffer until he chose to relieve that suffering.

If he was to speak with Kim, it would have to be in private. He did not want to disturb Robin. He went downstairs, flicking on the hallway light as he advanced, then the kitchen light, before raising the telephone from the wall and pressing Kim's number.

"It's down to one hundred and one," he blurted out as soon as she answered, an instant after the first ring.

"Great." She gave a sigh.

Joseph pictured Kim shaking her head, shaking off the possibilities of the tragedy that might have stricken them. A close call. "I'll stay up. I'm up keeping an eye —"

"You'll be exhausted."

"It's okay." The black window, still dotted with droplets of rain, reflected a faint image of the room from the inside. He shifted his eyes away, expecting a face to appear on the other side, a wet face pressing against the glass and grinning with cryptic knowledge, smearing the window with its putrefying hands.

"You won't be able to function tomorrow. You'll be a mess."

"Function?" He gave a short laugh, then was silent for a length of time he lost track of. "We're coming home tomorrow."

"You shouldn't drive without sleep. It's no problem for me to come out."

"I don't think that'd be a good idea."

"Robin needs her mother."

Another lapse, through which Joseph drifted in essence only. He sighed and was grounded in his body again. He noticed his feet on the wooden floor. His grey socks. He sucked on his lower lip and peeked at the window. Nothing. Blackness fading to deep grey as if a fog had rolled in. He glanced around the kitchen — the two glass doors in the built-in cabinet where the dishes were neatly stacked, the old-fashioned white and black enamel stove, the chunky wooden table. He had chosen the house with Kim in mind, hanging onto faint hope that they would resolve their differences and spend the summer together.

So why was he resisting? A twisted effort to cling onto control, to pun-ish Kim for making him leave and divide their family.

"Joseph?"

"I don't know."

"Don't know what?"

"It could get complicated. I don't want to disapppoint Robin."

"It'd be good for her to see us together."

"Then what? More disappointment?"

"Anyway, okay. Whatever. That's fine. You decide." She hung up.

Joseph held onto the receiver, disabled by Kim's sudden withdrawal. The receiver was mute, plastic and empty. He was alone again. No, not alone, but fully reconnected to the anxiety of this place and its people. Kim had drawn herself back through the wires. She had been his protection of sorts.

A moment later he hung up, feeling as if he had accomplished nothing other than further injury to his already damaged state. He turned toward the window. Nothing. What did he expect? He edged nearer the glass, as if to doom himself with the fright of a face rearing up, one of those bodies from the depths of the ocean. What were they doing? Had they even been there?

All at once, another burden of rain was released from the sky, striking the roof as hard as a shower of bursting stones. He imagined how the rain must be beating against the surface of the ocean and how all the drowned bodies with their heads tilted upward were watching the pinpoints strik-ing the division between air and water, the barrage of piercings that might fully fragment the surface and, subsequently, free them.

~֍

When Tommy Quilty was two years old, shortly after he had been taken by the fairies and returned as a changed child, he began witnessing the coloured swells clinging around people's bodies. Babies were surrounded by the sturdiest, most spectacular colours, but so were numerous older people. As the babies grew, their colours either faded or remained brilliant. It seemed to depend on what an individual did with his or her life. Those who were selfless preserved the health of their colours, but those who were concerned only with their own gains devoured even their most basic colours. It didn't take long for Tommy to realize that the people without light were mean and careless. They lacked an inner quality that generated the coloured swells. Tommy suspected that this inner quality was compassion. These people were to be avoided, for they would cause a person extreme unease. Miss Laracy had told Tommy that these coloured swells were called auras. She saw them too, so it was okay to see. He took great consolation in Miss Laracy's presence, but when she wasn't near, he often felt bullied by his own powers of observation.

What grieved him most, throughout the years, was the gradual disappearance of the auras in people. The trees, the grass, the ocean and sky all continued to possess their living colours, hues different from what most people perceived. Yet fewer and fewer people actually possessed auras beyond infancy. Of course, Tommy wondered if it just might be him, if he was losing "the sight" or if the auras were actually dying. Miss Laracy, too, had noticed the fading of the auras and had explained it this way: "It be da dyin' belief in da fantastic dat cheats a person o' dere colours." He assumed Miss Laracy was correct, yet he couldn't help but wonder if it might be his belief in himself that was actually dying, for as special as Miss Laracy claimed him to be, he was still made to feel that there was something wrong with him.

The decline had begun decades ago, and was made most evident following the disappearance of the spirits and the fairies. Tommy had been eight years old when it all happened. He had gone grinning into the woods to visit the fairies' secret gathering place. Checking over his shoulder to make certain no one was trailing him, he pushed back the evergreen bows and saw the place where the blueberries, cranberries and partridge-berries all grew, the beaming colours vital and near-bursting with life. The fairies loved to eat and play with the berries. They would toss the berries around like miniature balls, flitting about in their game of catch, until a berry exploded upon an unlucky participant and the drenched fairy would hit the ground. Tommy had been looking forward to watching their games. He had brought along a knob of hardtack, which they broke into sheets and used to build houses until rain rendered the houses soggy and washed them away. Of course, the houses would simply be re-built.

The fairies were never disheartened, never discouraged or made cheerless by adversity.

Tommy had parted the evergreen boughs, expecting to see the fairies engaged in their frivolity, but there was no sign of them. A dragonfly fluttered past, its wings stirring a sound similar to those of the fairies. This briefly lifted Tommy's heart. Perhaps the fairies were hiding, playing a game on him. He stepped farther into their secret place and waited, shutting his eyes and saying, "Come out, come out." But, upon opening his eyes, he found himself alone. The fairies, who never ever wandered far from home, were gone. The fairies' homes were everything to them. They never travelled from their community or went away.

There was a silence in the woods, a new joyless silence. The playful texture of the air was muted, lacking the whizz and buzz of the fairies' merriment, and the colours of the leaves seemed dusty, for the fairies no longer polished them each morning. Tommy Quilty stood on that spot, the place where the fairies had sprinkled him with magic and changed him, made him ugly to all others but special in his own right. He knew that he was a test of others' character. How they saw him, how they treated him, dictated who they truly were in their hearts. The fairies had told him as much, although a few of them were snickering behind their backs while the others explained. The snickering ones were just jealous, Tommy assumed, because like humans the lesser fairies were capable of great jealousy.

Now, almost forty years later, the fairies were still gone, the spirits had been driven higher into the skies, and the men and women with the coloured swells stuck to their bodies had grown scarcer.

Tommy sat at his table, his charcoal pencil firmly pressed to the expensive off-white sketching paper. With precise scribbles, he drew a sea brewing with creatures so spectacular that the sight of them made his jaw gape. On the wharves there was chaos and panic as people hugged one another or pointed in disbelief.

The shapes on the wharf were known to him, each a member of the community. When he was done sketching the head and body of one small figure, he recognized it to be Rayna. Streams of hazy light, spectres, filled the night sky above her.

Tommy paused, bewildered by the sight of Rayna. Was this a good or bad thing? He feared that it was bad. Over the past few months, he had noticed the layers of Rayna's coloured swells thinning. She had been drinking too much, sinking too deeply into herself, severing her union with the world.

Tommy returned his concentration to drawing. He dabbed the tip of the charcoal with his tongue before returning the pencil point to his sketch. He drew with determination, unable to stop, even as his hand grew shaky and he felt that he must rush to the bathroom to pee. He remained in his chair, needing to finish the sketch, not wanting to step away for fear that it would have changed when he returned, advanced beyond the stage that he was presently depicting, his hand drawing images over other images, blurring the picture. He feared the confusion of going beyond this vision.

For years, Tommy had caught dim flickerings of these images in his mind, but now that they were full and complete in his art, they would most certainly exist. He dropped his pencil, the sketch absolute. He wanted to call Rayna, to see that she was okay. It was Saturday night. Was she home or had she gone to the dance at the Caribou Lounge? He rushed out to the kitchen and into the bathroom that adjoined it. He peed with a sigh of spectacular relief while watching the water in the toilet bowl flicker and waver. When he flushed, he stared as the water level sank only to pause at the midway point. The mechanisms in the toilet tank fell silent. He jiggled the handle. That didn't seem to help. He jiggled it again and the water began rising toward the rim. Tommy grabbed up the plunger, but refrained from shoving it into the bowl. It would only force the water level, which seemed to have paused again, this time at the near spillover point. He waited and steadily watched, holding the plunger at the ready in both hands, like a talisman of protection, until the water gradually sank with a few big gurgling bubbles.

In the kitchen, Tommy stubbed his fingers against the telephone digits. The line connected and the phone rang four times before it was answered, the receiver making a lot of noise as it was smashed against something or dropped and carelessly retrieved.

"Lo?"

"Rayna?" Tommy beamed at the sound of her voice.

"Yeah, who's 'is?"

"Tommy."

A wet sloppy laugh came from the other end. "Tommy, Tommy … how ya getting on? Nice talkin' to ya, Tommy."

"Rayna?"

"Yeah's my name. Want my address?" Raunchy laughter.

"Rayna?"

"Wha', Tommy, wha're ya sayin'?"

"When I were a little boy, da fairies took me."

"Sure I know that."

"Never was always ugly like dis."

"Tommy, sure you're priceless, a prince."

"No, I'm not."

"You're the bestest prince I ever clapped eyes on, 'n I loves ya ta pieces."

"Rayna? Ghosts are comin'."

More sopping laughter. Disbelief. "That'll be sum'thin' diffrnt."

"Da water's rising and ghosts are coming, Rayna. What'm I supposed ta do?"

"Send 'em over here for a swally of rum."

Tommy couldn't help but laugh outright. Rayna never failed to give him delight, no matter what her state. It was her gift.

"I'll get 'em good n' plastered. Bunch 'a drunk ghosts. Whooo-hoo. Hauntin' da hell outta me. What a friggin' party, Tommy. Send them ghosts right over now. Send 'em 'n we'll all get sloshed!"

SUNDAY

Sergeant Chase usually enjoyed Sundays. He maintained a slow pace, cruising through Bareneed, appreciating the silent houses, a stray horse or cow grazing here and there. No need to hurry on a sunny Sunday. Individuals, lulled by the notion of God hanging over them in some sort of brighter, more profound way, laid down their tools and set aside their feelings of animosity toward one another. Well, it was nice to think that way.

Yet this Sunday held no peace. A teenager from Bareneed, Andrew Slade, was dead. He had fallen on the road, hit his head, and stopped breathing. The paramedics were helpless to resuscitate him. He was rushed to the Port de Grave Hospital. DOA. When Chase had contacted Dr. Thompson on the doctor's cellphone, to gather the specifics of the death, Thompson had informed Chase that two new cases of the breathing disorder, similar to the one that Donna Drover was suffering from, had just arrived in the hospital.

Chase had to admit that three deaths in a matter of days, and the possibility of some sort of viral outbreak, was more than a simple shake of the dice for a small community like Bareneed. There were already rumours of a full inquiry. Another death would guarantee that. The area would be flooded with experts. They would arrive from St. John's and then, if matters continued to deteriorate, they would fly in from across the country. Something in the water. Something in the air. Something in the soil. A virus. A plague. A message sent from the Creator. Doom and gloom. Or simply a coincidence. Three deaths. Was that anything at all? This is nothing, he tried to reassure himself, thinking of his wife, Theresa, hoping for her sake that calm would prevail, that news of this would never reach her.

Chase flicked on the radio, listening to Bruce Springsteen singing "Glory Days." It reminded him of a specific period in his life that he valued as much as his present life, if not more. Drinking with the guys and not yet married to Theresa. Friday nights in a pool hall. An attractive woman in tight jeans eyeing him. He had no problem attracting women. They seemed drawn to his dark skin and size. He smiled to himself as he recalled the sound of the pool balls clicking together. Turning up the song, he then rolled down his window, passed alongside the fenced-in war memorial and the Bareneed post office flying its red and white Canadian flag. He cruised beside the long red building that housed the community hall and the volunteer fire department. There were two army vehicles parked in the narrow lot. He watched the vehicles in his side mirror, wondering what they might be doing there. Soon the curve of the harbour was directly at his left. Water. He felt his stomach shrink and sway with nausea. Seagulls and crows were flocked above the wharf. Birds were consistently at the scene of a death. Birds and bugs. You could always count on the scavengers.

Up ahead, cars were parked on both sides of the road. There appeared to be some sort of commotion at the large community wharf. A crowd of thirty or forty had gathered and were staring at an object laid out on the concrete. Chase pulled up behind a string of parked cars, on the gravel shoulder, and removed his sunglasses. Nothing as obnoxious as a police officer wearing sunglasses in a crowd. He laid them on the dash and climbed out of his cruiser. He put on his hat, fitted it snugly and checked his gun to make certain the protective hasp was fastened.

Approaching the wharf, he caught bits and pieces of conversation from the people lingering on the outskirts of the crowd: "Never saw … what a sight … Hauled up from under …" He reached the edge of the gathered group and pardoned himself to get through. Each person glanced at him first, before opening a path, bodies shifting out of the way until he had a clear view of the centre — the focus of everyone's attention. A shark, pure white and radiating in the sun with such intensity that Chase was forced to squint and shade his eyes. This might be something, he told himself. Might very well be. He bent and studied the shark's head. Its eyes were pink, like two raw fleshy rings set in a glow of white light. An albino.

"Sumtin' else, dis be," an old voice said from above Chase. Chase inquisitively glanced up to see an elderly woman, wearing a housedress and a bandana, staring down at him. He stood as she winked and tilted her head, turning it slightly in the gesture of greeting specific to Newfoundland.

"Ye ever set yer eyes on such a t'ing?" she asked.

"No, I can honestly say —"

"Naw, ye never did, did ye?"

"Where'd it come from?" he asked, watching a young boy poke at the shark with a stick, then run back to his buddies who, no doubt, had dared him.

"Dat boat," said the old woman, pointing to the green and white crab boat. "Dem mighty jaws latched onta a crab pot and wouldn't let go. Dey had ta beat it off widt a staff. Weren't white first." The old woman grinned, exposing gums as pink as an infant's. "It turned white when dey beat it."

Chase recalled the sculpin that had become bright red, as if in reaction to the air itself. From beside his feet there rose a quavering retching sound, a beast caught between a moan and a growl while vomiting. A stench wafted over Chase, making him grimace and press the side of his hand to his lips. The old woman clutched hold of his arm. A number of people backed away and a few others gasped as the shark's jaws opened mechanically, the rows of sharp twisted teeth parting. A flesh-coloured fluid seeped loose to pool in the bottom of its jaws. In such abundance, the fluid smelled identical to the rotting flesh found at a murder scene. The putrid scent was invasive to the human core.

"Where's the doll's head," Chase muttered to himself, trying not to breathe.

"Doll's 'ead?" the old woman asked. "Are ye off yer noggin, or at wit's end?"

Chase kept his eyes fixed on the pink hollow of the shark's opened mouth, the muscles of the throat-hole expanding and contracting in an unsettling rhythm, as if attempting to dispel its trouble. A mucousy clot of hair jammed in the throat, the wet arc of a skull slowly forcing itself into the air, the sheening forehead, opened eyes and whiskered cheeks. The head dislodged and rolled out to settle unevenly, like a warped turnip, at Chase's feet.

Chase, despite his unspoken pledge to hold it together in the midst of catastrophic upheaval, took an uncomfortable step back. More people gasped and scrambled to put distance between themselves and the head. A buzz of conversation travelled through the crowd. "Mother of God!" said one woman and blessed herself. Another grimaced: "Oh, my sweet Jesus!" and shielded her eyes with her fingers, only permitting herself the briefest peek. It was not a doll's head at all, but a man's head; the expression on the mottled green face was startled, the hair damp and clotted.

The old woman, releasing her grip on Chase's arm, now slapped it and professed, "Mudder a' Christ, dat's Kevin Pottle. Edyth's 'usband."

"No," challenged a shocked younger woman.

"Yays," argued the old woman.

The name Kevin Pottle strayed forward and back through the gathering as the noise of conversation mounted.

Chase, dumbfounded and delicate in his stomach, peered at the old woman. "What?" was all he could manage.

"Kevin Pottle. He be lost at sea four or five year ago. Never retrieved 'is body. A starm rose up like dey be wont ta do. Many a crew frum 'ere lost at sea. Many more ta be." The old woman nodded in resolute certainty. "'Tis an omen, da 'ead of a departed one in da belly of a fish."

"An omen?" Chase could barely believe the words he was hearing: talk of superstition in this day and age. He noticed that the eyes of the head were watching him intently.

"Ye'd never guess what such a t'ing portends." The old woman leaned her lips near his ear and whispered wholeheartedly: "A time o' da most wicked reckonin' fer all in its midst."

⁓◦

Even though it was Sunday, the medical examiner, Dr. Basha, a short, cinnamon-skinned man with black hair and a thin yet pleasant face, had been brought in from St. John's by the Chief of Medical Staff at the Port de Grave Hospital. Dr. Basha had instructed the hospital to hold Lloyd Fowler's body for review. Upon arriving, he evaluated the information and performed his own extensive autopsies on both Fowler and Andrew Slade.

Muss Drover's body was to be exhumed tomorrow. Basha had also examined blood and tissue samples from Donna Drover and others suffering from the breathing disorder who remained connected to respirators.

Autopsies on Lloyd Fowler and Andrew Slade had already been conducted by Dr. Peters, the resident pathologist. Nothing out of the ordinary had been discovered. Fowler's death had been ruled "of natural causes" and Andrew Slade had died of a head injury hematoma resulting from his fall. As for Donna Drover, there were no signs of virus or infection. White cell counts were normal. A CAT scan had detected no scar tissue or tumours in the brain stem, which controlled automatic functions such as breathing, heart rate, blood pressure, swallowing, sleep patterns and body temperature.

Staff at the hospital had been relieved to hear the news and kept their fingers crossed, hoping for no further fatalities. The last thing they, or anyone, needed was a panic situation. Phone calls to Emergency were already on the rise. There was growing concern about respiratory problems and fear that something viral or chemical was troubling the air around Bareneed.

Dr. Thompson had been notified of the forthcoming autopsies by Dr. Basha and had requested a presence at the procedures. He had been one of the first, along with the Chief of Medical Staff, to hear Dr. Basha's observations while the pathologist probed the bodies of Andrew Slade and Lloyd Fowler laid out on separate tables beside one another: "Lungs show no obvious signs of trauma." Basha had removed the skullcaps and taken out each brain to observe the stem. "No abnormalities in the brain stem." Basha had proficiently discounted a long list of possibilities while slicing open or weighing slivers of organs and marking notes on his clipboard.

"Hematoma killed Andrew Slade," Dr. Basha said with bright eyes and a bright smile. "Lloyd Fowler died of natural causes. Simple as that."

Despite the fact that Dr. Basha had confirmed Dr. Peters' judgements, Thompson left the hospital unconvinced. He climbed into his four-wheel drive to visit Bareneed, to call on the Slades as he had intended to do the previous day, before Andrew's untimely death.

Thompson had been in the hospital most of the night yet had managed to catch a quick nap in the interns' quarters shortly after 5:00 a.m. He needed a shave and proper rest but, most importantly, he felt it essential to speak to someone about the deaths. He required more information to settle his mind. Despite Dr. Basha's supposedly consoling report, these recent deaths troubled Thompson in a way understandable only by someone living, day in and day out, in the community. Two of the deceased had been his patients. He had treated shortness of breath in Lloyd Fowler's case. Andrew Slade had been treated for shortness of breath as well, the night prior to his death, then sent home from the hospital.

Thompson would pay his respects to the Slade family and inquire as to whether they had noticed anything peculiar about Andrew's behaviour. If any of the family exhibited shortness of breath then he would make certain they were rushed to the hospital and placed under observation. Driving down Shearstown Line, Thompson spotted a green army jeep racing toward him in the opposite lane. Within seconds, it zoomed past. He glanced in his rearview and wondered what might prompt an army vehicle to travel that fast. He thought of calling Sergeant Chase on his cellphone to lodge a complaint, but what good would that do? He only hoped that the jeep would not run over a child.

Shearstown Line was a barren strip of virtually treeless land with small houses standing alone in lumpy, rocky yards. Dilapidated barns, tilted in various angles of decline, stood in unfenced backyards. Long sticks of firewood were leaned against the sides of the occasional barn, and car wrecks deformed the yard of every eighth or ninth house. The area appeared abandoned but it was not. It spooked Thompson and yet put him in awe of the people and their brutal stark lives. He knew many of the residents from his practice. They survived on a diet of deep-fried foods and meat killed with their own hands.

Thompson let up on the accelerator and took the turn down into Bareneed. The landscape changed noticeably. Evergreens, dogberry and maple trees flourished along the sides of the road and around the well-kept houses and small barns that the locals referred to as "stores" because the outbuildings were once used to store fishing gear.

What a difference between Shearstown and Bareneed, Thompson reflected. The two communities were like "chalk and cheese," as his mother used to say. Yet Thompson had seen Bareneed sliding downhill since the elimination of the cod fishery. People moving away to the mainland, others becoming bitter or passive about the grave injustice the government had perpetrated against them, cutting off their livelihoods. Many residents still retained the fiery Newfoundland spirit and the ingenuity of true islanders, but a lifestyle had been destroyed for approximately half the community, and the despair was palpable.

The driveway sloping up to the Slades' house was a long, potholed stretch of gravel. The gradual incline led around to the rear of the house where two old, but seemingly functional, cars were parked. A rusty snowmobile was abandoned on the grass and, farther away, a yellow all-terrain vehicle was positioned facing the rocky hill that rose toward the blue sky. Everything seemed in its own particular stage of disrepair, a bit of Shearstown invading Bareneed.

Thompson parked the four-wheel drive and stepped out. He turned to survey the community, the harbour at his left and the houses spread out before him in the cupped valley between the two ranges of hills. He could even see the Critch house, against the hill on the opposite side of the community, where he had visited the Blackwood child last night in the blowing gale. Not a sign of rain now. He assumed the girl was fine. Otherwise, he would have heard different. Farther to the east, he caught sight of the steeple of the old church poking out through the treetops. A beautiful panoramic view that most would kill for, but lost on the dim-witted likes of the Slades.

Thompson scolded himself for thinking lesser of the Slades while he trod up the back wooden steps. Once on the landing, he was jerked to the left as one of his feet went through a hole, and he violently twisted his ankle. "Holy cripes!" He caught his balance and hopped to one side, staring angrily down at the gap where a rotted board had given way. His ankle panged horribly. There would be swelling. "Cripes, cripes, cripes!" He kept hopping until he had to stop, leaning his head against the clapboard while he tried squinting the pain away. He could sense the threshold coming. There it was. He scrunched his eyes tighter. There it was. Here it is. Yes, here it is. He remained perfectly still, his muscles clenched, and waited until the pain receded and the sweat sprang out on his forehead. He pulled a handkerchief from his back pocket and swabbed his forehead, taking a few moments to regain his composure. As he raised his hand to knock, the inside door was swung in and the outer screen door flung open, smacking him square in the head. Cursing again, he stumbled back and grabbed for his forehead with both hands, the ferocious stinging drawing tears to his eyes. "Christ Almighty!"

A child giggled on the other side of the door and Thompson felt a savage fierceness rise in him, burning his cheeks. His eyes shot open. The smack had really hurt. Standing there was Bonnie Slade, a pudgy six-year-old, stark naked and with an index finger shoved firmly up one of her encrusted nostrils. She stared at Thompson, her index finger digging and probing, bending elaborately at the knuckle, before scooping out her prize. Thompson looked away but heard Bonnie's fat lips smack together and then her giggle as she spun and ran back into the house, blabbering a string of utterly nonsensical words.

﹈

Joseph had not slept a wink. Throughout the night, he had kept vigil at Robin's bedside. He had not eaten, had rarely moved, yet had managed to take his pills. How many, he could not possibly recall; enough to satisfactorily calm himself. His body enjoyed this submersion in inactivity, and his mind appeared to enjoy it even more. He had taken the Ativan and he had taken wake-ups to keep from dozing off. Pills were a modern-day blessing, a tribute to human technological ingenuity. Tiny white tabs created by humans to relieve the stress that humanity created for itself. What genius! He only hoped that he had enough to do him the rest of his life.

The sun had come up in a gradual and grand wash of light that was the very essence of enlightenment. The epiphany of sunrise had filled him to the point of bursting. Where once the room was dark, it was now brilliant with light. He stood and, instead of finding movement strenuous, he found it liberating.

Out in the open air, with Robin still sleeping soundly in her upstairs bedroom, Joseph glanced toward Claudia's house. It was of such a specific construction. Made of modern fable rather than legend. The air was fresh and benign. How could anything possibly be unjust anywhere in the world, let alone here in this place, in the magical land of Bareneed? Suddenly he was aware that he had something bundled in his arms, something soft and almost blocking his view of where he might be going. He remembered that he was carrying blankets from his bed. He had been going to shove them or himself into the trunk of the car and depart this frightening place.

For reasons he could not fully understand, he was exceedingly interested in the solar house. Its architecture. All that glass reflecting the blue sky. He valued all the glass, the water in the walls with Claudia nestled in there like a wan swan. During the night, Claudia had crossed Joseph's mind a number of times. Around 5:00 a.m., he had considered going over for a visit. He even thought that he had risen to walk there. Coming to his senses, he had discovered himself sitting still. Nothing before him except Robin's bed.

He dropped the blankets into the trunk. They took up most of the space. Would he be able to fit everything in there? He stared back at the Critch house. It was large. Solidly built. What was he taking? Only the things that he had brought here. None of the furniture. He would require a truck if he was to claim ownership of everything. The house itself would need to be disassembled, the windows removed first.

Again, he stared toward the solar house. Was that Claudia in the upstairs window? It must be. The figure was too large to be the more diminutive dead daughter. He waved expressively, but his forthright enthusiasm evoked no reply. It was not Claudia after all, but merely a glimpse of reflected objects — light, clouds and sky. "Uh-oh," Joseph said, experiencing the strain of inner sinking. "Time to eat something." Perhaps Claudia had breakfast on the griddle. Flapjacks and maple syrup. He chuckled at the image of Claudia flipping flapjacks, standing there in her Gothic nineteenth-century slippers. What would Gothic nineteenth-century slippers look like? No doubt they'd be too tight for her feet. They were about pain, after all. Repression. Claudia's own enduring sense of separateness, both from her physical self and the world. The slippers would be made from the skin of past lovers, stitched together with the twine of their sinews — the only part of the lovers of any true use. That would be Claudia's secret and, once she was confronted by Joseph, she would stare at him with eyes that burned, searing two holes straight through his suddenly bloodless heart. And as the icing on the cake, the lard in the larder, the dust on the family mantel, her sluggish incarcerated smile would sanction the bedevilling fact that she was lost to him, that he was merely a tool in her tirade. The flapjacks would be made of pulverized grubs and spiders. The syrup composed of profane fluids which Claudia would lick from her fingers with spasmodic delight. Shut up, he warned himself. Had he spoken aloud? Or was the shout merely ringing in his head? The caw of a crow. Shut up. The ding of a telephone. The crack of a book slammed down.

Yet how could he shut up, stop, desist? Claudia was pure intrigue: both forlorn and erotic; fiercely, destructively artistic in a manner that smeared a grin across Joseph's lips. Truth be told, Joseph had stolen a few glances at the novels Kim read. He had secretly skimmed a page now and then, and, when Kim was not in the house, had actually finished several chapters. He believed they furnished him with penetrating insights into female nature. While Kim loved to read nineteenth-century novels, Claudia *was* a nine-teenth-century novel. She was a high-strung bearer of misfortune, misery, anguish, all the juiciest bits, waiting to plummet to the ground, and Joseph wanted to be a part of that, yes he did, to be gashed by the fallout of Claudia's shattering descent. He deserved as much. It would be the most beautiful, tragic and heartbreaking spectacle imaginable.

He might live as Claudia's ruined and mad lover, locked in the crawl space of the solar house and permitted to roam only at night, to haunt the oppressive forest with its rotting secrets, while inside the house, fat candles in pottery holders or longer tapered ones in wrought-iron floor stands were positioned toward the corners of the spacious room. Claudia in a sheer nightdress, standing in the wash of that light, hands stretched out, beckoning him in from the forest, pining for him, just as he was, loving him not for his deformity but for his uncivilized and unrequited love of her. Together they yearned for the touch of warm skin, the snug fit of body to body. He would willingly be further deformed for her, a cryptic hermit, a ghastly misfit, a ghoul with a severed pecker.

It had been such a long and tedious battle with Kim. The deterioration of their relationship and then the legal maelstrom that had sucked the spirit from him. Lawyers. Rats and pigs. It was time for a blush of comfort. It was time to start thinking of himself and the exquisitely passionate pain that might, once more, be his when love failed him again.

I'm staying, he defiantly told himself. Yes, it was a beautiful morning, a beautiful morning to be brought to one's knees in a world of invention. The sun was just up, gentle orange shadows everywhere. Down toward the ocean, the sun, low in the sky, warmly brushed the water. One of the shrimp boats was offloading something large and white. A number of people had gathered on the wharf. No mystery there. He would not allow it to be a mystery. The grass was dry and Joseph could smell the ground warming, the silent heat hinting at a day of extreme temperature. *Why not stay? It's perfect here. I have everything I need. Everything real and everything imagined. What an opportunity. Don't be such a scaredy-cat. Rise to the occasion. Have you no virility?*

Leaving the trunk open, he turned toward the house. The word "virility" had made him wonder if he had taken condoms along for the journey. Would he have packed any? No. The thought hadn't occurred to him. He pulled out his wallet and searched through it, remembering the condom he had bought a few months ago in the washroom of a downtown bar after striking up a conversation with an alluring woman. But he hadn't had the stamina to go through with anything. His heart just couldn't force itself to betray Kim. Digging in, he came across a photograph of Robin and Kim taken two years ago. He had raised the camera, centred the two of them and pressed the shutter button. And there they were now. Robin was sitting on Kim's lap on a wooden recliner he had built in their back-yard. The recliner was positioned in the shade, beneath the wide splay of dogberry trees. Robin and Kim were smiling, hugging each other. Kim was beautiful. If he didn't know her, he would say that she was the most beautiful woman he had ever laid eyes on. Unfortunately he wasn't a stranger who could walk up to her door and knock, watch her appear there and see her as she should be seen, removed from all the emotional detritus. And there was Robin. Always vibrant and beautiful, no matter what. Was she up yet? It had been only a few minutes since he had come downstairs with the blankets, and she had been sleeping. Her forehead had felt normal and she was breathing easily. The fever was gone. Where did it go? It was energy, right? Or was it? Robin was not dying. That was extremely important, for her not to die. That was a good thing.

He found the condom, slid it out, held it between his fingers. Protection. Protection from disease. Protection from conception. Protection from complications. He slid it back into the leather pocket and shoved his wallet away. Suddenly, he was overwhelmed with the conviction that they had to leave. Finish loading the car and leave. Protection from complications. This was stupid. A stupid idea.

Inside, Joseph entered the kitchen and stared around. They hadn't even finished unloading all the groceries yet. Hunger gnawed at his pasty stomach. When his gaze fell upon the box of cereal, he tore it open and scooped out a handful, ate it dry. Dust. He yanked open the refrigerator door, expecting to face a row of drowned heads neatly arranged on each rack, watching him with numbed expressions, simply waiting. Why he thought such a thing he had no idea. *Perhaps it has something to do with my radical insanity*, he proposed. *Might have something to do with my need to rip the refrigerator door off its hinges*. He was gritting his teeth and it felt proper. He wanted to bite something, bruise something.

The refrigerator racks were occupied by food he had brought along for the vacation. Absolutely no human heads. Not even a single small one that he might stomp like a pumpkin. He slid the milk carton out from the top shelf, and raised it to his lips, began chugging. It was cold. It was milk. Cow's milk. Why cow's milk? Why not human milk? Milk from women. Milk of human kindness. He felt completely fried, as if he were a teenager who'd stayed up all night drinking beer and listening to music. He was in the grip of a crystalline discharge. He knew that this vividness, this almost manic precision, would soon implode into jagged irritability. He would have to sleep and his nervous system would be all the better for it. If he still had a nervous system. Tweezer it out from beneath his skin, thread by thread.

The phone on the wall. He was staring at it. Why? It was a phone like any other. It was grey. Hadn't it been blue? Kim. She had been smiling in the photograph. She had looked so enticing. Familiar and easy. He might call her after he finished chugging the carton of milk, tell her they were coming back for certain. Maybe there would be reconciliation. Laughter. A gush of canned laughter. Who knew? Again, his thoughts shifted to Claudia, alone in the house. A missing daughter. Eerie string music. Why did he feel as though he were abandoning Claudia? Claudia, of all people. He continued gulping down the milk. Boy, it was good. Whatever it was. Cold, chilling his insides. Why did he feel as though he were abandoning himself again? He wanted to stay, but not in this house, he realized. He wanted to stay with Claudia. He wanted to learn new facts from her, be invigorated by the details of a life unsullied by a shared past. A new lover. Fresh knowledge and a virgin body to paw. Shopping together for wicker furniture in the mall. Visiting the lingerie store. Picking out matching shotguns.

Joseph heard Robin clump down the stairs. Lowering the near-empty carton, he dashed out to meet her. His daughter. Father and daughter.

"Good morning, honey," he called before reaching the stairway. "What a great day to be alive." He was smiling, licking the milk moustache from his upper lip, his eyes scanning the hallway, seeing that no one stood there nor on the stairs.

"Robin?"

He listened for her presence. Eerie string music. A hush of wind. Nothing. A low bass drum rumbling.

"Robin?" He started up the stairs, grabbing the bannister and yanking it as he ascended. On the second floor, he turned for Robin's room and entered. His daughter's bed was empty. "Robin?" He pivoted and lurched out into the hallway, checked his room. And there she was. There was Robin sleeping in his bed, her head against the pillow, her lips slightly open, but the tremblings of a smile there. Who had moved her? Had she moved herself? Had she been hiding?

Joseph slowly sat on the edge of the bed. It was a game. She was play-ing. It was fun, but it was disrespectful too. He couldn't help but smile at her. He smiled until his jaw ached, then nudged her, saying: "You faker, that's not nice." He expected her to burst into laughter at any moment, to be caught in her game. "Wake up, you faker." But she wasn't waking.

Joseph gave her another shake, this one slightly rougher, desperate or demanding. "Robin?"

His daughter opened her eyes, sleepily dismayed as she shifted to squint at him. "What?" she asked in a perturbed groggy tone, rubbing one eye.

"Morning," he said. "It's morning."

"Morning, Dad," she replied, her irritability giving way to a waking smile that warmed his heart. She yawned: "I'm tired."

Joseph would return to the city, drop Robin off at Kim's. No, why drop her off? She could stay at his apartment. But if he dropped her off at Kim's then he could come back here and visit Claudia, continue losing his already piddling mind without the worry of dependants.

"It's nice out," Robin said, her eyes on the window.

Immediately, Joseph stood from the bed to watch out the window. He noticed that a larger crowd had now gathered down toward the wharf, no doubt to study whatever brand of insanity had been unloaded from the shrimp boat. He felt it had something to do with the red sculpin Robin had reeled in. There was even a police car there. Or maybe it had something to do with the bodies he had seen. All of it. It had to do with all of it. Out beyond the wharf, a small dory was leisurely floating along. Joseph's eyes followed its wake. He didn't like the way he was thinking.

"What're you watching, Daddy?" Robin asked.

"A boat," he said. "A little tiny boat going out to sea."

~⌀~

Doug Blackwood was thinking of catching a few nice codfish as his dory slowly putted along. He steered the bow straight toward the open mouth of the harbour, glad to be off land and on the water, in this true and treasured place.

Earlier he had boarded his pickup and ventured from his home on Codger's Lane, headed west toward the community centre, passing by a bit of a commotion on Atkinson's wharf and even a few army men farther up the road. The army men had studied his pickup but hadn't done a thing or said a word. They just kept their eyes on him while he passed. Loved to watch things, those buggers. Was the army actually brought in to keep the fishermen from fishing? Had the bastards become that rotten now? Doug had flushed with anger as he drove by, hoping they would wave him over and start pestering him with questions about whether or not he had plans to fish for cod. He'd tell them a thing or two, launch into a tirade that'd scald the ears right off them. Bramble, Doug's white husky that he'd found abandoned out behind the barn years ago, stuck in the raspberry bramble and bawling like a baby, had commenced barking at the army fellows from where she sat in the passenger seat. That was peculiar because Bramble never barked at anyone and was utterly harmless. The dog had been acting strange of late, lazing around and raising her head to whine at nothing at all. And she had taken a particular dislike to those soldiers.

What in the name of Christ was the army doing in Bareneed, anyway, Doug asked himself once more, the wake of his dory trailing away from the stretch of community wharf. Watching the unoccupied slat across from him, he felt a slight pang of loneliness. He usually took Bramble with him on the water. But considering her behaviour of late he had decided to leave her in the truck with the window down for air. If she started barking and bounding around in the dory she could drown the both of them.

To his left, the abandoned fish plant sat at the base of the massive headland. He had cruised by the headland for years, yet he still felt a reverent thrill while passing beside the imposing majestic tower of rock high above him. Atkinson's wharf, used by the larger crab and shrimp boats, was at his right. A fair-size crowd was gathered there now: people gawking and gaping at something that had been hauled out of the water. Doug paid them no bother. They were just gossipmongers. He wouldn't give them the pleasure of showing that he was even slightly interested in what they were up to. It was probably just the commencement of some sort of stunned celebration. The town was always holding fairs and festivals and soirées and jamborees and jubilees. Might even be a celebration of wharfs, lorded over by some bunch of snotty monarchists. The Royal International Day of the Imperial Wharf or some other brand of nonsense. The frigging council was always trying to drag in a crowd of tourists to show them the beauty of Bareneed. Like anyone needed to be convinced. Christ, this was always the most glorious spot on Earth. God's country. Why did they take it upon themselves to ram it down people's throats? Why did they assume they had to peddle the beauty to everyone, try to make a fortune from it when the fortune was already here? Put the people of Bareneed on display like they were museum pieces, the last of the fisherfolk done up in period costumes for some arse-backward reenactment. Have a good look, ladies and gentlemen. Step right up. See how they wiggle like fish on the ends of a hook, gasping their final breath. Bait for you to nip at. See how their boats are rotting and their children don't have a clue what a codfish even looks like. No more children going out to sea with their fathers, no more passing of the trade. It was a crime against existence itself.

When Doug was ten years old, he had climbed into his father's skiff to fish for the very first time. The night had been pitch-black as they departed the bay with the other boats sailing ahead or behind them, their lamps swaying with the motion of their crafts. As they left shore far behind in quiet and darkness, Doug had the peculiar feeling that he was actually floating, not on water but into the air, to and fro, up and down, floating like ghosts drifting over the ocean. His eyes were learning to see in a new way.

For two hours or more — he could not rightly guess at the exact measure of time — they sailed in blackness, until tiny pinpoints of light shone in the distance like fireflies. Doug gazed up at his father at the skiff wheel and saw him patiently staring ahead. Fireflies weren't to be found in Newfoundland, but Doug had heard tales of the fairies and the lights that illuminated them at night. From his vantage point in the boat, he suspected they were approaching a secret cluster of fairy homes, far out on the ocean.

"Fairies," he had said to his father, who merely smiled.

The size of the lights had deceived Doug. Soon they appeared to be growing brighter, bigger, until Doug and his father not only drifted close to those lights but into them, sailing among the blots of illumination that hovered at either side of their craft. These were the lamps belonging to the gathered boats, anchored and floating on the waters, awaiting the first light of day to cast their nets.

The voices of the men in the dark air, the dialect of fellowship, was something Doug had never forgotten. It was as though they were in a huge casual room, yet unlike in a room, the voices were softened by the cushion of the velvety sea. The voices all around him spoke briskly to one another, joking, laughing. They were all waiting to fish and there was no sense of animosity or competition among them. They each had their space and they were content to be a single part of the community, afloat.

Doug had no recollection of beginning to whistle a tune. But as he did so, the voices, one by one, and the movements in the boats, began to drop away until there was not a sound. Utter silence save for his whistling. The yellow lights from the crafts bobbed around him and it was as if the men and boys in their boats, all darkly outlined against the vaguely brightening royal-blue sky, had perished on their feet and existed now only as silhouettes; or perhaps they had simply quieted themselves to honour his whistling which travelled in all directions, its beautiful pitch hovering over the dark water and even filling the vacuous sky. He was enjoying himself in his rapture, his lips puckered while he belted out a tune, when he felt a mighty grip on his shoulder and gazed up to see his father's vexed expression in the spill of lamplight.

"Shush," warned his father in a grave tone. "'Tis da worst sort o' luck ta whistle on water." And, sure enough, the catch had been less than expected that day. Doug's carelessness was singled out and blamed.

Regardless, Doug had suffered only a few days' regret for it. He had remained a fisherman all of his life. His father was a fisherman and his father's father was a fisherman. His only brother, Peter, had been a fisherman, too, but he had given it up and moved to St. John's to live the slack-arsed life of a townie.

Now Doug was the last man left in his immediate family. The only fisherman. And to make matters worse, his nephew, Joseph, his last living kin, had mustered up the unmitigated gall to land himself a job as a fisheries officer. What sort of frigged-up thing was that? And now Joseph was in Bareneed, right up the road from him. He'd heard the word from Aida Murray who'd heard from the woman who bought the house and

rented it out to townie gawkers every summer. Doug's nephew, Joseph —
a government fish spy.

The government had ordered everyone to stop fishing for cod. They
had banned the cod fishery. Banned it. Fisheries officers now patrolled
the waters in greater numbers to make sure that folk weren't swindling
from the sea. You can't fish any more, a bunch of pasty-faced bureaucrats
proclaimed. Tie up your boats. Simple as that. Stay on land and learn a
new trade. Train in Technology. Train in Business Administration. Train
in Pet Grooming. He could see himself styling the fur on a poodle. He'd
sooner shave it bald and give it a swift boot in the hole. The government
had given fishermen money to help them get through the transition from
life to no life. Handouts, that's all they were. Bloody handouts from the
government. No better than welfare. He'd be damned if he'd let those
bastard government clerks, sitting in offices all day turning peskier and
paler by the moment, have a file stuffed full of personal information
about him. None of their goddamn business. He refused to take any of
their stinking money. They couldn't tell him what he could or couldn't
do. If he wanted to fish for cod, then he'd fish for cod. Who in the name
of Christ were they to tell him different? Who gave them the high-and-
mighty right?

The same went for hunting moose. What did a fellow need a moose
licence for, or a hunting season for, when the moose walked right into your
backyard? You could shoot it with a 12 gauge pointed out your window, the
barrel steadied on the sill. Boom. And the beast would fall over. There was
your moose for the year. A fellow only needed one. Cut it up and freeze it,
hand it out to family and friends who enjoyed a bit of moose meat, and
that was that. That's why nature was there, to provide for the people of the
community. That's why the Lord Almighty put animals and fish on earth
and in the oceans. For us to fill our bellies with. What was the Christly
point of living otherwise, eating things out of cans made by scientists?
They were making animals now. They were playing God and if a fellow
ate those things made by scientists then what would happen to the fellow
who ate them? What would he become?

Mark my words, Doug told himself. Trouble a'brewing. But best not dwell on that foolishness. He shifted his thoughts to the nice codfish he'd soon be bringing home. A fine feed of fish 'n brewis. He'd catch a couple of extra cod and cart one up to Joseph. The thought of the look on Joseph's face made him grin. That'd be good for a laugh or two. Or maybe he'd just leave the fish in a bit of water in the kitchen sink, hoping Joseph would drop by and catch sight of it. What could his townie nephew do? Arrest his own uncle? Maybe he'd give Joseph a call when he got home. He didn't have the number but it had to be somewhere in the book.

The sun was climbing in the blue endless sky and the tint of sunrise orange was gone. Not a speck of wind. The water opened up at his left as he cleared the headland, revealing the stretch of land that was Port de Grave off in the distance. At his right, to the east, the ragged brown cliffs of Bareneed loomed above him. Doug chuckled at the perfection of it.

Whenever anyone asked him what he was doing going out in his boat, he'd assure them that he was fishing for sea trout. "Oh, yes, my brother," he'd say. "Sea trout. A nice catch of sea trout. No question." Smacking his lips together. "Finest kind." But the askers weren't fooled by his shenanigans. They knew Doug was lying by the roguish glint in his eyes. He had caught a good few sea trout in his time. Big ones, silver like salmon but with a V-tail instead of the salmon's straight one. The ones he caught were four- or six-pounders. Dandy size for slicing up into steaks.

There were still others in the community, besides him, who fished for cod. There were plenty of cod still in the water and plenty of them being robbed from the waters by foreign trawlers anchored outside the two-hundred-mile limit. Foreigners sucking up all the fish. They were the worst kind of thieving bastard cheats. Perfectly legal for a bunch of foreigners to drain our waters, but not legal for decent folk to catch a single codfish from the waters that had provided sustenance to generations of their forefathers.

As Doug reached the smaller grey and brown headland at the end of Bareneed, he cut the engine. The church was high up there, at his right, even though he couldn't see it; the wall of cliffs barred his view. Port de Grave sat off to his left and the bow of his boat pointed toward Blind Island, straight ahead about ten kilometres and flat as a pancake.

Blind Island had once been one of the most prosperous iron-ore-mining towns in the world. Doug had been over there a few times in the 1950s and seen how cosmopolitan it was. They even flew famous singers in from the States. Iron ore ships had been torpedoed by Nazi submarines during the Second World War, just off the coast. They were still resting on the bottom of the ocean. But now the mines on Blind Island were shut down and the town was a mere shadow of its former self. The island's riches had been sucked dry by foreigners, too.

Doug lifted his fishing rod from where he had it tucked away beneath the slat he was sitting on. Out here on the water it was a different world entirely. A man who had never been in a boat could never understand the true meaning of what an ocean was. Doug adjusted the bill of his cap and leaned to have a look over the edge of the boat. The water was clear and green. He had given up using his cod jigger. That was too obvious to the Fisheries' choppers. Instead, he used his trouting pole with a big three-hook red devil spinner attached to a heavy-gauge line.

Raising the pole, he flipped the casting bar and let the lure drop. It plunked in the water, the line unfurling in loops as the red devil sank.

Enough line out; Doug gave the reel a quick turn to snap the cast bar over. He jigged the pole, then jigged it again. Glancing around, he paid little attention to his line. He stared up at the sun. It was high enough now to be blazing hot and furious. If he wasn't careful he'd get a burn on the back of his neck. Good thing he remembered his hat. The heat was full on it.

A low pesky whining, like a mosquito, but too mechanical, sounded near him. He suspected a speedboat. Turning toward Port de Grave, he spotted the high craft with its sharp nose jetting over the water, bouncing as it zoomed along its pointless course. What sort of retarded fellow would drive a thing like that on the water? Someone who had no respect for the sea. Someone who was looking to get killed. Why did the boat need to go so fast and make such a noise? The sound increased and then receded as the boat turned back the way it had come. Doug wished it was a mosquito so he could reach forward and bat it out of the water.

Again silence settled, and Doug gave his reel a few extra-slow turns. A big splash behind his dory forced him to take a puzzled look. He thought it might be a trout jumping, although it was too early in the day for trout. They usually showed themselves late at night. Might be a flatfish slapping the water. They made a mighty big sound doing that. The water was rippling away from the area where the splash had landed. When it reached Doug, his boat rocked ever so gently.

"Big friggin' fish," he muttered, blowing out a breath of disbelief and amusement.

Another splash from the front. He shot a glance in that direction to witness a huge tail, slim and green with broad bluish scales, slide under the water.

"What the Christ?" Could it be a tuna? No, not thick enough. The tail was too long and tapered.

"Douglas," called a spirited woman's voice, and he heard another louder splash behind him. He twisted around, his movement so frantic he rocked the boat and nearly tore every muscle in his neck and shoulder. His dory now swayed from the ripples that surged from both directions. He turned to face front again, as if to catch the creature jumping, and there it was in all its glory. The sleek orange hair wet and dripping, the wide adoring brown eyes, the face of an angel and the bare breasts shimmering with cascading water in the sun. The creature raised her coral-pink supple arms above her head and curved her spine, diving backward, her turquoise tail rearing out of the water and then flicking into the air as she disappeared with a mighty splash that sprayed water in Doug's flinching face.

"Sweet Lord Jesus Suffering Christ Almighty!" he sputtered.

～✺

Robin felt tired, even though she was awake. Whenever she dreamed, and the more real the dream was to her, she would wake and still be very sleepy. She yanked down the hem of her nightdress where it was all bunched up and twisted around her legs, and stepped over to the window to see what her father was watching. She searched toward the harbour for a boat, but there wasn't one there. Out of the corner of her eye she saw a green army jeep coming up the road. Her father's head turned to watch it too. The jeep stopped in front of Jessica's house, and a soldier climbed out the passenger side. He walked fast down the path, a clipboard held behind his back. As the soldier stepped nearer the house, Robin lost sight of him.

"What're you watching?" she asked her father.

"Seems we're being invaded," he said as if talking to himself.

In a little while, the soldier came into sight again. He strode up the road toward them while the jeep followed faithfully behind.

"It's a soldier," Robin said. "He's coming here."

Her father glanced toward the bedroom doorway. Robin heard foot-steps approaching the house, then a loud quick knocking from downstairs. She ran toward the doorway and waited, watching her father pass, before following him down the stairs.

When the front door was opened, Robin saw a soldier who seemed very young. He had a thin face, his hair was perfectly combed and he had a bunch of pimples across his forehead. He stood straight with his hands behind his back.

"Morning, sir. My name's Able Seaman Nesbitt. I'm with the Canadian navy."

"Morning," her father said in a voice that sounded as if he was worried but trying to hide it. "What's up?"

The soldier looked down at Robin and smiled, his good colours, yellow and pink, growing brighter, before shifting his eyes to her father again.

"We're visiting people in the community, just to make certain everyone's okay."

"Oh, we're okay. Just fine, we are fine-fine."

The soldier watched her father, seeing more than Joseph was letting on. The soldier could see things, just like Robin. The full glow of his pink colours told her as much. They were the same shade of pink that had been around the old woman who took the lilacs.

"Why's that?" her father asked. "Why are you checking, I mean. Is it us? Did we do something untoward?"

"There's been some sickness and we've been advised to visit everyone and make certain it's nothing that's going around." Again, the soldier offered Robin a kind smile, then winked to double the point.

"What sort of sickness?"

"We're not certain, sir."

"Serious sickness? A plague or something?" Her father laughed nervously and glanced at the jeep. Its motor was still running. Another soldier sat behind the wheel. He was looking at their car, then writing something down. "A plague would be a major inconvenience."

"Really don't know, sir, but I expect not. We've just been asked to check."

"Well, we're really fine here, though my daughter had a fever last night. But the doctor came and now there's not even a cough between us. Neither one of us is even bow-legged. All our own teeth, too."

"Yes, that's good to see." The soldier smiled, raised a clipboard from behind his back and made a few notes. "If I can just get your names, I'll be done here."

"Our names?"

"We're establishing an inventory of the residents. That's what we've been told to do."

"By who?

"Orders, sir."

"Orders?"

There was silence for a while. Robin watched her father's face, then the soldier's.

"I just need to get your names, sir," the soldier repeated.

Her father sighed, "I'm Vladimir Zandmark and this is Quintata," he said quickly, flashing a secret glance at Robin. "Her mother's Mexican."

The soldier wrote the names without asking how to spell them. "You're father and daughter?"

"Yes, naturally. She's the father. I'm the daughter." Her father's laughter seemed more hearty than he had intended.

"Anyone else in the house, sir?"

"No. Not that I know of. Maybe a few ghosts. You know. Old place like this." Again and again, he licked his lips while talking. "Full of ghosts. Not that we humour them or anything. Are you partial to ghosts? I'm not insulting you, am I?"

"No, not at all." The soldier gave a shy little smile and read over his clipboard. "And are you from Bareneed?"

"No. We're from holidays. I mean, on holidays."

"I see." The soldier turned his eyes toward Robin. "Having fun?" he asked her. "It's a pretty place."

Robin nodded.

"Good." Then to her father, "Can I get your home address?"

"Why?"

"In case we need to follow up."

"Follow up what?"

Toward the harbour, a bunch of vehicles were moving along the lower road. Robin saw that they were jeeps, like the one in front of her house, and they were heading toward the red community centre. A number of jeeps were already parked out front. The soldier at their door glanced over his shoulder.

"Home address please," he said toward the harbour.

Robin's father was watching the jeeps too. He focused his attention back on the soldier. He spoke a mishmash of numbers and made-up road names, then watched the jeeps again. Robin saw that three soldiers were about to enter the community centre, when another stepped out. The new arrivals paused to salute him.

"Were you planning to leave Bareneed, sir?"

Her father's brow webbed. "What? Leave. Why?"

"We're just asking residents to remain in the community until we discern the nature of the sickness."

"Is this a virus or something? Should I not be breathing the air?"

"I have no idea, sir. I really don't."

"Stay here? Here, in this house, you mean?"

"Yes, sir."

"Are people allowed in?"

"Your house, sir?"

"No, Bareneed, coming in from outside?"

"Yes, sir."

"Well, that doesn't make any sense."

"That might be so, sir. Just following orders."

"Okay, then." Her father nodded. "I might see what you're saying. It's a particularly confusing job that you have."

"Thanks for your time. Sorry for the interuption." The soldier turned away and headed for the jeep, where he opened the passenger door. Before climbing in, he turned to say, "Have a nice holiday," to Robin.

Her father waved and smiled. He continued waving until the jeep was gone. Then, glancing at Robin to see that she was not looking (but she was peeking anyway), he gave the departing jeep the finger and slammed shut the door.

"Why'd you lie, Daddy?" Robin asked, because she liked the soldier.

"I didn't lie. I was just making things up."

"What's the difference?"

Her father shrugged. "Depends on your religion. Besides, they were soldiers," he said, as if that explained everything. "Soldiers don't operate within the same moral field as us. They kill people. We don't kill people. So, therefore, we can lie to them and not be held responsible, by a court of law even."

"Oh." Robin considered that bit of information for a moment. "My name's not Quintata."

"No kidding?"

"That soldier was nice."

"He was a soldier."

"He was nice."

"Why don't you go draw something."

"I want to go see Jessica."

Her father stopped to think, then said: "You'd have to find her first."

"I know where she is."

"Where's that?"

Robin raised her finger as if to point at something, but then brought her fingertip to her temple and tapped there. She tapped and tapped.

"Why don't you go draw something," her father said again. This time he didn't seem happy.

"I already am," she said. "Can't you tell?"

⟡

Kim stared at her computer screen, an illuminated page from the research paper she was struggling to write for *BioJournal*. The paper had to be submitted in less than two weeks. With tired eyes, she read over the words she had just rewritten: "The behaviour of sea life is constantly affected by the intrusion of environmental factors, such as toxins, over-population, underpopulation, water temperature fluctuations and electronic signals. Sonar, for instance, has been linked to inactivity in whales, a decrease in game playing and whale song." The words were awk-ward and, what was even worse, there was nothing she could do to confer them with grace. Not now. Not the way she was thinking and not when she was so concerned about her daughter. She raised her mug and took a sip of tepid coffee. No amount of coffee could hone her focus. She found herself hoping that the telephone would ring. And, if it did, when she picked up the receiver she wanted to hear Joseph on the other end, insist-ing that she join him and Robin in Bareneed. To give her a sign that it was okay. A-okay, as Joseph always used to say. It would make things so much easier than just showing up on his doorstep.

Kim laid down her coffee mug. Sighing, she eyed the telephone beside a framed poem Robin had written for Kim in kindergarten. The poem was about a whale:

Whales are big and blue
Mommy I love you.

The paper on which the poem was written was coloured in streaks, a multitude of crayon shades. A rainbow arcing over a whale in the water.

Last night, while Robin's fever was still high, Joseph had indicated that he and Robin would be returning to St. John's, but Kim knew what he was like. In a situation like this, a situation that required firm and decisive action, he could be counted on to change his mind a dozen times every half-hour. Plus, he probably hadn't had any sleep. When things were on his mind, he never slept. No doubt he would be sitting over Robin, watch-ing her, making certain she was okay. Say what you would about him, he certainly was a caring father.

If Kim knew for certain that Joseph and Robin were actually staying there, she would jump in her car and head out, invitation or no invitation.

She didn't need an invitation to see her daughter. *Her* daughter. What was she thinking? Yes, of course she'd go. But what if she just ended up passing them on the highway, driving in the opposite direction? Call first. Call.

Kim stared down at her keyboard in its slide-out tray. Joseph had used drawer rollers to fasten the tray beneath the top of the old wooden desk that had once belonged to her great-grandmother, a feisty woman who had worked for the suffragette movement in St. John's. Joseph had designed and built the tray himself; it worked beautifully. "Cheaper than buying a new desk," he had cheerily proclaimed. Saving money always made him happy. Kim had been vexed at him for being such a cheapskate. However, studying it now, she realized that it was much more endearing than a new desk. Joseph had made the tray with his own hands, and the desk had sentimental value. She eyed the power button on her computer tower. She'd love to press it, shut the system down, lose everything she was working on. Forget about it all. If only. She snorted at the impossibility. She tilted her head one way, stretching her shoulder muscles, then squeezed the back of her neck. What I wouldn't do for a neck massage, she thought. Drive to Bareneed?

As the notion lingered, the telephone rang. She snatched up the receiver.

"Hello?" she said, shortly.

"Hi, Kim." It wasn't Joseph.

"Luke?"

"Yeah." Luke Tobin, an old boyfriend and colleague. He'd been calling her since hearing news of the separation. On two occasions, Kim had agreed to go out for drinks, but on their first so-called "date" Kim knew immediately that she no longer had feelings for him. Whatever had first attracted her to him was annihilated. In fact, there was such a void of feeling that Kim had been confounded by the idea that she had actually slept with him for six months. It must have been the sex. Luke was athletic and had plenty of stamina. Regardless, the thought of having sex with him now made her stomach churn with nausea. On their last "date" their conversation had degenerated to talk of various acquaintances. Gossip. Kim hated gossip.

"What're you doing?"

"Working?"

"On what?"

"A paper."

"What about?"

"Complicated." She shifted her eyes from the calendar on the back of her door to her computer screen, reading over a few words and becoming more and more disgusted with herself. She felt a headache begin to root and stretch along her forehead. She would need to pop three ibuprofens if she was going to survive the afternoon.

"As complicated as me?"

"Way more. That's not hard." She chuckled, felt slightly better. She had forgotten that Luke could make her laugh too.

"I can tell you're just rearing to get back at it, so I'll cut to the chase. I just wanted to let you know I'm heading out of town."

"Okay," Kim said. "See ya." She swivelled her chair to search the floor-to-ceiling bookshelves for the bottle of pills she had poked there for those extremely special work headaches.

"No, that's not it. Getting rid of me isn't the special offer. There's been this amazing discovery in Bareneed."

"Bareneed?"

"Yeah, you been there before?"

"No, not really."

"You know where it is?"

"Yeah, northwest. Joseph's family is from there. Actually, Joseph and Robin are there now. What discovery?"

"An actual albino shark. White as anything. The genuine article. Pink eyes —"

"That's not possible."

"I beg to differ. Got it from a trustworthy source. Boyd lives out that way. He's been there, seen it, got the T-shirt."

No amount of mental effort could help Kim pull words together. As a marine biologist, she had heard stories of the albino shark. In fact, just yesterday she had been reading about the history of sightings by fishers in an article in *Marine Nature*. But there had never been any conclusive evidence put forth. In fact, she was surprised that such a loosely researched piece of writing could have made it into publication in *Marine Nature*. Their standards were slipping, no doubt in an attempt to attract more readers with sensational stories.

"Is that you gasping?"

"I … No."

"I'm going out to have a look. It's magic time, Kim. The stuff of legends."

"It must be some kind of hoax." Kim's mind reeled at the possibilities. She glanced out her window and saw the grass in the yard, the blue summer sky, Joseph's bird feeders. A few finches fluttering around there. She stared at her computer screen. Words.

"I don't think so. Interested in coming along? Fast ride in a fast car, blow those journal-paper-writing cobwebs clear out of your head."

Kim smiled despite herself. A trip to Bareneed with a legitimate purpose. An albino shark! Well, Robin was legitimate reason enough, but this was something entirely different. A Sunday-afternoon drive and back again later in the evening, after checking on Robin and putting her own mind to rest.

"Thinking?"

"Yes."

"Maybe too much? Well, here's the best part." He coughed to clear his throat then continued in a regal voice: "I'm supervising the transfer of the shark. We're loading it on a flatbed to transport back to the centre."

Kim glanced toward her roll-top desk in the corner. It was where she sat to pen handwritten letters to friends. Sighting the framed school photo of Robin, Kim hesitated. There was no way she wanted Robin to see her with Luke. That would be hurtful. Regardless, her thoughts were drawn to the albino shark. With that and the opportunity to see Robin, how could she possibly stay away? She could always drive out by herself. And she would get a chance to inspect the house where Joseph and Robin were staying. She was curious about the whole set-up.

"Kim? Are ya there, Kim? Earth to Kim?"

"Yeah, sorry. When're you leaving?"

"About half an hour, but if you need more time —"

"I'll call you back in a few minutes."

"Okay. Great. I'll be here."

"See ya." She hung up and reached for the issue of *Marine Nature*, flipped open to the artist's conception of the giant albino shark. Was the Bareneed shark dead? She had not even asked. Life drained out of it. Colour, too. She wondered if there was film in her camera.

What would Kim do if Robin saw her climbing out of a car with Luke? It would be fine to be seen talking to Luke, after all he was her colleague, but she would have to drive her own car. She shut the magazine, called Luke back to explain that she would meet him out there.

"What about the fast ride in a fast car?"

"Not interested in dying on the highway."

"I'll drive really slow. In fact, you can get out and push if that'll make you feel better."

"No, thanks. It wouldn't."

"Okay." He sighed expressively, then continued in a mock-defeated tone. "I'll meet you at the wharf."

"Okay. I'm leaving in a few minutes."

"See you there, I guess."

Kim hung up and stared at her computer screen. She leaned forward and shifted the mouse, clicked the "X" to close her document, clicked to save the changes, then clicked the "shut down" icon. She waited for the orange words to pop up on the screen, giving her permission to turn off the machine. At the press of the power button, the screen went black. There was a sudden quiet in the room and her tension eased a touch.

-◊-

Dr. Thompson watched the blank entranceway where the naked Slade child had stood. He waited for someone else to attend to him. His ankle was hot and panging cruelly. He suspected that the joint would swell nicely in the hours to come. A television was on inside the house. Thompson heard the dramatic music of a soap opera, then the channel appeared to be changed and there were shouts through a speaker, two people shouting at each other, words being bleeped out, boos and wild cheers from an audience. Thompson raised his hand and rapped on the screen door. His patience was running to an end.

"Who's at that door?" a man shouted. No one answered his question, so the doctor brusquely called out: "Dr. Thompson."

The man coughed, but there was no sound of movement.

Thompson knocked again, a tighter, quicker succession of raps. The man cursed, then Wade Slade's slight wiry body appeared in the doorway. Slade was no more than twenty-five and had the most peculiar hair Thompson had ever come across. It was halfway between orange and blond, and it was thick, like his moustache. He had sad eyes, large freckles cluttered his face, and his nose had obviously been broken, how many times Thompson could not possibly guess. Slade was wearing a black World Wrestling Federation T-shirt featuring a snarling face above a biblical quote.

"Got something on yer forehead, buddy," said Slade, pointing a freckled finger.

"The door struck me."

"Needs a spring." Slade grinned, showing his front teeth, both chipped. "Must be blood den."

"Yes, I guess it is."

"Don't have no Band-Aids."

"Who's that," a woman's voice screeched from behind Slade. He paid no mind to the sound, as if it were a common enough occurrence. There was no mistaking Aggie Slade's fierce cry. Whatever disease was in the news that week Aggie had invariably contracted, in its most wretched form of advancement. Thompson imagined the woman sitting in front of the television, glued to the news as if watching bingo numbers lighting up on the board, and popping up from her chair when the announcer informed the viewers that there was a malaria outbreak in New York. "That's it! That's what I got. That's it exactly."

"I'm sorry about your brother," Thompson managed to offer. The pain in his ankle was now billowing in less intense waves.

Wade Slade stared, the grin fading, his eyes dipping toward the floor. Then he carefully lowered his head and commenced weeping. He made no motion to cover his face, but merely turned and pushed the inside door half-shut. Thompson stood there waiting, but no one came in Wade Slade's place. The doctor raised his hand to knock again on the screen door. As he was doing so, the inside door swung open. This time, he jutted back to avoid a second smack on the forehead. No one was standing there. Thompson turned to check for wind. Nothing. He knocked.

"Who's at that goddamn door?" It was the female screech again.

Thompson considered turning on his heels and fleeing. He had truly reached his limit. But then Aggie Slade came stomping from the living room. She was a short stick of a woman with a graceful smile. No one would ever have believed that she, in all her five-foot glory, was capable of making all that noise. Mrs. Slade was a devout churchgoer but could stick a knife through a pesky cat in the blink of the eye, then attend communion the following day, blaming the stabbing on one of her faithless conditions.

"Morning, Doctor," she said.

"Mrs. Slade. Sorry about your trouble."

Mrs. Slade stared. "Stupid, isn't it? Trip up and die. He wasn't even sick, like me."

Thompson could think of no reply. He noticed that his lips were parted. He thought this might be the closest he had come to actually having his jaw hang agape. He sucked in breath and said: "I was wondering if Andrew had any problems. Physically."

"He was fat as a pig."

"No, I mean, with breathing."

"What?"

"Did you notice him struggling to breathe."

"Drawing breath?"

"Yes."

She shook her head. "He had allergies."

"Possibly. But did he have a history of breathing troubles?"

"Wha?" Mrs. Slade turned her head and screeched, "Wade, you notice if Andrew had trouble drawing breath?"

A sob issued from within the house.

Dr. Thompson cleared his throat. Mrs. Slade looked at him as if something might be the matter.

"I'm not meself today," she confessed. "I got spots." She held up her arm, showing him a rash. "From them mice. What's that disease called? Hint of Vara?"

Thompson glanced at her arm. "Looks like a rash, Mrs. Slade. New soap? Lotion?"

"Got new liquid soap at the flea market in Port de Grave. Five cents for the bottle."

"Might be your problem. An allergic reaction."

"I'm 'lergic to everything."

"When did you last notice Andrew's allergies?"

Mrs. Slade gave it some thought. " Three or four day ago. He was crying the first time. Scared shitless."

Thompson gave a tight smile. "Well, sorry for your troubles. If you need anything come see me."

Mrs. Slade nodded. "Get these spots checked out. Might be deadly."

"Most likely. You should have them surgically removed." Thompson shifted back, conscious of the burning, throbbing pain in his ankle. He glanced down at the rotted boards in the veranda, hoping he would not break his neck on the way back to his car.

⁓〽

Joseph thumbed the digits on his cellphone, dialing his old drinking buddy, Kevin Dutton, who now practised law in St. John's. After a few rings, and after navigating the convulsion-inspiring labyrinth of the legal firm's directory, he succeeded in reaching Kevin's voice mail, but when the time came to leave a message, Joseph's brain jammed. Too much information to relay. He suspected that if he opened his mouth a jumble of words would roll out, an indecipherable wall of sound clunking to the floor. With cellphone still in hand, he paused a moment. It appeared that he might have fallen asleep on his feet for he soon heard the explosive broken sound of a man's voice, as though the volume of a radio or television had suddenly shot up and then been switched off, all in an instant. He had

experienced this noise before, waking from dreams to consciousness. It
startled him, made his skin prickle. He listened, heard only the hum of his
cell. After hanging up, he tried Kevin's home number. No answer. No
voice mail or answering machine either. What was the world coming to?
Joseph wanted to question Kevin about the legalities of being advised not
to leave Bareneed. He assumed the army or navy could do whatever it
pleased, but didn't a state of emergency need to be declared first? A wave
of dizziness spilled over him. He rubbed his eyes, saw the sparkle of grey
and white pinpricks behind his lids as he forced his palms against his
sockets. When the dizziness had dissipated, he opened his eyes and
watched the channel static fading. Grey and white crackling to a clear
scene. He was in a kitchen. The Critch house. Bareneed.

He glanced at the cell. Who else to warn? He hadn't called his Uncle
Doug yet. Although he had thought of contacting Doug on several ocas-
sions, something had always come up to either divert his attention or
frighten the crap out of him. Clutching the chair beside him, to catch himself and hold steady against a sinking sensation, his thoughts flashed on
the drowned people underwater. Dead, yet not dead, only their eyes
moving, watching him. Must be the pills I'm taking, he assured himself.

Joseph pulled out his wallet and fingered through the cards and folds of
scrap paper, finding the note on which he had scribbled Doug Blackwood's
phone number. Reading the digits, he carefully pressed them with a shaky
thumb. What should he call the man. Doug? Uncle Doug? Dad's brother.

The line rang five times before being answered gruffly.

"Yes?"

Hello Dad's Brother. "Doug ... Blackwood?" Joseph stammered.

"Could be," the voice said. "Who's this?"

"Joseph Blackwood." He was going to add "your nephew" but thought
that might be a tad too familiar, too clingy.

"Joseph Blackwood. That be my nephew, Joseph?"

"Yes."

"The fisheries officer?"

"Yes."

"From St. John's?"

"Yes."

"Hmmm." Silence. "Haven't ever heard your voice, I don't think."

"I'm in Bareneed with my daughter, Robin."

"Heard as much. Got a daughter?"

"Yes."

"Makes sense. How old?"

"Eight."

"Eight … Hmmm. Eight's a pretty age."

A nice age for a child-eater, Joseph couldn't help but reflect. "Yes, it is."

"Well, you coming down to see me? Or you going to be a stranger all the rest of your maggoty life?"

Joseph was both intrigued and chilled by how much Doug's voice reminded him of his father's. It was as though he was talking to a fatherly distortion. "No, we'll come down."

"You're staying in the old Critch house, up on the higher road."

"Yes."

"On holiday?"

"That's right."

"Would be a holiday to the likes of you." Doug laughed outright, so loud that Joseph was forced to hold the crackling cell away from his ear.

When Uncle Doug's laughter finally diminished to a few low chortles, Joseph asked: "Have you heard about the military going around —"

"Sure I have. But have you heard about the two fellers from St. John's who froze to death at the drive-in movie?"

"No, I —"

"They went to see *Closed For the Season*."

Joseph was perplexed. Was this an actual news story? It wasn't winter. How could they have frozen to death. He wondered if he himself had seen *Closed For the Season*.

"It's a joke," Doug said. "Are you that stunned?"

"Oh … Have the soldiers been to your door?"

"Don't be talking. Bunch of nonsense. A few people get sick 'n the government thinks they can move in and bar up the place. They're scared to death of sickness these days. I never saw the likes of it in me life."

"So, you can leave if you want?"

"Leave where?"

"Bareneed."

"What you wanna leave here for? Didn't you just get here? I've got a lovely feed of codfish down here if you want to drop by. And tomorrow I'm goin' out in the boat 'n your daughter's more 'n welcome to join me."

"She's taking a nap. A little under the weather." Joseph wondered where Doug might have acquired the codfish. Perhaps his uncle was only teasing.

"Under the weather? What in the name of Christ does that mean? And I'm talking about tomorrow. She'll be napping till tomorrow? Will she?"

"No."

"Well, come see me when you get a chance. When everyone's not scared and everyone's feeling fit. Get some vitamins or something and some books on how to cure yourself, and when you're all smiling and comfortable and happy as two pigs in their own filth drop down and we can chew the fat."

Chew the fat. Joseph couldn't help but grin. Uncle Doug had his father's irreverent sense of humour. "Where are you?"

"Ask anyone, they'll know."

"Okay."

The phone was hung up at the other end.

Joseph shut his cell, poked it away in his pocket and decided to wake Robin. She would be delighted at the thought of going in a boat. But would she go alone with Uncle Doug? Joseph hadn't been invited. Was there room in the boat? Even the smallest boat could hold three.

No, what was he thinking? The mild sunny day was only a screen of deceit. Once night fell, the hallucinations from the medication would take hold again. He had phoned Uncle Doug for advice and had received none. What had he been doing? He turned to discover he had been packing up food in plastic bags. That's what he should continue doing. Uncle Doug could wait.

As Joseph crouched by the lower cupboard and began filling a plastic bag with canned goods, it occurred to him that maybe he should just leave the food there. If they left, they could come back in a week or so and the house would still be rented. It was paid for, in advance, for the next three weeks.

He stood briskly and was overcome by dizziness. He shut his eyes as the wall phone rang. The room was wobbling when he opened his eyes and reached for the receiver.

"Hello?"

"Hi." A woman's voice. Kim's.

"Hi."

"I'm coming out to Bareneed to see the albino shark and to see Robin. How's Robin feeling this morning?"

"Shark?"

"Luke Tobin said there's an albino shark in Bareneed."

"Oh, really?" Joseph glanced around the kitchen. Shark. Luke Tobin. Luke Tobin had been with Kim, of course he had. No doubt he had moved in with her by now. No doubt he was presently clipping Kim's lawn, trimming her bushes. No doubt he was bringing presents. They had probably gone cruising in his sports car with big plastic smiles on their faces, waving to everyone and singing stupid songs while they accidentally ran over dogs and cats but never stopped. No, they wouldn't bother stopping, would they?

"I'm leaving in a few minutes," Kim informed him. "I want to drop by and check on Robin."

"Here? We're just about to leave, coming back to St. John's." He couldn't get Luke's face out of his mind. Perfect face. Perfect hair. Perfect pocketbook. "I'm packing things in the car. I have to go now."

"Why? Is Robin okay?"

"Yes, she's fine. It's just too … weird here."

"Weird," she laughed. "Just wait till I get there, okay? I want to see the place." Joseph let the silence gather. "Are you coming with your new friend?"

"I'm coming out by myself."

"I don't want him around Robin."

"Who, Luke? Joseph, don't worry. What do you think I am?"

He was about to say "you mightn't even be allowed in the community," but he didn't want to alarm her. Besides, Joseph had no idea if people were still allowed in. He hadn't seen any barricade, even though the soldiers down by the community centre appeared to be stopping the occasional car and asking questions. He was fairly certain that a soldier had come to his door. Robin had been there, too. She had seen the soldier.

"Joseph?"

"Okay," he said. "But once you get here we're going back."

"Why?"

"Because …"

"What's the matter?"

"Nothing. I just want to go home. Sleep in my own bed."

Silence. The word "home" meant so many things. The words "my own bed."

"You get any sleep last night at all?"

"Yes," he lied.

"What? Ten minutes?"

"No, four seconds, at least."

His tension diminished at the sound of Kim's laughter. Life was so easy when they were laughing. If only they could just keep laughing, mouths open, tonsils wagging, flies swooping in, laying eggs. Maggots. Wagging maggot heads laughing. A cacophony of squeaky cartoonish laughter. Rotting necks snapping off. Oh-no!

"I've got to go check on Robin. She's napping."

"Napping. Robin?"

"Yes."

"She doesn't usually nap, Joseph."

"Well, out here she does, must be the country air."

"I'll be there soon."

"See you." He hung up just as Kim gave a slow heartfelt "Bye."

That "Bye" warmed and snagged in his heart. If Kim was here, and things were patched up, then they might stay another night. He could show her the sights. Lock her in the barn with the ghost of the bearded man. Take her to the harbour, shove her in, make her see the floating underwater dead. Open the jaws of the albino shark and stuff her head in there. Joseph's Chills and Spills Tours. But what about Claudia? Supposing Claudia walked in and started being intimate with him in front of Kim? All hell would break loose. No, they should head home immediately. Quit while I'm dead. I mean, ahead.

He went to the parlour to check out the window, but there wasn't a clear view of the wharf or any albino shark. He headed upstairs, watching the rich tapestry runner blur beneath him. His footsteps made not a sound as he ascended. When he reached Robin's room, he saw her bed was perfectly made. Empty.

"Robin," he called, striding to his bedroom. The sheets were rumpled. Robin might be lost in the jumble or hiding as she often did. Pawing the sheets back, he discovered that she wasn't there. He checked out the window and saw some sort of commotion down by the wharf. A large crowd. The albino shark?

He rushed down the stairs. At the bottom, he slipped on the floor and almost lost his balance. There seemed to be water on the floor. He hurried into the bathroom. The tub was filled to the brim, but no one was in there. The floor was wet, and a trail led through the kitchen and out the back porch. Had Robin drawn a bath? Had he told her to get one? Had he filled the tub? He didn't remember and he was scaring himself. His heart thrust wildly and his breath caught as he bolted out the back door and scanned the field of tall grass that led toward the treeline. He never would have feared the trees, but now he did. Christ, what if she's lost in the woods? As the panic mounted, his nostrils filled with the blood-metallic scent of fear. Robin? Had he taken her with him at all? Was he really alone, had he been alone out here all the time? Here to get away from everyone. Absolutely everyone.

"Robin?" he called in fright. Two birds sounded back and forth in the forest before one of them flew free, rustling branches. Joseph rushed from the house and caught sight of the barn off to his right. "Robin?"

She was standing in the doorway facing in, her small back still. She made not the slightest movement when Joseph called.

"Robin," he said again, this time with a harshness provoked by his fear cloying to anger. He hurried toward her, gripped her shoulder, but she would not turn to face him. Her shirt seemed damp. Joseph heard her talking in a rhythmic secretive whisper: "Fish in the sea. Fish in the sea ..."

"Robin." He spun her around and saw her white face, the skin puckered as if she'd been in the tub too long, her shivering lips blue. "Robin!"

"Fish in the sea," she droned, her teeth chattering like dominoes rattled in a bag. "Fish in the sea ..."

～෯

It was well over a year since Kim had last been on the highway. When she and Joseph were still together, they often went for drives on the weekends; they took one of the highway off-ramps that connected to a two-lane road and followed it for desolate kilometre after kilometre until reaching a small community by the sea. They'd view the houses crowded together around the arc of a bay or built on steep cliffs that dropped a hundred feet to jagged rocks and the ceaseless surge of water. The sun on the ocean, charging the scene with gentle and simple clarity. Kim often marvelled at the seemingly endless stretches of roads that were put in place to connect tiny communities once accessible only by water.

Since her separation from Joseph, Kim had been preoccupied with taking care of the fundamentals: cooking, cleaning, working and attending to Robin's needs. No highway drives. Her and Robin's leisure time was spent shopping at the mall or visiting the park. It was liberating to drive with the land opening up around her, barrens and boulders instead of furniture, distant treelines of clustered evergreens instead of the strictly vertical enclosure of walls. She had not expected to feel this good simply driving in a car.

Weeks ago, when Joseph first told her about his plans to rent a place in Bareneed, she had wanted to rush out there at once. The older communities fascinated her. She took immense pleasure in wandering around the once-thriving grounds that surrounded abandoned houses, some of the structures built more than a hundred years ago; peeking in the windows, discovering how the interiors were still in order, the antique furniture and rugs, the dishes and lamps. All of it just sitting there with no one willing to lay claim to it. A style of life abandoned. On a few occasions, Kim had checked the back doors to find them unlocked and had stepped in, moving as if through the outlying, yet romantically forsaken, world of a time-honoured novel, embraced by a ghostly affection for life that had once been lived in the now dusty and damp space that seemed both mourning and awaiting the return of its occupants.

Kim switched on the radio just as the announcer said: "Two-forty on a beautiful June afternoon. We've got twenty minutes of music …" She checked her watch; it was set to the same time. It would be close to supper when she arrived. Maybe she'd be able to wrangle a dinner invitation out of Joseph, or — better yet — an invitation to spend the night. The idea of sleeping in an unfamiliar house gave her a sharp twinge of excitement. That was one of her most powerful fantasies, to make love in strange enclosures, amid the ruins of other people's lives. She smirked to herself. Maybe the house would even be haunted.

The uptempo opening notes of Van Morrison's "Brown Eyed Girl" sounded from the speakers. Kim twisted up the volume, feeling more sure of herself than she had in months. She cracked the window and the air refreshed her face. She felt as though she were gliding back to better times, back to Joseph and Robin, back to an affinity with harmony and reconciliation.

-◠-

There was no answer at Kim's. Joseph reached her voice mail but refused to leave a message. What would he say? Robin's acting like she's a dead girl now and I've got static in my head. I'm receiving signals. I don't know whether I'm dreaming, in a television sitcom, a horror movie or my own life. One way or another, I'm angry about something and I'm not certain what that might be. When he had dried Robin off and asked her about how she got wet, she had simply said: "Playing with Jessica." Jessica! Joseph had already called Dr. Thompson and been connected with his service. He left a brief message. That was easy enough. Name. Phone number. "Help." Hanging up, he stared at Robin lying on the couch. She seemed fine now, changed into dry clothes. She was calmly drawing a picture. But with this latest development he feared there might have been some permanent damage to her head from that rock, and his entire body ached with anxiety and grief.

"How you doing, sweetie?" he gently asked, wiping his palms on his jeans. They were damp. Had he too been in the water or was he simply sweating? He checked his clothes. Dry. A rush of fever overcame him. A hot flash. Energy entering him from other sources. The sound of a man's cough. Perhaps his own. Then he was fine, settled.

"Okay."

"You should stay in the house now," Joseph insisted, trying to pull his eyes away from Robin's drawing, hoping that the man she was sketching was not him. The image was so real that he suspected she had clipped photographs from a catalogue.

Robin frowned and glanced up from her drawing. "Why?"

"Because I want you to. We might need to go back to the hospital. And besides I told you not to go out already. I need you to stay —"

"You said it was okay."

"What?" A pulse in his temple, a tremble in his left eyelid that he scratched. A noise like laughter or applause in his ears, the hiss of a kettle. Had he put the kettle on? "What was okay?"

"I told you I was going outside and you said okay."

"No, I didn't."

"You did. I walked right up to you, you were on the telephone talking to someone."

"When?"

"Before I went out." Robin sat up all the way, balancing a book beneath the drawing on her knees. "You were talking to someone."

"When I was talking to Mommy?"

"No."

"Yes." He gave a serious laugh, one that he meant, one that maintained he could not possibly be wrong. "Yes, I was. I was talking to Mommy."

"No, it was Claudia, I think."

"Robin, what're you saying!?"

"You said her name and you said other stuff." Robin blushed, shifting her eyes toward the polished piano against the far wall. No doubt it would soon start playing by itself. No, that would have to wait until nightfall. Midnight. Blood on the ivory keys. The man with the face you could not see.

"What stuff?"

"You were whispering bad words."

"I was not." Joseph stood up straight, and fixed his daughter with a shocked and indignant look. "What are you talking about? I don't even have her number."

"The phone rang here."

There was a knock on the front door. Joseph spun toward the sound, making Robin giggle. Or was that the static again? He peeked at Robin and saw that her expression was even. No sign of amusement. She was watching the door.

"Who's that?" he asked. "You think that's funny. Ha-ha. I'm funny now."

"It's not funny. It's Claudia."

Joseph studied Robin. How could she know? That bump on her head. Had it made her clairvoyant? "I think we should get you to the hospital."

"You?"

"You," he snapped.

"You?"

"You." He headed for the door. Yanking it open, he faced Claudia standing there, her large fascinating eyes locked on his. She was wearing a white cheesecloth dress, the material hanging to her ankles. In both slim hands, she held a box wrapped in decorative paper that appeared to have been hand-painted and featured grey whales against blue water.

"I brought you a housewarming present." She held up the gift and smiled edgily, the skin stretching on her face, her eyes sinking deeper. She seemed to have lost ten pounds since Joseph had seen her yesterday, yet her belly was slightly distended beneath her tight-fitting dress. Joseph wondered if she might be pregnant.

"What could be in such a small box?" he asked, imagining himself kissing Claudia's lips. They now seemed fuller in her thin face. He thought about prying his tongue past her lips to smear her teeth, prying past her teeth to wag at her tongue and finding it shockingly cold and dry.

"Is it a bad time for a visit?" she asked.

"Yes." He waited, wondering what might come next. "No."

"May I come in?"

"Yes," he said, briskly stepping aside. "Come in." He glanced anxiously past Claudia's shoulder. "Anyone with you?" he asked in a worried tone that he tried to hold reasonable.

"No," replied Claudia, venturing into the house. "I'm alone."

"Good. Alone is good. I was alone once. It's okay if you can stomach it." Joseph gave the outside another sweeping inspection and, finding nothing that could possibly alarm him more than the comings and goings already in his head, he swung shut the door.

⟁

The sound of his cellphone going off worried Dr. Thompson more than usual. The fact that it was Sunday did nothing to quell the atmosphere of death that lingered over Bareneed. Thompson had just limped back into his Blazer after examining the albino shark. One of the strangest things he had ever witnessed. After leaving the Slade house, he had come upon the crowd and climbed out of his vehicle to investigate.

Presently he opened his cellphone and pressed the button, checking his forehead in the rearview. The cut that the Slade child had inflicted on him was not serious at all. More like a bad scrape.

"Yes?"

"Dr. Thompson, this is Betty at AnswerTel. We just received a call from a woman in Bareneed, extremely upset. Her son is having breathing troubles and she was wondering —"

"Who was it?"

"Edyth Pottle."

"On Pottle's Lane?"

"Yes. I've called for an ambulance. And you have another call from Joseph Blackwood. They came right in, one right after the other. He said 'Help' but it wasn't like an emergency. He wasn't shouting or in pain or anything. It was strange."

"Did he leave a number?"

"Yes."

Betty read out the digits.

"Okay, thanks." Thompson pressed "End," then dialed Blackwood's number.

"Hello?" It was a girl's voice.

"Hi, is your dad there?"

"No, my father went to sea …"

"Went to see what?" Nothing but silence followed, until Thompson felt he should ask: "Is everything okay?"

"Yes."

"Where's your dad? This is Dr. Thompson."

There was no reply.

"Hello?"

"My father's feeling a little under the weather."

"That's too bad. How's the bump on your head?"

"I don't have a bump on my head."

"Good. It's better then."

"All better. I'm all better. And I'm not so cold anymore."

"That's nice to hear. Tell your father that Dr. Thompson called."

The little girl began to flatly hum a tune.

"Okay?" Thompson asked.

The humming kept on. "Okay," the girl finally said. "Goodbye, Dr. Thompson."

"Goodbye."

Thompson shut the cell and stared ahead a moment at the crowd beyond his windshield. A group of boys were pointing out toward sea. One of them was jumping up and down and calling with his hands cupped around his mouth. Thompson looked where the boys were pointing but could see nothing that might warrant attention. He engaged his engine and backed away from the crowd, a few of whom turned to watch him go. He then pulled a U-turn in the middle of the road, raced off in the direction of Edyth Pottle's, suspecting that the key to the breathing disorder was to catch the stricken in time and get him or her on a respirator. Otherwise, there might be death. Why? He had no idea. Once the patients were under observation, there didn't seem to be degeneration. Not yet. Not that the medical staff had noticed.

Pottle's Lane was farther west, back the way he had come, not more than a minute away and directly across from the community centre. Suddenly he was upon two soldiers positioned beside the barricade. One of the soldiers was trying to wave him over. Distracted by his thoughts, he saw and understood the direction too late and was forced to swerve, jamming the brake while crashing into the rear of an army jeep parked at the side of the road. Fortunately, he was strapped in by his seat belt. No damage done, except for a searing pain in his neck. Whiplash! Just what he needed. He started rolling down his window, but decided to open his door instead. Shifting, he tugged at the door latch, but was restrained from moving. His seatbelt. He grunted, unclipped it, and tossed open the door just as a soldier was approaching. The top of the door frame nailed the soldier in the head. With a startled gasp, Thompson reached back into his vehicle for his black bag. The soldier stood there dazed, a set of fingers to his head. Thompson gave him a quick look over. No damage. Not even a scrape. The soldier's eyes were focused on the cut on the doctor's forehead. "You're fine," Thompson said and hobbled off, pointing ahead. "I'm a doctor," he called out, biting back the pain from his ankle while weaving around the barricade. "I've got a medical emergency, watch out."

-◊)

The green highway sign loomed up ahead. No chance of missing it. White letters and a slanted arrow pointing right. The sign read: *Shearstown, Bareneed, Port de Grave, Exit 44, 1 km.* Moments later, Kim headed her white VW for the off-ramp and was on Shearstown Line. The land around her was breathtaking, rolling pastures of a rich green wrapping around distant ponds. She shook her head in awe. The landscape could change in an instant in Newfoundland. She had just left the moonscape barrens of the highway and was now in a stretch of pasture that reminded her of the lush fields of Ireland. Grey woolly sheep grazed on a low hill. She could see for miles beyond the pastures on both sides of the Line. The pastures dipped and rolled before meeting dense forests of spruce, fir and pine. The ocassional low rocky hill interfered with the otherwise sprawling quality of the land.

In a few moments the road dipped into a valley so steep that she was forced to apply pressure to the brakes. Within that valley, the landscape turned desolate. Rundown houses and shacks were set apart by wide patches of rocky unworkable land. The road then rose and inclined left, the weather-worn houses becoming even more dilapidated, practically sinister. No sign of life. Not a cow, horse or sheep. The trees behind the houses grew denser, tangled, blacker. She felt she might be lost and hoped that she would not have to stop, that no mechanical problem would overcome her car, delaying her journey forward. Her palms grew sweaty on the steering wheel. A tension headache threatened. She noticed her jaw was clamped tightly. She slackened it and checked the speedometer. Too fast. Up ahead, she spotted a green sign with a white arrow pointing right: BARENEED.

"Bareneed," she said hopefully, laughing with relief.

Along the road into Bareneed, as the landscape became more picturesque, Kim wondered about her fear, which now gradually dissipated. She tilted her head from side to side, stretching the muscles in her shoulders. She had been working too long on the computer. Plus the uncertainty of her route had added stress. Now that she was nearing her destination, she could travel at a slower speed, comfortable to take her time and study the land and houses with a new sense of communion.

A massive headland towered above the distant harbour. Beyond it lay the ocean. So fantastic to see the ocean again. The expanses of land between the houses soon narrowed as Kim navigated deeper in the community, passing old treasure-packed square houses that she would give anything to enter and explore. She noticed one of those obnoxious satellite-TV discs mounted on the side of one of the houses. The sight never failed to make her heart sink, the way the grey disc intruded upon the old architecture. Every fourth or fifth house had one secured near the roof and pointed toward the sky.

Soon, she was so preoccupied with trying to catch glimpses of old furniture through front windows that she no longer noticed the discs. Nor did she catch sight of the soldiers stationed in the road, until she was upon them. They looked so out of place in the historic town. Why were they there? To protect the albino shark? That seemed a touch drastic. One of the soldiers raised his hand, forcing Kim to slow and stop, roll down the window.

"I'm sorry, but the area has been closed." The soldier was wearing a black wire-microphone, the tip close to his lips.

"Why?"

"A cautionary measure, ma'am."

"Because of the shark?"

The soldier gave no reply. He pointed to the gravel parking space beside the community centre. "You can turn around there."

"I'm here about the shark. I'm with the university. Biology. We're moving it, back to the university. Plus …" Kim fretfully cast her eyes ahead. "My daughter's here with my husband."

"You live here?"

"Yes, a summer place."

"Could I please see some identification?"

"Sure." Kim rifled through her purse. In her rearview, she caught sight of a car pulling up behind her. One of the soldiers stepped close to the car and spoke with the driver, who soon turned his car around. Kim discovered her wallet and handed over her driver's licence. The soldier carried the ID to another soldier who made note of the information on his clipboard. They exchanged a few words, then the soldier watched her, his lips moving almost imperceptibly. He was speaking into his microphone, listening, then speaking. He came toward her and returned her ID.

"You're in the old Critch house." The soldier pointed toward the ridge.

Kim looked there, thinking: *I should know where I live. I just told him that we have a summer place. He knows I lied.* She nervously regarded the soldier's steady eyes.

"Your husband's Joseph. Daughter Robin?"

"Yes."

"Give your husband a message for us, would you please? Tell him the next time he wants to change his identity he should change his licence plate first."

"What?"

"That's fine, Mrs. Blackwood. You can drive on. We're still letting relatives of residents through." The soldier patted the top of her car, stepped back and glanced up the road.

"Thank you." What had Joseph told the soldiers? She left her window rolled down; the sea air was enlivening. She drove on, past the post office and community centre. Was there an army base close by?

Sixty feet ahead there were lines of parked cars on both sides of the road. This must be near the wharf. She couldn't shake the feeling of being rattled by those soldiers. They knew her husband. Change identities? They had probably asked Joseph his name and he had given them a false one. Joseph was like that, didn't take kindly to giving out personal information to authority figures.

There was the wharf. Kim had to park back a distance and walk the rest of the way. Her emotions grew unsteady as she stepped toward the crowd. She noticed a big police officer standing beside a cruiser. Another officer was at the wheel, elbow out the window. She was beginning to have doubts. She had travelled from one place to another and the movement had been exciting, yet actually finding herself in a new place, suddenly being here, made her feel dislocated.

A few old-timers stood chatting on the periphery of the crowd, checking out who was coming and going, trying to decipher from which community the visitors hailed, so they could guess at the visitors' complete lineage and history. One of them was smoking a pipe, chewing the stem while adjusting the bill of his salt and pepper hat. Kim heard him saying: "I saw one a' dem once. Out on da water. I tol' da crew but no one took it fer da truth." The second old-timer smoked a home-rolled cigarette and wore wire-rimmed spectacles. His fingers were stained with nicotine. He started with his own tale, "Yays, I knows exactly what ye be on about. Widt me own two eyes I saw dat very creature dash 'longside me vessel. 'Twas over fifty year ago."

Kim had to skirt the crowd, which spanned to the far edges of the wharf. It was a tight squeeze to get by without tumbling into the water. She turned sideways to slip past two older women chatting quickly and nodding with the utmost conviction. "Oh, yays," said one, tut-tutting. "It were a bad bit of fortune, dis calamity."

As Kim tried worming her way nearer the centre, she noticed heads turning and checked to see what might be drawing their attention. A yellow crane had just pulled up in front of the wharf and had come to a stop, the driver, no doubt, wondering where he was going to park. From the crowd, a man pushed free and walked decisively toward the crane, where he paused to speak with the police officer. Before she saw his face, Kim knew that it was Luke. She had been with him long enough to recognize his walk and body movements. She knew them by heart.

"Through here, me ducky," Kim heard an old voice say. A soft hand touched hers. She turned to see a toothless elderly woman with a broad grin and small, vivid blue eyes peering at her. "Watch yer step." The old woman was wearing a green and white dress, and a bandana tied beneath her chin. She nodded encouragingly as a space had opened along the edge where Kim might get through. "Ye wanna clap yer eyes on dat shark ghost?"

"Is that what it is?" Kim asked, good-humouredly.

The old woman laughed, gave Kim's hand a little squeeze and continued holding it. "Me fiancé tol' me 'bout da albino shark years ago. Dat 'n da blood-red octupi and da mermaids."

"Is that so?" Kim said, regretting sounding so formal. But how was she supposed to respond to such a statement? From where she was standing, the shark was ten feet away. She could see it through the gaps between the shoulders ahead of her, but to get any nearer she would need to be forceful. She had no intention of upsetting people here. If she went over with Luke she could become part of the removal team. Get as close as she wanted, bend down to the shark and run her palm over its sleek glassy skin. Regardless, she shied away from the attention. Feeling as though she were hiding, she scanned the crowd for Joseph and Robin.

"Ye frum St. John's," the old woman said, nodding solidly, convinced beyond a shadow of a doubt. "Townie."

"It's that obvious?"

"Ye look confused 'bout yer intentions 'n whereabouts. Dat be da sign o' a townie."

That's for sure, Kim chuckled to herself.

"Bit o' a run frum da city ta dis ol' village."

"Yes." Kim continued searching the crowd.

"Never saw nuttin' like dis, 'av ye?" The old woman tutted fiercely, sucking in breath. "Oow, terrible sight."

Kim glanced down to see her hand cradled in one of the old woman's small wrinkled hands. The old woman was softly, absent-mindedly, patting Kim's hand.

"No, never," Kim finally said.

"Ye never 'erd da fish tales."

"I've heard a few. My husband …" She trailed off, not wanting to let the woman know her husband was a fisheries officer. The information was private, after all. A gurgle of hunger sounded from her stomach. She suspected it was loud enough for the old woman to hear.

"Wha'? Wha' were yer 'usband?"

"Nothing. No, we're separated."

The old woman touched Kim's arm. "Ohhh," she said lamentfully. "I were separated too. Long, long year ago. No spell o' time 'av showed me 'eart any mercy."

"I'm sorry."

"'T'all work out, me ducky, betwix ye 'n yer man, betwix da jigs 'n da reels. Dun't ye worry 'bout dat stuff. Yer a true beauty 'n dat's one o' da greatest consolations."

"Thanks."

The sound of the crane engine revving caught Kim's attention and she turned to see the rigid yellow arm of the machine facing them. It edged forward and the crowd shifted farther down the L of the wharf and out into the road to make room for it.

"Bloody t'ing's gonna squish us," scoffed the old woman.

"Probably." Kim laughed while shifting back with the crowd. The old woman released Kim's hand and took hold of Kim's arm for support while she shuffled daintily in reverse.

Luke called out to the crowd, waving his arms above his head: "You're going to have to clear the area."

No one listened to him. A few people whispered disparaging words while others stared blankly at him as if he had given them incomprehensible instructions.

"Me fiance wrote down a lot o' 'is fish stories, were gunna print dem in a book."

"Really?"

"Truly as I be standing in dis spot, may God strike me dead. Ye wanna 'av a gander at 'em?"

"I ..."

"Come 'av a bit o' dinner 'n a nice cup a tea widt me. I'll show 'em ta ya later. Dey'll dazzle yer wits."

The idea of exploring the old woman's house appealed to Kim; no doubt it was filled with all sorts of antique riches. Plus she was hungry. If she left with the woman it'd give her an excuse to avoid Luke, who was so in control of the situation now that she couldn't bear to be anywhere near him. I can see the shark when they get it back to the Marine Centre, she convinced herself. And she could ask to use the old woman's phone to call Robin.

"Sure," she said to the old woman. "I'd love to. Thanks."

"Finest kind," proclaimed the old woman, winking, her wrinkled hand quietly reaching forward to again take hold of Kim's and give it a warm gentle press. "An 'andsome young woman like ye," she said with soft impish eyes staring up. "Would be a treat ta 'av ye over fer company. Ye tell me 'bout yer troubles, me love, 'n I can offer some tolerance ta yer woeful heartache."

⁓ϟ⁓

"He's a fisheries officer."

Robin's voice, from out in the parlour, reached Joseph while he was filling the blue and white speckled kettle at the kitchen sink. Joseph glanced at the phone and wondered if he should call Dr. Thompson again. How long had it been? Hours? Days? Weeks? He should call again, if only to pin himself to a point in time. It would be reassuring to see a doctor, to have one near, someone who understood anything that might intrude itself upon his psyche and would proficiently explain everything away with a neat string of unfamiliar yet authentic and thus comforting words. Joseph stared down at the tap. The flow gushing into the kettle. Too much water. The kettle was overflowing, heavy. He shut off the tap, dropped the kettle in the sink, and flinched at the calamitous racket of metal slamming against stainless steel.

The kettle sat at the bottom of the sink, weighted there like an anchor. An anchor filled with water, moored in open air. Joseph picked it up again, poured out a long steady gush of water, until every drop was drained, then turned on the tap, started all over, filling the hollow vessel. It was a real chore. He might be at it for years. Sisyphus' kettle.

Trying to boil water. Why did he need to boil water? Make it so hot that it could burn the skin right off the body. Who in their right mind would do such a thing? He thought of the sea. Black and peaked with whitecaps. He shut off the tap and poured out a measure of water. He had put in too much again and the weight of the kettle strained the muscle in his arm.

"But you already knew that," Robin continued from a distance. "Jessica told you, right?"

No reply from Claudia as Joseph held the kettle suspended over the burner and twisted the switch to maximum. He stood and watched the swirl of the electric element begin to glow faintly, like a mechanical spectre making its presence known, then deepen to angry red, then flush with the pure radiance of barely contained fire. The glowing swirl that had been in so many of Robin's drawings from the time she was a small child. Was she afraid of the stove? Of fire?

Joseph slammed the kettle down on the fiery rings as though to smother them. He turned to check out the window. Nothing but grass, the woods and the solar house across the way. No dead people waving soggy freshly dug-up arms while sporting terrifying grins and man-eating teeth. No dead people staring at him in ill-tempered camaraderie. Hoarsely, crustily professing with a wink: "You're one of us now, Mr. Nothing." A few crows swooped along a straight line in front of the trees and a brown and white beagle raced past, sniffing the ground, its ears flapping, and was gone. All normal enough. All was well in Bareneed.

"Jessica says she knows a secret about my dad. But she won't tell me yet. She said that you know it. About why we're here."

"What is she saying?" Joseph murmured, cautioning himself. He turned to look toward the open kitchen door. He could see down the hallway, but not into the parlour. No view of Claudia and Robin. He glanced back at the window. Nothing. No more crows. No more dogs. Strangely, he almost wished for dead bodies. Come on, he challenged. Come on, dead bodies. After all, weren't they dead? How more insignificant could a person get? What sort of fight could they possibly put up, foaming at the mouth and crapping their pants? How much strength could they possibly muster from their rotting disassembled atoms?

"Jessica told me that my mom's coming here. But you can't be friends because you have to sleep with my dad. You have a really major plan to get him in the sack."

With webbed brow, Joseph stepped down the hallway and into the parlour, directing a cross look toward Robin, only to find her drawing a picture of a woman who resembled Claudia. The woman wore the same dress Claudia had been wearing. On the belly of the dress, Robin had drawn the swirl of amber. Behind the woman, the land sloped steeply toward the water, the walls of cliff rock flattened. Houses were plunking into the ocean and being enclosed by the limbs of bizarre sea creatures.

"Robin! I don't think you're being very nice," he said, searching the room for Claudia. Where was Claudia?

"Why?" Robin asked, blamelessly staring up from her drawing. She blew a strand of sandy-blonde hair away from her eyes, then hooked it behind her ear.

"Where's Claudia?" he asked worriedly. The room seemed to be flickering frenetically, or perhaps it was simply an electrical nerve stutter in his eyeballs.

"Who?"

"Claudia." He gave a nervous laugh, slapped the sides of his legs as if the joke was a fine one indeed. "You know, from next door."

Robin shrugged, continued drawing. Streams of amber shooting down from the sky like a shower of meteors. Sparkly crayons.

"I'm going to play in the backyard," Robin said, without glancing up from her work.

"I'd prefer if you stayed in."

"I want to go."

A form drifted into the space beside him, crossing the parlour threshold, startling Joseph. Claudia so near him he could smell her perfume. Roses and lemon and a million other scents of flowers and weather — lightning, rain, fog and blazing, deafening sunlight. The scent nearly melted his knees, tore a crevice in his heart that leaked and mainlined infatuation straight to his brain and groin.

"I used your washroom."

"That's okay. I don't think I was using it."

"Oh, you were present." Claudia slipped past him, too close, too too too close. The frail way she spoke, the manner in which she was dressed, her white dress with the embroidery stitched down the front, three buttons running vertically from her throat, each one perfectly fastened, the way the material lay against the swell of her breasts, the way her belly was slightly distended, it all drove Joseph out of his mind. He wanted to lay his hand on her belly, press to feel the stirring as though it might be connected to him in unimaginable ways that he would openly accept.

Claudia caught Joseph's eyes watching her. For his intentions, Joseph was scolded by her with a feeble yet wicked glance. With grace befitting a bygone era, Claudia carefully sat on the lip of the couch and lifted the box with the decorative wrapping from the coffee table. She rested it on her lap, between her legs. Joseph stared at it, thinking: clutch swallow. Wasn't that the name of a bird? It had a beak that never shut. Its throat inflamed, layered and pink. Clutch swallow.

Shifting in her seat, Claudia inclined her head back, as though she might swoon, while she tucked the dress under her legs; the material became tauter across her breasts, the cloth between the second and third buttons gaping, revealing the lacy trim of her brassiere and the lovely white round of cleavage above the horizontal edge of a rib.

"Stay out of the barn," Joseph instructed Robin without shifting his eyes. "Just in the yard. No farther."

Robin nodded happily, jumped to her feet and held the drawing up to his eyes.

"See?" she said as Joseph stared directly at Claudia's image.

"Promise?" he said, tilting his gaze to face his daughter, surprised by how much older she appeared to be, more mature, more capable than him. "Promise me because you know that a promise is sacred." With these words, he had to restrain himself from snatching her by the throat to squeeze the wished response from her. Fortunately, it came on its own accord.

"Promise." The girl tossed down the drawing, and charged out of the room, off toward the kitchen.

Joseph heard the sound of the back screen door shutting on its spring.

Alone. In a strange house. Perfume lingering in the air. Alone with an unusual and weak woman in a room that did not belong to him, with articles from a lifetime that the dead had affectionately handled and would be heartened to fondle once again.

"I'm sorry," he said to Claudia, fixing his hostile eyes on her. The kettle began hissing on the stove. Soon it would be bubbling, boiled, spouting steam.

"Sorry?" Claudia gave no smile but merely shifted her attention around at the wallpaper and polished furniture. Her eyes alighted on the piano. The presence of the object seemed to fortify her. "This is a charming room."

"You've never been here before?"

"No," she said, bluntly, continuing her survey of the surroundings. "The Critches passed on before my husband built our home." She paused to moisten her chapped lips. Her mouth was dry and thick as if from persistent worry. "The various people who then rented the place kept very much to themselves ... They were usually older couples." Again she paused, this time to place one set of fingers along the wrist of her other hand, as if seeking the vibration of her pulse. "The previous tenant was an elderly woman from abroad who carried a basket of aborted fetuses around with her. A retired nun, I believe." Claudia then absentmindedly ran the fingers of both hands over the box, snuggling it firmly between her thighs. "The owner wouldn't allow children, you understand? Far too complicated to have them full-blooded and present in her home. The living, far too complicated."

"Oh." What he wouldn't give to be able to smash her in the mouth, and then kiss her pained swollen lips. It would make her better. No, him better.

"I imagine fashionable people of this age assume children accomplish little other than destroying everything in their path." Her fingernails absentmindedly dragged along the box, scratching the paint. Coloured flakes caked beneath her nails and crumbled against the pleated white of her dress. Pigment.

What was pigment made from, Joseph wondered. The flesh of plants, of animals, of minerals, of men?

The kettle was whistling. It was not his head after all.

"It's come to a boil," she said and swooned, her body slumping toward the armrest of the low-backed couch. Joseph's eyes scavenged over Claudia's pale unconscious figure. The wretched and the horrible, their will might be done. Desecration of desecrations. His fingers writhed like sniffing insects. He fell to his knees, pressing near her.

With a low moan and whimper, Claudia soon returned to herself.

This vision of her being revived was dreadfully romantic. What a charming creature for a victim, thought Joseph. No longer lecherous but full of amorous, tight-lipped affection, he asked, "Do you want some water?"

Bracing a hand against the armrest, she managed to straighten in her seat. "No," she said.

The kettle continued whistling, shrieking.

Joseph rose from his knees and turned for the kitchen, his fuming thoughts snagging on what Robin had said about her mother coming out here. Robin's mother. That was his wife, too. He forgot her name for a second and his stomach collapsed in on itself.

Someone was screaming horribly. He was close to it. The kettle. He noticed that the toaster was unplugged. He plugged in the cord and felt better. How had he moved to the kitchen so quickly, sparked ahead? Kim. That was her name. Through the kitchen window, he spied Robin standing at the corner of the house staring toward the harbour.

The screaming persisted. He watched the steam pour from the spout. How to stop the scream? How to clap his hand over it without being harmed or implicated?

The telephone receiver was in his hand, so he assumed he must have picked it up from its cradle on the wall. Perhaps someone could tell him how to stop the screaming. He quietly dialled Kim's number, then snatched two cups down from the glass cabinet. On the fourth ring, or was it the first ring? How did he know for certain? It might have been the fourth ring coming first and working backward to meet itself. Was it? On what he suspected to be the fourth ring, Kim's voice announced that she was busy or away. Her voice was mechanical, uncaring. Her voice knew absolutely nothing of him. It was for anyone.

Cursing, Joseph slammed down the receiver, then froze in his tracks. There had been an explosion of noise in front of him. He grimaced, shut his eyes, opened them, held still for a while, then snatched hold of the kettle with a shaky hand. The screaming slowed, dying breath, dying. He poured the boiling water onto the tea bags. Wisps of coppery-red seeped out, swirling and leaking into the clear water, tainting it, staining it redder. He would take it all back if he could. What was it that Robin had said? His eyes toward the window. Robin was not there. Alone at last with Claudia. He grinned as the black humourless satisfaction bubbled up from his heart, catching stickily in his throat. There was a tickle in his lungs. He felt if he coughed he might spit out a tribe of black-clad barbarians on miniature horses. They would gallop around his feet, brandishing their weapons in the air, urging him on toward the banquet of rape and pillage. No, wrong sequence. This was about horror, he reminded himself. The ghoulies have made off with my daughter. A tremor of relief rushed through him as he anticipated the chaos that might need to be mended, might fill the bedroom scene. But then — tearing away from his reverie — he started for the back door, almost colliding with a child who was rushing in.

"I was coming out," he barked.

The child was bigger than he remembered. No, smaller. She was four or five. Standing there, smiling, her two front teeth missing. It was that all over again: her growing up, this time in black and white. A screen propped up before him, the channel dial glued to the spot. The Family Video Network.

"Mommy's here," the child actor said, her voice a wavering crackle. When did this happen, Joseph wondered. When did this really happen? The child was grinning and clapping her hands. "She's down on the wharf with that guy you'd like to kill from work."

Joseph grunted in agreement at the word "kill." "Kill" was a word that had been squat behind his rib cage for far too long. It had the potential to be so big and full of itself. It was getting musty. It needed airing out.

—⟲—

Limping up the gravel driveway, Thompson slipped into the cool shade that pooled around the Pottle house. The smell of cooking drifted out to him. It was suppertime and he was hungry. Mrs. Edyth Pottle, a diminutive grey-haired woman in a floral housedress, was standing in the doorway, holding open the wooden screen door, anticipating his arrival. Her eyes were bloodshot, her nose pink, and her lip swollen and scraped in one corner as if she had been struck.

"Doctor," she said, eyes lowered.

"Mrs. Pottle, are you all right?" Thompson inquired, curiosity and concern welling up inside him.

"Yes." She meekly moved aside. "Come right in, sir."

Thompson stepped up into the house, his lungs awash in the scents of Sunday dinner: boiled cabbage, other vegetables, chicken and salt meat. Glorious! The house was dense with humidity, the painted walls sweating in the hallway. Off to his right, in through the kitchen, the cover of a boiling pot was rattling on the stove, and the window was steamed with mist.

"What happened?" he asked, his inquisitive eyes noticing a line of abrasions on Mrs. Pottle's forehead. The doctor laid down his bag and moved to touch her face, but she leaned away in mortal dread and embarrassment.

"It's nothing … Darry." On speaking the name of her son, her voice quavered. "He's upstairs, in his room. He won't come down." She pointed toward the stairs at the front of the house as Thompson glanced down to pick up his bag. He hadn't taken off his shoes, hadn't even wiped them on the porch mat. Too late now. The urgency of the situation suspended common courtesy. He followed Mrs. Pottle toward the stairs, where she stopped as though in fear of rising.

"Is he conscious?" Thompson took the first two steps at once, the pain in his ankle slicing through him in such a crippling manner that he feared he might go over. His knees also ached fiercely. He winced, yet there was no time to pause.

"Yes. Won't let me call an ambulance."

"Is he violent?"

"No, no. Not Darry, sir. Darry's a good boy. You know how quiet."

"You need to call the police," Thompson instructed, hand on the worn bannister as he edged up the stairs. Ascending, he checked back over his shoulder. Mrs. Pottle took a step in reverse, shifted back against the wall. So much fear. He regretted having left his cellphone on the dashboard of his vehicle. He could contact the police and an ambulance. Where was the ambulance the telephone service had called? "Call the police."

Mrs. Pottle nodded, then shook her head.

Another two steps. "Has he had any heart troubles?"

The old woman clutched the neck of her housedress close to her throat, watched Thompson's legs, then the carpet. Again, she shook her head. "No, never, sir. He's only twenty-two year old."

Finally, Thompson made it to the top landing. He knew the location of Darry Pottle's room. He'd been there before, over the years. Childhood fevers, violent stomach sickness, the usual. He passed the first shut door, stepped toward the second. It was ajar, the room seemingly calm in late-afternoon light. Through the crack, he made out a small colour television playing images of turmoil in some distant country. The volume was turned down. He reached forward and pressed the edge of the door, leaned his head in. Darry was lying on the bed in his Sunday suit, his arms rigid at his sides. He must have come right up to bed after church.

"Hello, Darry," said Thompson, noticing the smell of mothballs. There was a wall-mounted font beside the light switch. Holy water. They used to be in every room in practically every house once upon a time.

Darry would not regard Thompson, but simply said "Sir." He remained motionless, as though bolted to the bed; only his eyes shifted across the tiny blue flowers on the cream wallpaper.

"Are you in pain?"

"No, sir."

There was a silence and then Darry drew a deep breath.

"I'm going to sit on the edge of the bed, okay?"

Darry nodded, eyes fixed on the ceiling.

He's ashamed, Thompson thought, as he settled on the bed. Mortified with shame. "I'm going to check your throat." Carefully, he set his fingertips along the front and sides of Darry's throat, pressing lightly, checking the glands. No signs of swelling. He opened his bag and lifted out his stethoscope, fitted the earpieces in and leaned over Darry. "I'm going to have a listen." Slipping the head of the stethoscope beneath the lapel of Darry's suit jacket, Thompson watched Darry's face for hints of coming movement — quick injurious movement. He heard a regular heartbeat, a trifle fast, but that — no doubt — was from fear. Fight or flight. He noticed a small nick on Darry's face where he had shaved for church.

"Take a deep breath."

Darry did so.

"Another." The lungs were clear. No fluid. "No pain in your chest?"

Again, only the eyes stirring, trying not to meet Thompson's, "No, sir."

"Christ, it's hot up here!" Thompson blew breath up at his forehead and checked the window. The glass was fogged up. Someone had drawn a childish picture of a fish in the mist. Streams of condensation ran down from it. A commercial for cat food was presently playing on the television and Thompson thought of Agatha. He had been away for a while and she needed food and water.

"Sunday cook-up." A weak nervous smile from Darry. "The heat's something."

He's only a boy, really, Thompson thought. A good boy, from what he remembered. He curled his stethoscope away. "Were you napping when this happened?"

"No, sir, walking home from church with mudder." His muscles contracted and he drew a deep breath, his fingers clutching the bedspread. A tight sound rose from his throat, the yelp of a puppy.

"Did you have pain just then?"

Darry, lips pressed together, eyes shut, shook his head.

"Speedy heartbeat?"

"No, sir."

"Did you have a strange feeling, like you aren't really here at all. Scary feeling like you're fading away from yourself, going to lose your mind?"

"No, sir."

That ruled out panic attacks. "Any gas, feeling like you're bloated?"

"No, sir. It's just …"

"What?"

"Like I can't catch my breath."

"Any burning in your lungs?"

"No, sir."

"Tell me then, what is it?"

"It's just like I can't breathe without … thinking about it. It won't come. I lay here waiting. It won't come. And …"

"And what?"

"Nothing … I'm really angry. Mom …" A tear bulged in the corner of Darry's eye, spilled down his cheek, collecting in the strands of his hair. He made no effort to wipe it away. "I'm not myself, sir."

Thompson studied Darry. The young man was scared and confused. He'd seen it before, but usually in patients confronted with news of a serious illness. He had no idea what this was. Just then, he heard the siren of the ambulance travelling from afar and glanced toward the window. Strangely enough, there was a police car racing down the street on the television screen.

"I want you to go to the hospital, just to be on the safe side. There doesn't seem to be anything serious, but just to be safe."

Darry swallowed. "Skipper Fowler died, right?"

"Mr. Fowler was an old man," Thompson said, reassuringly. "There's no reason for you to die. Just keep breathing."

⟆

As the crane raised the albino shark above the parted crowd, the old woman squeezed Kim's hand tighter. Fluid gushed from the shark and the crowd pressed back as the liquid sloshed and spattered onto the concrete, spreading a large pink stain.

"Sweet blest virgin," cried the old woman, releasing Kim's hand to pluck a handkerchief from up the sleeve of her green dress and cover her mouth with it. "Da stench'd turn yer guts."

Kim felt her stomach and throat muscles contract, saliva pool in her mouth. She backed farther away.

The shark rose high in the air as the crane swivelled toward the huge grey plastic container that lay on the back of a flatbed. A few cars were lined back up the road in both directions. Three boats were anchored in the bay, facing the road, watching the spectacle. Gulls followed faithfully above the suspended shark, gliding weightlessly, as if attached by guide wires.

"Turn dis way if da stench still be bodderin' ye, me ducky."

Kim shifted to face the water. She glanced at her watch: 4:55. She sighed at the lateness of the hour.

"Wha's da matter? Ye need ta be off?"

"I was hoping to see my daughter."

"Where be she?"

"I don't know. My husband took her."

With a gasp, the old woman clutched Kim's arm and said: "Kidnapped 'er?" A few people in the crowd shifted their interest toward Kim, scanned her up and down.

Kim turned away and the old woman swiftly shuffled to keep in plain sight.

"No," Kim said. "They're on summer holidays out here. Maybe you saw her."

The old woman grinned in delight, and her pink gums glistened. She smacked them together and nodded enthusiastically. "Yays, I believes I 'av. She be seven year old, 'n he be a 'andsome man widt sandy-blond 'air, goin' a tad bald up da fore'ead?"

"Yes." Kim took closer interest in the old woman, who now pointed toward the ridge across the road.

"Dey be up at da Critch 'ouse. We had a chat. Dey were fishin' on dis very wharf. Dat blue 'ouse up dere, next ta da queer-lookin' one where dat hartist widt da missin' 'usband 'n daughter 'as 'erself locked away." Continuing to point, she shut one eye to be exact. Kim felt overwhelmingly self-conscious as a man nearby glanced at her and then at the house that the old woman had singled out.

After a moment's contemplation, the old woman lowered her hand and offered it to Kim. "Me name's Eileen Laracy, 'n I knows evertin' 'bout dese parts."

"I'm Kim Blackwood." She gave her married name, not her birth name which she had often used since the separation, thinking a married name more fitting in the presence of this old woman whose soft, loose-skinned hand she now shook.

"Dat be a right peculiar name. Pretty as a plucked canary, though 'tis."

"Thanks." Kim removed her hand from Miss Laracy's lingering grip.

"Dey call me Miss Laracy, because I never wed. In da church o' da Lord dat is. I wed in me 'eart. Never loved anudder human bein' as much as 'e. Me sweet'eart were lost at sea."

"Oh, I'm sorry."

Miss Laracy lowered her head briefly in recognition of Kim's sympathy. "I used ta see 'im all da time beyond da grave, but den … he wandered off widt all da udders." She gave it no further mention, but merely turned away and sniffed bravely as if to stifle a stab of pain. "Let's go 'av a nice cup o' tea, me love, 'n a bit o' dinner." Tilted forward, she started off fast, faster than Kim had anticipated, jostling people in the crowd who briskly moved aside for her. They were out of the gathering and across the road before Luke had a chance to notice her. Glancing back, she saw him listening attentively to one of the old-timers who had pulled another man from the crowd. The second man, in his mid- to late-forties and appearing to have the features and expressions of a simpleton, was hugging a large notebook while timidly casting his eyes at the ground.

"Dat's Tommy Quilty," exclaimed Miss Laracy. "'E draws da t'ings dat be comin'. He prawly drew dat ghost shark two or t'ree year ago."

"Really," Kim said, watching the man with the large notebook strain back against the old man's grip, free himself and sink into the crowd, which seemed to swallow him up protectively. The old man spoke quickly to Luke who, no doubt, couldn't understand a word. Kim was even having a hard time making out all of Miss Laracy's words. The dialect was

difficult to follow, fast and clipped, with "h" sometimes dropped and sometimes added on in the strangest places. Kim watched Luke grin in disbelief,
shake his head at the old man. He then excused himself to continue with
the supervision. A busy man. Kim liked him even less after that.

She was coaxed away by Miss Laracy's insistent hand. They journeyed up
the road, passed the soldiers and the barricade and soon entered a yard abundant with flowers. Miss Laracy headed around back of the old two-storey
house while Kim tried to keep up. The old woman certainly could move.

"Come into me 'ome," Miss Laracy beckoned from the back step. "Yer as
welcome as da stars on a night widt no moon."

-⋒-

Tommy watched the crane operator staring toward the sky while the
man's hands shifted the levels, carefully lowering the albino shark into the
container. At first, the shark's tail poked out, but it soon slid in, sloshing
water down over the sides. The grey lid was lifted and set in place. Chains
were flung across the top, then fastened to the thick metal rings welded
along the sides of the flatbed. The truck idled for several minutes while
men exchanged words, confirming the delivery's destination and the anticipated time of arrival. The driver took off his work gloves, then climbed up
into the truck's cab.

Tommy shuffled back a few steps and clutched his notepad tighter to
his chest as the vehicle pulled away, engine revving and gears grinding as
it navigated the main road west, on its way to the marine tanks at
Memorial University in St. John's. That's where the shark was going.
Tommy had heard the men saying as much.

The truck rolled away from the community, and the crane, too, soon
departed, releasing the traffic to gradually flow freely and prompting the
majority of the crowd to disperse. Yet Tommy remained stood there, in
the centre of the road, until he was eased off to the side by a policeman.
He continued staring up the pavement, watching where the truck had
gone. He could still see it moving in his head even though it was now
out of sight.

He saw inside the container, the motionless shark bobbing around in seawater. Patches of faint grey intermittently appeared on its tail, like bruises, as it bumped against the sides. The patches faded and then reappeared, until finally they set as permanent markings.

Eventually, as the shark was transported farther away from Bareneed, the grey patches leaked to spread across the entire length of the shark, nose to tail, melding and darkening to completely restore the shark's natural shade of grey.

~⦿

Joseph's eyes were glued on Claudia while he cordially sipped his tea. The Sunday sanctity of the parlour was being violated by his voracious smut. A racy loop kept replaying. In his mind, he was caught in a copulating stutter, humping away at Claudia like a maniac. It was modern-day courtship. The mating season captured in all its real-life intensity. Televisceral flickerings behind a pulled screen. Prime time ensured. The audience would be anticipating Kim's arrival, would delight in her staged gasp as she nonchalantly strolled in on their animal antics. The audience would bellow a collective "Oh-no" or sounds in keeping with their astonished bemusement. Kim's fingertips would shoot to the shocked circle of her mouth, her cheeks flushed red. Too racy, perhaps. Too carnal. That was easy enough to get around. After all, it was seconds we were talking about here. Seconds and minutes. In such a world, who could not be easily forgiven, or forgotten?

Claudia gave no sign of noticing his lascivious intentions. There was nothing modern about her. She wanted no part of action, instead desiring words. A man of words who found the body clothed more erotic than the body undressed. Despite her suspected leaning toward suitable discourse, she sure as hell didn't say much herself, just sat there with that box on her lap that Joseph could not reach for. Not gabby enough, that one. Not empty enough. Her innards rarely tickled by giggles. Her hair unaccustomed to the wispy dye-wand of the bottled blonde. Introspective sort. No doubt she preferred foreign films to the frilly mechanics of sitcoms.

Subtitles to canned laughter. Bottled-up frustration just yearning to bust out, claw and gasp and tear into him with her fingernails. Rage as tempestuous as a storm sweeping across the moors.

By the looks of her, Claudia might faint away again at any moment. What she needed was a good lashing, a fist wound with a belt hammering her awake, pounding until she was not only fully in this world again but larger than life, huge, twice as big as Joseph so that she might crush Joseph efficiently. It was the mommy thing all over again. Crush and then cuddle. In such a state, what sort of incantations might stream out of her? What sort of dance under moonlight might be her fancy? A graceful flailing of limbs that would awaken nature. Belches from hallowed tree trunks. The strangling tangle of roots inching up her ankles. Birdies tweeting on her slender shoulders at some god-awful hour while she sported a harrowing grin.

Joseph shifted in his seat and sucked on his bottom lip. Eyes dazed, slipping in and out of focus, he imagined the absolute worse. And what might that be? Opening her up completely to bob for apples. He thought his supply of pills might soon be exhausted. That would end it for him. He took another noisy slurp of his tea. It was cooling.

As if sensing Joseph's mistrust of the proceedings, Claudia raised the box from her lap. "I forgot," she said, leaning toward him. He was now sitting closer to her than he had realized, actually within reach. "Your housewarming present," she stated, or was it: "You're a housewarning pheasant." Or, worse yet: "Peasant."

Joseph accepted the box with his shivering fingers, smiling with reassurance at how the bottom had been warmed by Claudia's thigh. He noticed that her fingers were perfectly tapered and ringless.

"Thank you," he said. "It's not really our house though. Any of them. Mine, I mean."

"For a short while." Claudia straightened in her seat and joined her hands in her lap, brightening a touch, so ladylike. "Or maybe longer."

Longer, Joseph echoed in his thoughts. Longer. Yes, it could always be longer. Above him, something thumped. Robin was up in her room, probably trying to escape through her window. Smart girl. Bright girl. He recalled that Robin's mother was coming. His wife. He saw her face and it was bloodied and bruised. Who would solve the murder? His guilt was crushing, even though he had committed no crime that he knew of.

"I don't want to ruin the wrap. It feels hand-painted." Standing, Joseph tilted his head toward the kitchen, hoping Claudia might divine his strategy and track the flesh-crumb trail of his butchering thoughts. "I'll get a knife … Or did I already say that?" If she did not follow in his footsteps, then she would *have* to be the victim.

With polite obedience, Claudia stood to shadow him into the kitchen, paling even more.

"You know," Joseph said over his shoulder, feeling a confession coming on, feeling that these words he was about to speak would realize the mood of a bitten-lipped kiss. "I'm often scared of my own reflection. I don't mean coming upon it suddenly, but just looking at *it* in the mirror, knowing that *it*, what I see, is me." With this, he paused to listen to the inactivity in his body. His lungs. They seemed empty. As if to test what might be wrong, he drew a breath. It worked. He worked.

"I once knew a gravedigger who thought along those same lines," Claudia conceded

Joseph broke out in a sweat, gave a little laugh as they crossed the threshold of the kitchen. "And what happened to him?"

"He buried himself."

Once more, Joseph gave an uneasy laugh. The sweat had stopped and now chilled the fabric of his shirt. They were in the kitchen. Had he even left there, he wondered. What had happened to their tea? He laid the box on the counter and opened the drawer, fishing out a filleting knife. What was he going to do with it? Cut larger into small to fit sideways into his mouth? Saw through the bridge in the newly existent divide in his head, the bridge that carried him through himself?

"Slice it." Claudia's face, her dry lips parted, contained catastrophe within.

Joseph thought of lip balm, moisture. Not to utter a word, but to construct a Byzantine structure where silence glided through the arches like doves. To squeeze two doves into one without ruffling a feather. Magic without tricks or mirrors.

He was going to slash the box open. Dump the introspection and cut to the chase. Claudia stood near him as he clutched the wooden handle and held it up so that she might admire the tip.

"Yes," she purred, stroking it with a fingertip, her breath deepening, all the way to her bowels as her breasts rose in longing, pressing beneath the fabric of her dress.

Joseph lowered the edge of the blade. Gently, he sliced the spaces where the tape had fastened the wrap. The corners sprang up once the tape was severed. He took his time unwrapping the gift. It became an adventure of such complication that he found himself lost, so disoriented that he had to stop. Origami in reverse. Gathering his wits, he began again with his hands. Soon, the paper was deconstructed and a box sat at its centre. He raised each flap to reveal wads of flimsy blue tissue paper. Reaching in, he pawed deep beneath the blue, until his fingers struck bottom. He took another laboured breath, carefully gripping the object. Glancing over his shoulder, he saw Claudia standing nearer, giving him one of her closed-lip smiles, a smile that insinuated outings to secluded beaches that had been planned and anticipated for months, children in Sunday dresses hand-stitched from fabrics no longer obtainable in this world.

Joseph carefully removed the tissue paper. A black tiled peak and the darker lines that indicated lengths of blue clapboard became evident. It was the Critch house, an exact miniature. He thought of his reflection, condensed, made smaller. He raised the house free of the box and held it in the flat of his palm, tried to peek in and see himself. No such luck. He turned to face Claudia.

"The roof comes off." Claudia's long pale fingers curled to remove the lid. "It's a candle holder for when the lights go out."

Joseph gawked at Claudia, standing no more than a foot away, her eyes mirroring the precise sentiment in his. He should kiss her. Where? On the cheek? On the lips? On her soft distended belly where he might lay his head and sleep, breathing the scent of her skin, such fragile scent implying that her flesh would slice so freely, like dough in the oven for mere minutes. He was reaching for her, extending his hand as Claudia extended hers, warmly taking hold. Her grip lingered. Gently, she stroked the insides of his fingers and his fingertips, a caress, as she withdrew. The knife. It had been in his hand. He had gashed her deeply. Claudia watched her hand but there was not a drop of blood.

"Oh," she said, dismayed, delicately fingering the gash.

Joseph tried searching Claudia's eyes, but they were shut, her expression one of epiphany, her breath still. What a beautiful vision, Joseph thought, fixated on her pink eyelids, so thin that the mesh of veins was discernible, her chapped lips still plump, full of moisture waiting to be sucked to the surface. They were lips like none he had ever seen. Lips that reawakened chaste sentiments of love.

Footsteps sounded beyond the kitchen. Joseph looked toward the hall-way as Robin entered the room. Her hands were covered in blood. Had she cut herself on the bedroom window while trying to escape? Joseph had heard no explosion of glass. No, the blood was actually red ink from markers. She was always drawing on her skin, always running out of paper, always creating something of herself.

"Look what I made for Mommy," she said, holding up her scarlet hands.

The canned laughter was deafening.

~❦~

Miss Laracy was seated on her purplish-grey couch with the photo album balanced on her knees. Along its back, the couch was covered in colourful swirls of embroidery. Red knitted coverings were neatly hung over the armrests. Miss Laracy held one twisted finger above a black and white snapshot of a young girl aged eleven or twelve.

Kim leaned her face nearer the photograph, pressing arm to arm with Miss Laracy. She eyed a cranberry-glass dish on the coffee table. It was filled with a collection of colourful hard candy. She imagined that the candy might be stuck together in one big clump. Kim's stomach panged with hunger.

"Dat be me sister, Tamer. She were blest widt da sight." Miss Laracy tilted her head to thoughtfully consider Kim. "'Er blood turned though. Poor soul. Bless 'er sweet 'eart."

"Blood turned?"

"Yays, affer she 'ad 'er first daughter, 'er blood turned and she fell sickly. Me sister saw spirits wherever she set 'er sight." Miss Laracy quietly blessed herself. Her eyes lingered on the photograph while she reached for the thin gold chain around her neck, carefully drew on it until a delicate gold crucifix emerged from inside her dress. She kissed the cross, then let it slip hidden again. "Tamer were high-strung, nervous. I used ta see 'er ghost."

"Really?"

"Yays, she would come ta me near mornin', appear as da child she once were, sit on da chest at da foot o' me bed 'n watch over me. Never uttered a word. She were a lovin' child."

Kim shook her head once. "No one sees ghosts any more."

Miss Laracy examined the side of Kim's face, her wrinkled expression turning sombre, her forehead a thick clump of wavy lines. The old woman's eyes darkened as she squinted as though she were under the weight of more complicated thought. "Ye knows why, don't ye, me love?"

"No, not really."

Miss Laracy shut the album and placed a hand over Kim's, leaving it there for comfort while drawing a steadying breath. "I 'member when da spirits started roamin' off."

"Really?"

"Yays. I truly does. Da year of 1952." Miss Laracy paused, awaiting reply from Kim.

"Why 1952?"

"'Twas da year da television came. Black 'n white. Da spirits were aplenty den, every'n had dere own ghost story ta tell. But da spirits, dey kept vanishin' more 'n more as da television went t'rough every 'ousehold in Bareneed. Sometin' in da air." Her eyes quietly searched the upper corners of the room as if seeking out a presence.

"Maybe it had something to do with imagination. I read an article once, I think, that —"

"Yays, dat too, but stuff be in da air dat slice da spirits ta pieces. It pains dem." Miss Laracy lifted her hands into the air and wiggled her fingers. "Dey rise higher, up ta da heavens where dey wail 'n moan widt no comfort.

Stuff in da air keeps 'em frum da livin'. Only in dreams do dey visit ye now. I were tol' such t'ings."

"Microwaves, you mean?"

"Dat what ye call it, me love?"

Kim nodded attentively. "From televisions and cellphone and computers. Everything electronic, I guess."

"Dat stuff dry out da body too. Make a person wickedly t'irsty. I used ta watch da television many a year ago and I'd be all shrivelled affer. Craved water like nuttin' else. Ye needs a glass a water by da looks of ye. Yer colour's off."

Kim's throat was parched from talking. She swallowed, finding she was, indeed, thirsty. "I'm okay," she said, not wanting to put Miss Laracy out. She checked over the living room; all the furnishings and articles from years gone by gave Kim a sense of domestic peace, yet she couldn't help but think she should call Joseph, to set her mind at ease about Robin. She glanced around for a phone but saw none. A framed reproduction of Jesus, his heart radiating beneath his held-open robe, caught her attention on the wall above a glass-doored cabinet.

"Wha' can I get ye? A drop o' water?"

"No, I'm fine. Actually, I was wondering if you have a phone."

Miss Laracy shifted the photo album to the coffee table and groaned, struggling to rise from the couch. Kim stood and extended her hand, aiding the old woman to her feet.

"I can get the phone," Kim said. "Just point the way."

"Naw, sure I'm up now." Slightly stooped, Miss Laracy ventured out into the kitchen, calling back: "I'll warm up a bit o' dinner." Soon, after the clanging of pots and the gushing of water from a tap, the old woman returned with a cordless phone. She handed it to Kim, who was caught by surprise. "I bought it on da count o' me knees, gettin' up 'n down." She sat with a huff and leaned near the phone. "Press dat button dere," she said, pointing specifically. "'N den da udder ones."

"Thank you." Kim did as instructed, and dialled Joseph's number. "It's a local call."

Miss Laracy raised her hand and screwed up her face in an expression of indifference. "Ah, no matter. I got me pension. Never spends it. Call China if ye wishes."

The line connected. Kim drifted toward the front of the living room, where she could see the harbour through the lace curtains. The wharf was practically deserted now, save for a few old-timers still chatting. The telephone rang three times, resonating deep in her ear, before it was raised at the other end.

—⟋⟍—

"Hello, Mommy." Robin held the receiver with both hands and spoke into it. She knew it had to be her mother on the line because no one else had the number.

"Hi, baby. How you doing?"

"Fine."

"How you feeling, sweetheart?"

"Okay."

"You sure?"

"Yup."

"What're you up to?"

"Nothing." Robin toed her sneaker against the wooden kitchen floor and twirled the phone cord.

"How's your head?"

"Sore on the back. I've got a bump."

"Ohh, I know. It must be sore. You taking it easy? Having fun?"

"Sort of."

"There must be plenty to do. You been fishing yet?"

"Yeah, we caught a sculpin and it turned all bloody red when Daddy tried to get it off the hook."

"Really? Yuck. So, what're you doing now?"

"I was looking at the little house Claudia gave us."

"Claudia?"

"Claudia's an artist."

"Really? Where's she from?"

"Claudia's our neighbour." Robin lowered her voice to a whisper, looked around for Jessica but she was nowhere to be seen. "The one with the dead daughter. Claudia thinks she's missing, but she's not really."

"Really? Hmm. Can you get Daddy for me, please?"

"Daaaddddyyy?" Robin called, bending toward the kitchen doorway. When she turned back, she was surprised to see Jessica standing there with one white arm reaching for the telephone. Robin covered the receiver. "What?" she asked Jessica.

Jessica nodded toward the phone, as if in explanation.

Robin shook her head. "No. That's my mom."

Jessica smiled with wide, yellow teeth, the spaces between packed with brownish-green guck. She leaned toward Robin and whispered in her ear. Robin gasped playfully, then became serious, but giggled all the same while shaking her head, "No."

"Robin?"

"Jessica wants me to tell you something. It's a bad word."

"Who's Jessica?"

"She's my friend. The girl who's not really dead. Claudia's her mommy."

"Can you get Daddy for me, please."

"I think he's busy."

Jessica whispered in her ear and Robin gasped again, shook her head more adamantly. They both giggled uncontrollably.

"Call out to him again, Robin."

"Jessica says he wants to … you know, the 'f' word … her mommy."

"Robin!"

"I didn't say it." She heard her father coming down from upstairs, her father mumbling something about the foundation of the house, how it was made of slate rocks and they could be stacked and stacked. The house could go high into the sky.

"What?" Kim said.

"Are you coming here? I saw you —"

"Can you please get your father, Robin? Right now."

"Daddy, the phone's for you." Robin handed the phone over and ran from the room, racing up the stairs. "It's Mommy. Come on, Jessica. Mommy's coming."

⌇

"Hello?" Joseph said, wondering who it might be wishing to speak with him at this point in time.

"What the hell is going on there? What's the matter with Robin?"

"Who's this?"

"What'd'you mean, who's this? Who the hell do you think it is?"

"No one."

"I'm here, Joseph. I'm right here in Bareneed and I'm coming to get Robin, right now, Joseph. Right now, you hear me?"

The quavering voice stopped. The line went dead.

Joseph shook his head and wondered where Kim might be. Hadn't he killed her already? Buried her in the floorboards under the barn out back? He checked his hands. One held a telephone receiver, the other Claudia's small house. One should fit into the other, he thought.

Giggling came from upstairs. Two little girls at play, singing a rhyme: "Myyy fawwther went to sea-sea-sea to see what he could see-see-see and all that he could see-see-see …"

Joseph quietly sang along, "… was the bottom of the deep blue sea-sea-sea."

⌇

The ambulance arrived and the attendants, ignoring Darry's intermittent shouts of protest, carried him from his house on a stretcher. After fixing an oxygen mask over Darry's mouth, one of the attendants, a short man with a crewcut and one black eye, said, "The last guy gave me a smack." He had noticed Thompson's judgemental eyes watching the safety straps being brusquely yanked tight. Darry's mother stood to the side, uncertain of what to do. She whimpered and held out her hand, trailing the stretcher down over the stairs, through the hallway to the back door and out into the road.

"He's not in any danger," Thompson assured Mrs. Pottle. "I want to keep an eye on him, just in case." He gave her a wink and held her shoulders. "We've seen this before. As long as there's oxygen, it doesn't get much worse."

Dr. Thompson chose to ride in the back, guarding his patient. The pain in his ankle intensified, crouched as he was, but it was important that he be there at every moment, to see what complications might develop. This was the mystery right before his eyes.

Darry stared toward the white ceiling as the vehicle sped up. Through the back windows, Thompson saw Mrs. Pottle in the road, watching the ambulance glide away. In no time, she was a dot as they zoomed through Bareneed, toward Shearstown Line. Thompson caught bits of the ambulance attendant's conversation with dispatch. It was not the standard conversation. The attendant had been advised to switch to a different frequency. Thompson thought he heard the voice at the other end identify itself as a military figure. Major something or other. First, soldiers on the roads. Now, a military leader communicating with ambulance attendants. The attendant stated the specifics of Darry's condition. Minutes later, a jeep raced up behind the ambulance and overtook it, remaining slightly ahead. An escort.

Darry's condition didn't appear to be deteriorating. His blood pressure was stable. Heartbeat fine. Darry coughed behind the mask, his fists clenching tighter. His chest rose and then fell, remaining flat for seconds before rising again. Not pain, thought Thompson, but intense fear. Which of the two was worse?

As soon as they arrived at the hospital, Darry was briskly removed and wheeled through the sliding doors into Emergency. Hobbling after the stretcher, Thompson caught a glimpse of the military jeep as it headed off, two soldiers up front, not looking back, needed elsewhere.

Inside the hospital, there was a soldier stationed before the swinging double doors to Emergency. The army is taking this, whatever it is, seriously, Thompson told himself. If this is why they're here.

The Emerg doctor on duty checked Darry over and found no signs of cardiac or pulmonary distress. He ordered blood work and when the results were returned — and Thompson came back from grabbing an egg sandwich and milkshake in the cafeteria — all signs indicated there was no infection or contamination in the blood. Chest X-rays were carried out. Nothing. A brain scan was next on the roster.

In the meantime, Thompson insisted that Darry be put on a respirator just to be cautious. The Emerg doctor, after fixing Thompson with a stare that said, "Is this another one? What's going on?" concurred and Darry was sent up to the medicine ward and assigned a bed in a room occupied by three other men suspected of also having contracted the breathing disorder. Thompson had already ordered that a quarantine sign be posted on the door, with all visitors cleared through him. Donna Drover's room was just next door. Thompson, having followed Darry up in the elevator, limped toward the provisions room and tightly bandaged his ankle with a roll of Elastoplast.

"You want a hand with that?" asked a passing nurse.

"I'm a trained physician," he huffed, his breath cut off from bending over.

Done with his self-treatment, he navigated the corridor to Donna Drover's room. The support provided by the bandage did seem to make a bit of difference. He would pay Mrs. Drover a visit before heading home to finally feed Agatha.

The drapes were pulled in his patient's room. It was almost entirely dark, save for the thin slant of light spilling in from the corridor. There was no movement beneath the sheets, only the hiss of oxygen being administered. They had removed the respirator and put in a trach tube. It was more comfortable, limited possible damage to the vocal cords and lessened the chance of lung infection. Mrs. Drover was facing the curtains. When the doctor coughed lightly, the patient languidly turned her head toward him. He came to stand beside her bed.

"How you feeling?" he asked in a hushed voice.

Mrs. Drover watched him with blank eyes. She did not seem to recognize him at all and her face was changed from the last time he had visited her three days ago. On that occasion, she had asked the doctor: "Who am I?" Thompson had told her and she then seemed to remember her name and the vague details of her condition. Thompson assumed she had been confused, having been awoken from a dream and perhaps still lingering in that realm.

Presently, the doctor realized that Mrs. Drover had lost a noticeable amount of weight. He raised her chart from the foot of her bed. Vitals all normal. Loss of weight noted. He sighed and slipped the clipboard back into its metal slot.

"Can I get you anything?"

Mrs. Drover observed him without expression. Her dry lips stirred, but no words came. Thompson managed his way nearer her bedside and leaned his ear to her lips.

"Water," she hissed through an arid throat.

"Sure." Thompson hobbled to the ice machine at the end of the corridor and returned with a paper cup of ice chips and a baby-blue plastic spoon. He scooped up the chips and tried feeding them to Mrs. Drover, but she shook her head, tightly shut her lips.

"Water," she said.

"Ice chips," he countered, raising the spoon. "It *is* water." Regardless, she would not accept what he offered, and so he set the cup and spoon on the night table.

"Am I …" Mrs. Drover made a slurping noise, then swallowed with difficulty. "… Some … where?"

"You're in a hospital in Port de Grave."

Thompson had trouble making out the next words, but they sounded like: "I can't … see."

"You want me to turn on the light?"

Mrs. Drover seemed not to know what he meant. "What?" she asked, pausing to shift her eyes toward the foot of the bed. "Is this?"

Thompson inspected her gaze as it skimmed toward his face. Her visual acuity seemed fine, her pupils contracted, focusing on him.

"What … am … I?"

"You're in a hospital. You came here by ambulance."

"What am I?"

"How do you mean?"

Mrs. Drover said nothing more; her eyes grew dimmer, vacuous, the pupils widening to solid black spheres framed only in white, then contracting back to normal.

Christ! He had never seen that before. Shifting, he went over on his ankle, refreshing the pain. He glanced at the button for the nurse to sound the alarm.

"Mrs. Drover?" he asked.

But she said not another word, merely blinked and watched him. The pupils were fine again, no further expansion. Mrs. Drover stared at his face.

"I'll come see you again tomorrow."

The hiss of the respirator was the only reply.

"Okay?" He waited, wanting to prompt further reaction from her, wanting to reassure himself that her condition was not deteriorating, although he now knew that it was. His heart sank at the prospect of what might become of those inflicted with the condition. "Okay, Mrs. Drover?"

"Did I kill him?"

The remark took Thompson by surprise. A moment of charged silence followed. "Who?"

"My son. See him …"

"Muss?"

Dazed, Mrs. Drover stared slightly to the left of the doctor. "I see him …"

Thompson checked over his shoulder. Nothing.

"… when I shut my eyes."

"It's just your thoughts."

"What am I?"

"You're a woman. Donna Drover." He kindly placed a hand on her arm. "Donna Drover."

"No … *what* am I?"

Thompson watched his patient's eyes, the look of utter blankness that made his skin prickle. "I'll come see you again tomorrow." He needed to get out of the room. He felt as though he were suffocating.

In the elevator, on his way down to the main floor to head home and feed Agatha, he thought over Mrs. Drover's question: "What am I?" not

"Who am I?" It was the first time he had heard such a thing from a patient. His stomach grumbled. The egg sandwich wasn't enough. He needed a feed of pasta, lots of butter and garlic and a big glass of Cabernet. His cellphone rang. He answered it briskly. It was Sergeant Chase; his voice seemed amused as he informed the doctor that he was down at the Bareneed wharf.

"And what's there now? A school of talking cod?"

"There's a body."

"Another shark?"

"No, human, on the road. Flung on the road from the water."

"What?"

"It's ..."

"Flung?"

"... an old body."

"On the road? Old man, woman?"

"No, not like that. You better come. Older than that."

"Fine." He shut his cellphone as the elevator doors slid open. "Older than that." What could that possibly mean? "Older than that." "What am I?" "*What* am I?" He went to step off the elevator, but heard several voices calling out or gasping in warning. He stopped dead in his tracks, noticing he was about two feet above the main floor. The elevator had stopped before reaching the level. Three people were gawking up at him.

"Cripes!" He tried crouching with one hand braced against the elevator floor, to spring down, but he knew that would hurt. All he could do was sit on the floor and dangle his legs. "Give us a hand." He reached out to two men, another doctor and a male nurse, who stepped forth to help him down. "Bad ankle," he told them. "Otherwise, I would've leapt Tarzan-like." He limped off, putting more limp into his walk so they might get the point.

Outside he scanned the parking lot, wondering where he had parked his four-wheel drive before he recalled that he had left it crashed into an army vehicle. What pizazz! He'd have to bum a ride from one of the ambulance attendants. Again, his stomach grumbled. Maybe the egg sandwich had gone bad before he ate it; maybe the mayonnaise was off.

"Fine," he muttered. "Just fine. Let me starve to death." Heading back into the hospital to seek out a ride, he felt a clutch in his stomach, then lower, in his bowels. A watery sensation letting go. Squeezing his buttocks together, he raced for the washroom down the corridor. It was right beside the gift shop. Hobbling and huffing, he crossed the threshold mere instants before his trousers might have suffered the flood of a spectacular indecency.

-◌)

Doug Blackwood was reading a book written by a Newfoundlander about life on the winter trapline up on the Labrador. It was a book concerning survival and gave a decent depiction of life in the woods: burying the food deep in the snow to prevent animals from eating it, always the need to keep a fire going at night to stave off frostbite, and keep dry, always keep dry. Then there was the constant lack of sleep and the animals ever-present around you day and night. Deep in the woods with no modern contrivances to bother a person. Doug revelled in imagining that feeling of forest solitude. He had been on the trapline himself and read every book he could get his mitts on that detailed the adventure. Most of the books were published locally but he had read a few written by mainlanders too. It was always interesting to read about how mainlanders got everything all arsed-up about Newfoundland. Uppity snobs, most of them, looking down on the dumb Newfs.

Staring at his book, he focused on the print and had to read the same sentence over two or three times, unable to absorb the words, distracted by remembrances of the creature he had seen out on the water. He refused to call it a mermaid, because that would be fairy tale foolishness, yet he assumed that was exactly what the creature was. Then there had been the army fellows stopping him when he was heading back up the road. Bramble had gone mad again, barking at the soldier and trying to get at him from the passenger seat. Doug had to keep shoving the dog back.

The army fellow had asked a few questions about seeing anything unusual while out in his boat and Doug had shaken his head and told the soldier he'd seen nothing other than the great big blue sky and great big blue water. The army fellow stared hard at Doug's face and then told him that he could drive on.

Frigging pests.

His thoughts shifted from unwelcome recollections of the army back to his story of the mermaid. Who to tell? Maybe he'd call his great-niece, Robin, and secretly pass the tale on to her. She'd be delighted to hear the news. Yes, a child would understand. Not something to detail over the phone. You had to be there to hear this sort of yarn. Plus he hadn't figured out the best way to tell it yet. That was the trick to the story. It wasn't just having information to pass on, the tale had to be laid out and arranged so it grabbed the person's attention right off. *I was out in my boat and it was a fine day, too fine to foresee it staying that way. I was out on the water, expecting nothing other than a nice catch of cod. I'd left the harbour, seeing those army fellows standing on the road, and I boarded my boat and stared ahead to the horizon. Not a ripple on the water. Not a breath of air.* But what about those army fellows? They had questioned him about seeing anything strange, like they already knew what he had witnessed. It wasn't about codfish. There was something afoot, something in the wind.

Doug imagined the ocean and the sun and the movement of his boat as if journeying out to the place at that very moment. *My boat sailed without fault, without stutter in its noble progression. I left the wharf with the jagged cliffs looming over me, cliffs as old as Adam, beaten down by centuries of water, but faithfully remaining solid. Something out of the ordinary was awaiting me beneath the massive weight of water. There was always something down there. Something to catch or something that would cause a man peril.*

Doug was engrossed in the grand contemplation of his tale when he heard a banging noise from the backyard. It sounded like the barn door slamming shut. Bramble rose from where she was sleeping by the parlour stove.

"Who's that, Bramble?" he asked, first glancing toward the curtained window, then toward the hallway and wondering about the wind. Was there a gale brewing? He hadn't heard anything about it on the fisheries broadcast. Maybe someone was in his barn, had shut the door. He hadn't left the door open, not that he recalled. He'd been in there earlier checking his stock of paint for the south side of the barn. It took the brunt of the weather and so was in need of a good lick of paint. Its shabby appearance was getting on his nerves. While he was there he had also added a bit of white paint to the replica of the wooden church he was building for a fellow from Heart's Delight. The fellow had been driving by Doug's place and spotted all the boats, churches, and brightly painted birdhouses Doug had built and arranged on his front lawn, and had come knocking asking if Doug would build him a church like the one in the yard. Doug had agreed and named the price, to which the fellow readily agreed. People were often coming in and asking him to make one of the items. He also built wooden men with arms that spun in the wind, and furniture from the heavy limbs and twisted, gnarled trunks of trees.

With book still in hand, he rose from his chair and approached the parlour window. The light outside was mellow and the shadows were stretching toward evening-length. There was no one he could see, only his constructions in the front yard and, on the other side of his white fence, the bench that his wife, Emily, had asked him to place there, where people might take a sit down if they so desired. She had painted the sign in her own script: SIT AWHILE ON YOUR JOURNEY AND REST YOUR WEARY BONES. Each year, Doug painstakingly repainted the script in Emily's favourite shade of blue.

Doug let the curtain fall back into place and went toward the kitchen at the rear of the house. He wasn't expecting anyone. Of course, it could be Joseph and Robin, but he hadn't heard a vehicle or the slam of a car door. Perhaps they were on foot. Bramble was on Doug's heels, then past him, whining, wanting to be let out. It was after supper and the scent of Doug's rabbit pie still clung to the air. The leftover pastry remained on the counter. He thought he might make tea buns later. He usually baked on Sunday. A good feed of fresh tea buns slathered with gobs of melting butter before bed.

Doug peeked out the kitchen window and was miffed to see the barn door wide open. Were Joseph and Robin in there, poking around? He'd had plenty of people trying to do that, townies coming out from St. John's wanting to search through his barn to see what was there, steal all his old pop and medicine bottles, old wooden tools and trinkets. He'd sold a case of them to a fellow years ago. The man had given Doug an amount of money for the goods that seemed generous enough. In fact, Doug was grinning inside, telling himself that he'd taken the fellow to the cleaners. A good bit of cash for a load of old junk. But later he'd learned from Willy Bishop that the man was selling the stuff in a shop in St. John's for a fortune. Since then, Doug had run off any men who came snooping around for antiques, despite their boldness and their claims that they had plenty of money.

"Christ," Doug muttered, tossing the book on the kitchen table, and heading for the back porch. He yanked open the inner door, flicked the hook latch on the wooden screen door, pressed his fingers to the slats, and pushed it open. Bramble bolted off and ran straight toward the barn, leaping up over the threshold. Doug caught a breath of fresh late-afternoon air and a view of the dark evergreens in his backyard beyond the small red-brown barn.

"Bramble," he called, "get back here." Doug peered out, opened the door wider and searched around the yard. Shadows were on the recently mowed grass as the sun hung low in the sky. He stepped out onto the back landing and had a more careful look around his yard. His imagination seemed to be getting the best of him. No one was there after all.

A racket sounded from inside the barn. Paint cans were being tipped over.

"Bramble," Doug shouted, "get out of that." He thought of pulling on his shoes. His eyes lingered on the barn's south wall. It definitely needed painting. It was beginning to flake in areas. Shameful. He'd tend to that tomorrow, weather permitting. He gave a shrill whistle, expecting Bramble's return, listened but heard no other sound from the barn. Moving forward in his stocking feet, he trod over the grass, wincing when he stepped on a patch of gravel, and soon stood in the barn doorway. The scent of freshly cut pine lingered in the air. The light was dim inside, yet he could see that cans had been knocked over toward the back, on the left end of his work table. Something silver and mercurial shifted at the base of the cans. Bramble was sniffing at it, backing away. The silver arced and flicked and thudded softly against the wooden floor. Doug discerned a small round eye aimed at him. He reached for the light switch by the door and flicked it on. The single bulb revealed a space immaculately clean and ordered. Over by the paint cans there was a puddle of water and in the centre of that puddle lay a huge codfish that looked to be more than twenty pounds, its head practically as large as Doug's. Bramble stared at her master, wondering what might be done about it.

Doug, not trusting his eyes, approached the fish. Its mouth and gills spread and shut rhythmically, gasping for water. Its tail flicked once as Doug knelt down beside it. He glanced overhead and around the barn for a clue. Nothing. Everything in its place. Bramble inched nearer, dipping her pink nose toward the fish; it seemed entirely unharmed, fresh from the sea. Doug slid his hands under it and stood, the weight pressed against his belly. It was much lighter than it should be, considering its size. The fish needed to be gutted and then frozen. Doug headed toward the house with Bramble running and jumping beside him.

In the kitchen, Doug laid the cod in the sink, its head and tail curved up over the edges. He opened the cutlery drawer and extracted a thin filleting knife. The codfish, still full of life, jerked half out of the sink. Doug made a snatch for it, but it slid from his hands and off the counter. Thudding to the linoleum, the fish flapped violently, spasmodically, in a way that Doug had never seen before — never such force or frantic behaviour. Doug jutted back as the fish convulsed toward his shoe. A bark came from Bramble as she crouched, shuffled in reverse, and barked again.

"What the Christ?" Doug muttered in awe.

The fish tossed itself against the bottom cupboard doors, smacking wood against wood. Its tail slapped Doug's leg with such vengance that he jerked back out of the kitchen. The fish arced its body and held it curved in a U before snapping in the opposite direction and flicking itself high into the air. Booming to the floor, the fish arced again and sprang higher, at least four feet off the ground. Doug glanced out into the hallway. This was his house all right. He seemed to be awake. A thundering boom shook the floor beneath his feet and drew his eyes into the kitchen.

The codfish was still. Scarlet red oozed from its mouth, pooling darkly on the linoleum, sheening wetly toward Bramble's paws.

Doug rushed the fish and, grunting, stuck his fingers through its gills, and raised it to the counter. Immediately, he stabbed the tip of the blade into the soft belly before the fish had another chance to carry on with its shenanigans. Piercing the flesh, he noticed how smoothly the blade went in. He caught a whiff of roses and he wheeled around looking for its source. For some reason, he suspected his wife, Emily, was present. No, she wasn't there. She had been dead for more than twenty years. The perfume sent shivers up his spine; it seemed to be the exact scent that Emily had worn. Bramble appeared to notice too, for she sat and whined, watching the air above her. A moment later, she stood and wandered down the hallway. No, Doug would not follow after her. How could he? Nonsense. He reset his attention on the knife in the fish's belly and drew it fully toward the tail. It slid effortlessly, as if through butter. No slosh of entrails. He peeled back the two sliced edges and caught the full scent of the perfume. Flower petals of every conceivable shape and colour were stuffed within the fish: purples with yellow centres, reds spotted with dusty orange, greens trimmed with black edges … And the scent. It was glorious, enrapturing to such a degree that it sent him into fits of moaning pleasure.

Doug stood in silence, suddenly realizing the profane sounds that had come from him, his brow gradually lining with confusion, his cheeks flushing with embarrassment. Two white paws slapped the edge of the counter as Bramble rose to sniff at the codfish.

"Where's the sense in this, Bramble?" Doug muttered, numbly shaking his head. He poked two fingers into the slit, felt around the silky petals and pulled out a baby-blue flower between two fingertips. The colour was the exact shade of the dress his wife had been buried in.

"Emily," he whispered, twirling the bent flower. The warm fullness of a tear rose in each eye, blurring the spectacle before him.

Doctor Thompson spotted the police cruiser parked lengthways across the road by the wharf, blocking the inquisitive from venturing beyond. Two army jeeps were pulled to the side of the road farther ahead. Yellow police tape had been strung in place between two wooden makeshift posts, and two additional police cruisers were glaringly present. One was parked on a slant in the road with its blue and red lights flashing. A soldier stood behind the strip of yellow tape, watching an RCMP officer wave his hand in circles, beckoning cars to turn around. The third police cruiser was parked on the opposite side of the road, making it impossible to pass at that point as well. What was the army doing here? In the back of his mind, Thompson tried to coax out the emergency response measures he had studied in medical school. The specifics were fuzzy, yet he recalled something about the army being summoned should the general population be at threat. When the ambulance Thompson was riding in reached the officer directing traffic, the attendant rolled down his window to state that he had a doctor on board who had been contacted by Sergeant Chase. The police officer spoke into his wire-microphone and glanced at a nearby soldier, who gave the slightest nod, then waved the ambulance over to a clear spot of gravel beside a forensic van.

"Thanks," Thompson said to the attendant.

"No problem. I'll be needed here soon, anyway."

Thompson lifted his black bag from his lap, and climbed out of the ambulance, biting down on the tweak of pain from his ankle and hoping his bowels would behave themselves. Where was the nearest washroom, he wondered, scanning the houses across the road while he limped ahead. People stood in their windows, eyes trained on the curiosity. A crowd of residents had gathered in front of the police tape and spoke in quiet respectful voices to one another. The mood was grimmer than Thompson recalled from the albino shark. People had been delightfully intrigued about the discovery of the shark. But this was different. This was a human body.

The soldier at the barricade briefly questioned Thompson and then permitted him access beyond the tape, where a young photographer in green army fatigues was packing away his equipment in a shoulder bag.

Sergeant Chase was speaking with a soldier in his early fifties whose face appeared etched out of granite by six haphazard strokes. No doubt an officer, thought Thompson. The officer was wearing a black earpiece and a thin wire-microphone. He steadily scanned up and down the road, listening intently and nodding. Chase raised his arm and swept it out over the ocean. The officer stared toward the water, squinting. There didn't seem to be any end to Chase's explanation. When Thompson was ten feet away, Chase caught sight of the doctor and excused himself from the officer's company.

"What's going on?" Thompson asked, his eyes taking in a rectangular arrangement of khaki green curtains hung on metal rods around a spot in the centre of the road. Thompson assumed the tall screen was set up to conceal the deceased. What was the body doing there? Had it been struck by a vehicle?

"Body," Chase said, his eyes flickering with interest. "Drowned."

"How'd it get there?"

"Not certain. An old man, a witness, said it was flung there."

"You mentioned that — flung."

Chase pointed toward the water and made an arc in the sky toward the place where the concealed body now rested.

Thompson gripped the handle of his bag tighter. "Drowned?"

"Yeah, but that's not it."

"What then? Flung? How was it flung?"

Chase gave no reply as he led Thompson nearer the curtained rectangle. The officer held back one of the curtains. The doctor entered and bent to the body, which was laid out on the asphalt. The man was not blue, bloated and with skin clumped away from its bones, as Thompson had expected, but had pale unwrinkled skin. Thompson touched the man's throat just to be certain. Cold and no pulse. The drowned man was dressed in thick garments that sparked curiosity in Thompson's mind. The body looked like an actor commissioned to portray a character in a period drama. An actor or a man outfitted in expensive costume for Halloween.

"There shouldn't be anything left of him," Chase commented.

"Why's that?" Thompson asked. Standing, he faced Chase, who was still holding open the curtain, seemingly unwilling to enter the confines of the space. Beyond Chase, the army officer was speaking with a young soldier who was relaying information from a clipboard.

Sergeant Chase stared down at the body. "Look at the way he's dressed."

"Yes." Thompson took note of the clothes: thick corduroy overcoat with fur collar, knitted grey woollen sweater, heavy black pants tied with a belt of rough rope, and boots made of some sort of animal hide. Thompson suspected sealskin.

"It's an old body," Chase stated.

"How would you know that?" Thompson regarded the police officer, wondering if this might be a joke. "That's impossible. It must be someone dressed up."

Chase shook his head, smiling as if it might be a joke after all.

"What?"

As if taking his cue, the army officer stepped in beside Chase and extended his hand. "Dr. Thompson?"

"Yes." Thompson almost winced at the man's crushing grip. The bones in his hands were paining him of late. Perhaps he was developing arthritis there as well. Time for another X-ray.

"I'm Major Rumsey. I'm the commanding officer here for army and navy."

"Pleased to meet you." Thompson recognized the name Rumsey. It was the one that had been given over the ambulance radio as they were transporting Darry Pottle to the hospital. He noticed that Rumsey's free hand was clutching a zip-lock Baggie. In it, there was a small leather-bound book with embossed lettering on the cover. The cover was worn and the pages deeply yellowed.

Rumsey held Thompson's hand for a longer time than Thompson thought necessary before finally releasing it. A cool breeze had just come up, off the water. It rattled the metal curtain rings against their poles. "We understand you're familiar with most of the residents in the community. You've lived here for twenty-three years. Is that correct?"

"Yes. I'm one of the doctors —"

"Exactly." The officer cut Thompson short. "So, we'd appreciate your help in identification."

"I don't recognize …" Thompson found his eyes drawn back to the body. "There's no way I would …"

"Through the others, elders. You're in their confidence. You might suggest they come forward and lend a hand. They might have snapshots or sketches of this individual."

"Yes, of course, I'll do what I can. But, you're assuming this body is … I mean, these period clothes are available now, in museums, theatres." Through the slit of the curtain, he noticed a boat calmly floating between the wharf and headland. There were two divers in the craft, using binoculars to scan the waters surrounding their vessel. From farther down the road came the sound of hammering. Sheets of plywood were being erected along the shoreline to keep people from visiting the beach. The construction of the barrier was making its way toward them. Soldiers hammering the framework in place. Again, Thompson glanced at the Baggie in Rumsey's hand. *What … am … I,* he thought.

The major stepped nearer and the breeze swelled to mild wind. Holding the Baggie up, he regarded it and lowered his voice to a confidential hush: "This journal was found on the body. It authenticates the period of death. Mid-1700s."

Thompson chuckled despite himself. "That's not possible. That's just a book. A museum could have it just as easily as the clothes. They're always staging these historical pieces about Newfoundland."

Chase stepped nearer, allowing the curtain to fall shut behind him, so that the three men formed a tight triangle. He said, "It tells a fascinating tale of a many-headed sea creature that was trailing their boat for three days. I read it before Major Rumsey arrived on the scene."

"He's an actor," Thompson professed, staring down at the body with the vague humour of disbelief in his eyes. "Isn't he?"

Chase continued with his explanation as Major Rumsey attentively looked on. "Seems the creature destroyed their ship. Last entry — 1746."

"This is ludicrous," Thompson said, compelled to bend near the drowned man and place two fingertips to the corpse's throat again. Still cold. Still no pulse. "He hasn't been dead that long," Thompson muttered, glancing back up at Rumsey and Chase who watched him without further comment. "How could you possibly believe …"

Major Rumsey coughed to clear his throat. He reached for his belt and shut off the power pack for his wireless headset.

"There are others," the major claimed. He turned his granite head to stare toward the fish plant across the harbour. "Over there on ice."

~⟢

Kim was in a such state of agitation that she was out the door before she even knew what she was doing. The wind was rising. It cooled the burning in her cheeks.

Up ahead, there was another commotion at the wharf, plenty of police and army, too. They had already taken the shark away. Earlier, Kim had heard the truck rumble past Miss Laracy's window and had stood behind the glass to investigate. Had there been another fantastic discovery? She paused at the edge of the yard to search through her purse for her keys, but could not find them. When she shook her purse, it gave up no metallic jangle. She must have left them in her car where it was parked, down nearer the wharf. Compelled to glance back at the doorway, she saw Miss Laracy standing there with the cordless phone to her ear, calling out and pointing toward the wharf, "Dere's a body been flung onto da lower road."

Just then a gust of wind came up and snatched Kim's scarf, which was loosely tied around her neck. The silky material was carried off on an uplift of air, toward a tree where it lodged itself in high pointy branches. Kim had no time to chase after it. It was a gift from Joseph, and right now she hated him.

The old woman called out: "Carry yerself back 'ere, in case dere be any affliction."

Kim waved, "Thank you!" and hastened along the road to where she had parked her car. There was a string of yellow police tape across the street. Five or six faces from the crowd turned to watch her as she opened her car door. She leaned in, her hands pressed against the driver's seat, relieved to see the keys dangling in the ignition. Yet her relief was short-lived; a cutting pain pried itself into the space above and behind her eyes, making her cringe and squint fiercely. Migraine. She hadn't had one in years. How long would it last? God! It was crippling. She managed to slide into the car and pull in her feet, but barely had the strength to shut the door. If she stayed there long enough, with her eyes jammed shut and her forehead against the steering wheel, she was certain to be approached and investigated, perhaps sent back to St. John's or to a hospital.

Her fingers fumbled for the keys. Finding them, she engaged the engine. She backed away slowly, then curved into a patch of gravel to turn around. The higher road was thirty feet ahead. When she reached it, she veered left, then straightened, rising on a slight grade toward a church steeple poking out above the evergreens in the distance. The light from the setting sun in Kim's eyes was hurting her head more than she imagined possible. The pain intensified as she ascended the road, her stomach churning with nausea. She thought she might vomit as she caught sight of the solar house and then the blue house that the soldier and Miss Laracy had both called the "old Critch house." She spotted Joseph's car and the pain gouged deeper, cleaving down the centre of her head, jamming her eyes shut. She began seeing double, images shifting over one another. She could not stop now. Could not let Joseph see her this way. She would seem frail, incompetent, needy. Easing up on the accelerator, she drove past the house, kept going until the pavement turned to gravel and she could no longer bear the pain.

A graveyard was twenty feet ahead. *How appropriate*, she thought. She parked abruptly with the nose of her car pointing toward the chain-link fence, then shut off the motor and sat perfectly still. The pain was so excruciating, the acute whiteness so glaringly unsteady behind her shut eyes, she feared she would lose consciousness at any moment.

⬷

As Thompson stood on the road staring at the body, a call sounded from toward the shoreline.

Dr. Thompson, Sergeant Chase and Major Rumsey turned in unison. A soldier, down on the grey rocks, waved his arms in the air and pointed at the beach. It appeared as if something had washed up, something soaked through its clothing and roughly the size of a man.

The crowd of onlookers all stared in that direction, the chatter increasing a few decibels.

Major Rumsey sighed. "Doesn't that man have a wireless?"

Thompson noticed the major check the button on his power pack and press the switch, unwilling to admit by gesture or word that his headset had been shut off.

Dr. Thompson mumbled, "God Almighty," under his breath as Sergeant Chase nodded his head, seemingly baffled by the prospect of yet another drowning victim.

The echoes of hammering ricocheted in the air. Farther up the beach, three more soldiers had joined the effort. The plywood barrier was quickly working its way nearer.

⟿

A gust of wind dislodged Kim's scarf from the upper branches of the maple tree in Tommy Quilty's front yard. The scarf drifted skyward, then hung slackly, suspended in the air, high above Tommy. He stood watching down the road where soldiers were stationed beside an orange barrier by the community centre.

The gust of wind held still as the scarf lingered motionless. A seagull flapped nearby, circling to investigate the article. The gust expanded like a pulse of breath, held again, then released. The scarf wafted lower, the silky material forming valleys and hills and creases as it drifted down toward Tommy Quilty. He had opened his notebook to study a drawing of a man who might have been himself with a seagull sailing above him. Prompted to look skyward, he tilted back his head and the scarf settled gently on his face. Form-fitted.

Tommy Quilty remained in that position so as not to disturb the cool thrilling sensation of the silk against his skin. The perfume on the scarf conjured an image of a lovely woman with dark hair. She was arguing with someone but that only made her beauty more fierce. He felt the sense-lessness of the argument. A second image appeared to him: Miss Laracy standing in her doorway waving at the woman. Now Tommy knew where he might find the woman who had lost the scarf. Miss Laracy was his dearest friend and he would pay her a visit. He kept his head tilted back, breathing through the silk, drawing in all that lovely perfume. His lungs couldn't help but shudder with a laugh, and then shudder again. Soon, he had to snatch the scarf from his face while he sputtered and pawed at his tickled lips.

~⟋⟍~

The full ferocity of the migraine had locked on Kim's brain, making her disoriented and sick to her stomach. Blinking hurt her eyes. She was seeing double again, ghost images of everything, the graveyard fence, the tombstones, the white church. Three other times she had experienced migraines, and on each occasion they had knocked her on her back for an entire day. The only affliction that ever came close to matching the pain was a sinus infection that had troubled her two years ago. Light pained her. The slightest sound was unbearable. Movement hurt her faltering eyes.

Opening her purse with unsteady hands, she searched through the clutter for the bottle of ibuprofen, popped the cap and shook out three pills. Her hand was trembling noticeably. The pills would do no good. Regardless, she popped them into her mouth, wishing she had water; her throat was so dry she could scarcely pull together enough saliva to swallow. An acute energy, squatting in on her brain from all directions, forced her eyes shut.

The pain was just too much. She reached for the door handle, fumbled with and pulled the latch, then shoved open the door. The air that swamped the interior was sweet and welcome, cooling the sweat on her face.

Pale, flimsy, fading, she retched while leaning out the car. Another wave of nausea gripped her and she opened her mouth. Gagged. Nothing came. The pills were burning her throat. There was noise in her ears. The noise of suffering. A tingling white creeping in, compelling her thoughts to recede. She fell after them.

If I don't get out of the car, she reasoned, *I'm going to faint. I need air.* The notion grew powerless, more removed from conscious thought. She shifted her legs out and set her feet against the gravel parking lot. Standing, she noticed the open graveyard gate just ahead. A place to sit. There was grass in there. She walked for the gate, hoping that movement might save her. The sparkling whiteness that had been sweeping in cleared somewhat. She grabbed hold of the steel gatepost and shut her eyes, held on.

When she opened her eyes to face daylight again, the tingling whiteness not only remained but a buzzing mounted in her ears. Just move, she told herself, circulate. She took three steps into the graveyard. A row of gravestones just ahead. Focus. Try to see the names. The one that first caught her attention was Newell, the next one Bishop. The third one — Blackwood. The strength in her limbs let go. Tumbling forward, she dropped in a rush and, with a sharp thud, soundly whacked her head against the edge of Emily Blackwood's gravestone.

⁓◑

Joseph stood in the parlour window watching for Kim. The sight of the ocean, off in the distance, was causing him distress. It seemed there were boats on the water, navy divers, groups of people on the wharf, army, police, old and young sightseers. It also appeared as if bodies were floating to the ocean surface. Would the bodies speak of him in an ill manner, claiming he had already laid eyes upon them and was keeping their existence a secret?

Joseph checked his watch. Numbers built to be arranged in some sort of strategic order. They were all about planning something. After a few minutes of ardent calculation, he determined that fifteen minutes had passed since Kim's telephone call. A car had driven by that resembled Kim's. In fact, the woman at the wheel bore a startling resemblance to Kim. Robin had even wanted to run out and chase after the car, but Joseph had stopped her. It wasn't safe outside. Don't take yourself into the outside and don't let the outside in until you recognize it as something inherently connected to you. And, of course, there was always the possibility that what was coming in from the outside, what you thought you recognized as something that was attached somehow to your life, was actually a forgery of feeling. A pretender. Kim. What did she really look like, Joseph wondered. The woman at the wheel of the car. A commendable impersonation. Would he even recognize Kim? And if he did recognize her, what exactly would that prove? Did he know her at all any more, other than as a target?

"What did Mommy say on the phone?" he asked Robin, who had abandoned her habitual drawing to play with a brown-haired action figure on the parlour carpet behind Joseph.

Robin shrugged. "Not much."

"You were talking to her."

Robin laughed, "Yeah. She just went by in the car. She must be turning around. You said that."

"Just a while ago."

Robin shook her head and rose to her feet, gripping the action figure by the hair; the action figure hanging by the hair, suspended. Not a scream out of her. She watched Joseph. Both of them did, the action figure and Robin, before they turned away as if to leave the room.

"Why don't you get a snack," he suggested, his nerves crackling, static in his eyeballs that must be dusted away. "You look hungry. Mommy'll be here soon."

"Can I have cereal?"

"Sure, anything. It's treat day. As long as it goes in your mouth."

"Yay!" Robin skipped from the parlour, down the hallway toward the kitchen, leaving Joseph to turn and face the window. He thought of a bowl filled with cereal and a glass of juice; how they might shatter and cut Robin if she should drop them. She might cut herself on the shards. He might cut himself before his daughter was cut, just to protect her, or harm her. Which was it? He nibbled on his bottom lip. A tiny piece of skin tore loose and he chewed it delicately between his upper and lower front teeth. *How horrible do I look?* he asked himself, rubbing a hand over the stubble on his chin. *Who do I resemble? What will Kim think when she sees me? Where is she? I was talking to her, or was that Claudia on the telephone? No, Claudia came to drop off a gift. She has big lips, sweet lips. Kim had thinner lips, but nice lips too. Where is Claudia now? Or are they one and the same? If they're fooling me,* he raged to himself. *If they're fooling me, so help me God, I'll kill them both.*

"Stop making so much noise," Joseph called back over his shoulder.

"I'm not doing anything," Robin said. Now she was standing beside him, watching the back of her right hand while she drew on it with her left. She spelled her name in blue ink: ROBIN.

"Did you get your snack?"

"I'm not hungry, Dad."

"You said you wanted …"

"What?"

"Nothing." He felt himself plunge another permeable layer deeper into himself, closer to his scalding core. When he looked at his daughter, he saw her as being too small. So much trouble from a little body. A face that held ghost traces of Kim. He clenched his fist and thought of striking her across the head for her devilish complicity in the semblance.

"Get out," he said.

Robin took one step back.

"Get out," he shouted, straining to hold himself in check, straining with such anxiety that he began trembling, convulsing. "Get out. Get out …"

-◊)

On Doug Blackwood's evening walks, he often traveled past the old church, reliving memories of his wedding and various funerals he had attended before the church was shut down six years back and the new one constructed closer to the harbour. Often he would stand contemplatively in the graveyard and study the names of the people he had known. Names etched in stone. Memories etched in a similar fashion. The names conjured up funeral wakes and parties that lasted well into the morning. Accordion and fiddle music and, later, with a group of the last hangers-on gathered in the smoky kitchen, the pure heartbreaking sounds of voices, unaccompanied by instrument, forlornly singing ballads they had learned from their mothers and fathers. "My Old Man," "Galway," "Bound Down For Newfoundland," "Fare Ye Well" … until there was not a dry eye in the place.

In the graveyard Doug would visit his wife's headstone last, desiring to linger over the honour of her memory the longest. Emily. Dead from breast cancer twenty years ago. The doctors could do less for a woman back then. They could have probably saved her life now. A waste of the finest woman who ever lived.

Doug was treading up the slope of Codger's Lane when he noticed Bramble running ahead. From his position he could see the tip of the church tower with its missing tiles. Further up, as the slope began to level off, the church roof came into view and then the church itself. He was heading for the graveyard's chain-link gate when he spotted a white car parked at a peculiar angle, the driver's door wide open. No one around. He checked toward the graveyard. People often parked in the lot while tending to relatives' graves. It was then that he saw the body, right there beside his Emily's headstone.

"Mother of God!" Doug hurried his pace in through the gate. Bramble had already arrived by the woman's side and stood waiting, her tongue hanging out while she watched her master's approach.

Nearing the body, Doug saw that it was a woman lying on her side, and bent to her. His own heartbeat had increased twofold and he reached to check the woman's, but decided his hand had no place there and tried her nose instead. He set his palm in front of her nostrils and, feeling a puff of warm breath, went to lift her head. There was a cut on her forehead, near her temple. It was trickling blood. A bad spot to be injured. She's breathing though, he assured himself, pulling his handkerchief from his back pocket and pressing it to the woman's cut.

Standing, he glanced down the upper road. No sign of a car. He bent again, not knowing if he should move her. He checked the cut. It was still bleeding. Bramble started licking the woman's face and Doug swatted her away, "Get out of that!" He flicked his fingers at the woman's cheek, patted it, faster, more desperately. "Hey?"

The woman made no movement. Bramble stuck her head in to lick the woman's face again and Doug nudged the dog aside with his knee. "Bramble! G'wan, get your filthy gob away." The dog backed up and whined.

"Missus?" Doug tapped her face harder and her eyelids flinched in unison. "That's it." He smiled, nodding to himself. He shouted, "Missus. Hey, missus." And tapped her face harder so that she flinched more dramatically and her eyelids fluttered open and shut. "That's it."

The woman made a low groggy sound as she attempted to move her head. This movement seemed to pain her fiercely. Her lips parted stickily, emitting a moaning breath through both lips and nostrils: "Uuunnhh." She stared vacantly at Doug. "Wh … ere?" she asked, sputtering as Bramble wetly licked her face again. "Where … am … I?"

"Bareneed." Doug said matter-of-factly. He glanced back toward the woman's car, thinking she might have a cellphone in there. "Stay right where you're at. Don't move." He headed for the car while Bramble sat in wait.

Leaning in the driver's side, his eyes caught sight of the parking permit photo ID hanging from the rearview on a loop of string. He reached for the ID, read the name.

"Christ!" Doug gasped. "'Tis yet *another* Blackwood."

-◀))

From her studio window, Claudia watched a woman being aided into the Critch house by an elderly man. Claudia thought the man might be Doug Blackwood. The woman had shoulder-length brown hair and appeared, from a distance, to be exceptionally attractive. This distressed Claudia, for she had begun to believe that there was hope for her family. She and Joseph and Robin and Jessica. The girls were already playing together. Friends. In time, they might be like sisters to one another.

Claudia knew Doug Blackwood from the community; his front yard was littered with folk art. Years ago, one of Claudia's artist friends, on a visit out from St. John's and having seen Doug Blackwood tending to an item in his yard, had marvelled at the texture of the old man's rugged face and had wanted to photograph him. But Doug Blackwood, in a fit of suspicion, would have no part of it.

Turning toward the miniature village on her desk, Claudia saw that it was nearing completion. The houses and people were lit by candlelight. Quaint and cozy. How long had she been sculpting the scene, she wondered. It seemed like years.

"Who's that, Mommy?" Jessica asked, toying with one of the small pottery figures of a man, newly formed and still moist. The child then shifted a finished yellow house to a different angle and lifted the roof to peek inside.

"I don't know," Claudia quietly replied. Listlessly, she gazed at her daughter.

"That's too bad," sighed Jessica, replacing the roof.

"What is?"

"It's Joseph's wife, isn't it, and that's too bad." She picked up a glazed figure of a woman, turned her around to face the ocean, then set her down again.

"For who?"

"I don't know … Are you still going to hurt him?"

"I don't want to hurt anyone —"

"Daddy says you are, because of what happened to us, to me. It was Joseph's fault." Jessica slid a miniature cow nearer a horse.

"Not his fault, Jessica."

"If it wasn't for —"

"Joseph's only a man. Even in death, your father won't accept …"

Jessica watched the pottery houses and people for a few moments longer, then regarded Claudia. "Daddy says you're going to kill Joseph anyway and I'm going to kill Robin."

"Don't talk like that," Claudia said shortly, troubled by the open spite she felt toward her daughter. This wasn't her daughter. It couldn't be. Jessica was changed, a mixture of her true self and other elements. Unsavoury elements. A corruption.

"If I kill Robin, then she can be my friend always. And Joseph can be your friend when you're dead."

"Stop talking like that, Jessica. Please, stop."

"It only hurts a little while and then it's nothing but a nice feeling, like you're floating all the time, lifting up, but staying in the same place. It's okay."

With numb wonder, Claudia studied her daughter. She felt herself smiling distantly. "You're so clear," she said, her voice choking with anguish, "in the night."

"Once upon a time, it was only the sun blocking spirits from coming here. Daylight. But now it's different, even worse."

"Worse?"

"The wirewaves. They're going through your head right now, millions of them. Not as many at night, though."

"I can't feel anything."

"You just don't know it. The water in your body moves the wirewaves all through you. The wirewaves make you sick. They make you feel like you're never at peace, don't belong, and you never know why."

"Do they hurt you, too?"

Jessica nodded. "I'm just energy, Mommy. And what's in the wirewaves changes me." She paused as her voice turned wet with emotion. "That's why sometimes you don't even know me."

"I know you, Jessie"

"No. Everything's going through me. People talking, all these people talking and channels, billions of channels, radio and TV. The noise!" She pressed her hands over her ears. "I can't be your daughter," she shouted. "Not down here."

Newly preoccupied, Claudia stared toward the Critch house.

"You can't be a family again," Jessica whispered, reading her mother's intentions. "Not this way. You should die, Mommy?"

A lamentful silence passed before Claudia, regarding her daughter, spoke again: "I think I should."

"It has to be soon. I know it does. That's why you can see me. A part of your body's dead already. A hole that must be filled. I can fit in there. It's easier to get in. But more of your body needs to be dead for us to be the same."

"I know," Claudia mourned, shifting her dry eyes toward the window. The Critch house. Windows alight. A family inside with the darkness kept at bay beyond the walls. A family that was once apart, now reunited, made stronger.

⸺◊⸺

The body on the beach appeared to be from the 1940s: a woman wearing a velvet and chiffon evening gown with one matching elbow-length glove, the other missing. A soaked marten stole was wrapped around her throat like an ugly drowned thing, barely recognizable. The woman's feet were bare and her hair was clipped short. The manner in which the body lay there in the quickening dusk was sinister. She might have been something out of a gangster film, dumped on the beach as a warning.

The soldiers and police officers, gathered in a half-circle, stared down and exchanged a few words. Dr. Thompson felt the surreal pull of the scene and wondered if he might be lodged in a bizarre dream powered by a late-night snack of brie cheese or roast pork. He often had strange, intricate dreams when he ate pork after six o'clock in the evening. The sun was setting across the water to the west. Hammering ricocheted through the air. The barrier now being constructed almost directly behind them. Thompson secretly pinched the skin on the back of his left hand and felt the sharpness of the sting, the reality of it.

A garbled sound in the distance attracted Major Rumsey's attention. He spoke a few words into his wireless microphone and listened. For a moment there was no reaction and then he shut his eyes as if relenting. The sound resembled a lawnmower slowing to a stuttering percussive wharp. Because of the contours of the land enclosing the community, the sound appeared to be coming from all directions at once, bouncing off the rocky hills to either side. The noise grew louder as those gathered on the beach stared toward the headland across the harbour. A large orange helicopter rose from behind the enormous formation; it was coming from the new military base in Cutland Junction.

The gathered people on the beach, wharf and road all watched as the helicopter approached and hovered over the wharf. A rope was dropped and a soldier in navy-blue fatigues and helmet shimmied down, letting himself fall the remaining four feet to the wharf. At once he was giving directions to a young soldier and police officer on the scene. The soldier with the helmet, obviously a high-ranking officer, pointed toward the road. The police officer, a high-ranking officer of his own order, pointed toward the beach where Dr. Thompson and the others stood. The helmeted soldier pointed to the road again, this time more adamantly. The police officer, seeming to yield, went toward the road and instructed a female police officer to stop traffic while the soldier looked out toward the water then shifted his attention to the draped enclosure that concealed the body.

The noise from the chopper made it impossible for Dr. Thompson or Sergeant Chase to pass comment. Chase shrugged when Thompson raised his eyebrows in speculation.

When the traffic was cleared back, the rope dangling from the helicopter was retracted and, in a slow hover, the chopper inclined toward the road where it mechanically lowered itself, kicking up dust and gravel and blowing the enclosure's green curtains until it finally rested on the asphalt.

The chopping sound of the rotors soon diminished to a whipping-whoosh and then the blades of the rotors became more obvious and soon stopped completely. The whining engine was shut off.

Dr. Thompson turned to Major Rumsey for reaction.

"That'll be Lieutenant-Commander French," said the major. "Navy specialist." He watched French with a look of reverence and vague trepidation. "They've called in French," he muttered, sighing with open concern.

They all stared toward the wharf as Lieutenant-Commander French pulled off his helmet. No one noticed the third body popping up from under the water farther out in the harbour, a diving mask fastened to its face, rusty oxygen tanks strapped to its back.

SUNDAY NIGHT

The wharf was lit up like daylight. Two helicopters hung over the harbour and searchlights swept the black water. Three small navy boats patrolled the area while a fourth larger boat was anchored further out in the harbour. Doug Blackwood watched one of the boats flip up, hang in a vertical position for a moment, then tip over and smack the water upside-down. Something had struck it from beneath the surface.

"Did you see that?" Robin asked in astonishment, standing beside Doug at her father's bedroom window. They had been in Robin's room at first, but had moved next door for a better view of the commotion.

"Probably a whale," Doug ventured. He watched a helicopter descend, the violent wind from its blades rippling the surface. A harness on a rope was tossed out and one of the soldiers from the capsized boat rose from the ocean. "The whales are in feeding on the caplin," he explained, regarding Robin. "Tons of 'em in here spawning."

"What's spawning?"

"Laying eggs."

"Can we go see them tomorrow?"

"Proper thing." Doug winked. He glanced back toward the harbour as another helicopter descended to retrieve a bundle floating in the ocean. The helicopter then tilted off toward the fish plant across the harbour at the base of the headland, where it lowered and settled into the parking lot — a makeshift landing pad.

Working amid the noise and light of the helicopters, the remaining two small boats diligently approached the objects that resurfaced, and pulled them aboard. One of the boats started away from the activity, steering toward the fish plant, but was soon batted out of the water by the giant black glint of a tail.

"Wow!" Robin cried. "Did you see that?"

"Yes," Doug said, glumly.

"What was that?"

"Don't know," Doug bluntly replied, fearing that he did know exactly what was happening. Bodies rising from their watery graves. The sea giving up her dead. And the whales trying to prevent the bodies from being taken. Why? And what of the mermaid he had witnessed? He looked at his great-niece's face, the pure skin, the expression of wonder, and felt close to her, although he had met her for the first time only a few hours ago. A kindred spirit, linked to him through a duplication of sensibilies, despite the distance of years. He felt comfortable in her presence.

As if sensing his thoughts, Robin gazed up at him and smiled. "This is really exciting." She heard adult voices from the room down the hall, and her smile turned to concern.

"Your mom'll be the finest kind soon," Doug said. "Just a little bump on the head."

"The finest kind?"

"Good as new. Fit as a fiddle. Right as rain. All better."

"I know."

"A bump on the head. Nothing to it."

"I had a bump on my head, too." Robin turned to show him, lifted her hair so that Doug could see the small bluish-purple marking. "See. Me and Mom are twins now. Don't touch. It hurts."

"I won't." He felt a stirring in his heart and said: "Bless your cotton socks." She was a sweet child, not one of those spoiled brats, saucy as dogs, he often saw out in the world, whiny brats who wanted everything they set their eyes on and had no respect for their elders. Robin was mannerly and tender-hearted. He had to restrain himself from hugging her. Instead, he turned to face the window. "This place is becoming right famous," he muttered, glancing farther west.

Up the road, about two hundred feet along, a glowing line of headlights wound back toward Shearstown Line. Floodlights glowed in Mercer's Field.

No doubt the media, reporting on the unfolding events, sucking every bit of tragedy out of the proceedings. He wondered how long they had been there in the field. From the rise of his own house, he could see no farther than Atkinson's wharf. And he'd rarely watched the television since Emily had passed on. Some of the vehicles were vans with spotlights aimed toward the harbour. A good few people were out on Mercer's Field, which had, it seemed, been transformed into a lookout point for curious specta- tors. "There's queer things afoot."

"Like what?"

"I saw something in my boat today." He lowered his voice to a mythical hush, paused for effect, then turned his head to regard her. "I don't know if I should be telling you."

Robin grinned, "Why not?"

"It was a magical bit of business."

Robin backed away and sat on the edge of her father's bed, her smile widening expectantly. Doug came away from the window. He tried to con- tain the tremblings of fear that menaced his heart, for he knew something unheard of was happening in Bareneed. Regardless, he wanted to give an impression of calm, if only for his grand-niece's sake. He wouldn't have her thinking he was a coward.

"What?" Robin begged.

"I don't know if I should be telling you or not. How are you at keeping secrets?"

"The best. Pleeeease, tell me." She twiddled her feet and clutched her hands together in a gesture of pleading.

Doug settled in the old wooden rocking chair in the corner. Sighing, he measured the space between himself and Robin, pausing as if to col- lect it all up and use it to effect in the dispatching of his tale. He set his hands on the armrests of the rocker, the wood smooth beneath his palms, rubbed by generations of hands, aged and young alike. Most of them related by blood.

Doug rocked the chair a few times, before saying: "I was taking the boat out to fish for some cod."

"You're not supposed to fish for cod."

Doug feigned shock. "No, really?" He stopped rocking and leaned forward, hands remaining on the armrests while he eyed Robin. "Who told you such foolishness?"

"My dad."

"Sure, he's no fisherman," he said dismissively, leaning back in his chair and rocking. "Not like me and my father —"

"He's better than a fisherman. He looks after the ocean."

"Who told you that?" Doug snapped. The rocking chair abruptly stilled.

"Dad did. That's the way he says he carries on the tradition or family stuff or something."

"Hmmm."

"He's trying to protect the fish."

"So, anyway," Doug continued, tilting the rocking chair into motion and gently leaning back his head to measure the tale. "I was sailing my vessel and the ocean was calm and beautiful blue. You remember today? Lovely day. Not a bit of a breeze and all."

"What'd you see?"

"Patience, my love, patience."

⁓◉⁓

Joseph listened to the radio in the kitchen. The radio had sensational news that both fascinated and angered him. The news was more astonishing than anything he had ever heard. Reports about bodies discovered in Bareneed harbour were being updated every fifteen minutes. There appeared to have been a nautical accident. A shipwreck or a plane crash, according to the news. At this point, they could not confirm the exact nature of the tragedy. He had been right about the bodies in the water. No one knew exactly how many had been retrieved but they guessed at least nine at this point. The on-scene reporter spoke with urgency, almost nervousness. Even the reporters were uneasy, not an encouraging sign. Regardless, Joseph felt vindicated, stronger, meaner. He was right. Right about everything. What could make him more right than believing something to be a hallucination and then having it turn real? Definitive exactness.

Between news reports, the radio played music that was so sugary it stuck to Joseph's teeth. He pulled back his gums and furiously wiped his teeth with his sleeve. The unexplained deaths on land, in the community of Bareneed, stood at three. Three was a hideously uneven number. He wanted more deaths, if only to even the digits. And the hospital was dealing with an outbreak of some sort of virus that interfered with people's breathing and resulted in an inexplicable form of amnesia. There were four new cases at the hospital. A special emergency ward had been established and respirators were being flown in from other areas of the province and country. The military had taken over the site and was supervising the fishing of bodies from the harbour.

"Sources close to the scene have confirmed that the bodies in Bareneed harbour appear to be from decades and even centuries ago. We have yet to verify the existence of a downed aircraft or sunken vessel."

Joseph sensed disbelief in the radio announcer's voice as she relayed the details. Joseph could practically feel her itching to crack some sort of weak-spined morning-show joke about the predicament, but she restrained herself, employing a tone she slid from the drawer labelled "tones of concern and decency." Joseph wanted to cheer her on, encourage her to crack those jokes. They would be hysterically funny at this point. He would openly guffaw, like a thick-headed moron.

"Only emergency vehicles are permitted to enter and leave the community until the source of the illness is determined."

Joseph stood before the kitchen sink, his face, pale and thin, reflected in the dark window. Focusing, he saw that his mouth was slightly open. He shut it. Sneered at himself. How he hated his reflection. It was never substantial enough. He despised it, and *it* he was.

Before he could stop himself, he had yanked the radio plug from the counter socket and then clutched the telephone receiver to strike himself on the head with it. The blow hurt more than he expected. He had already dialled Dr. Thompson's cellphone again, yet all he managed to get was a voice mailbox, not even a live operator any more, Thompson's voice informing callers that the line was engaged. Joseph wanted to ask about Kim. Robin. Himself. What would he ask the doctor? What could the doctor possibly do for him? What did a doctor do anyway? Nothing. Offer comfort. A blessing. Absolution of illness, shame and guilt. Pills. No doubt Thompson was implicated in issues relating to the outbreak of whatever it was that had gripped Bareneed. Whatever sort of drama. It was inconceivable. Joseph could not fathom the plot line.

He hung up the receiver, checked it for blood. There was none. He then stared at his feet. Kim was upstairs, lying down in the spare room. His Uncle Doug had brought her here, and now he was visiting with Robin. If only his Uncle Doug would leave.

Joseph was glad to have Kim near, but not under these circumstances. Under these circumstances, he wished that she were dead. Not only the house, but the community as well, was becoming a place of illness and contamination. He needed to hug Kim, hug Robin. Tightly. Hug them tighter and tighter until he strangled them into his body. The thought of it brought tears to his eyes. He wiped them away and caught his breath. It was all too overwhelming. Why did he feel as if everything was his fault? No, it was not he who thought that way, but them. He was bursting with excruciating love. He sobbed and caught himself, wiped away the tears once more, snatched at another breath. I'm getting sick, he thought. I *am* sick.

They are making me sick. They should all leave, but as of tonight the community was sealed off. There was a new virus. It was to be expected, with all the toxins in the air and being dumped in the water, all the screwing around that scientists were doing with nature. *They* were the ones who should die. He thought of Robin; the possibility that she might have contracted the supposed virus made his heart stop. Robin had been acting peculiar since their arrival at this cursed house, sinking deeper and deeper into the fantasy world of her drawings. The thought brought more tears to his eyes. He smeared them away with the butt of his hand and stepped out of the kitchen, blubbering like a baby. This house was a foreign space. A space not his own. Not his home.

He heard Robin's voice from above. There was so much grief in the world, too much grief to allow a gentle voice like that to survive. Wouldn't she be better off if she escaped the pain that would most assuredly find her, if she was prompted to drift away from the ugliness that the future held?

Joseph could hear Robin gasp in disbelief, "Not true."

"Yes," Doug replied adamantly. "True as I'm sitting here."

Uncle Doug, a colourful character. A fraud. He was just another man, full of criminal wants and evil thoughts. How could he possibly be any different?

Joseph crept along the hallway, gaining strength as he advanced. He reached the stairs and laid his hand upon the bannister, looked up toward the second storey. Should he check on Kim, make certain she was okay, numb and cold and dead, yet okay? Perhaps he could hold her hand, plead to resolve their differences. Smother her with a pillow. The time was right to end it, begin again. The time was now. Was she still angry with him? She had quite a temper, but it was no match for him now.

He raised his foot to the first stair just as he heard a loud knocking on the back door. Gasping, he wondered who it might be. Claudia? The pregnant Victorian whore. Wouldn't she have the sense not to come? She usually entered through the front door, as city people often did. It was the outport people who used the back doors as the main entry and exit point. Sneaky people, trying to get into your kitchen and see what you were cooking, stick their fingers in your pudding. Whoever was knocking on the back door was a resident of the community. Or someone coming to him in secrecy. The trollop. Claudia.

Spinning around, he headed toward the kitchen. As his eyes caught sight of the back door, the lights flickered once, twice, then went off. He stopped dead in his tracks.

"Perfect," he whispered, grinding his teeth. He rummaged through his pockets and lifted out the book of matches he had brought along for just such an eventuality. He tore off a match and scraped it against the flint strip, the yellow light glowing around his hand. A peaceful offering that, at once, eased his muscles and temper.

Out in the porch, the chill increased as Joseph neared the door. The knocking came again, this time lower, as if the knocker somehow sensed his approach. He watched his other hand rise into the arc of matchlight. It seemed as though the hand was not his at all, but something from a painting. He was suddenly stilled. Serenity permeated his body, a calm and composure that emanated from the simple flicker of that matchlight. His fingers were reaching forward, reaching and holding the knob, then carefully pulling open the inner door.

He started. The outer screen door was already held open, an old woman gripping it, an old woman he vaguely recognized, her wrinkled face framed by a wall of night blackness, staring up at him, wavering as the breeze tickled the flame.

Grinning, the old woman held the knot of her kerchief beneath her chin, smacked her toothless gums together and winked, raising up a beautiful silk scarf a moment before a breath of wind snatched the flame from the match.

"It be yer cherished wife's," said the voice through darkness.

～◍～

"It must be something in the water," Chase speculated, his gaze fixed on Dr. Thompson.

They were seated at one of the rectangular stackable tables in the community hall, which was in the midst of being transformed into an emergency base. There was constant noise as tables and chairs were dragged into place, the scraping sounds amplified in the long hollow room. The clamour made it difficult for Chase to concentrate.

"Something in the water all right," Thompson countered. "Bodies."

Along the far wall, soldiers were erecting partitions, metal rods, stands and khaki-green curtains, identical to the ones used to conceal the body on the road. That body had been taken to the fish plant. Chase assumed the partitions would act as makeshift offices. Toward the corner, a small room with wooden walls had already been built, no doubt the commanding officer's office. Two soldiers wheeled in a portable blackboard that must have been taken from an old school. Elementary math sums were still drawn in white chalk against black: $2 + 2 = 4$; $2 + 3 = 5$.

Chase was regarding the sums when the lights suddenly flickered off, and the emergency light toward the canteen window dimly glowed. The activity in the hall slowed to a standstill. Soon, the loud noise of an engine clamoured from outside the centre. Lights, brighter than those that had previously illuminated the hall, came on, and the commotion was reengaged.

"Lights out," said Chase, slightly perturbed, and squinting in the brilliance. "Lights on."

"They've got generators, it seems. I guess they're needed for their high-tech equipment." Thompson nodded toward the blackboard.

"They probably have a few computers too. Just a guess, though." Chase flipped open his notebook and studied the names he had written there, the names of the dead and the names of the people who were confined to hospital. What stuck in his mind was one fact: the patients had all become violent prior to the onset of illness.

"Why would these people turn violent?"

"Brain tumours. Cancer can be a personality modifier, but we found no tumours of any sort in the corpses or patients. Brain chemistry change, or some sort of swelling on the brain stem."

"Bodies drowned," said Chase. "Bodies floating. Swelling."

"Something in the water," Thompson said. "I keep thinking about that albino shark." The doctor shuddered, then sneezed loudly. "It's chilly in here."

"Not really."

"I must be coming down with something."

The doctor's words reminded Chase of his wife, Theresa. Coming down with something. What a strange expression. News of the bodies and a suspected virus had already reached Theresa. Earlier that evening, when Chase's first shift had ended, he had gone home in his uniform. He hadn't even bothered to change, knowing that he would be called back shortly. In a state of deep-seated unrest, he had walked in on Theresa lying on the couch, following the crisis on television. Seeing her on the couch in her bathrobe made his heart plunge and his stomach knot with despair.

"What're you watching?" he had asked. She had merely looked at him with a dullness in her eyes.

"Bodies," she had said. "They've come here now, Brian."

"And what about the red sculpin you mentioned?" Thompson was asking.

Chase drew his attention back to the doctor. "And the albino shark. Both of them with heads in their mouths. A doll's and a man's."

Chase stared at the list in his notebook, trying to focus. The noise was really getting to him. He took a careful sip from his coffee and grimaced. "This was bad enough when it was warm," he joked, smiling feebly. He noticed Thompson's eyes on his list, and so he turned the notebook around for the doctor to glean a better view. Chase glanced over the names. "Male and female."

"Right."

"Young and old."

"Right."

"Live in the same area, everyone from this community."

Thompson nodded, his eyes shifting toward the canteen.

Following the doctor's gaze, Chase saw a table with sandwiches laid out. They had been delivered by some of the ladies in the community. There were also cookies and gooey treats on platters covered in plastic. Chase wondered why the food had been displayed like that, considering the threat to the community. If this was, in fact, a virus, mightn't the food have been contaminated by the people who made it?

"Hungry?" Chase asked.

"Starved."

"Grab a sandwich."

"No, I'm not that hungry. God only knows how long they've been sitting there." Thompson pointed at his belly. "I've already got problems down there."

"I was thinking …" Chase glanced toward the blackboard, where Lieutenant-Commander French spoke with an anxious young soldier. The lieutenant-commander, a man of average height, neither slim nor stout, and with average looks, turned in their direction and the young soldier immediately looked their way as well.

"Thinking what?" Thompson asked.

"If this is something contagious," Chase said, refocusing on the doctor, "would they have laid out that food from the ladies auxiliary?" He peeked over his shoulder at Lieutenant-Commander French, who now stood facing the blackboard, reading the sums over. The young soldier was heading in their direction.

Chase said to Thompson: "Contamination from a common place of gathering. One place."

"Where they might've all been at once?"

"Yeah. Let's start with church." Chase placed his fingertip beside the first name and spoke it.

"Anglican," Thompson affirmed. "And the next one's Roman Catholic."

Bodies, Chase thought. Theresa's words: *They've come here now.* His eyes checked toward the young soldier, who stood beside him with his hands behind his back.

"I'm just observing," said the soldier. "Name's Able Seaman Nesbitt, sir."

"Why don't you pull up a chair?" Thompson suggested, nudging the metal leg of a chair with his foot.

"I'd rather stand, sir." Nesbitt licked his lips, glanced warily around the room. "Thank you."

"Bad for the back," Thompson chided. "You'll tire your muscles."

Nesbitt gave no reply. He merely fixed his eyes on the names in the book.

Chase studied the names as well. He addressed Thompson: "So, it's not church. How about work?" Chase slid a pen from his shirt pocket and clicked down the tip. "Donna Drover?"

"Unemployed."

Chase wrote "unemployed" beside Donna's Drover's name.

"Muss Drover?"

"Unemployed."

"Lloyd Fowler?"

"Unemployed."

They continued down the list to discover that all of the dead or suffering were unemployed.

"No common workplace," Thompson observed.

"But they were all unemployed."

"What were their previous occupations?" interjected Nesbitt.

"They were, let's see …" Thompson wondered, studying the list. "Donna fished; her son, too. Mr. Fowler was a fisherman. Darry … fisherman … Fisherman … fisherman … fisherman …"

"Fishermen," said Nesbitt, again licking his lips. He briskly raised his fingertips and brushed at a spot on his forehead, as if shooing away a fly.

"Well, not all men, I guess."

"Something in the water?" Chase suggested. "That they caught."

With this, Nesbitt turned and walked briskly toward Lieutenant-Commander French, who was erasing the math sums with vigorous elaborate sweeps of his arm. He listened to the young soldier, his face expressionless, then he snatched the stick of chalk from the narrow wooden ledge, tossed it up and caught it with his palm. He began writing large looping white letters that spelled: FISHERMEN. Underneath that, he wrote, in a flourish of smaller letters: Fishers of Men. With a whip of his arm, he underlined the words.

The actions of a swashbuckler, Chase thought. A sword-fighter ballerina. A pirate.

"Fishers of men," Thompson said quietly.

Chase turned to face the doctor. "What does that mean?"

Thompson shook his head, "Not a clue."

"Tommy Quilty used ta sell picture frames," Miss Laracy patiently explained. She had dragged a wooden chair in beside Kim's bed to keep vigil over the troubled soul. "'N religious pictures too. 'E weren't all dere." She tapped the side of her head with her wrinkled finger and glanced at the candle flame in the holder on the bedside table. "Some t'ought 'e were just stunned." She then turned to give notice to Joseph, who was seated in a wicker chair beside the bedroom doorway. The chair appeared to be too small for him. Joseph was staring directly at her, a smile ticking on his lips. He nodded and raised his eyebrows, winked, then wiped his palms on the legs of his trousers, gripping the material and pulling. He seemed to be having troubles with his face. One moment he was smiling, the next pursing his lips and opening his mouth wide, stretching his lips as if attempting to rid them of numbness. Observing Kim again, Miss Laracy lowered her voice. "Yer 'usband, 'e's a bit o' a queer stick."

Miss Laracy watched Kim's gaze shift toward Joseph and knew that she was deeply concerned for her husband. Regardless, Miss Laracy continued on with her tale: "Da fairies stole Tommy from 'is crib 'n put anudder back in place o' 'im, anudder widt a face only a mudder could love. Dere were dose who said 'is mudder took a scare when she were carryin' 'im. 'E were born widt a bloody-big birt'mark on his cheek. But when 'is mudder passed on, I seen ta 'im takin' da cure."

"The cure?" Kim asked, carefully turning on her side to better face Miss Laracy. She paused a moment as though in pain.

"I took 'im ta 'is dead mudder's bed 'n put 'er lifeless hand ta da birt'mark. Ye needs da touch o' da dead. 'N den, da birt'mark fades whilst da corpse rots in da grave. O'er time, da birt'mark shrunk smaller 'n smaller 'n smaller, den vanished." Miss Laracy pressed her lips tightly together, opened her eyes wide and held them that way, regarding Kim. "Da God-blest trute!"

Kim stirred slightly, her eyes shutting for a spell of time.

Miss Laracy leaned nearer, her voice a cryptic whisper. "Tommy see t'ings like me 'n me sister did. Dat white shark dey found. I seen dat 'fore swimin' in da ocean n' glowin' by night. Everyone knows dat. Like da fish tryin' ta fly. 'Twas only we before, we who were blest widt da sight, but now udders sees too. Da sight be giftin' everyone."

"Who's Tommy Quilty?" Joseph piped up from his chair near the door.

"'E discovered yer wife's scarf," said the old woman without bothering to turn. "'E say it floated ta 'im. Da wind lifted it from 'er 'n carried it ta 'im. Da one I brung back. But 'e also one o' 'em who seen da shark at night. 'E tol' me I were needed 'ere."

"Who else sees the shark?" Joseph asked, nibbling his lip. "All of you people?"

The old woman whirled about to size Joseph up and down, then returned her soft blue eyes to Kim's. She paused, searching through her thoughts. "Ones."

"Still alive?"

"Yays, still alive." On this, she spun bluntly toward him again, her arm hooked over the back of her chair, and said: "Once, I knew a skipper who hailed frum down in Burnt Head. 'E took sick 'n weary. 'E never felt like 'imself 'n narry could rest. At dat time I were noted fer me sight 'n da skipper paid me a visit. I soon learnt dat 'e were ill at ease. Frum da smell o' 'im I learned why." Miss Laracy fished her handkerchief from up her sleeve and blew her nose with determination. She folded the handkerchief, blew again, then lowered it, staring into the creases and folds. With a huff, she shoved the handkerchief up her sleeve and became more and more content, to the point of almost nodding off.

"What smell?" Joseph asked.

"Eh?" Miss Laracy raised her chin.

"The smell off him."

"Who?"

"The skipper."

"Yays. Da skipper." Newly invigorated, she continued on: "Da smell o' timbers. I could see lengths o' timbers curved like ribs 'n strapped by planks o' siding. I asked him: 'Ye be buildin' a sea vessel?' 'Yays,' was 'is reply. ''Tis almost done,' says 'e. I says: 'Ye be buildin' a coffin fer yerself.' Da skipper went white as a sheet 'n stood 'n left. 'E never drove anudder nail inta dat craft 'n 'e had no mind ta sell it. 'E let 'er rot where she be. Years wandered on 'n da craft rots until only da ribs remain 'n skipper salvages enough timber frum da hull ta build 'is coffin. 'E lay in it every night ta settle 'imself before settlin' in 'is feather bed. 'E wore out t'ree coffins before 'e gave 'is final wink. An old codger were 'e when he perished."

"You think the boat would have sunk?" murmured Kim.

Miss Laracy spun toward Kim, but then offered a gentle smile, and nodded kindly. "Oh, yays, me ducky. Sunk like a sack o' stones."

Kim smiled in return.

Joseph laughed.

Kim and Miss Laracy both studied him.

"I don't get it," he said.

"Ye," accused Miss Laracy, "what are ye buildin'?"

"I don't know … Courage?"

"Ye be buildin' no craft, 'n dat be da coffin ye are buildin'."

"She's gone off," said a deep voice from the doorway. Joseph flinched and

Kim gasped and Miss Laracy chuckled at Doug Blackwood standing there solid as a rock with a candle in his scarred and callused hand.

"Drifted off. Young one loves the stories."

Gazing up at his uncle, Joseph regarded the man's face.

Miss Laracy noted that Doug Blackwood's face was a strong one, lined by wind and weather, the etchings deepened by the angle of the candle-light held in his hand. She knew that Joseph felt weaker, paler in his uncle's presence. His suddenly shrivelling aura attested to that.

"How ya doing?" Doug asked Kim, shifting across the threshold. With candle in hand, he created large wavering shadows that fully occupied the room. Him and the shadows cast from his body.

"Better, thanks." Kim sat up straighter in the bed and tried a smile. "Bit light-headed, but okay. The pain's not so bad now."

"Get da girl a nice cuppa tea," Miss Laracy instructed Uncle Doug.

"No, thanks," Kim said.

"How about a snack?" Joseph piped in. "You need to eat something."

"No, my stomach's upset," she said coldly, in a biting manner that made plain her lingering resentment toward him.

Miss Laracy leaned forward and patted Kim's belly. "Is not yer stomach doin' dat. Is yer mind, me love. Ye needs ta clear out all dat old townie junk frum up dere. Den ye be well again. It be clear roads fer ye. Dis bit o' old michief'll soon blow over."

⟿

The night sky was deep blue and unclouded. Stars amassed in their precise patterns. There was no light from the land or from houses or street lights in the community, yet across the bay, Port de Grave shimmered with electricity. Claudia had just come in from the second-storey terrace of her studio. From there, she had plainly heard sounds from the wharf as helicopters continued with their seemingly endless work. Vehicles were arriving at and departing from the community centre. Farther west, along the road, blue and red police lights flashed every hundred feet. Mercer's Field was lit up and there was constant activity.

Watching the movement, she had thought she heard a dog barking toward the water. She wondered what the helicopters were doing, lifting things out of the water. Perhaps there was some sort of disaster, a ship-wreck off the coast. That would explain the commotion in Mercer's Field. Perhaps the large vehicles belonged to television crews. Claudia owned neither a television nor radio, so she was powerless to check the news.

Two ambulances, pulling away from separate houses in the community, had raced along the lower road, dots of strobing red, sirens wailing, as they sped toward Shearstown Line. Calamity. It all seemed perfectly natural to her; everything around her was nothing more than the culmination of her grief. She had hoped that her situation might turn worse, darker, intolerable. Since the disappearance of Reg and Jessica, she had prayed that the world would fail around her and thus, through crueller tragedy, offer her relief.

Presently, Claudia faced her studio. The electricity had gone off some time ago, and now candlelight flickered from five of her miniature houses and barns. She moved toward her work table and sat, raising a bisqued barn in her hand. It was greyish white and brushed by the orange shadows of the flickering candle flames that gradually settled now that she was at rest. She uncapped several bottles of paint-on glaze, dipped her brush into the cobalt blue and began painting the lines of clapboard. She thought of her mother's hands, of watching them when she was a child, while they carefully worked a needle and thread through the cloth of her needlepoint. The delicate gestures of her mother's hands blended in her memory with those of her father's, carving from walnut or pine, then smoothing and rounding the sculpture, polishing it with oil. The scent of an oily rag and the stains forever on his fingertips and in the grooves of his fingernails.

"I know what you're thinking," Jessica said from the enveloping dimness.

"What's that?" Claudia muttered, or thought. Of late, the distinction was of minor significance.

"You're wishing you were one of the drowned ones, like us."

Claudia continued stroking the tiny slats of clapboard. She dipped her brush into the bottle, wet the bristles, then dabbed them against the rim, draining off excess wetness. The candlelight imbued her movements with an exact delicacy that melded with the beating of her heart.

"You try so hard," Jessica said.

Claudia rinsed her brush in a glass of water, the thin wooden stem tinkling, the water rippling. She watched the clear fluid turn murky, then dipped the brush tip into another bottle, mustard yellow. She commenced painting the trim along the eaves and around the windows.

"You try so hard to find my love in what you do."

Claudia's hand grew still.

"You feel it, don't you, Mommy? When you make things with your hands it does bring me back."

Claudia continued with her brush strokes, which had grown unsteady.

"I'm going to play with Robin."

With a scant shake of her head, Claudia laid down her brush.

Jessica's voice came louder, distorted, wavering the candle flames: "I want someone to play with."

"Don't," Claudia whispered. "Please."

"They're losing their grip on her. They're not paying attention. They're against each other, not for."

Claudia listened, wondering at the silence, wondering how long it had gone on, until her doubt was contested by the voice of a little girl.

"I'm taking her," said Jessica. "Then I'm taking you."

─◦◦─

The small pottery barn, the gift from Claudia, sat on Robin's mantelpiece, encasing a dim candle flicker. Robin lay on her side, facing the wall, unable to sleep because of the events taking place down in the harbour and in the house. Presently, Robin listened, worrying about her mom, hoping that she would be okay. Robin had wanted to climb into bed with her mom, but her dad had stopped her, saying that her mom needed to rest by herself, to get better. Although, by the looks of his colour, he didn't mean what he said. He was glowing a liar's shade and this brought tears to her eyes. Why was he keeping her from her mom?

Her father had made her go to her own room, get in her own bed. He was outside somewhere now, probably gone for a walk. She wanted to get into bed with her mom. She wanted to get up and run into her mom's room.

Just then she heard someone moving in the room across the hall. The person gave a little cough and Robin knew it was Uncle Doug. A moment later, she heard his steps going down the stairs. Her Uncle Doug was a good man. He'd saved her mom and brought her to be with Dad. Now there was only the old woman in the room with her mom. Miss Laracy.

Earlier, the old woman had asked Robin again about the flying fish, which Robin hadn't seen since her first few sightings. But Miss Laracy was delighted when Robin anxiously explained that she had drawn flying fish only a few weeks ago when she was home in St. John's. She had also, in anticipation of her vacation, drawn a town that had a harbour and old square houses that were surrounded by hills. The drawing looked an awful lot like Bareneed.

Presently, Robin had an urge to pick up her crayons, which were secretly tucked under the blankets with some sheets of paper, but her hand was tired from filling so much space with the same colour on her last drawing. All that blue. The bedcovers, pulled up by her father before he left, were snug around her. She breathed deeply and evenly through her barely parted lips. Minutes passed in breathing. She was fretting for her father when her breath caught in itself and only the vague sounds of Miss Laracy's measured voice could be discerned from across the hallway.

The candle flicker grew brighter within the pottery barn, pulsing shadows across the ceiling and casting the large shadow of a head onto the wall that Robin was facing. A voice hummed to the tune of: "Myyy fawwther went to sea-sea-sea ..."

Robin turned to see Jessica staring intently at her. Jessica reached down to lovingly touch her hair.

"You're so warm," whispered Jessica.

"Hi," said Robin, smiling. "Why aren't you in bed? It's late."

Jessica grinned. "I am in bed."

"No, you're not."

"I'm tucked into the seabed? See?" She raised her hands and tiny sparks glimmered across her skin. She rubbed one hand over the other and a cloud of sand sprinkled to the floor. Then she brushed her hands over her soiled clothes and the sand ran off her.

"Let's go to the playground." Jessica tilted her head toward the window.

"Where?" Robin propped herself up on one elbow. She glanced at her door, where warm candlelight glowed from the room across the way. "Where's the playground?"

"In the water," said Jessica. "It's the best kind of playground. There's the most things to see that you never saw before."

"But I can't swim."

"Me neither. That's not important, though. You just have to know how to float."

~🜚

Tommy Quilty lived alone yet was never lonely, despite what people thought of him. *A lonely child, a lonely forsaken man.* Moments after he was born, Tommy had been laid out by the midwife, who assumed — as there seemed to be not a flicker of life in him — that the infant was a stillborn. He offered up not a breath. He had been laid out on the sideboard and the women in the room, the midwife and an elderly aunt, had stood a moment in miserable grief, their hearts swollen by a bruise of loss. The midwife was about to summon Tommy's father and deliver the sorrowful news, when all of a sudden the baby gave a gurgle, then a cry.

Tommy was barely crawling when he scrawled his first pictures across paper. The sloppy crayon drawings soon matured into elaborate sketches made with coloured pencils sharpened diligently to fine points. The sketches were of the sea, all that sailed on its surface, and all that lay beneath — its countless monsters.

Tommy's father decided that it would be pointless sending the boy to school. "No sense tryin' ta h'educate da child," his father had professed. So Tommy was left to focus on his one talent, which was encouraged by all around him and praised beyond the required tolerances. There had even been a story written about him, TOMMY QUILTY — ARTIST PRODIGY, in the *Compass*, the regional newspaper. He had become a bit of a celebrity and had begun selling his paintings, at the age of ten, in a shop in Port de Grave.

As he grew older and word of his talent travelled across the island, other stores, and even two galleries, had contacted Tommy to carry his work. The money he received for his paintings he sent to the addresses beneath photographs of starving children he saw in advertisements in the various art magazines that he bought secondhand at the Second Read bookshop. The owner would make a point of bringing the magazines in from St. John's for Tommy.

When he was twelve, Tommy began fishing for cod with his Uncle Edward. Tommy's father remained at home with a back injury that had left him in a wheelchair. He was tended to by Tommy's mother, Agnes.

For many years, Tommy painted and sketched and fished the sea, until the government shut down the cod fishery. He honestly missed going out in the boat and seeing down into the water, watching the creatures lurking beneath the surface, smoothly gliding near, but only rarely revealing themselves to the faithful.

Even though Tommy had his own van, Rayna drove him to the bank in Port de Grave once a month to cash the cheques he received from the four galleries that sold his work across Newfoundland. After paying the light and telephone bill, buying groceries and sending money orders to his charities, he used the remaining money to purchase art supplies. He worked in charcoal, pastels and watercolours. He liked pastels best because of the feel they left on his fingers and the way he could smear them to change the picture, to make it look the way he sometimes saw, particularly when peering into the ocean.

He tried not to let the things he drew frighten him. They would come regardless. They always did. Tonight, the noise of the helicopters to the east didn't frighten him.

Sitting at his dining room table, under the light of an oil lamp he had lit after the electricity went out, he convinced himself that there was nothing to be scared of. It was night and he was alone, but he saw Rayna in his head and he would call her soon, call her and see that she was okay and that would make him okay too. He pawed at his pads of art paper, counting them, one to seven. The others were stacked away in the drawers of the sideboard and in bedroom closets upstairs. He reached for the book second from the bottom and tugged it out. Nodding assuredly to himself, he opened the cardboard cover and stared at the first picture. It showed the albino shark on the wharf, a yellow crane parked on the road, a crowd of faceless people. The people were distinguishable by only one feature — the auras glowing around some of them. Some were lavender, others pink or faint yellow.

On the next page, Tommy's stained fingers pressed against the image of a woman of forty or so, the same age as Tommy. There was no glow around her and this saddened Tommy. Soon, tears warmly blurred the image. He smeared them away with his sleeve.

"Rayna," he mumbled, shutting his eyes tightly and turning the page. Helicopters in the night sky, hovering over the harbour; spotlights glaring at the water, revealing the faces and hands of bodies, the clothes flat and indistinct. Tommy turned a page to a drawing of a hospital room, the beds filled. The nurse had a pinkish-yellow aura, but neither of the patients had one at all, not even the faintest bruised purple.

Tommy peeked at the next image then hurriedly shut the book. He slid it back into its place in the stack, second from the bottom. He knew where each book belonged, and he knew when the sketches had been created. The sketches he had just studied, depicting scenes that had occured in recent days, were drawn more than a month ago.

He knew what would happen next. Bodies everywhere in a big tin building that must be the fish plant. Golden streaks raining from the sky like falling stars.

And then waves, followed by blackness. He had devoted many full sheets of paper to the particular shade of black that he saw in his mind. It was tinged with the faintest amount of cobalt blue. He wondered if it was the sky. There were no details. Just darkness, as black and sheening as a soaking-wet night.

⁂

Robin and Jessica walked, hand in hand, toward the abandoned church, where Jessica paused to watch the dark graveyard.

"There's no safety or comfort in the ground," said Jessica.

"Graveyards make me really sad," responded Robin.

"You should know better."

"Why?" Robin felt chilled, out in the night air without a sweater or jacket. She wished she had brought along her white sweater, the one with the pink flowers embroidered on each side that had belonged to her mother when she was a girl.

"Bodies buried there, once rotted and turned to sludge," explained Jessica, in a new voice that confused Robin, "are eventually displaced by rain seeping into the earth and underground springs, and carried, gradually, toward rivers that empty into the sea."

"I don't understand. You're talking too old."

"The rain is just part of the sea," continued Jessica in the same strange voice. "It knows. Water drags back to water and in its course carries the lot. In time, particles of everyone and everything end up down there." Jessica tipped her head toward the ocean. "There's not a single exception. Sea level."

Robin glanced around the darkness, not understanding her friend, not warming to the graveyard the way Jessica did. Jessica pressed up against the chain-link fence and stroked the cool pole running horizontally along the top. Robin turned to stare back the dark way they had come. She felt Jessica's damp chilly hand take hers again and they moved off, down Codger's Lane. It led into lusher darkness, toward the beach at the head of the inlet. The road was uneven and Robin watched the shadowed ground for potholes. "It's too dark," she protested, hearing the air-chopping noise of a helicopter down toward the harbour. The sound grew louder, rounder, and then faded.

"It's not. It's fun," Jessica insisted. "There're all these animals everywhere, watching from the dark bushes. See their green and red eyes? They're keeping themselves very still. They don't want to disturb our smell." She paused to sweep her sight along the treeline across the road. With a look of admiration, she purred: "The creatures in the trees are glowing. You've never seen anything like this."

"I've seen animals. I've got books —"

"You've never seen these. Sometimes people see the creatures, a glimpse of them, but only when they're frightened because being really frightened is like you died a bit. You died and you caught a peek and then you came alive again. Or if they catch a handful of real death before it lets them go … I haven't seen the woods in a long time. Not in a long long time."

"Why?"

"I need to go with someone. Someone who cares. I need their energy. I can't go alone. I can only go in the places of love where someone cares for me."

"What's that?"

"Places of love?"

Robin nodded as she stepped along, the soles of her sneakers scrunching pebbles and sand. Everything was so quiet and still. There was only the faint hum of wires above them, a noise that went off and on, drawing Jessica's attention. Robin felt Jessica's hand tighten its hold on hers. Then the hum stopped and stayed that way.

"Places …" said Jessica, her voice trailing away. She pulled her eyes from the wires and her mouth opened slightly as if in a grimace.

"Places of love," said Robin, as though repeating this phrase might somehow help ease Jessica's discomfort.

Jessica stared at Robin as though she were lost. "Places that are warmed by my mother's hand … or the hands of others leading me. Hold my hand tighter, please."

"Why? Can't you go where you want?"

"No. Not in this place."

"Why not?" Robin turned her head toward the returning sound of a helicopter. There came a squawking, a voice through a loudspeaker. It reminded her of a circus, a carnival. Rides and spinning colours in the night.

Jessica shrugged. "Because I'm dead. It's the rules." She smiled.

Robin returned her smile hesitantly, in uncertain friendship.

"Come on, there's a path up here." Jessica led Robin closer to the side of the road. "See the opening? I used to play in here when I was alive." She nodded toward a dense blackness and entered it, stooping beneath the bows of two towering evergreens that led into a woods path. The path was well-worn and smelled of sap warmed by sunlight but now cooling; the area felt damp and was brimming with night.

"This is too scary," Robin said, her trembling turning to shivering as Jessica pulled her along. The way everything felt and the way Jessica was talking made Robin think that she might be dreaming.

"Don't be such a baby."

The narrow path soon opened up at a clearing and there was the smell of salt air and the constant breeze that never settled on the water. They were free of the woods, on a cliff so high above the black ocean that Robin's stomach was gripped with a dizzying sensation. Gazing ahead, Robin saw the tiny lights from houses far across the water and, above them, specks of stars in the deep-blue sky over Port de Grave.

Jessica stared solemnly at Robin. "Out there," she said, fluid dribbling down her chin, catching moonlight as it crept, seeping like something alive and mercurial. She pointed off toward Port de Grave, its lights glowing sharply across the water. "That's where it happened."

"What?"

"It," said Jessica, her voice a gargle as water sloshed from her mouth. She coughed once, bent slightly forward; her shoulders slouched and bucking as water gushed from her mouth onto the grass as though she were vomitting, steadily, without effort.

"Jess?!" Robin said, her voice tight and frightened. She stepped back so her sneakers wouldn't get wet.

Jessica coughed again, her head jerking down. A beam of bright orange light flashed between Jessica's lips, strobing deep-orange brilliance across the grass.

Again, Jessica coughed, retching breathlessly, her face straining, her eyes bulging, her arms straight and pushed back, as the orange glow shuddered against her lips.

The flickering tail of a fish.

Jessica gagged for a long steady time before the orange fish slipped freely from her mouth, thumping onto the grass, where it flopped around, glowing like muted fire illuminating the blades of deep-green grass.

Stupefied, Robin watched the fish. It seemed electric, like a lantern you plugged in. She looked up to see Jessica's dark eyes staring at her in silence. The only sound was of ruffling in the grass as the fish's gills opened and shut in mute spasm. It jerked toward the edge of the cliff, where it found its freedom in the weightless tumble toward life-sustaining water.

Robin listened but heard no splash. When she looked up, her jaw slack in wonder, she saw that Jessica's eyes were now remarkably larger than usual. A strip of brown slime, like rotted leaves caked with mud, was stuck to Jessica's left cheek, and her skin seemed green and bursting-soft.

"I'm full of fishes," said Jessica sadly, then spat a small grey fish from her mouth as an afterthought. Her face bulged and settled, ripples of motion beneath her skin.

"I want to go."

"Fish in the sea," Jessica breathed, her eyes swelling fatter, her skin breaking out in a rash of sucking dots that reminded Robin of pimples with lips, but as they grew larger resembled nibbles, bites; her skin splitting, being eaten in flecks before Robin's eyes.

"Fish in the sea," said Jessica, her voice clotting, a loud underwater garble, each word sealed in a bubble of spit, "Fish in the sea."

A terrified scream flinched in Robin's chest but was clamped in her fear-shut throat as she stumbled back to counter Jessica's advance.

"Myyyyy fffawwwther went to sea-sea-sea to see what he could see-see-see —"

Spinning, Robin was ready to run, but lost her footing at the very edge of the grass sod. Her wet sneaker-bottom slipped and, painfully, she did the splits while grabbing for a nearby bush. The branches were thin and twiggy and the tiny leaves came free in her frantic hand as her weight pulled her backward. She plummeted straight down, her shrill scream fading until being silenced by a face-smacking splash.

⁓◌

Lieutenant-Commander French had given Dr. Thompson a special reflector sign to post on the passenger side of his windshield. The sign displayed the shield of the Canadian Armed Forces with a series of wide red numbers beneath it. Thompson had rolled down the front windows to let the air in, to convince himself that — at the very least — the sweet summer air had not been sucked away. As he drove along the lower road, with the helicopter and boat engines making a racket as they went about their business, his eyes lingered here and there on the dark houses to his right. Only a few houses had lights moving through them. Lamplight and the flickering of candles in one room or two. A flashlight beam sweeping an interior and then disappearing. How much longer for the power outage, Thompson wondered. He had asked Lieutenant-Commander French but the naval officer could give no answer. "We're investigating the cause," he had said halfheartedly, his eyes trained on the computer screen that had recently been unboxed and set up on his desk.

Thompson suspected that the military was the cause, and so standing in the doorway of French's makeshift office, he had asked outright, to which French had replied: "We are here to be of assistance. If a loss of power is required to assist the people of this community then that would be an action sanctioned by those involved in this operation."

"Is that a yes?" Thompson had asked with a challenging smile, vying for openness and, more importantly, camaraderie.

"What I said was not a forthright 'yes,' but a statement perhaps, and I say only perhaps, leaning toward the affirmative." With this, French gave a grimace. He cleared his throat dismissively before returning to the information on his computer screen. Thompson had noticed a giant volume of sea legends on the lieutenant-commander's desk.

"Are you searching for something particular in that book?"

"Strictly a pleasure read," French said, without looking from the screen. "Print." He gave the order into his wireless microphone and the driver inside the printer across the room began to whir.

"Any idea yet what's going on?"

"Probably just a bad case of the flu."

This statement made Thompson burst out with a single shotgun laugh. French did not bother regarding Thompson. He simply stood to collect the pages from his printer. Thompson caught sight of the bold words "Electromagnetic Hypersensitivity" on the top sheet.

"Mind if I have a look?" he had asked, gesturing toward the book.

"Go right ahead." French sat and read over the printed papers.

Thompson raised the book and turned a page, perusing the old mariners' drawings of creatures rising out of water. Giant octopi, three-headed monsters, and fish with human heads were featured on the glossy pages.

"This is quite the mystery," he commented, to which French replied, with a tap of his fingertip to the side of his head: "Mystery. Conundrum. Quandary. Enigma. Those are fighting words. We won't let them beat us, will we doctor?"

A second army barricade had been set up halfway down the lower road, between the community centre and Codger's Lane. Now Thompson's headlights illuminated the soldiers stationed there. The soldier closest to the left side of the road, and thus the water, held up his hand and aimed a flashlight beam at Thompson's windshield, forcing the doctor to squint and shirk away. Sighting the military pass, the soldier waved Thompson on.

"That's okay, doctor."

"Evening," said Thompson through his window as he passed.

"Evening, sir."

What exactly was he supposed to be doing? French had instructed him to patrol the area and keep his eyes open for any signs of possible distress. Was it simply a ruse to get Thompson out of French's hair or did French actually expect Thompson to see into houses, see through walls? How was he supposed to recognize distress? And wouldn't he be more useful over in the fish plant where they were stockpiling the bodies collected from the ocean? He had put forth such a question but French had plainly said: "There's no need for doctors over there. Not presently. The bodies are altogether dead. I, too, am a doctor, doctor. A doctor of environmental biology, and I can assure you that medical science will not benefit those unfortunates who have been hauled ashore. What will greatly benefit the living in this situation are astute eyes in the community. You have those eyes. My eyes are all wrong. They're shrouded in a uniform."

Thompson passed two black-windowed houses and tried to recall who lived in them. In the dark, it was difficult to place the dwellings. Up ahead, light was pouring through the windows of one particular house. Every room was lit, and the shadows of people frequently skimmed over the panes. Out on the front lawn, a few wooden chairs had been arranged to face the harbour. People sat there in the near-darkness, occasionally illuminated by the glare from helicopter floodlights. Others came and went from the open doorway. Children ran at play in the yard and around the road. As Thompson neared the house, an engine started and a pickup truck backed out of the crammed driveway, then headed farther along the lower road to another distant illuminated house.

Thompson knew where he was now. This was Wilf Murray's house. He understood exactly why people had gathered at Wilf's. Wilf was highly regarded as a mighty fine storyteller and a source of inspiration to many in the community. The old man must be in his eighties but he still chopped his own wood and built dories to sell around the province. He was a skilled boat builder. Even in the best of times, there were always a few men and women dropping by for a visit, to listen to him spin his yarns.

Thompson pulled his vehicle over behind a grey van. A few cars were parked along the side of the road and the driveway was almost completely blocked. About to leave the four-wheel drive, Thompson reached for his kit bag on the passenger seat, a gesture of habit, but then decided against it. Why would he be taking that along? His stomach grumbled. He thought of the pills in his case. What did he have to settle his stomach or, for that matter, what kind of pill did he have to settle a totally surreal situation? Perhaps Mrs. Murray would have a cook-up going. No, the electricity was out. But, if he remembered correctly, she had an old wood-and-coal stove in the kitchen. The Murrays had never bothered acquiring an electric range, willfully rejecting all things modern. The last time Thompson had been here, Wilf was suffering from a bad case of gout which was eventually brought under control.

As Thompson limped up the path, his face came into the light of a kerosene lamp hung in a tree and a few men spoke up with their usual greetings. "Hello, doc." "Evening, doc."

Thompson acknowledged the greetings and paused a moment to turn and scan the harbour. A red flare had streaked the sky to the west and was languidly descending near the headland. The front door opened behind

Thompson and he shifted sideways to allow the departing man by. Doing so, he heard the clatter of plates and the ruckus of conversation, and his spirits rose substantially. Stepping in, he wiped his shoes on the mat. He was bending uncomfortably to unlace them, his gut cutting off his breath, when he heard an anxious voice moving in by his side: "Now don't you bother taking off them shoes. Don't worry 'bout that, Dr. Thompson. People been traipsing back and forth all day."

Thompson glanced up to see Mrs. Murray standing near him, her plump cheeks rosy red. She was wearing an apron featuring a big red lobster over her sensible, loose blue dress. Three children raced by behind her, chasing each other up the stairs, their footsteps thundering while they shouted with glee.

"Some shocking bit of business going on," said Mrs. Murray, tut-tut-ting. "Leave those shoes alone. I already told you." She swatted him with the dish towel that was draped over her shoulder.

"I've already got them unlaced," Thompson protested, gasping and bracing one hand against the wall while he stepped out of his shoes, one at a time.

"Stubborn or what?" she said. "I've got a cook-up going. Salt beef and cabbage. I'll fix you a plate?"

Standing, Thompson gave a sigh of salvation. "God Almighty, you don't know how starved I actually am."

Delighted, Mrs. Murray turned and anxiously led the way. "Come on," she said, waving an arm for him to follow. "Everyone's in the kitchen."

Another group of children rushed by, almost knocking Thompson off balance.

"We're minding after the children of the sick," said Mrs. Murray. "Poor darling souls."

The kitchen was sweltering with the smells of boiled cooking and the gathered warmth of bodies. The windowpanes by the table were steamed over, the condensation dribbling down.

"Fine bit of heat in here," Thompson said as those seated at the table or standing by the counter and stove regarded him and winked, tilting their heads, or offered stray greetings. One man laughed and nodded, said: "Yays, fine bit of heat all right." And a few others freely chuckled along.

Before he knew what was happening, a heaping plate of food was shoved into his hands. Mrs. Murray stood before him, nodding and wiping her palms in her apron.

"Eat up now, my love."

"Thank you. This is just fabulous." In embarrassment, he realized he had actually begun drooling as the scent from the meal reached his nostrils. Finally, a proper feast. He swiped his sleeve across his mouth and chin.

Mrs. Murray grinned and her cheeks proudly rounded to perfect plums. She turned away to snatch up a gravy-smeared plate that someone had just finished with.

Thompson stared down at the steaming mound of vegetables and cabbage, creamy pease pudding, red strands of chewy salt meat, a leg of chicken poking out beneath it all, the skin golden and crisp, and the whole heavenly feast smothered in perfectly concocted gravy. He was about to open his mouth to ask for a fork when one was slapped into his hand by Mrs. Murray. She had returned from disposing of the plate and now blew a breath up at her forehead. Her face seemed redder and she fanned herself with one hand. "I'm perishing with the heat," she said.

"Thank you," said Dr. Thompson with a massive grin, wondering how Mrs. Murray's blood pressure was doing. Standing exactly where he was, without offering another comment or taking one step forward or back, he dug his fork in. Bliss, he told himself as his taste buds were slathered with the first forkful. Bliss. Bliss. Bliss.

"Wilf was just telling 'bout the sleet storm of '65," explained Mrs. Murray, nodding toward her husband. Thompson glanced at the table and saw Wilf tucked into the seat closest to the wall. The old man adjusted the bill of his red and white baseball cap and, without word, raised his hand to Thompson, then turned back to his conversation. Thompson tried to listen as he shovelled the food into his mouth, but the clicking of his jaws and his moans of adoration drowned out the specifics of the story. As much as he was enjoying the meal, and, perhaps because of his profuse appreciation, he couldn't help but feel a pang of guilt at his gluttony. He should be at the hospital, speaking with the other doctors, diligently working to determine the source of the illness. He glanced around the room to see that all eyes were on Wilf. Any one of these people could stop breathing at any moment. No, they didn't seem as if they would. None of them appeared to be even slightly aggressive. They were all smiling, grinning or waiting for the right moment to laugh. Thompson watched them as he ate. The words "What am I?" came to him. He definitely should return to the hospital. But wasn't the fact that these people were well just as much a part of the mystery as the state of those afflicted? Wilf Murray was describing the ice-coated trees violently snapping in half beneath the weight of frozen water.

"Like icicles plucked off an eave," he explained. "And da wires were dancin' across da roads, spittin' fire. Alive, dey were." Wilf raised his hands in the air and flicked his fingers like a hail of sparks going off. "Like dey were alive and hissin' at us for being so bloody stunned, us thinkin' we could snatch hold of 'em and set dem back together. Set things right again. Who got control over that? Who? No one." He steadied his eyes on one man, then the next. "No one."

~❦~

Uncle Doug stood in Robin's dim doorway, softly humming an old Irish ballad while watching the rumpled sheets of the candlelit bed. In a hushed resonant voice, he began singing to distract himself:

> "There was an old man who was lively yet dead,
> they sent for the doctor to check through his head.
> And in his late head they found a cool spring,
> where thirty-nine salmon were learning to sing."

The candle in the barn-holder on the mantelpiece flickered, the breeze from Doug's appearance in the doorway only now reaching it. The wavering light lent the bedsheets new dimension. Something appeared peculiar about the jumble of sheets; the head against the pillow was entirely too small.

Mutely, but with mounting concern, Doug entered the room. Robin could easily be lost in the bedcovers. After all, she was a small girl. But, no, as he stepped near he saw that the head against the pillow was none other than that of a sleeping doll.

Doug yanked back the sheets to be certain. Only the doll's body rested there. And beside the body there were sheets of paper and a container of crayons. Snatching up the top paper, Doug saw that it was covered entirely in one dark colour. It seemed to be blue without any definition. Blue with ripples of white. Startled, he tossed down the drawing and turned toward the doorway. No one. He thought of calling out, but stifled the urge in favour of checking in Kim's room. No need to put the fear of God into people yet. The girl might have crossed the hallway and crawled into bed with her mother while Doug was downstairs getting a drink of water.

Doug made his way to Kim's room and stood over her bed. He leaned nearer to examine the space between Kim's back and the wall. Nothing. He noticed Kim's eyes twitching, sensing his presence. He stepped back as her eyes fluttered open.

"Is Robin in there with you?" Doug asked.

Kim turned and half sat up to check the space behind her. She slapped at the blankets.

"No," she said, grogginess in her voice. "Why?"

"She's not in her room."

Kim threw back the covers and rose, still in her street clothes. She hurried toward the door on unsteady legs, passing Miss Laracy, who had dropped off in the wicker chair. Before Doug could reach the threshold himself, Kim was back in the room, her eyes fully awake, frantic.

"Where is she?" she curtly demanded, her gaze shifting toward the dark window, then down to the candle that burned in its ceramic holder.

"I don't …" Doug shook his head.

Kim turned and screamed "Robin?" at the top of her lungs. She stood still, alert, listening. Not a sound. The noise of Kim's cry had awoken Miss Laracy. The old woman straightened her head and squinted as Kim grabbed the candle beneath the window and turned for the door.

"Da girl be in da water," Miss Laracy mumbled.

"What?" Kim asked, halfway out of the room, her free hand grabbing the door frame so she could catch herself and peer back.

"Da girl be in da water."

"What?" Kim checked Doug. "What?"

"Be quiet with that foolishness," Doug snapped at Miss Laracy.

"But she be fine," Miss Laracy insisted with a pink-gummed grin. "Right as rain."

Kim's eyes lingered incredulously on Miss Laracy for a moment. Then Kim turned and bolted from the room, shouting: "Robin? Joe?"

Doug shook his head, chastising Miss Laracy while Kim briskly searched the other rooms, the sound of her distraught voice echoing through the house: "Joe?" Doug continued watching the old woman. But Miss Laracy was having no part of it. She winked and grinned. "Dey'll search, but dey won't find 'er where dey be lookin'. 'Twas a spectre dat led 'er astray."

"Be quiet with that codswallop." Doug departed the room and headed down the stairs just as the front door was flung open and Joseph stepped in, a blank expression on his face.

"Is Robin with you?" Kim demanded.

"No." What little colour remained in his face drained away, leaving his skin ashen. "Where is she? Someone harm her already? Whose turn is it?"

"What?!" Kim stormed past Joseph, slapping his chest on the way. "What're you saying?" She rushed out into the night, her voice carrying in the still air, carrying above the sounds of retrieval from the harbour: "Raawwwwwbbbiiinnn?"

"If someone killed her already," said Joseph, "that's way sooner than it should be, 'cause the show's not over yet."

⁓๑⁓

The internet broadcasts, originating from St. John's, were reporting that the electricity had now gone out in Bareneed, further complicating the bizarre state of affairs that was already grieving the community.

Sergeant Chase, seated in his chair with a damp towel wrapped around his waist, was secretly plugged in, fascinated by the news. After taking a shower, he had left Theresa watching a gardening channel in the living room, and had snuck to his computer in the spare room and slipped on his headphones. The spare room had once been a bedroom; he had claimed it as his office and given it new gyprock walls, over layers and layers of yellowing wallpaper. Nail dents were still evident in the gyprock — they had yet to be filled with plaster — but for all intents and purposes the room was finished.

Of course, he already knew that the electricity had gone out, but what he now learned was that the head of Newfoundland Power was quoted as saying they could find no technical reason for the outage. As far as they were concerned, the electricity was still flowing through Bareneed.

Chase minimized one of the windows and maximized another, checking a national broadcast. The news had even made that site, as a small story, seven or eight down from the main feature at top. He clicked BODIES DISCOVERED OFF NEWFOUNDLAND COAST and watched the broadcast. It was just a repeat of a local broadcast he had already viewed. A syndication. He warned himself that he should go to bed; it was getting late and he had no idea how long he had been on the Net. But, should he decide to turn in for the night, he would only be lying in bed alone, staring at the ceiling. Theresa would not come to bed until 3:00 or 4:00 a.m., if at all. She might just stay on the couch. There was no need to worry about sleep for another few days. He didn't need sleep. All he needed was a shower and he'd had one.

Chase minimized the site he was watching, then maximized another, switching windows to obtain a different perspective, but the stories were pretty much the same. The information was scarce and there were few answers. Doctors were being interviewed. Specialists postulated and endeavoured to appear professional and authoritative in the face of something they knew absolutely nothing about. Some claimed the problem was in the water. Others claimed it was in the air. No one admitted anything for certain. One-hundred-percent speculation.

Chase felt peculiar watching the community on the computer screen. He had been in Bareneed only a short while ago. If he went outside his door, out into the backyard, he could see Bareneed across the water, the back of the headland that sheltered the harbour. The broadcasts were bringing him a live view. He could watch what was going on. Live.

How many bodies now? No one knew for certain. He shook his head, and brought up another site. Slipping his headphones off one ear, he listened for Theresa. Not a sound from her. He had escaped the mayhem of northern Saskatchewan only to find himself in the worst scenario he had ever experienced. In Saskatchewan, Chase could always seek solace in the fact that the rest of the world was functioning — more or less — as it was meant to. Even with the serial killings that he read about in the paper, life went on around him. But this mess in Bareneed was of catastrophic proportions. No one knew what was to happen next. Whatever was affecting Bareneed might easily spread to Port de Grave.

He slid his headphones back on and listened to the theories. He knew something that the reporters did not: a notable piece of information that Lieutenant-commander French had told him. It was the reason why Chase had been permitted to leave Bareneed. This was not a virus that was passed from person to person. That's all the information French would supply. He refused to elaborate. Chase suspected that French knew more than he was letting on. The lieutenant-commander had suggested that Chase, the assigned RCMP liaison for the tragedy, go home for a rest. Perhaps French just didn't want the police in his way. When Chase had countered with "But the town is quarantined," French had simply said: "This isn't about a virus. The roadblocks remain only to contain the scene." French had stared at Chase, deadpan. No further words. Chase knew better than to press the matter.

He brought up another site. The same video feed. A long shot of the Bareneed harbour at night. Helicopter lights sweeping the air. Streaks of red flares, rising and leisurely descending, fading to pink. The scene had the atmosphere of a war. And there were casualties as well. Bodies in the water. Never mind that some of them had been dead for years.

The telephone icon on his computer flashed and he quickly clicked it, aware that the line was ringing in the kitchen. He didn't want to disturb Theresa.

"Hello," he said, eyeing the microphone extended from the top of his screen.

"Sergeant Chase?" It was a female officer from dispatch in St. John's.

"Yes."

"We have a report of a missing person in Bareneed. A girl, aged eight. Hair: sandy-blonde. Eyes: blue. Height and weight unconfirmed at this point. As you're the search-and-rescue liaison for that area, we thought you should be notified."

"Who's the contact?"

"Joseph Blackwood, father. Address: Higher Road, Bareneed. The only precise address I have is the Critch house."

"I know where that is," he said, recalling the father who had helped his daughter reel in her line on the wharf, the red sculpin hooked at the other end.

"How long has she been missing?"

"One to two hours. Should I code you back in on CIID?"

"Yeah, contact Mr. Blackwood. Tell him I'll be there right away."

--①

When Joseph called the police, he was informed that an officer would be sent as soon as one could be assigned. The voice had been machine-like, heartless, unforgiving, no doubt secretly blaming him for his daughter's disappearance.

Joseph had cursed and slammed down the receiver. Uncle Doug then brushed him aside and raised the receiver, dialled a number and listened. He pressed the disconnection tab, waited, let it up. Pressed it again, listened.

"What?" Kim asked.

"Nothing," Doug said. He hung up.

"The telephone?" Exasperated, Kim watched Doug, then snatched up the receiver and listened, her eyes shifting toward Joseph. "It's dead." She hung up, and faced her husband: "Were you talking to someone?"

"I was," Joseph shouted, clenching his fists. "They just didn't hear me."

"What?"

"Let's go. We'll search." Ignoring his nephew, Doug rushed toward the front door with Kim and Joseph close on his heels. Miss Laracy was seated on the couch in the parlour, a yellow and white crocheted blanket over her lap and legs. She said, "Da girl be safe," as they passed. But no one except Joseph paid her any mind.

Outside, Joseph stared toward the activity in and above the harbour. He had it in his mind to go back and smother the old woman. She was old enough to appreciate dying. She would go easily, although a bit of kicking and clawing would be nothing to turn his nose up at. There were pillows upstairs.

Toward the west, huge lights had been erected along the hills and flashes of silver came to Joseph as something enormous and metallic was lowered in place by two helicopters. He noticed Doug standing by Kim's car. A beam of light flicked off and on. A flashlight. Perhaps the old man was going somewhere and needed illumination to find his way. The farther away, the better. That would make Joseph feel relieved, under less obligation. The old man, being a family relative, was keeping Joseph from doing exactly as he desired, and desire was becoming larger now, purer, more lethal.

"Who wants to drive?" Doug asked.

"How far will we get?" Kim fretfully shifted her body, eager to search, her body so anxious for the return of something that had been taken from it. "She has to be near. Where could she go?" She cupped her hands around her mouth, "Rawwwwbbbiiinn?"

Neither of them had an answer for Kim, although Joseph suspected that Claudia's daughter might know something. The dead girl. No doubt the dead girl had taken Robin out for a romp. The dead were like that. Greedy and caring for no one other than themselves. Being dead, what could they possibly be but greedy? He assumed Robin had been led somewhere by Jessica. Where? He had already checked the barn. The woods behind the house were too thick and dark to enter. Surely, a child wouldn't get far into the brush without being snagged in the hooked branch tips. Should he tell them that? Tell his wife, if that was who she was, and this man, Uncle Doug, the brave and hardy Newfoundlander, the stock character? Tell him Robin was off playing with a dead girl? Maybe everyone would just throw up their hands and exclaim: Well, why didn't you just say so in the first place. That makes sense. She's safe with the dead girl. After all, the dead girl is dead, isn't she? Dead and dead. Double dead. What harm could possibly come of that?

All would be accepted. The people out here seemed to have an affinity with ghosts. Life in the city didn't hold such myths sacred; they were something to roll your eyes at. Joseph's eyelids fluttered, stuttering his view of the outdoors. The back of his hand was pattered by something wet. He raised his hand to study the lined skin bound around bone. A clear drop of fluid. He put his tongue to it. Water. He gazed toward the sky. Not a cloud. The blinding sharpness of stars. Another droplet burst against the top of his head, sluggishly seeping through his hair. Another drop on his cheek. Then nothing. He thought of the old woman in the house. He still had time to murder her, rip her to shreds with a nifty selection of domestic cutlery, and document the effort with a series of photographs he could sell to the highest media bidder. Wasn't his disposable camera in his car? The old woman deserved to die for being so goddamn old. The young would understand. He would be a hero to them.

Kim wandered farther up the road, "Rawwwwwbbbiiinnn?"

Watching Kim, Joseph considered breaking her neck, smacking her in the back of the head with a two-by-four. Winding back and … WHAM! That recoil action would make him feel better right about now. Or he might choke her, get her on the ground with her arms thrashing at him, with her shirt torn and already full of maggots and bash her head in with a rock. That would show her true colours. The childless bitch. What was she good for anyway? The dead baby had been her fault. She couldn't hold it in long enough. Robin had been her fault. If Kim had been there to watch over Robin, then Robin would not have gone missing.

He considered going to check Claudia's house. Claudia was the sort who wouldn't mind dying either. She would be expecting it, waiting in her burial dress, flowers clustered in her hands, a crucifix fastened around her pale throat. His daughter might be there. One already dead, one to go. But, no, he had already been over there earlier, standing outside the house, peeking in the windows, planning his assault, and there was no sign of Robin, only Claudia in the window of the living room, standing there behind glass, as if shadows were attracted to the features of her classic, otherworldly face, her sunken eyes staring down at him with a look that beckoned pity for how her heart had been perpetually mislaid. Kill her and make her feel better. That was what she wanted. Give her what she wanted. Shotgun barrel in her mouth. How hot could she make it?

Joseph noticed Uncle Doug, who was watching him with suspicion, clicking his flashlight beam off and on, sweeping it over Joseph's body, then into his eyes, so that Joseph raised his hand against it. The old man shook his head and straightened the bill of his baseball cap, cursing under his breath. "You with us?" he asked.

"I'm going," Kim said, back closer to Joseph but with one foot and her body leaned toward heading in the opposite direction again. She regarded Joseph, making up her mind about the worthless state of a man he truly was. She pointed up the road, in the dark direction of the church.

Joseph roughly grabbed hold of her arm and squeezed. "Nowhere," he spat.

"Oww!" She yanked her arm away.

Joseph grinned at her, a consummate leer.

Kim shouted, her voice a teary angry shiver: "What's the matter with you?"

"What the hell're you doing?" Doug barked at him.

Joseph curled a lip at Doug while imagining poking things through Kim's flesh, making holes in her so that she would be more accepting, easier to lift. He exhaled, waited, snatched a breath through his nostrils. What was that, he wondered, in his lungs? Something was in there, or had been taken out. A chunk of required something.

"I'll go this way," Doug said, tugging his ire clear of Joseph to face where the road gradually dipped back toward the community. "You take the flashlight." He approached Kim and handed her the instrument. Kim clicked it on, swept its beam into the trees.

Joseph's eyes were fixed on the hills. Three different sets of lights, three different projects: monstrous things were being erected. He glanced back at the house. Should he stay at home and be alone, just to be with himself, hide in a closet, waiting for the others to enter? The old woman was there. She could be practice.

Uncle Doug and Kim continued off in different directions. Should he go with the man? Or should he be the man and go with the woman, his wife? Slash out her beating heart and eat it in a conquering fashion, be the chow-down man, the man with a hearty appetite. He heard Uncle Doug treading back up the road in a huff. Approaching, Doug pulled off his baseball cap and used it to whack Joseph in the side of the head.

"Go with yer wife," he cursed. "Don't be so bloody useless."

Kim, lingering nearer and nearer the darkness that would soon swallow her, turned and viciously called out: "Are you coming?"

Joseph assumed the woman was speaking to him. What were his plans? He was supposed to be doing something, searching for something. But he had found it, the pure urge in him. No frills. That was what they were looking for, wasn't it? The pure urge.

The old man was moving off down the road, his head turning one way, then the other, checking purposefully into the bushes and calling out a name. Joseph stepped and his legs felt wobbly, as though sinking into silt. The faces he had seen in the ocean, the faces that had been watching him, as if in dumb underwater allegiance, reared up in his mind. They stared imposingly at him. One of them, with a face that bobbed forlornly nearer, was a little girl he recognized as having been connected to him. Someone he was once attached to in a way that made no sense to him now. His "daughter," they called her, if that was a word.

Joseph stared ahead, seeing the back of the woman fully disappear into the darkness, yet a beam of light stretched out in front of her, leading her forward. He started off after her. It was easy to follow because she was calling out, making noise, giving herself away. How was she supposed to be hiding from him like that?

⁓❀

When Sergeant Chase arrived at the Critch house, he made his way through the dark yard to the front door, where he knocked and waited. There was faint orange candlelight filtering through the lace curtain on what he assumed to be the parlour window. He glanced over his shoulder at the street light. Out. He then regarded the solar house to his right. A large black dog was seated on the doorstep. He knocked again. No reply. They must be out searching for the lost girl, he assumed. Then he heard a frail aged voice, singing:

"A girl on shore many tear will shed,
fer 'im who lies on da ocean bed,
where above 'is 'eart da whale will hiss,
'n 'is pallid lips da fish will kiss."

Not certain if the voice was originating from within the house, he tried the knob. It turned smoothly. Easing the door open, he hesitantly leaned in. The parlour at his left was, indeed, lit with candlelight. At first, the room seemed completely deserted. Not the slightest bit of movement. The old piano was standing against the far wall and the waxed antique furniture held the highlights of candlelight. Shifting his eyes toward the chesterfield, he saw a white-haired old woman watching him directly.

"Hello," he said, starting at the sight of her eyes fixed so resolutely on him. The old woman then nodded and grinned, singing:

"'Oh bury me not' — 'is voice failed dere,
dey paid no heed ta 'is dyin' prayer,
dey lowered 'im down o'er da ship's dark side
n' above 'im closed da dismal tide."

When she was finished, the old woman stared mutely at Chase, as if expecting mournful affirmation.

"Is this where the little girl is missing?" Chase asked, stepping fully into the house and shutting the door. A calm, mellow sensation overcame him. Perhaps it was the candlelight reminding him of the days of his youth when he burned candles and sweetgrass and tried so hard to be a sensitive soul. Perhaps it was the song, which he had never heard before, and was wonderfully tragic and beautiful.

"Yays."

"Have they had any luck?" Chase removed his hat and held it in his hands, feeling awkward in the presence of the old woman.

"Not widt da girl missin'. No luck dere, me ducky."

"I meant in finding her." He stepped ahead, fully into the parlour with its odour of ancient upholstery and solid wooden furniture.

"She be fine."

"They found her?" Chase asked hopefully, noticing a sheet of paper on the coffee table, beside a blue vase of wildflowers. The paper featured a drawing of a woman with long strawberry hair. If it was a child's sketch then the child had exceptional talent.

The old woman stared.

"Where are they now?"

"Searchin'."

"Right." Chase glanced around the room. "Do you know the exact time of her disappearance?"

"Yays," the old woman chuckled warmly. She wiped at her dry lips with the edge of her finger and chuckled again. "Disappeared she did, at an exact time."

Chase watched the old woman, his eyes fixed on her face. Her frivolous attitude was beginning to get on his nerves. "Are you her grandmother?"

"Dey be searchin' on land," spoke the old woman portentously. "Always be searchin' on land. But da girl be in da sea. No point searchin' on land, when da answers be in da sea."

MONDAY

Rayna woke to the sound of the telephone ringing. Shifting in bed, she felt as if her head were stuffed with wet rotten cardboard that weighed a ton. The telephone, ringing. It must be 9:30 a.m. Tommy Quilty called every Monday at 9:30 to make certain she was okay. Since her husband Gregory's death by drowning six years ago, Rayna had considered herself both fortunate and cursed to have Tommy looking out for her. He was sweet, but he was a bit of a nuisance at times like these.

Rayna didn't miss Greg that much. He'd been a brutal heartless man who abused her whenever the urge came over him. Tommy knew about Greg's brutality firsthand. Greg had laid a beating to Tommy one afternoon when he caught Rayna and Tommy together, just talking over a pot of tea at the kitchen table. Greg had dragged Tommy by the scruff of the neck out into the backyard, where he laid the boots to "the retard," as Greg called Tommy. It had been a pitiful sight, Tommy rolling around on the ground, whimpering. Rayna's attempts to pull Greg away had only got her two black eyes for her troubles. There was no missing that, although she still felt that she pined for something she could not actually name. Not Greg himself, but maybe his presence. Or the presence of the man she thought he had been.

The telephone continued ringing. Her head hurt from the bottle of rum she'd finished off last night. Her mouth was bitter with nicotine. She vaguely recalled stumbling around her backyard and falling over, trying to chase something away. A cat was it? Or was she trying to get it to come to her? Either way, she had a sinking feeling that she'd wanted to harm whatever it was.

She hugged the pillow, pressed her face into it and groaned. Recently Tommy's calls had increased to every second day. Rayna suspected it had to do with the trouble in Bareneed, the deaths and the strange sightings.

Last night, she had been watching the news where they were reporting from Bareneed. She had even seen Clarence Pike and Alice Fitzpatrick being interviewed about what was going on. They didn't have a single clue between them. They just stood there saying that it was "something awful" and "a nasty kettle of fish." Things like that. Rayna had chuckled to see the reporters from St. John's and other parts of Canada not understanding a word but nodding right sincerely like they were the most compassionate people to ever walk the face of the earth. Then the lights had gone off and the electricity hadn't been restored since. For that matter, the telephone hadn't been working either. She had tried to call someone last night. Who? Was it Tommy? And the line was dead.

She glanced at the electric clock-radio by the bed. It still said 10:30 p.m. She reached for the phone and pulled it to her ear. "Hello," she said, groggily. She set her hand on her forehead, only now realizing the full extent of her pain. She drew in a deep tired breath. Movement was always a problem. It was best to stay still. Listening at the receiver, she heard Tommy sigh.

"Tommy?"

"Yes," he said, quickly. "Rise 'n shine, me beauty."

Rayna smiled and shut her eyes. She coughed and moaned briefly, in a clutch of anguish, turning her head toward the dresser at the other side of the room. The air seemed thick. It must be hot outside. Humid. "What're you at, Tommy?"

"Talking."

"No kidding," she chuckled, her shoulders tightening, refreshing her pain. She caught a whiff of ashes. The ashtray was overflowing on the night table. The sight of it turned her stomach. She waited, accustomed to Tommy's silences. Then she grabbed a breath.

"Wha' you doing now?"

"In bed." Again, she heard him sighing. "I'm getting up … Maybe."

"Me too."

"You in bed?"

"No."

"Oh." Her smile softened. Tommy was like a big child. He was the only person who never wanted anything from her. He just cared for her, wanted to be near her, needing her. "You know something?"

"No."

"I was in Port de Grave at the … grocery store yesterday and I went over to Maxine's. I saw your new paintings there." Silence at the other end. She waited, about to reach for a cigarette, when she noticed she wasn't breathing. She sat up under the covers, tingling and startled. Drawing a breath, she listened to herself. Everything seemed fine, except for the sweat that had broken out on her skin. It was a booze sweat. She could smell the grimy odour off her body. Time for a shower. "Tommy?"

"Yeah?"

"I got to go."

"Okay. Can I come over?"

"Sure." She drew a deep panicky breath. "Jesus," she muttered, touching her chest. "Is it humid out?"

"Wha'?"

"There's no air in here."

"Huh?"

"Nothing. Come over," she said, distracted, "whenever you want." She hung up and tossed her legs over the edge of the bed. Clear of the sheets and pulling her long red T-shirt away from where it was tangled at her legs, she felt the air on her arms and was frightened by the sensation. And she was scaring herself even more by assuming she now had that virus people were talking about, or was it just the cigarettes? Her knees started trembling as she stood. She sat back on the bed, an emptiness rearing up inside of her, rushing straight toward her head.

She drew a breath, sweat sheening on her forehead, collecting in her eyebrows. A drink, that was all she needed. A straightener. She lifted up the end of her T-shirt and wiped her brow, held the fabric to her face and shut her eyes. Nothing.

"I need a drink," she said, hearing the words she had just spoken, but forgetting them instantly. She stared around her bedroom, a rush of incomprehension careening through her nerves. For a split second, she did not recognize her surroundings. Whose house was she in? A stranger's? *Where am I?* Then, she remembered. The room was familiar. More than familiar. It was hers.

~◊

Doctor Thompson stood in the emergency waiting area, scanning the people sitting or standing around. No doubt most of them were relatives of those afflicted with the breathing disorder. Mothers and fathers. No, not mothers and fathers, because there had been no children admitted with the symptoms. No children. Only adults. Why was that? Diseases particular to age. What were they? He could think of nothing relevant to this situation.

Donna Drover was now non-communicative, and Darry Pottle was experiencing memory lapses. Amnesia rarely came in stages like that. It was usually the result of a single traumatic incident or trigger. Other patients were displaying similar symptoms: mental degeneration without apparent brain pathology.

Thompson had been at the hospital all night. The previous evening, while he was enjoying his respite at the Murrays', feasting on his meal, shovelling in the food and trying his best to suppress his moans, his cellphone had gone off for the thirtieth time that day. Talk in the kitchen had collapsed into silence as all heads turned to look at him. The ringing of his cellphone was an alarm, proclaiming the full thrust of Thompson's intrusion. The faces watched while he stood there, both cheeks stuffed with food. The kitchen utterly still as Wilf Murray adjusted the beak of his cap and tilted back his stubbly-grey chin. The cellphone rang again. Thompson chewed once, lifted the phone from where it was clipped at his belt. He flipped it open while holding his plate with his free hand. The faces examined him with new interest. Turning away, he had struggled to swallow the load of food in his mouth while speaking, almost choking himself. Coughing, he had caught enough of what was said at the other end to know that Donna Drover had recently slipped into a coma.

Following a quick stopover at his house to feed the appreciative and miserably alone Agatha and to bring his cherished pussycat along on his journey in the four-wheel drive, Thompson had headed straight for the hospital and hurried to Donna Drover's room. His hastened pace exacerbated the pang in his ankle, making him nauseous, and so he was forced to slow down or lose the supper so hospitably provided by Mrs. Murray.

Two more beds had been crammed into Donna's room since his last visit. The bed toward the window was Donna's. Thompson hobbled toward it, and stood over his patient. She should be in ICU, but there was no room down there.

Thompson considered the other beds: two women from Bareneed on respirators, no trach tubes in yet. One of them had her eyes shut; the other, a younger woman, was watching him with a vindictive expression. Her wrists were tied to the bed rails. Thompson heard Donna's voice in his head, "What am I." He then recalled the words Lieutenant-Commander French had written on the blackboard: "Fishers of men."

"How are you feeling?" Thompson asked the woman watching him. The woman simply shook her head, her hateful countenance shifting to one of sinking desperation and helplessness that deeply affected Thompson. After studying Donna for a few moments, he left the room and proceeded to the doctor's lounge. There were two other doctors present. Thompson knew neither of them; they must have been from outside the region and they were engaged in their own conversation concerning the situation. One of them, a slight, middle-aged female physician with long brown hair, was convinced that Bareneed was contaminated by a toxin that targeted the brain stem. The other doctor, a man in his early thirties with curly black hair and wire-rimmed spectacles, argued that it could not be contamination, as no toxins had been found in any of the patients' bodies. He argued that it must be a psychological condition, a form of mass hysteria.

"The bodies are *not* physically ill," he contested.

"But how does that explain the deaths?" the woman countered. "How can hysteria kill?"

"I don't know," said the man. "Do you? That's just it. We don't really know, do we?"

Thompson had already given consideration to the notion of hysteria, but it didn't hold water. He was too exhausted to join the conversation.

The two doctors glanced his way, hoping that he was paying heed to their conjecture, but soon gave up on him. He thought of Agatha out in the vehicle, wondered if he had cracked the window. Yes, he remembered doing so. His side, his window. He then considered the new stage of the condition. Coma. The progression: aggressive or violent behaviour. Loss of breath. Loss of sense of self. Amnesia? Coma. And none of the sufferers were children. He thought through this sequence as he slid into sleep, and was soon snoring away.

A couple of hours later, he stood in the waiting area, waiting, but for what? Thompson recalled how he had been in that exact place, two days ago with Sergeant Chase, and had been struck by the way the men and women scrutinized him. The meanness in their eyes, the seemingly wicked intent. However, unlike two days ago, a soldier now stood guard beside the main sliding doors, hands behind his back, legs sturdily spaced. No weapon. Thompson had expected him to be holding a rifle. They were in a state of emergency where chaos might erupt at any moment, spilling from the walls, floorboards and ceiling. Thompson burped, tasting the meal of last night that still sat in his stomach. Fond memories.

The waiting area was blocked with adults and children; most of them had blank expressions. A few older men or women leaned toward each other in their seats, talking, nodding or shaking their heads, no doubt having seen their fair share of tragedy and rating the present course of events against past incidents. The heat coming off the crowd was suffocatingly human, overwhelming.

Thompson glanced from face to face. No sign of ill will. Had he been imagining the malice the other day? He turned toward the sliding doors and thought he heard a siren in the far distance.

Other heads were turning. Thompson listened, then hobbled toward the doors while continuing to scan the people in the waiting area. There were the usual number of sprains, flu and minor cuts. Relatives of the stricken were not permitted to visit the sick, yet they waited regardless for any sort of word. A few had approached him with questions, but all he could offer was a string of hopeful yet evasive words, nothing definite. The sixth floor of the hospital had now been completely quarantined.

The double doors slid open as Thompson approached. The morning air was cooler than he expected for a summer morning. Refreshing. He watched the evergreens that rose in the distance. A single crow sailed along, high above the treetops. The siren grew intensely loud, then was shut off as the ambulance pulled up, blocking Thompson's sight of everything except the white hull of the vehicle with its orange stripe and lettering. The attendants leaped from the front and raced to open the back doors. The stretcher was slid out. Thompson saw a girl, seven or eight years old. He watched the stretcher roll past him and then trailed after it.

"What happened?" he asked.

"Hypothermia," announced one of the paramedics. The stretcher rattled through the double doors. "Temperature's not moving."

"She was in the water?"

"A navy boat fished her out, took her to the fish plant, thought she was just another of the dead." They were rolling up the corridor, heading for the Emerg doors. "Then they noticed she was wearing clothes from present time, from now." The paramedic looked at the doctor, shook his head as if unable to believe what he was saying. Thompson watched the child's face behind the oxygen mask. She was definitely familiar. One of his patients? No, the child from the house in Bareneed. What was her name? Something like an animal. A bird. "Blue," he muttered as the stretcher hit the Emerg doors and passed through. The doctors were waiting, the nurses in their blue garb. "Robin," he said as the Emerg doors swung shut on him. "Her name's Robin."

~๑)

On Sunday night, Kim had stumbled over a pothole along Codger's Lane and the flashlight had flown from her hand into the trees. She had tripped and just managed to catch her balance when she was bowled over from behind, slammed to the gravel on her side with the full weight of a body on top of her. A man was roughly struggling to shove her onto her back. Then Joseph's face was in her face in the darkness, his eyes slitted and wavering in the shadows of trees cast down from moonlight, his hands pinning her arms flat against the ground while his foul breath made her twist her face away in disgust.

"You slut," he spat through clenched teeth. "With that man. The fish man."

"Get off me," she winced, lifting her hip to thrust him off, only to discover it ached horribly from where it had been rammed against the ground. "My hip! Get off me!"

"You won't leave me any more."

"Get *off* me!" She continued shoving, despite the pain, yet failed to budge him.

"Slut." His hand, freeing its hold on her right arm, rose to his lips. He licked a finger and rubbed her cheek as though trying to scrub something off. "What're you under that? Makeup. Pull out your teeth." He pinched her front tooth and yanked. "Drill holes in your head. Find out who." His hand left her face and went for her throat. His fingers toyed with her windpipe, not squeezing hard but pulsing and releasing as if testing the resilience.

With one hand free, Kim had taken the opportunity to grip a rock and smack Joseph in the side of the head. Upon impact, he loosened his grip on her windpipe and his unfixed eyes watched her for a few wondering moments. His face slowly lowered nearer to hers. She thought he might pass out, or bite her, and so she raised the rock, about to strike him again. But instead he kissed her with such delicate emotion that it genuinely alarmed her. A goodbye kiss with the prickles of his unshaven face hurting her skin. Then he jumped up and ran off into the trees. A trail of cracklings and snappings, and a series of animal grunts, marked his progress into the woods.

Kim had lain there on the gravel road, pebbles in her back and legs, the pain in her hip making itself evident again. A sob shook her chest. She felt weak, then angry, stronger. She braced her hands to the gravel and carefully rose, tears of fright and pain in her eyes. She checked toward the trees for her lost flashlight but could find no sign of it. Calling out Robin's name, she trod forward. She was alone and terrified; nothing made sense to her. She had been attacked by Joseph, who then raced blindly into the woods as if he knew his way.

She had to pause to bend forward, her anxiety and the pain in her hip becoming so intense that she vomited in the gully at the side of the road. Weeping and gasping for breath, she continued descending the incline of

Codger's Lane, calling out for Robin, the sharp, deeply inner pain in her hip growing worse. She pressed on, her head swimming with dizziness.

At the bottom of the lane, she had caught sight of the scene along the harbourfront and could think of nothing but the word "nightmarish." Not far from shore two men, in one of the several boats on the black water, were pulling a bundle aboard. It was evident that the bundle was a body. A helicopter hovering overhead shone its searchlight directly into the boat, illuminating the men in black wetsuits and the pallor of the body in their hands.

Unsteadiness surged through Kim. She felt as though she were searching in an utterly foreign land, a land not made of soil, but landscaped entirely from the bleakest terrain of the mind; searching for her daughter who was lost or had been taken by strangers she could never find nor understand because this was a horrible horrible mystery that would not give itself up. It was so unimaginable that it made her feel invisible. She would not think of the reasons why Robin was missing. She could not bear to think of them. She could only continue searching.

A few steps along the lower road, she had stopped, hearing the snapping of branches and the sweep of footsteps over grass. She turned to see the shadow of a man following her, darting off the road and into the woods. Joseph. Had he completely lost his mind? He seemed to be stalking her like prey, about to strike. She hurried her pace, cringing while alertly calling out in tormented longing, "Rawwwbinn?"

No reply. If only her daughter would appear. Kim would give anything. She told this to God, assured Him that she would do anything to have her daughter returned to her. Anything. *Please,* she begged, again and again. *Please, God. Do this for me, for my baby. Please.*

When she reached the first barricade, heading west on the lower road, a cluster of soldiers with flashlights prevented her from searching farther, even when Kim screamed above the noise of helicopter rotors chopping the air around them: "My daughter's lost. She's gone."

A tall soldier who seemed to be in charge, or thought himself to be, took notice of her injury and radioed for assistance. He then indicated to Kim that residents were not permitted beyond the barricade. Another soldier, standing a little farther away, watched Kim with a look of concern bordering on fear. It was the sight of this frightened soldier that compelled Kim to begin shrieking savagely and clawing the soldier who was blocking her way. She was pulled back by a third soldier, her breath coming hot while she stared at the tall soldier with hatred, her eyes trying to avoid the frightened soldier, his appearance hunched while he studied the water with dread.

"I'm sorry," the tall soldier said.

And Kim backed off, still glaring at him. She was about to turn away when headlights approached beyond the barricade. Kim was forced to shield her eyes as the vehicle came to a stop, then flashed its blue and red lights. The form of a police officer climbed out to stand in the strobing lights. He was taller and sturdier than the tall soldier.

"Are you Mrs. Blackwood?" called the silhouette.

"Yes," Kim uttered, shuffling forward, then called "Yes" again, louder to compete with the air-chopping noise from a helicopter that was now hovering directly overhead, as if watching down on them. She took a step toward the police officer, but, again, was halted by the tall soldier. She shoved him with both her hands and he stumbled back.

"That's okay," the police officer said loudly, moving ahead to take her arm. "I'm Sergeant Chase." He glanced down at her feet. "Did you hurt your leg?"

"Have you found my daughter?" Kim asked.

The officer opened the back door of his car for her. "No, I'm sorry. Not yet. A search-and-rescue team is being assembled. They'll be here soon."

Kim climbed into the police car, wincing as she settled. The heat was on and the air beyond the windows was cool. Late at night. Cooling. The heat was comforting, too comforting. Kim's hip was aching deeply, the soreness troubling her stomach again. Sergeant Chase climbed in the driver's door. Kim stared back, through the rear window, watching toward the hills where, under the glare of floodlights, house-size silver discs were being erected by helicopters.

"Are we looking now?" she asked the officer.

"Searching?"

"Yes."

"It's useless at night, just us."

"It's not useless." Kim slapped the seat ahead of her. "Christ!"

"It's better if everyone stays in one place. Keep things in order. The search has to be systematic." His eyes flicked toward the rearview. "Children behave differently than adults when they're lost. Children tend to hide in the one spot. They don't wander." Kim followed the officer's eyes, then caught sight of Joseph. He stood briefly on the road, before leaping into the woods. The tall soldier had taken an interest and was going after him.

Sergeant Chase took Kim back to the Critch house. On the way, he asked if Kim required medical attention for her injury. Kim refused the offer, claiming that she had simply stumbled and fallen down in the dark.

"I'm fine," she said dismissively.

At the Critch house, Sergeant Chase used his radio to contact the army base at the community centre for word on the girl. There was sketchy information that a child had been found, but they were not positive who the child might be. Boy or girl. Dead or alive.

"Where's the child?" Kim demanded.

"I'm not certain," Chase replied. "We have to wait here. Word will come to us, right away. I'll make sure."

How long ago had that been now? A night, a week, seconds ago? It was still dark outside, smothering, the parlour lit only by candlelight. Kim had taken three pills, but they didn't seem to be working and so she'd taken another two. Her mind was burdened in a drug stupor that was occasionally infused with panic. When the pain rose, she attempted to get up from the couch in the parlour, as if the pain was stirred by the urgency of Robin's need, but then she fell back again, useless. She couldn't even do something as basic as walk.

Miss Laracy sat in a rocking chair across from Kim. She had asked Sergeant Chase to move the chair down from Joseph's bedroom and he had kindly obliged. The old woman was seated by the parlour window, rocking and humming. Kim guessed the song might be "Silent Night."

Sergeant Chase sat with them for a while, not saying a word, not knowing what to do. Then a call came on his radio, a message notifying Chase that the search and rescue team was now on site.

"Where's your husband?" the officer asked.

Kim shook her head. "No idea."

Chase excused himself to make a few telephone calls in the kitchen. Kim listened but heard nothing distinct, only the deep murmur of his voice. He returned without a word and sat on the piano stool, watching the window, waiting in silence for the first signs of daybreak which soon began to brighten the room.

"Time to go." He reached for his hat where it sat on the coffee table. He fit it on his head and stood.

Miss Laracy took a break from her humming to say, "Da girl's fine."

Sergeant Chase said nothing in reply, merely watched the old woman before stepping past her.

Kim followed him to the door, favouring her right leg to keep the pressure off her hip.

"I'll see if I can find your husband."

"Find my daughter."

As Sergeant Chase's vehicle pulled away, Kim looked toward the dim harbour. There was no activity: no boats and no helicopters. The sky was brightening from black to deep blue. The water was calm, clear, as if the scene from last night had been nothing more than a fantasy, an extravagant cinematic endeavour.

Kim glanced up and down the road for sight of Uncle Doug. He had not returned during the night. There was no sign of him. He was the sort who would not be discouraged by darkness. Kim took comfort in the idea that he was still out there, searching, with friends or neighbours and flashlights. They knew the land. They knew where a girl might be lost. Lost. Taken. Harmed. Kim could take not much more of this. The hours ticked on and hope died and died and died … She went back into the living room.

"Da girl's fine," said Miss Laracy.

Kim sat on the couch and shut her eyes to hold back the tears. She clenched her jaw, then regarded Miss Laracy. Who was this old woman?

And why was she there? She was a bad omen. An evil person. A witch with a wizened face that grinned at her. Grinned!

"Da girl's fine."

"Please," Kim said, placing a hand to her forehead. "Please, just …"

"Naw," said Miss Laracy, raising her voice. "I won't quiet down fer ye. Ye lose yer fait' 'n dat's it fer ye all. Christ, almighty! Clasp hold ta yer fait', young maid."

Kim glared at the old woman.

"Put da peekture in yer 'ead. See yer liddle girl." Suddenly, Miss Laracy looked at the ceiling. She said: "Dere's sumtin' travellin' t'rew." She watched toward the harbour, then up at the ceiling again, down the wall. Her eyes alighting on the telephone on the side table beside the couch as it rang.

Kim leaned to snatch hold of it. "Hello," she said, desperately clutching the receiver, her hip throbbing from the sudden twisting movement.

"Is Joseph Blackwood there?"

"This is his wife. Is this about Robin? I'm her mother."

"This is Dr. Thompson at the hospital in Port de Grave. I've been trying to call, but the line's been dead."

"Is Robin okay?"

"Please come to the hospital. You should come right away."

Often, I clutch hold of the place where I am sitting or standing, for I feel the earth tipping me toward water. Gravity shifting, lilting, leaning. I might slide through trees and grass and over craggy rocks to plunge into the sea. Is this where I belong? Where we all ultimately belong? If so, why do I continue to hold on? Let the pull of the sea take me.

I have been sitting and watching through the window in my studio. The harbour is beautiful. At night. At day. A painting that continues to revise itself. The images, the colours, the light. The light persistently shifts the contours, a seamless advancement of time and energy that manifests its own reality with each second that changes me and all matter in my line of vision. But it is not reality. It is merely the view through my window, framed by a wall on which hang other paintings and photographs that do not change. A pretense, a masquerade. Realism to abstract.

I woke this morning and Jessica was not sleeping beside me. I wonder where she has gone?

I am eating the last of the dried apricots and pears. So sweet. I continue with my sculpting of the barns and house that make up the community. Miniaturized. I have begun to sculpt tiny people. Fishermen in ceramic boats and soldiers in jeeps. Every single house and person nearing completion. These sculpted people come to knock on my door. I do not answer. They go away. I wait for someone to intrude.

The dreams of Reg are becoming stronger, my emotions rawer. As I wear down, Reg appears to strengthen. I will not shut my eyes. When I dream, he is more distinct than when I awake. I see him in Joseph. A man like a man who was once mine. Not to love. Never to love again. I have a compulsion to rush downstairs and throw open the cutlery drawer, snatch up a blade and race across the grass to the Critch House, stab Joseph until he is dead, stab him again and again until I am free of these thoughts.

Why does my mind persistently draw me toward longings for a man? I might kill Joseph, but how do I kill Reg? If I do away with myself, will I be forever bonded to Reg, husband and wife, holding hands while he drags me around perdition, beaten to a pulp, hauling me after him like a rag doll, leaving a smeared trail in my wake?

A knocking on the front door plucked Claudia from the stream of words. She listened to hear the sound, to assure herself of its actuality. Then it came again. Sighing, she waited for it to stop. She set the tip of her pen to paper and waited for words to flow, but there was only knocking. Loud knocking.

Unable to bear it any longer, Claudia stood. The knocking grew thunderously more insistent, the urgency compelling Claudia to hurry her pace down the stairs. Who might it be?

Flinging open the door, she saw a young handsome man in uniform with a clipboard held at chest level. Distinctly nervous and tense in her presence, he raised his pen over the clipboard, ready to take notes.

"Good day," he said.

"Hello."

"My name's Able Seaman Nesbitt."

Claudia glanced over his shoulder toward the harbour. A plywood fence had been erected all along the shoreline. No doubt, to keep people from entering the scene, or seeing in from close up. Helicopters continued their work on the hills to the west, where giant metal discs were being erected. Claudia could make out numerous sparklings of light where the discs were being welded, assembled on the spot. What were they for? Satellite dishes for the media?

"We're checking to make certain the residents are in good health." Nesbitt glanced at his clipboard. "You're Claudia Kyle?"

"Yes." She was struck by how young the man appeared to be, eighteen or nineteen, practically a child. "Someone was already here."

Nesbitt checked over his left shoulder; he'd heard a car door shut. The sound arrived from the direction of the Critch house. An engine started and the car sped down the higher road. A woman was driving. Joseph's wife, swerving slightly. The soldier seemed to be about to race after the car; he raised a hand and opened his mouth to call, but held himself. He returned his gaze to Claudia's face, his cheeks flushing with embarrassment.

"I guess I'll get to her later," he said, licking his lips and offering a faint boyish smile.

"I suppose so."

Nesbitt checked Claudia's chest, then peeked at her eyes. "Are you in good health?" he asked, the flush in his face deepening.

Claudia shut her eyes, gripped by slumping weakness, and frowned. The young soldier continued speaking: "Specifically your respiratory function."

"My breathing?" Claudia opened her eyes and the colours seemed a touch more vibrant than before. The face of the young soldier was so clean and eager. She examined his lips. They were not thin, but not too full. If only she could kiss him. Plummet back to that youth, be saved. That's all. Kiss him and, perhaps, hold his face against her bosom. Hold his warm head, his warm hair. Kiss him and watch his face for years without moving. No complications to appropriate her heart.

"Yes, your breathing."

She took a deep breath, in, then out.

The soldier glanced rapidly at her chest again, not wanting to let his eyes linger. Convinced, he nodded, ticked a small square on his clipboard, then wrote a number next to the tick.

"Thank you, m'am. Sorry to bother you. If you need assistance you can call this number." He handed her a card. "It's a sticker. You might want to stick it on your telephone. The telephone in a central location. Oh, is there anyone else in the house with you?"

"No, no one." She accepted the sticker and studied it without interest. "I don't have a telephone." She noticed the soldier's eyes on the sleeve of her nightdress, the words she had scrawled there, up and down the length.

The soldier shifted his eyes from her sleeve but gave no indication of judgement or blame for the state of her nightdress. "I need to put this on your door." He slid a larger sticker out from under his papers. It was a green symbol of three thick waves stacked atop one another. He peeled off the back and stuck it to the upper panel of the door.

"Thank you," said Claudia.

"That's okay." The soldier smiled and tipped his head. "So, there's no one else in the house?"

Claudia stared, not saying a word. She thought of a quote from somewhere: "My house is never empty, my heart is always full."

"No," she finally said.

Again, the soldier nodded, offered her a beautiful honest smile that said he appreciated her or knew her better than she ever expected, then turned to leave. He was on foot, heading toward the Critch house. She glanced at the green wave sticker, nibbled on her bottom lip, then shut the door with both trembling hands.

Back upstairs, she sat at her desk and wrote:

I am here again. I was downstairs and there was a soldier at my door. I spoke with him and he left me a sticker which I now stick here. A telephone number in case of trouble. I am to be saved by contact. The soldier stood in front of me only a minute or more ago. And now he is gone. But the soldier still occupies a space in my head. An optical echo. I visualize him handing me the sticker and I can see him smiling at me. He has left my life, but he has remained. Once I have seen him, face to face, he is with me. Everyone I have ever seen remains with me as if they are all required to keep my life from wandering away from what it is. They make me from their lives, their needs. My life. What is my life, alone?

There is a dull hammering above me that is rhythmic and then sporadic, then rhythmic again. A bird banging its beak against the roof. No doubt a crow, pecking as if I am already sealed within my casket, food for the dark ones that creep, slither and travel by wing. I will make myself into dust. I will hold no rot for them.

Why must I be the tragedy?

⁓◑

When Able Seaman Nesbitt reached the Critch house, an old woman answered the door before his raised knuckles could impact a single knock.

"Yays?" asked the woman, her tiny face grinning up, pink gums catching sunlight. She squinted at him and touched the back of his hand in greeting, patted it encouragingly. "Tell me wha' ye be after, me ducky."

"This is the Critch house?" asked Nesbitt, finding peculiarity in the old woman, the colourful warmth that swelled from her touch, the way her eyes seemed to see right into him and clutch at the beats of his heart, tenderly hold on. It was a sensation he had experienced before only in love.

"Yays, but da Critches be dead fer many a year."

"This is a rental."

"Yays."

"A man and his daughter."

Nodding: "Yays, 'n udder ones now, too."

"Other *people?*" asked Nesbitt, for the tone of her voice implied something otherworldly. He hoped for no further unsettling episodes, for he was already scared beyond belief, what with the bodies and the creatures in the water. The flying fish. The things he saw were troublesome to him. The others soldiers seemed not to see the entirety of what he noticed.

The old woman shrugged. "Townies out fer a lark."

Nesbitt attentively checked over the clipboard. The words were there, yet he had trouble focusing, reading them. They offered no clarification. He feared they were there merely to confound him. "We don't seem to have any record of you," he said, frowning in forced concentration.

"Fine widt me," answered the old woman, giving a lighthearted chuckle, then pointing toward the hills. "What're dey buildin' over dere. Big silver t'ings."

"I don't know, ma'am." Nesbitt continued searching his clipboard. "This is the Critch house, right? Are you Mrs. Critch?"

"I jus' tol' ya dat da Critches be passed on fer many a year. Are ye daft, or just stunned as me arse?"

Nesbitt stared at the old woman. He could not pull together an answer, and so he said: "Could you please give me your name? Please."

"Eileen Laracy." As though taking notice of his emotional turmoil, she patted his hand and mellowed her tone. "Ye be awright, me ducky. Dere's nuttin' ta be a'scared of."

Nesbitt watched the old woman's sympathetic eyes. If decorum had permitted, he would have pleaded with her to hold and comfort him.

"Da missus dat live here just took off fer da hospital. Da udders are out searchin' fer da lost liddle girl. On land, not da water."

"Oh." Nesbitt noticed something in the old woman's hands, a string of beads wrapped around her palm, a small silver cross and the medals of saints hooked together at one end. "Are you feeling okay? Your health, I mean. That's what I'm here to see about. I was sent here to see about."

"Da finest kind." The old woman grinned broadly and winked, extended her arm, offering her wrist. "Check me pulse, lover."

Nesbitt gave a quick laugh. "No, no, I don't think I need to do that."

"Well, wha' else ye be affer? Dere's sumtin' else stumblin' 'round in yer 'ead. I sees it in ye."

"Huh?"

"A question ye be wantin' ta ask."

"Yes, that's right. There is, actually. The navy'll soon be conducting an exercise to identify the bodies —"

"Hexercise? I gets plenty o' hexercise —"

"To identify the bodies that have washed ashore. The navy wants to enlist the services of the older residents in hopes that they might recognize some of the drowned."

Miss Laracy squinted. Again, she touched Nesbitt's hand. "Ye 'av ta slow down yer words. I can't follow ye 'cause yer tongue's too swift."

"Have you lived in Bareneed long?"

"Since da day I were born."

"Would you care to help us identify some of the bodies?"

"I'd prolly know dem all, sir. Each 'n ev'ry last one o' 'em."

"So, you'd be willing?" The idea of her possible compliance brightened Nesbitt's hopes. He felt in his bones that she was a key to much of what needed resolving.

"Is dere money in it?"

"Payment?"

"Yays."

"I don't … think so."

"Hmmm."

"You'd be helping us a great deal."

"Who be da 'us' ye speaks of?"

"Your community, I guess."

"Yer not me community," she huffed. "Yer just strangers, a big bloody nuisance."

"We're here to help."

"Dat's bullcrap!" Again, she pointed toward the hills. "Wha' da hell be dem monstrosities up dere?"

"I really don't know, ma'am," Nesbitt truthfully confessed.

"Ye'll kill us all widt yer high-tech gizmos. Nuttin' been da same since da snowmobiles 'n da chainsaws 'n all dat jewellery. Where be da horses 'n da dog sleds 'n da healthy men who could clear a forest widt a bucksaw? Automobiles killin' families 'n chil'ren every God-given minute of da day."

Nesbitt could offer no answer.

"All yer jewellery. It be da deat' of us."

⁓◊⁓

Tommy walked straight into Rayna's house. He had no time for knocking on doors. They were just hiding stuff. He stood in the back porch and bent to unlace his sneakers. He knew something was wrong by the smell of the house and the sounds and colours of uneasy light that told him the mood of things was all akilter. His sketch pad was tucked under his arm. He had brought it along to show Rayna his latest drawings of what came after the sheets of just one colour. She always said nice things. It made him happy to see how she really liked what he could do. And she'd think these ones were pretty. The way he drew spirits was pretty. Even he knew that.

"Hello," he called out, hurrying into the kitchen. An empty bottle of rum stood on the counter, dishes were piled in the sink, there were dirty pots on the stove. He thought of doing the dishes right away. The urge to clean up, to see things in order, tugged powerfully in his chest, giving him pause. Squinting, he shook his head once, smartly, as if chopping a thought in half. "Rayna?" he called out. He listened and heard a sound from somewhere in the house: a thud, something hard hitting a wall. He stared down at his socks, saw how the ends were loose, not snug to his toes. That bugged him. He had to bend down and pull them up, then fold the upper edges down evenly, along his ankles, so they were tight and perfect. That way they wouldn't bug him. It was a chore to do this and keep the sketch pad under his arm, yet he managed.

He stood and wasted no time rushing into the hallway. "Rayna?"

Another thud, followed by a low pained gasp.

Tommy blessed himself and clumsily sprinted down the hallway toward Rayna's bedroom. He had never been in there before yet he knew where it was. He'd seen her cross through the door to get changed or do other stuff. The door was open a crack. Hesitantly and with a flush of embarrassment already splotching his cheeks, he leaned toward the opening, then leaned back before he could see anything, shaking his head, displeased with himself. He shouldn't peek in there, not at Rayna. She might have no clothes on.

Another thud shook the floorboards under his socked feet. He bravely put his eye to the crack and saw only the wall, ragged holes punched in gyprock. He opened the door. Rayna was by the bed, staring at the wall and looking out of sorts. There was no colour around her. She turned her narrowed eyes on him, the knuckles of both hands covered in blood. She gasped for a breath and screamed, punching another hole in the wall.

Tommy flinched ahead a step, then back. "Rayna," he whispered worriedly, but she just made a mean face at him. In a flash, she spun and grabbed up the lamp by the side of the bed, and hurled it at his head.

Ducking, Tommy felt the sketch pad slip out from under his arm. When it hit the plaster-sprinkled carpet, it spread open to the most recent drawing of a multitude of golden spirits in the dark sky, spirits up high, descending toward the night water.

The noise from Rayna had stopped. Tommy looked up to see her staring at the drawing on the floor. Her face was not mean any more. She stared for a long time without moving at all, without even pulling in the slightest breath, like she was nothing more than a picture herself, captured, identical to one of the drawings Tommy remembered making of her; that look on her face. Then Rayna's body went limp. She fell sideways, landing on the bed with a bobbing bounce that reminded Tommy of floating.

⟿

Sergeant Chase was somewhere in the broad patch of evergreens between the higher and lower roads. It amazed him how he could be so deeply immersed in such density of woods with a community all around him. The woods engulfed you, secluded you, cut you off from your known life, as soon as you entered them.

Presently, all he could see were trees. Deep-green spruce mingled with the lighter-green pine boughs and the even-lighter fir, and the varied leaves of mountain ash, maple and birch. The trees in Newfoundland were smaller than those in Saskatchewan, the evergreens stunted by the wind, salt water and brief summer season. And there were fewer bugs, less heat, less humidity. These woods were much more enjoyable, but not under the present circumstances.

Chase was following as opposed to leading. Doug Blackwood was up ahead, calling out Robin's name and cutting through the taller bushes with a machete that he claimed was brought back from the First World War by his father. Chase recalled one of his previous search-and-rescue efforts. They had been searching for a little girl at night, and they had no luck finding her until the next day when she came out from hiding under a bush. Chase had spotted her through the trees, off in the distance, walking in a clearing as though nothing were the matter, her palms skimming over the tall blades of grass. When Chase had called out, she simply froze and waited for them to reach her. She had told him that she had been frightened because a monster was moaning her name all night, a monster with one glowing eye that kept passing around her, moaning and moaning her name. As it turned out, the monster with the one glowing eye had been one of the rescuers with a flashlight. How efficiently fear compels the mind to trick itself.

Another voice called off in the distance, somewhere to Chase's right. The voice kept bellowing the same phrase: "Wake up, wake up, wake up," before it fell silent for a short while only to repeat the same words again. Insects buzzed around Chase: clouds of white, barely visible flies lingering here and there, shifting in a hazy multitude. Other voices called persistently: "Robin? We're here to find you. Robin? We're here to help you." Occasionally, Chase could hear the branches snapping to either side of him, the efforts of other men and women forging ahead, people Doug Blackwood had recruited from the community along with members of the search-and-rescue team.

Sergeant Chase had come upon Doug Blackwood at daybreak. Blackwood had been on Codger's Lane, having just stepped out of the woods on the east side of the road, the woods that led to the cliffs and water. Doug was instructing a group of two men and one woman, pointing with the machete toward the woods on the west side of the lane. At once, Doug had recruited Chase, informing the officer that he had assembled the search party from the men and women gathered at Wilf Murray's, Honey Greening's and Bren Cutland's, the only three houses that contained people who were not sick. These people were the last healthy members of the community. They had gathered without fear of contracting the contagion, to seek out a lost little girl.

Why the three houses, Chase wondered. Why the people gathered there? Why were they well? His mind flickered over memories of the places where people had gathered on the reserve: in the longhouse where elaborate feasts were prepared, stories were told and songs sung. He recalled the sweat lodge ceremonies: steam rising from the heated rocks within the enclosure, each person singing a song of praise to the Creator, offering up devotion. Places of gathering. The idea nagged at him as he ducked through branches and kicked his black boots free of the lower growth tangling his step. The buzzing of a bee or wasp drifted near and he hoped no one would tread on a hidden nest.

He stumbled, alert yet lost in thought, and soon realized that there was a figure coming near in his peripheral vision. No doubt, one of the searchers. He turned to catch a better view. It was a man who resembled Joseph Blackwood, the father of the missing girl, the man he had seen fishing on the dock those few calm days ago. Yes, it was Joseph Blackwood, trying to keep pace, wildly thrashing through the growth with his arms, then falling to the ground with a grunt. Chase called ahead to Doug, who spun around expectantly and quickly trudged back along the path he had cut. Discovering the focus of Chase's concern, Doug sighed in disappointment, then reluctantly cut a path to Joseph with assured sweeps of the blade. Arriving where Joseph had fallen, Doug and Chase reached down to help the man up. He was pale, trembling, terrified.

"Take the trees away," he muttered. "Trees away. They're not needed. They're hiding … the water … drinking it … Down there." He stared toward the underbrush and stomped it with his foot. "There's water under everything. I don't want to fall."

Doug looked Joseph up and down then headed off without further word, vigorously slicing through bushes, making his way while he called to the men at his left, "Any luck?"

No word in return.

"You need medical attention," Chase informed Joseph. The radio clipped to the pocket of his short-sleeved shirt gave a garbled blast of static. He raised it while watching Joseph Blackwood's fidgeting eyes.

"Sergeant Chase. Go ahead."

"This is Lieutenant-Commander French. We've found the girl. Call off your search party. She's been transported to the hospital in Port de Grave. We have received confirmation of her identity. Copy that?"

"Copy."

Joseph Blackwood snatched the radio away and, using both weak hands, fumbled with it, stretching the coiled cord and pulling. Immediately,

Chase thought of his pepper spray, but at this close range he would get just as much of it as Blackwood. Instead, he reached for the extendable metal baton in the leather pouch hooked to his belt. He had it out in a second, flicked it to its full steely length. Joseph pressed the radio button again and again, but nothing happened.

"It's hollow," Joseph said, giving a suspicious laugh. He put it too close to his mouth, knocking it off his front tooth, and said a few words that made no sense. Then he bit it, his teeth working to pry into the casing. "Plastic." He laughed hysterically. "It's not authentic. You're not real."

Sergeant Chase snatched the radio. "Back off," he warned, eyes fixed on Joseph Blackwood. He then took a furtive glance toward Doug Blackwood, who was far ahead, cutting through the growth.

"They've found her," he called out, raising the radio when he saw Doug vigilantly stare back through the trees.

Carefully watching Joseph, Chase put the radio to his mouth while clutching the baton in his other hand. "What's the girl's condition?"

"Uncertain."

"Thanks. Copy." Sergeant Chase clipped the radio back to his pocket. "They've found her," he repeated to Joseph Blackwood, who simply nodded, then put a hand out in front of himself to examine it. It was covered in scratches, his fingernails lined with arcs of dirt. He licked the tip of one finger and attempted to rub the scratches off.

"They should come off," he said urgently.

Chase's radio squelched again. He raised it to his mouth. "Sergeant Chase. Go ahead."

"This is Lieutenant-commander French. Dr. Basha, the provincial pathologist, has arrived at base. All my men are occupied. Could you pick him up and escort him to the fish plant. Provide background. Copy that?"

"Copy. Not a problem."

Sergeant Chase continued studying Joseph Blackwood, who stood patiently in wait, staring at Chase's shirt. Blackwood's face was bloodied and lined with scratches and abrasions. There was a cut in the corner of his top lip that seeped blood. As the blood bubbled out, Blackwood licked it away. By the appearance of the vertical crease down the centre of his forehead and the pinched smile on his lips, he seemed to be concentrating on something painfully uncertain.

"Is that a real uniform?" he asked, examining the emblem patch on Chase's sleeve. "Or just a souvenir from the show?"

⁓∅

Tommy had rushed to the kitchen and called 911. When the woman who answered asked him the nature of the emergency, he had told her that Rayna was hurting herself and it was like she couldn't breathe. The woman had told him to stay with Rayna and that an ambulance would be there right away. Extra vehicles had been dispatched to the area to deal with the crisis. That was a while ago and the ambulance was taking a long time to get there. When Tommy had gone back into the bedroom, Rayna had regained consciousness and was sitting on the floor by the side of the bed, her face white, her chest heaving with panicky breath. She clutched Tommy's notepad and stared at his drawings. He checked her face to see if she was angry. But she wasn't angry while her eyes searched the amber forms of spirits. She kept watching them and paid no mind to Tommy.

When the ambulance arrived, the paramedic, Byron Quilty, a cousin of Tommy's, allowed him to ride in the back with Rayna as long as Tommy agreed to wear a white mask that he looped around his ears. The straps bugged his ears, bugged him until tears sprang to his eyes, but he kept the mask on anyway. He knew he had to, for Rayna's sake. He needed to be there, so he could look after his friend. If he watched over her then she might be okay.

Rayna lay still on the stretcher and tried breathing through the oxygen mask, but it didn't help her. She still jerked and shifted like she was uncomfortable. Tommy held her hand tighter. It was wet and slippery. But it was also warm and he liked the way it felt. It was only the second time he had held her hand. The first time, they had been on a walk and Rayna had taken hold of his hand like they were kids again, friends, and it was the most perfect feeling he ever felt.

As the ambulance sped along, Tommy knew there was something that he must do to make Rayna well, but he wasn't sure yet what it was.

One of the scenes he had painted a few weeks ago had been of himself, sitting by the side of a bed talking to a person who lay at rest. Other beds had been in the room and the people in them were missing parts of themselves. It was as if they were not all there. One of them even seemed invisible, fading away, the body becoming dark inside, but, strangely, the outline of the person still there.

"Da fairies carted me off when I were but a young nipper," he said, his distressed words muffled through the mask. He grinned worriedly, the mask stretching tighter on his ears.

Rayna was watching the white inner side of the ambulance. Hearing Tommy's words, she turned her troubled eyes toward him.

"I 'members it like t'were yesterday."

Rayna shook her head once, not understanding.

"Da fairies took me." He nodded faithfully to convince her. "Dey changed me 'cause dey were magical 'n I loved da fairies on a count of dem being like nuttin' else in da world. 'N den dey goes away 'n shows demselves no more."

Rayna let her eyes drift toward the side of the ambulance. A tear trickled from her left eye, spilling along her temple and catching in her hair, wetting the strands, making them sheen in the light. Tommy watched the tear. Another came and the way it left her eye and crept down her skin made his lips tremble. A sob pulled at his lungs while tears spilled freely from his own eyes.

"Da fairies," he said, his words sopping wet behind the mask. "Da fairies, Rayna, 'n da angels 'n all da dead belonged ta us. Think on dem. Think hard on dem, so dey can recognize ye when dey come."

-◌)

It was a little after 9:00 a.m. and Kim had to hold herself back from attacking the nurse behind the glass in Emergency. She had been in the waiting room for more than half an hour, trying to skip ahead in line, desperate to contact Dr. Thompson, but the nurse, who was wearing a headset and wireless microphone like the soldiers, insisted that Kim wait her turn, regardless of the fact that Kim pleaded: "It's about my daughter,

Robin. Robin Blackwood." Robin had been missing and now she was found. Didn't the nurse understand? Didn't the nurse have children of her own?"The doctor called me," Kim insisted."Where ... is ... the ... doctor?" she shouted, her voice quavering toward a screech. The static of conversation in the waiting area subsided and people in the line kindly or fearfully stepped back to allow Kim to take their place, but when she reached the window, the nurse informed her that Dr. Thompson was presently occupied and would be contacted shortly. Then the nurse had asked Kim to please step aside so that others might be assisted. That had been the near-breaking point, when Kim had to restrain herself from pounding the glass to get at the nurse.

Kim had then tried to enter farther into the hospital by the corridor that veered away from Emergency, but a soldier in green army fatigues was guarding the doors. No one was permitted entry without authorization.

"It's my daughter," she begged, leaning to step around the soldier, but he had blocked her path.

"I'm going to have to ask you to move back, please."

Feeling hands on her shoulders and suspecting that another soldier had been summoned, Kim spun around, hurt and worried. Her mind raced with the words "My daughter."

Uncle Doug smiled consolingly, and patiently guided her away from the soldier.

"It's okay, my old trout," he said. Kim's eyes flicked toward the Emergency doorway where Joseph stood hesitantly, scanning the interior with apprehension, sniffing the air. He was a mess, his face and hands smeared with dirt, sweating and covered in a multitude of marks and scrapes. Several days' growth of beard and moustache gave him the appearance of being destitute. An ambulance had pulled up behind him, making Joseph step back and then flee outside as a stretcher supporting a woman was wheeled in. A man with a mask, holding what appeared to be a sketch pad under his arm, wandered in to join the crowd.

"How's your hip feeling?" Doug asked.

"It's fine." Kim shivered with rage. She was so cold, her sore hip throbbed, and she could not even force herself to speak. She thought she might go mad, lose her mind, if she could not see her little girl soon. Uncle Doug slipped an arm around her shoulders and gave her a comforting squeeze that coursed warmth through her. Immediately, she hugged him, her eyes shut, her face against his blue and black plaid shirt. There was a strong smell of the woods off him and a faint smell of gasoline. When Kim opened her eyes again, Joseph had reappeared in the doorway and was watching the man wearing the mask.

"Is she okay?" asked a voice behind Kim. She turned her head to see the soldier who had been guarding the door. He was close to her, but his manner was not intrusive. He seemed genuinely concerned.

"She'll be all right," Uncle Doug said to the soldier. "Don't you worry about her."

"I'm looking for my sick daughter," Kim said with spite.

The soldier glanced at Kim's chest, eyes lingering until he discerned a breath. Then he stepped back.

"I'm not sick," she said. "Dr. Thompson called about my daughter. She was lost and now she's found and we need him paged and that …" she stabbed a finger in the direction of the nurse behind the glass, "… that … *thing* won't page him because I'm not in line."

"I'm sorry," the soldier apologized. "The place is very busy." With those words, he shifted his gaze toward the nurse, who was already watching the soldier. The soldier nodded and the nurse dipped her head down, pressed a button and spoke into her wireless microphone.

The paging system announced: "Dr. Thompson to Emergency. Dr. Thompson to Emergency."

"Thank you," Kim said at once to the soldier, a surge of emotion welling up in her.

"That's all right," he replied with a brief smile.

Uncle Doug nodded his thanks while Joseph inched a step farther into the waiting area, testing his footing as if treading on ice that was both slippery and likely to crack at any moment. Without a word to Kim, Uncle Doug stormed over to Joseph, grabbed him by the arm, yanked him fully in through the doors, and dragged him over to stand at Kim's side.

"Stand there, ya useless object," he lambasted Joseph, who stood cowering, without moving a muscle or drawing a breath, his eyes vacant.

In a small removed voice, Joseph asked Kim: "Where am I?"

—◌

"Have we identified any of these?" Dr. Basha asked, his breath steaming through his mask, lingering in puffs and wisps in the chilly air. He was a short slim man with black hair and a thin yet optimistic face. His deep-brown eyes took in the expansive fish plant where bodies, dressed in the colours and fabrics of various fashions, were laid out on long white filleting tables. Other doctors and military personnel milled about. A white lab coat here, a green or blue uniform there. Toward the rear of the fish plant, a row of computers had been set up. Four people sat, faces toward the screens, fingers clicking keyboards. One of the soldiers snapped a series of photographs of the dead, and then returned to one of the computers where he plugged the camera into the terminal. Another soldier carried a video camera with a bright light attached and was carefully documenting the features of each body. A third soldier held a metal wand that he passed over a corpse before examining a gauge held in his hand.

Chase, who stood lost in the sight of so many dead, noticed Basha now watching him. The number of bodies was far beyond Chase's expectations. Overwhelmed, he wondered what Theresa might be doing. She must not know about this. It would be the end of her.

"Sergeant?" Basha's breath wafted from around the edges of his mask, escaping like gas, as he stepped deeper into the chilly plant.

"Yes, it's Sergeant," Chase said, following after the doctor.

"Do we know any of these people?" Basha gestured grandly into the white-walled space before them, his palm opening, fingers uncurling. "In relation to things."

"One or two." Chase adjusted the straps of his white mask, which were tightly looped around his ears. He did not want to breathe in any of this. If he breathed it in, it might lodge deep in his lungs, to be exhaled into his home later. Chase imagined that Theresa was so thin-skinned she might actually absorb the germs of tragedy.

"Are there relatives?" Basha inspected a body lying on its side, outfitted in rusty scuba gear. The oval impression of the diver's mask — now hung around the corpse's neck — was embedded in the dead face. Basha tutted in disbelief. "This gear is not contemporary. The suit either."

"Nineteen-sixties," Chase confirmed.

"Really? That many years ago."

"I used to scuba. Not any more, though."

"I see." Basha turned his head, his expression slightly confused yet still spiced with good humour. He noticed a body across the aisle and approached it. It was dressed in the fashion of the late-nineteenth century. "These boots," said Basha, inspecting the cleats protruding from the bottom, tapping them with his pencil. "They're sealing boots. For gripping ice."

"Oh." Chase breathed and watched farther up the fish plant. The soldier with the video camera was now positioned at the far end of the aisle. There were more than twenty bodies to document while working his way down. The body presently under scrutiny was illuminated by the camera's bright light. A face glowing, then an arm, a leg …

The corpse beside Chase and Basha had a label, with the number "1" written on it, taped to the white slab on which the body rested.

"That's the first body to be retrieved," explained Chase.

"And now?"

"Close to seventy."

"All from different periods of time."

"Yes."

"Any particular relation? Theme?"

"None that we can determine."

"And not decomposed."

"No."

"This, of course, is rather unorthodox." Dr. Basha turned to look up expectantly at the police officer, his eyes blinking. "Generally water does damage. Bloating, slackening of the skin."

Chase said nothing. He felt no need to comment.

"This is absurd," said Basha.

"I guess so," Chase mumbled.

"This is ridiculous." Dr. Basha's head trembled slightly. He spun around. "Science just doesn't figure here. I'll admit that openly. Have there been any other pathologists dropping by? I assume there have been some, many more to come."

"I don't know, sorry." Chase followed Basha's line of vision, scanning the interior. Bodies laid out everywhere. It was eerie beyond sensation. A disaster, but more than that. A disaster that had taken centuries to evolve. Chase had seen nothing that even resembled it. There was no point of reference. A mass of dead bodies and no one to grieve for them.

Basha glanced overhead, squinting as if to fix the reality of his setting. He scanned the rows of fluorescent lights, the high windows letting in morning light, the long white walls. "Any single one identified for certain?"

"We think so." Chase stepped farther down the aisle, nearer the soldier with the camera.

"Thinking so is always a beginning."

"That's right." Chase led the pathologist halfway up the aisle to the body of a woman in her early twenties. Her pretty face was vaguely green, her long blonde hair tangled and damp. She was wearing jeans and a pale blue T-shirt. Chase noticed a pink starfish stuck to the woman's left leg.

"She's more up to speed," Basha commented in a welcoming tone. "Of course, I'm guessing. They all look recent to me. Fresh as daisies, in the chronology of the dead."

"She's been identified as a missing person from two years ago."

"Who is she?"

"Bonnie Pottle. The sister of Darry Pottle."

"And Darry Pottle is?"

"The third or fourth to be taken by this ... Whatever this is."

"The breathing disfunction?"

"Right."

"And who was the first?"

"With the breathing —"

"Yes."

"As far as we know, it was Muss Drover. He actually died. Shut himself off from the world. People suspected depression. He became angry. Violent. Then he died."

"Suicide?" Basha speculated.

"No. There's a history of violence, but only briefly. Before the breath gives out."

"I held a teleconference with Dr. Thompson while still in St. John's. He indicated there's no airway inflammation or bronchoconstriction in any of the patients suffering from this breathing disorder? No pathology in the brain stem."

"I don't know. What I understand is the breath just gives out."

Basha tutted. He stared Chase directly in the eye and tutted again. "The breath gives out. Like a machine that needs new batteries. We can only assume that the disorder and these bodies are somehow related. A virus from the decomposition."

"What decomposition?"

"Let's see." Basha regarded the young woman's corpse, then delicately tugged a pair of latex gloves from his pocket and snapped them on. He touched the woman's throat and raised her left arm, searching under it. "Quite limber," he said to himself. He raised the woman's t-shirt and Chase averted his eyes at the sight of her uncovered greenish-white breasts. "No wounds. Help me roll her over. Take her leg there."

Chase took hold of Bonnie Pottle's jeans, avoiding the pink starfish. The jeans were soaking wet and horribly cold all the way through. He pushed with the doctor. Dead weight. They held the woman on her side while Basha examined the perfect flatness of her back. "Nothing."

"She might have fallen over a boat."

"Possibly. Ease her down. Although I doubt it. Look at the way she was dressed." He ran his pencil through the air above the body. "It was sunny, calm. If she was in a boat she could be rescued. I suspect she drowned herself." Basha touched the woman's left ankle, then yanked up the jean cuff. "Ahh," he crooned. With the tip of the pencil, he pointed to a ring of indentations in her skin. "Rope burn. Rope around a rock. Rock into water. Water in the lungs. The end of the story."

A bright light shone against the side of Chase's face, glinting harshly in his left eye. Squinting, he looked to see a shrouded outline: the soldier with the video camera, aiming it directly at Chase. Basha raised his head from his observations and checked toward the brilliance as well.

The camera angled nearer, the two men motionless before its lens.

"Just act normal," directed the voice behind the blinding light. "Pretend I'm not here."

~⦿~

Tommy lingered at the edge of the waiting area, scanning the people who sat upright or bent forward in the rows of chairs. Others stood and seemed so painfully out of place, taken from their daily lives, trapped in a room with nothing but the buzz of conversation.

Rayna had been admitted for examination. That's all Tommy knew. He had been watching the woman who was looking for her little girl. He hoped the little girl was okay. The thought of sick children made him sleepy, drained him of any happiness he might be feeling. He could sense the happiness running out of him in a way that he had to stop by thinking good thoughts. There were sick colours wavering around the woman, purples and greens. The man standing next to her, the one Tommy thought was the woman's husband, had a grey aura that darkened toward the centre; he was lost to himself. No brightness for other people, no light to meld with their light and thus encourage comfort and peace. When the man and woman were near each other, the greys and purples and greens mixed, creating an ugly bruised colour that made both of them sicker. The older man who completed the trio was the purest, although not without anger and vigour. The light surrounding him was yellow with a shadow of orange. When his colours mixed with the woman's, the woman's colours were lightened; she became less body and more spirit. The deeper colours, the greys and blacks and browns and blues, were the colours of the body, the earth and water; the yellows and reds and goldens were the colours of the spirit, of the sun and its countless tints of light. Tommy was still wearing his white mask. No one had told him to take it off. The waiting area was full of people he knew. Some waved to him and he waved back. They were worried; their auras shivered pinks and blues and reds mixed with browns. Some men and woman watched the television that was high up on a pedestal toward the ceiling, while others paced. The elderly ones sat on seats, chatting freely and in strong agreement, staring at the worn carpet or watching the other people. Those with grey light hanging near them saddened Tommy for they knew nothing of what they had become, what they had allowed to leave them.

Tommy turned to the wall. It was white. He raised his finger and began tracing out the impression of hospital beds. He kept tracing them until his finger commenced outlining the number six. Then, beside the six, a zero. Then another six: 606.

Leaving the number in his head, he turned around and watched the people coming together to talk briefly or hug one another, their colours pulsing and merging in good or bad ways while they shared their experiences. The colours then pulled apart, bleeding away as the people went their separate ways. They were living life in a strange manner that was not natural. This was the place where the auras were damaged or set right. This place was so much like a church.

Tommy stood in the same position for a long time. The faces around him changed with movements that swirled colours inward and outward, colours that glanced off his colours as the people passed close by him, thrilling him or harming him in a barely felt way.

Overwhelmed by the particular vivid shades of colours seen only in such places, Tommy had to draw his gaze away and wander down the corridor. He paid the soldier no mind but simply brushed past him with his mask on and sketch pad under his arm. The soldier even held open the door for him, nodding and muttering, "Doctor."

Tommy found the elevator without problem. He had been in the hospital countless times over the years, visiting friends and family members or volunteering to sit with strangers, to help them mend, to listen to what they wanted to share with him.

The elevator whisked him to the sixth floor. Stepping off, he searched out 606, tracking the progression of numbers until he found himself at Rayna's room. There was a sign posted on the door that he could not read. His eyes searched up the corridor. A nurse passed in the distance, then disappeared around a corner. Tommy pushed open the heavy door and walked in. There were six beds on the ward and all of the people in the beds were attached to breathing devices that hissed and spat. Tommy found Rayna where he had imagined and sat in the orange plastic chair beside her bed. Hearing the sound of Tommy settling, Rayna slowly turned her eyes toward him.

"Hello," she said in a groggy voice, her flat tone suggesting that she took Tommy for a stranger. Perhaps it was the mask he was wearing. He pulled the strings away from where they were looped over his ears. He grinned and nodded, held his head bowed and nodded a few more times, bashfully and with reverence. He laid his sketch pad on the edge of the bed, then stared at the white respirator tube with its green plastic valve. Reaching into his pocket, he found a small stone. It was black with white veins, its edges worn to a polished smoothness.

"Wishing stone," he said, holding it up like a wafer. He carefully opened Rayna's bandaged hand and placed the stone against the gauze covering her palm, then closed her fingers around it.

"Thanks," she said, raising her fist to numbly look at it.

"Da fairies gave it to me. Six of dem carried it t'rew da air. It were a sight fer sore eyes, I'm telling ye." He laughed. "'Twas heavy as a bucket of nails for them."

Rayna said nothing, only squeezed her fist tighter.

"I used ta go fishing," Tommy said. "And I saw t'ings." Tommy nodded and anxiously licked his lips, grinning again but not without concern. "Stuff in me drawings. Other people saw 'em, too."

"What?"

"Dey tol' me. Did. But dey wouldn't tell other people. Some tol'. But people were afraid ta tell."

"Tell?"

"Because." He watched the white bedsheets, the shape of Rayna's body beneath them. He thought of the drawing he had made, the outline of the body all black inside, the person gone dark. Then he stared away, toward the other people on the ward, the curtains dividing the beds, the shadows beyond the hanging cloth, people not knowing how to breathe. Tommy took his time studying each shadow, trying to figure something through. He recognized Jacob Butler, Peter Newell, Bonnie Turnbull, all of them from Bareneed. All of them fisherfolk he had sailed past while in their boats.

"Dey were afraid?"

Tommy reached out and gently took hold of Rayna's hand. He held the wishing stone between their palms as he gazed down, worried that Rayna was not herself. Perhaps it was the drugs the nurse had given her. The way her hand was loosely holding his, fingers joined, made his breath catch in his chest, not from ailment but from the splendour of the touch. "Because ..." He squinted uncertainly and wiped at his nose, bravely tried to keep his smile intact. "'Cause ... 'cause people would t'ink dey were like me."

Rayna gave his hand a sweet squeeze, one pulse, one heartbeat. "S'okay."

"Retarded," he said, fat tears spilling from his eyes. "But dey're not here. Dose ones."

"Who's not?"

"Da people who saw, Rayna. Dey're not here. Dey're safe."

─◎─

The little girl was not sleeping. Her skin was too pale. The tubes in her mouth and up her nose proved that she was not sleeping. They could pretend that she was sleeping, but Joseph, standing at the foot of her bed, knew that she was not. Why didn't they tell him the truth? This girl was not his daughter at all, but a look-alike, a fabrication. This one was different. His daughter was alive and happy, her feet skipped along, her hands were always drawing pictures. This girl, not his daughter, this girl was not moving. He didn't believe she was sleeping. Sleep was closer to life, but whatever state this girl pretended to be in was not sleep. He felt something jam in him, a wedge of confusion and anger that stopped dead in his chest. He must have moved or made a sound, for the woman at the other side of the bed flashed her eyes at him.

Joseph blankly regarded the woman pretending to be his wife. Her face was strained, worn, almost ugly. She was older than he thought she should be if she was to play his wife. He remembered her younger, not so hard, with makeup softening the features of her face, not so bitter and corrupt. He could not think of this woman as ever being young. Her hair needed washing. Her clothes were ripped and muddied. She watched his eyes and what she saw made her hand rise to her mouth. Twin tears broke loose and ran down her cheeks. Big slow tears. She muffled a sob. God, she was so sorrowful. Brilliant in her impersonation of what someone might be like if they were his wife and he no longer cared for them any more.

The chubby, grey-and-white-haired doctor, hands in his lab coat, gave the woman a shut-lipped smile of compassion and understanding, then looked at Joseph. "She could come out of it at any moment," he indicated with his generous voice. "Or it could last years. She suffered massive heat loss. Water in her lungs. Her breathing has been compromised."

The woman sobbed and jutted slightly forward. This girl would die and the reality of life itself would be adequately served. A child's death. Joseph could hide from it no more. None of them could. A child's death. He sensed himself thinning and being drawn magnetically away, dissolving in sparkling incoherence. He glanced toward the window. How long before it would be dark? Black concealing everything, every living soul.

"I'm sorry," said the doctor.

Baffled, Joseph regarded the people in the room. He studied the machinery. The beepings and purrings and hissings further confounded him. He did not know why he was here. He could not pull the memory together and this struggle, this act of absolute concentration, seemed to pause his lungs.

The doctor's eyes had turned to him as he drew a deep breath. A gentle doctor, trying so hard to act concerned. He wasn't what Joseph expected. Where was the tall doctor? The cold doctor who was only in it for the money? The doctor scrubbed clean of death?

"Are you all right?" asked the man in the white coat.

Joseph surveyed the little girl in the bed. How was she connected to him? He felt his knees go wobbly and he clutched at the bed's metal frame.

"Whoa! You should sit down," said the man in the white coat, jutting toward him with one hand extended. "Are you having trouble breathing?"

The woman considered Joseph with mixed emotions, but the little girl did not open her eyes.

"Where am I?" he dizzily asked, as the man's hand took hold of his arm.

"He said that before," the woman claimed.

How would she know? Joseph wondered as the muscles in his neck weakened and his suddenly weighty head lolled back. *How could they possibly know anything about me?* Tumbling in reverse, he landed with numb noise in his brain, and faces and action above him. He had fallen. He was holding on. Hands were muffling his ears from the inside. Vision became more and more constrained until, swamping his mind with whiteness, the possible-all of unconsciousness blitzed him.

⁓𝄐

When Dr. Basha asked whether there might be someone in the community capable of identifying the bodies, Sergeant Chase had immediately thought of Miss Laracy, the old woman at the Critch house. She must be a hundred and ten years old, if she was a day. She might recognize any number of the bodies. The odour and chill from the fish plant was trapped in his lungs as he steered the cruiser around the arc of the harbour. He could use a bite to eat before visiting Miss Laracy, if only to smother that queasy feeling in his stomach. The community hall was just at the end of the harbour road, which ran perpendicular to the lower road. With any luck, there might be a leftover sandwich there. He had no concerns about how old the sandwiches might be. He'd eat a half-rotten caribou hide at this stage of the game.

Driving from the fish plant, with the harbour directly at his left, he scanned the ocean in the afternoon light. Activity was non-existent while the water itself was whitecapped. It rolled and splashed despite the absence of wind. There were no helicopters. Chase found this troubling, as if the chaos of activity had been sublimated beneath the surface, ready to rise at any moment.

The community hall was just ahead. At the stop sign, he took a sharp right and pulled the cruiser into the narrow fronting, behind an army jeep. There were three soldiers outside, discussing something with enthusiasm. As Chase neared, the conversation ebbed and he was refused entry by the soldier on guard at the door.

"Where's French?" he asked.

"Army personnel only."

Chase towered over the soldier. He removed his hat, neatly slid it under his arm, then pointed at the soldier's wireless microphone. "Tell Lieutenant-Commander French that Sergeant Chase is here. I'm the army liaison."

"No exceptions, sir. New orders. Sorry."

Chase looked hard at the soldier's face, his eyes carefully taking in every feature, until he noticed the nervousness in the soldier's eyes. Then he patiently backed off, placed his hat back on his head and returned to his cruiser. He sat behind the wheel, trying not to be aggravated, thinking of returning to Port de Grave to see Theresa. Why was he going out of his way to help French anyway? He should just go home. He was into his third straight shift, working overtime. A nice fat paycheque coming up at the end of it all, and things seemed to have calmed somewhat. He might live to spend the money.

He glanced toward the harbour, focused on his breathing. It seemed fine. Had all of the bodies finally resurfaced? Was the crisis almost over? Maybe the entire situation was a glitch, inexplicable. Try as he might, he couldn't get the image of Miss Laracy out of his thoughts. The drowned bodies needed to be identified.

Eight years ago, Chase had led a three-man search party looking for his own father around the shores of Skyhorse Lake in Saskatchewan. The man, last seen in a boat on the lake, had been missing for four days. Over the course of that time, there had been violently high winds and rain. There was no way to employ a boat, helicopter or plane. It had taken them another three days on foot to skirt the west side of the huge lake. They had camped in a tent with the rain pelting the canvas and the wind threatening to tear the shelter down. The two men with Chase, men from the nearby reserve whom he had known since he was a child, were quiet and respectful. They all understood what was coming. What the outcome would be. It was only a matter of time.

Chase was the one to find the body, beneath White Squaw Bluff, bashed countless times against the rocks. The body had been in worse shape than most of the drowned in the fish plant. The autopsy determined that the man had been blind drunk. Chase recalled one of the thoughts that had entered his head upon first laying eyes on his father's tattered body: at least the old man can't harm anyone any more. Relief one way or another. Then regret for the life that might have been.

The drowned bodies needed to be identified, if only for the sake of the living.

Dispelling his memories, he engaged the engine and, ignoring the soldiers, spun the cruiser around with a vengeful squeal of tires that struck him as childish, yet was deeply satisfying. When he reached the fork for the higher road, he veered onto it, climbing the gradual ascent above the harbour. The sun was glinting off the front panels of the solar house. As he passed nearer, the sun was golden, fiery in reflection as if a blaze was burning within. Chase noticed a black dog sitting still on the front step. He purposefully watched the dog to catch even the slightest movement, but there was none.

He pulled over in front of the Critch house, was out of the vehicle and slamming the door before his mind caught up with his actions. This would be his final chore before he packed it in and went home for food and sleep, to be with Theresa. He had done enough and now it was his time for rest.

Briskly stepping toward the doorway, he rapped his knuckles on the solid wood. No one answered. He listened, checked over his shoulder, saw his cruiser parked there, then knocked again. Nothing. He thought of trying the back door. The old lady might be in the kitchen, singing at the top of her lungs. He stepped alongside the house and found Miss Laracy outside, facing the barn, her nose pressed against one of the window frames.

She was dressed in the same green housedress and bandana as before.

"Excuse me," said Chase.

Miss Laracy did not turn. She continued watching through the barn window, unmoving, seemingly transfixed.

Chase trod nearer. Doing so, he had a wavering sensation that the old woman might not be real at all, that she was merely a cardboard cutout propped up in place. That feeling, fuelled by Miss Laracy's utter stillness, was so overpowering that he found himself reaching to touch her shoulder. Flesh and blood. Still, she did not move. He shook her gently.

"Miss Laracy?"

The old woman inclined toward him and her eyes opened wide as she regarded his face. "Ye again," she said, smiling with shut lips that trembled slightly with age. "'Twere watchin' t'rew da glass 'n I saw a liddle girl."

Chase said, "They found the girl."

"Naw, not dat one, buddy. Anudder."

"In there?"

"Yays."

Chase leaned to check through the window.

"She be wet 'n drippin', shiverin' ta deat'."

"Don't see anything." He cupped his hands, trying for a clearer view.

"P'raps I were dreamin'. I went inta convulsions or sumtin'. Wha' ye here fer anyways?"

"I was at the fish plant."

"Widt da bodies." Miss Laracy's attention was diverted as she heard a rustling in the grass, off toward the woods. "What da Christ be dat?" At once, she stepped toward the source of her distraction, hoisting the hem of her dress to make it easier to tread through the tall grass.

"Yes, there's a lot of bodies," Chase said, following in the old woman's path. "I was hoping you'd be willing to come help identify some of them."

Miss Laracy arrived at the spot of her consternation and stared down.

When Chase reached her, he was surprised to see a fish in the grass, a fish with long blades of hay stuck to its rainbow-coloured sides, its gills throbbing open and shut and its depthless eye glistening like a hard black bubble.

A shapeless sweeping shadow fell over the grass and Miss Laracy peered up into the sky. A crow languidly circled above, rising and lowering in a spiral. "One fer sorrow," she muttered.

"What kind of fish is that?" Chase asked as the fish flapped once, then twice, further tangling itself in dried lengths of grass.

"Sushi," laughed Miss Laracy. "Yays I'll go widt ye, buddy. Dere were a soldier ask me da same t'ing some time ago. But 'e weren't honourable 'bout 'is intentions. 'N 'e were frightened beyond all belief. I couldn't be too near 'im fer fear 'e'd turn me inta a bundle o' nerves. Ye be honourable, ain't ye." She regarded the fish and nudged it with the toe of her shoe. "Solid as a rock, ye be."

"I hope so." Hearing the muffled sound of a door shutting, Chase glanced toward the solar house. The black dog remained seated outside. "The car's this way." Chase offered his arm and Miss Laracy took it with a lovelorn sigh of delight, then followed his lead, leaving the fish where it lay.

"I'd save dat fish fer eatin', yet I suspects 'e's already 'af magotty. Alive or not."

Eyes on the solar house, Chase glanced toward the second storey, and saw the image of a small woman or young girl in the window, staring out toward sea.

"Ye see dat black dog?"

"Yes."

"No one knows dat dog. It be strange ta dese parts. No one seen 'im 'fore." She studied the glass panels of the solar house. "Dat queer 'ouse soon be grieved by deat' itself."

Chase felt the old woman tighten her hold on his arm, slowing him down. "Mark me words, da trute be made evident as da days lapse. Da appearance o' such a strange mongrel foretells occurrences o' woe."

"Let's hope there's no more death."

"'Ow many bodies ye got down dere?" She nodded toward the white-capped harbour.

"Seventy or more."

"Dey all be drowned?"

"It seems so."

"Trouble dere," she said, shivering with delight and rubbing Chase's arm, then giving it a gleeful squeeze. "Trouble dere, me ducky."

~⟲

"Canvassing of the area complete, sir."

Lieutenant-Commander French drew his eyes away from an illustration of a blue sea creature with the head of a giant-beaked bird and the spiny tail of a fish. Able Seaman Nesbitt stood before French's desk, awaiting a reply to his announcement. Nesbitt was a peculiar creature: thin-necked, long-limbed, with a rash of acne across his forehead. The soldier was nothing more than a boy, yet there was something knowing about him, something almost ancient that made him appear out of place or unaccustomed to his surroundings. The lieutenant-commander was about to inquire about Nesbitt's success when he heard the squelch of a communication arriving through his earpiece. He shifted his eyes toward the floor and listened to the voice: "Preliminary test of Blockage Sequence possible at twenty-two hundred hours, sir." It was Able Seaman Buckingham, up on the hill.

"North or south side?"

"North side, sir," Buckingham confirmed.

"The south side can wait. We'll test the first three macro-repellers on the north side." He heard the voice in his ear say "Copy," then looked up at Able Seaman Nesbitt, who remained in wait. "Any luck?"

"Sorry to report 'no,' sir. No volunteers."

"You checked every house?"

"Yes, sir, the houses with people." Nesbitt's shoulders shifted spasmodically while he spoke, as if he was putting too much of himself into the words. "The locals seem to resent our presence here, sir."

"That's fine, Nesbitt. Why wouldn't they?" French dipped his eyes back at his book. An illustration of a horned creature with hundreds of tiny swirls carved along the length of its scaly body. "We bring glad tidings."

Nesbitt said not a word. After a few moments contained by silence, French regarded him, wondering about his life, what the soldier might lose if his life was taken away from him, what his relatives might miss of him. A young man in a uniform, steadfast in his belief in nationalism, righteousness, democracy ... Was this how Nesbitt thought? Or was it merely a job to him? A paycheque to feed himself and whomever he supported. French wondered if Nesbitt had a house, a wife waiting for him, children pining for a call:"Daddy! When are you coming home?" He remembered it all. A wife who waited ... for what, for him to grow up and get old? No, she wanted more than that, and she had found it with another man, another life removed from his. His children, too. Taken, just like that, in a custody battle that scarred everyone. Of course, he had seen it all coming yet was powerless to prevent it.

"Dismissed."

Nesbitt saluted and sharply spun around, then disappeared.

French turned a page in his book. The tentacles of a monstrous creature held a wooden sea vessel in its grip, waving the vessel in the air above the sea. He frowned and coughed, reached for the package of cigarettes on his desk and lit up. Taking a deep draw, he shut the book and slid it aside, revealing another book — *Atlantic Tidal Waves*. He studied the cover, every inch of detail, while he smoked his cigarette. He then lifted the volume, glanced curiously at its spine, laid it down again, watched it.

"Sea monsters," he muttered. Leaning back in his chair, he observed the movements beyond his office. Soldiers were coming and going. A few of them carried boxes or equipment, others joked with each other. None of them had an idea of the magnitude of the situation. "This is French," he announced into his headset. "Be prepared for an evacuation order. This is a preliminary warning. This is not a direct order."

The action beyond his door halted. A few of the faces turned to peer in at him. Unwavering, he met their eyes, not giving anything away. He drew on his cigarette, realizing this might signify bravado. At once he regretted the movement, crushed out his cigarette in the brass ashtray then straightened in his chair and ran his eyes over the tidal-wave book. Opening it to the table of contents, he skimmed his finger down the list of chapters until he reached the word "Survivors." His finger then slid horizontally to the corresponding page number, to which he flipped. There were black and white photographs of people standing attentively near wreckage on shore and inland, faces indistinct. He noted the sharp contrast between dark and light. He thumbed the page, finding Margaret French, his grandmother; he knew her by the caption beneath the photograph. She was holding a baby, and both her face and the baby's were washed out, smears of vaguely grey white. He studied her face for what seemed like the fiftieth time in the past two days, not willing to accept his own suspicions. Margaret French was a pretty woman. He could see that much. Young and with a face that appeared to fit the times. How was it that faces assumed the qualities of a particular time? Was it simply the hairstyles? No, it was more than that. They somehow bore the characteristics of that age. Fundamental times; honest faces. Were people actually plainer in spirit and thought back then? Were they less troubled, less distracted? Or just worse off than today?

The tidal wave had hit Burin, on the south coast of Newfoundland, more than seventy years ago.

French recalled the words of his grandmother, spoken to him when he was eleven years of age (she had passed away the following year): "Dere were a boom out o'er da water, far, far off. Cups 'n saucers be rattled in da cabinet. Dat were it. No furder t'ought o' what it all amounted to. I were tendin' yer fadder, a wee infant he were. Den, an hour later, I were standin' in da yard, watchin' out ta sea fer yer grandfadder ta come in frum da fishin' grounds. 'Twere hard times widt da fish. Dey seemed scarcer den hen's teeth. We never reckoned why da fish were vanishin'. I had a view down ta da harbour. 'Twere all quiet, 'cept fer da radio in da house behind me, 'n da sky be slate grey 'n low upon us, gettin' lower in da silence. 'Twere enough ta spook da hardiest man. All o' us stood watchin' out ta sea. Dere were people up on da hills 'n banks 'n down nearer ta da water. We knew sumtin' were comin'. Not a one o' us stirred a muscle. Den da water started pullin' back frum da shore, like it were goin' out ta come back in 'n lap da shore again, but radder den returnin' ta us, it jus' kept goin' out, 'n I could hear da rocks 'n pebbles rollin' 'n clickin', rollin' 'n clickin' louder as da water kept being sucked back, slidin' away, 'n da grey sky dropped nearer ta our 'eads. Ye could see all da seaweed 'n fish 'n lost nets 'n da wreckage o' small crafts. Da sea kept pullin' away like it were givin' up on us, like it were poisoned widt da whole lot o' us. All bodies were stood still. No one budged

'n den yer fadder pointed wit' 'is fat liddle hand 'n giggled. Folks on shore
kept starin' off at da 'orizon, while da sea made its way out furder 'n furder,
until it were lookin' thick, a sorrowful grey bulging up, 'n den it got fatter
'n higher 'n higher till finally it reared right up, jus' like dat. Standing still,
da sea reared up, climbin' 'n climbin' t'ward da grey sky dat were lowerin',
till a mountainous wall o' sea 'n sky come chasin' forward, back t'ward land,
t'ward everyone who were standin' in wait, disbelievin'.'"

"Sir?"

Lieutenant-Commander French glanced up from his book, holding
his gaze steady despite his sense of dislocation at being abruptly disturbed
from reading.

Able Seaman Nesbitt stood erect, grinning, relieved, his face flushed
with pride and colour.

"Yes?"

"We've received a communication from Sergeant Chase. He's escorting
Eileen Laracy, one of the elderly residents, to the Chill Room, sir."

"Thank you." French continued holding his expression even. He
reached for a cigarette and lit it, thought of a drink. A solid shot of
Southern Comfort to smother the acuteness of what he was feeling, what
he was imagining. Sweet with a sting. A double shot in a nice clean glass.
"Dismissed."

Nesbitt saluted with such vigour that French suspected he might snap
his wrist or pop his shoulder out of its socket. Nesbitt spun and marched
away.

French shut his book. What good would come from identifying the
bodies? There had been bodies floating in Burin, too. The army had discovered them the morning after the disaster. It was classified information
to this very day. There were seven old bodies that they suspected were
uprooted by the tidal wave. One of the army reporters had recorded the
voices of the residents following the tragedy. French had listened to the
tinny and scratchy voices telling tales of sea creatures in the harbour.
Stories. Legends. Nonsense. A man could use these things to falsely
strengthen himself, to believe that he had come from a worthy heritage,

to bolster belief, to impose miracles upon mere mortals and make them seem mightier than they actually were. The legends were just another form of religion.

Around the time of the Burin tidal wave, there had been mention of a peculiar outbreak of tuberculosis. Fifteen residents had perished prior to the tidal wave, each of them somehow related to the bodies later found in the sea. Coincidence? How could there possibly be a correlation? Tuberculosis. No one had contracted it in this case, but perhaps there'd been a misdiagnosis all those years ago?

French flashed on that much-needed drink. He studied his cigarette ash and banished all thoughts of his past. If he was going to give the order to evacuate the community, it would be done so as a cautionary measure, not for belief in anything as laughable as old mariners' tales.

⟿

Miss Laracy stared at the police officer's face as he pulled the cruiser in beside the fish plant. His honesty and plain good looks reminded her of Uriah. The officer was dark-skinned and his aura was beaming yellow. Warm to be around. There was no fakery about him. Kind and reliable was he.

"Eighty-nine residents are on respirators," Chase explained to Miss Laracy as he twisted off the ignition. "That's what I've heard is the official count. Twenty-four still have no problem breathing. You included."

"Where be da sick?"

"Port de Grave Hospital." Chase reached between the seats for his hat, which was laid atop the portable Breathalyzer case. "They've opened some of the old wards they shut down years ago."

"Soon to be suppertime. Ye be needin' a nice big scoff in yer belly. Large feller like ye." She gleefully patted his stomach. "I'll feed ye when we're done widt dis bit o' nuisance."

"I'm fine." Chase smiled, his teeth white and even. Polite as an unwrinkled tablecloth.

"Me God, ye got some beauteous teet' in yer 'ead. Big, too."

Chuckling, Chase popped the handle on his door and climbed out. A few moments later, Miss Laracy's door swung open and Chase offered his hand. She was enchanted by the gentlemanly gesture and gave a shy smile.

"Sweet feller," she said. "Treatin' me so grand. Ye got yerself a honey?"

"Yes, I do." His previous spell of good humour soured. "A wife."

"She be unwell," said Miss Laracy, pitying the change in Chase's countenance. Offering a sympathetic nod, she reached high to place her hands on his cheeks. "It nar be yer fault. A kind soul like yerself. Always treat 'er well, ye have. Yer not capable of anytin' mean nor 'eartless. 'Tis just dat ... 'Tis ..."

"What?"

"Wha' ye were made frum. 'Tis confusin' ta ye."

Chase's brow furrowed. "Made from what?"

"Wha' ye were rooted in n' den wha' be expected o' ye. Dere's no consolation in bein' a 'afbreed. I mean dat not particular ta ye. We be all 'afbreeds dese days. Narry an idea where we come frum. Young'ns widt mouths on dem straight frum da television."

Chase watched toward the water. Miss Laracy noticed his colour deepening to orange, still warm and kind despite his uncertainty, which, in a more spiritless man, would have deepened his colours to a hue of brownish-purple, a shade that would inflict itself upon others. When Chase regarded Miss Laracy again, he was disheartened, yet he smiled despite himself. He offered her his arm. She walked along fine until she drew near to the fish plant door, where she stumbled and faltered, her legs wavy beneath her, her knees aching terribly. She had to be helped across the threshold by Chase and the soldier stationed at the entrance.

"I'm 'lergic ta fish," she confessed to Chase as they entered the plant. "Doctor tol' me. Everyone 'lergic ta sumtin' now."

Inside, Miss Laracy gazed out over the white tables. Years ago, she had worked there, gutting and filleting cod. All the Bareneed women had worked there, while the men were out in their skiffs and dories. The place had changed. Human bodies, requiring some sort of preparation, now lay atop the tables.

"Saints preserve us!" Miss Laracy gasped the oath as her jaw drooped in bafflement, not at the sight of such an unseemly collection of corpses, but at the spectacle of what plainly lingered above — amber spirits shredded to tatters. Each disjointed apparition, drifting like a fluttering sheet of cobwebs, resembled the body beneath it. The spirits moaned in a forlorn manner and, upon descending nearer their seemingly more substantial yet dead selves, became further disturbed and soon rose again, as though barred from entering.

MONDAY NIGHT

The needle was inserted into the tender underside of Robin's slim arm, the plunger drawn back. Robin did not so much as stir. Deep red blood, thicker than what Kim thought blood should be, pooled into the syringe. She fretted at the thought of blood being extracted from her little girl; how much blood could Robin possibly have in such a small body? Kim watched the lab person in her white coat with her green tray of blood vials laid to the side. The woman was respectful, kind and gentle, but was engaged in what Kim thought to be a barbaric act. It was all too unreal, her mind stung awake by the antiseptic odour that hung around her. She caught a whiff of rubbing alcohol and looked away, toward the bed beside Robin's. Joseph was lying there, staring at her with an expression void of emotion. He had been helped to the bed by Dr. Thompson and was presently hooked up to a respirator. What had happened to him? Kim recalled the day Joseph had picked up Robin to take her to Bareneed. It had been sunny. The trunk was packed with everything required for a vacation. He had seemed happy. Normal. Healthy. A shiver jolted her and her shoulders twitched in revulsion.

Kim turned toward the lab person, who gave her a sympathetic smile then directed an almost-loving look at Robin before leaving. Glancing at the heart monitor, Kim fleetingly thought of her computer, and the deadline for the paper that she had been so concerned about. She then recalled the discovery of the albino shark and how it had drawn her here. It was all meaningless. Trivial. Her feet on the tile floor, her daughter in a hospital bed. These were fundamental concerns that could alter her life in an irreparable manner.

Again, she turned her attention to Joseph. Dr. Thompson had quickly dealt with him, moving with agility for a man of his age. He had gripped

Joseph's arm and called for assistance while already guiding Joseph to the bed. A nurse from beyond the glass had hurried into the room. The doctor called out an order for a respirator and the nurse rushed out again and returned with a man rolling a respirator on wheels. Three hospital personnel had worked in perfect coordination to ensure that Joseph was in no danger. Breathing through a respirator, he now occupied the last remaining bed in the ICU. Dr. Thompson cautioned the staff to keep an eye on Joseph overnight. If his condition remained stable, he would be moved upstairs to the medicine ward in the morning.

Joseph stared as if he knew nothing of Kim, or was attempting to figure out who she might be. "It could just be exhaustion," Dr. Thompson had quietly informed Kim after taking her to one side. Stress. Joseph had been taking medication for stress, the doctor explained. Kim knew nothing of this. Joseph was not a pill-taker. He wouldn't even swallow a headache pill. All of the troubling events of late must have led to a breakdown. Thompson indicated that he didn't think Joseph was afflicted with the breathing disorder. He suspected it might be psychosomatic: a copycat reaction brought on by extreme anxiety. After all, Thompson indicated, Joseph was not from Bareneed and, up to this point, all of the victims were from that community. No outsiders had yet been diagnosed with the disorder. Kim had nodded in understanding, only to have her thoughts snag on the fact that Joseph's father had been from Bareneed. With quickening dread, she had passed on this information. The doctor, seemingly at a loss for words, had finally offered: "Try not to worry."

Watching Joseph, the way he lay there stricken with weakness, exposed feelings of love in Kim, despite his recent distressing behaviour. Would he die? Would he slip into the peculiar form of amnesia that those suffering from the illness experienced? An image of her home, its windows and front door, its flower garden, bushes and dogberry trees, burned in her mind. A savage need for Joseph and Robin to be with her in the way they once had been panged in her chest. There was nothing they could not work out if everyone was well. The blessings of health. Her home. Their home. If only they were in it, protected. Lying in bed in the morning, snuggled into each other. A family. They used to be a family.

Now she stood between two hospital beds, her husband and daughter sick, no one to comfort Kim, no one to give her strength as Joseph once had, even if that strength was drawn from argument. Why had they always argued? Why? She felt helpless and abandoned.

~◊~

Joseph shut his eyes and saw grey. Horizontal and dense, he was incapable of commanding his limbs to perform a single action. To rise from the bed and put one foot before the other was tantamount to changing form entirely. This greyness was what he had become. There was no division between it and him. He assumed his eyelids were no longer shut because he now saw a woman in the dim room. The woman's face scared him. The size of the little girl in the bed across the way scared him. The woman was watching the girl, stroking the girl's hair. For a moment, he was so completely removed from the scene that he felt concealed. A suffocating weight rested on his chest. In hopes of lessening the weight, he took a deep breath and turned his head toward the window. Something was attached to his mouth. It hissed a startling purity into him that could not reach his mind. It polished the grey to a sparkle in his throat and lungs. He watched the night outside. Its utter blackness pulled at his thoughts, luring away what he believed to be his self. Staring into the darkness, he understood absolutely nothing. He frightened himself into struggling to shift his eyes and face the two people across from him, a little girl and a woman.

Why was he in a hospital, consigned to a bed? Was he gravely ill? And if so, how was he dying? Dying of what? He thought it might have something to do with the woman and the little girl. Perhaps he had caught something from the little girl. He suspected she had infected him with an ailment so intricate and complex that it outclassed any known virus. The woman seemed equally stricken, although still standing on her feet, refusing to admit weakness into her heart. Through the large window behind her, another woman, this one in a white uniform, glided past. This seemed to be the place where he belonged, where he was safe.

Behind his head, the blackness in the window was magnetic, commanding his eyes there again. The blackness was a flat vacuity that negated belief, sucked in his listlessness so openly. If he could move from the grey clench, he would disassemble the barrier, let the purer blackness gush in through the open edges to spill thickly across the tile. Steadily, the room would be flooded by the inky deluge, submerging the beds, and drowning them in a paralyzing storm of the black-blunt-nothing that was kept at bay by a mere sheet of glass that was, itself, invisible.

⁓◐⁓

Miss Laracy could make out the vertical rows of tiny lights far across the harbour. They belonged to one building. The hospital in Port de Grave. She had wrapped the yellow crocheted blanket around her shoulders and stepped out of the Critch house to catch a breath of fresh air.

Down by the harbour, a single helicopter hovered over two boats, but there was no action in the water. A few moths fluttered around the oil lamp she had laid on the slate step by the door. It was chilly outside. Her eyes intently watched the hospital's tiny lights across the dark stretch of water. Members of the Blackwood family were all in there, gripped by calamity. The husband, the mother, the daughter. And here she was, an old woman, safe, alive and standing in the reassuring night air.

After seeing the cleaved apparitions hovering above the bodies in the fish plant, Miss Laracy had decided to return to the Critch house. She knew that she was needed here. The dead had something to do with the living, as they always did. She glanced at the fish plant at the base of the headland and replayed in her mind her visit there earlier in the day.

The policeman had asked her: "Do you know any of these people?"

Miss Laracy had carefully walked forward, gripping the edge of the first table upon which lay a man in his thirties, black hair, thick jawline.

"Dat be 'edley Jackman. 'Ee died of a Saturday, 1957. Lost at sea. His wife were Barbara from overseas. She died two year later. 'Art problems."

The soldier, who had kept close by Chase and Miss Laracy, wrote the name Hedley Jackman on the card attached to the arm of the body. He then wrote "Lost at Sea: 1957."

Miss Laracy noticed that the soldier had lovely handwriting for a man. She stared above Hedley and saw him floating there, not seeing, not knowing, as though he were misplaced. "'Edley Jackman's gran'son Christopher be one 'a dose dat took sick. 'E's in da 'ospital o'vr Port de Grave." Again she peeked above the body, her gaze apprehensive as if afraid of what might be staring back at her, but the spirit of Hedley Jackman seemed not even to know that Miss Laracy was there. Taking a steady look around the room, she decided this was true of all the spirits. They appeared sightless and mindless. She felt the soldier's hand on her back, the pressure of him coaxing her forward.

"Watch yourself, please," he said.

Turning to chastise the soldier, Miss Laracy's face softened when she saw a gurney being wheeled by, a drowned girl resting on her back, the girl's eyes staring toward the ceiling, her spirit floating above her, drifting higher but then drawn magnetically back to the body. "Alice," Miss Laracy muttered with a start, fingers to her gasping lips, "Alice Vatcher." The girl had been her play-mate. With tears already welling in her eyes and sprinkling down her cheeks, Miss Laracy was upon the gurney. She stopped it, and reached down to touch her dead friend, but allowed her fingers to hover above the child's face. In 1936, Alice had been running on the beach, her hands held high in the air, and been swept away by a single wave of such immense force that it had snatched the child and left no further sight of her. Miss Laracy had wit-nessed the spectacle. She had climbed to her outlook post on a large rock and shouted in panic, "Come back, Alice!" She remembered calling and calling. Over the decades, the tragedy had slipped from her thoughts, but she vividly recalled her friend now and the trueness of their love for one another. It was most definitely Alice. She was wearing the white gimp with the yellow and red flowers that Miss Laracy had always adored and wished to own.

"Did you say 'Alice'?" the soldier asked.

"Yays," she whispered, finally touching the child's face, finding the skin vaguely warm. There were tears on her fingers, tears that had dropped from her own face to patter and pool in her friend's eyes. "Oh, Alice, ye were such a true friend ta me. Look at ye now. I were once of such beauty, too."

The man in the lab coat who had been pushing the gurney tried wheel-ing it ahead, but Miss Laracy looked at him with tear-blurred eyes and quietly said: "Wha' be yer hurry?"

The man said nothing. He cast his eyes down and simply waited.

Again Miss Laracy regarded her friend. "Alice Vatcher died of a Monday, 1936. We were da best sort o' playmates. 'Er parents left Bareneed 'n I don't know where dey went off to. But dere son David came back. He 'ad a daughter who be named Rayna. She live in Bareneed."

The soldier checked the list. "Rayna Vatcher?" he asked.

"No, she married a good-fer-nuttin'. Gregory Prouse. God rest 'is soul."

"Rayna Prouse?"

"Yays. Gregory Prouse were taken by da water too." She peered across to the opposite aisle where another gurney was being wheeled past. On it there rested a man in a uniform dated from the First World War. The body was missing an arm. When the gurney was fully gone, she squinted at the length of table that had been obscured. "I believe dat's 'im over dere," she said. "Gregory Prouse." She gave Alice Vatcher another look, her heart flooding with acceptance of all that the presence of her friend had returned to her. She had reached for and touched the child's silky ringlets before the gurney was wheeled away. No more time for them. None.

Now, outside the Critch house, another helicopter joined the first one. The noise was mounting. Watching the machines hovering, Miss Laracy again recalled the sightless spirits in the fish plant who seemed to know nothing of their whereabouts. They were drawn to the bodies, but then refused entry. Why were they coming back? What were they missing that they desired shelter in their useless bodies? Why didn't they seek out their relatives instead, their living loved ones?

Miss Laracy looked toward the harbour, noting the plant across the inlet, beneath the headland. There had been other old folk like herself who had shown up to study the bodies. Miss Laracy assumed they had heard she was there and didn't want to be left out of the action. There was Zachary Dalton and Walt Boyd. She had spoken briefly with them and learned that, as far as they could tell, none of their relatives were there. None of her own people were there either.

The trick was to stay well, she assured herself, glancing over her shoulder at the Critch house, still warm with the lovely presence of a family, despite the fact that that family was at odds with itself. They remained a family — the parents joined, and a child from their union. There was no true separation beyond that point. And she could offer protection to that family should they return to the Critch house. The stories that she wished to share with them were welling up inside her something fierce.

She gazed up at the sky. Must be around midnight by the set of the stars. There was no sleeping through this. The two helicopters flew away and the harbour was quiet for the first time in several nights. Half an hour ago, through the parlour window, she had witnessed four jeeps driving off from the community hall. Two had headed west, and then up Slade Road toward the hills where those monstrous discs were built. The other two jeeps had cruised east, approaching the nearby harbour.

The discs, the one at the very top of the headland and the additional six running east toward where the crowd of media and onlookers was gathered in Mercer's Field, were glowing a dim green. Green was the colour of fairies. Miss Laracy searched in the front pocket of her dress for a piece of hard bread. It was next to the pebbles she had taken from the fresh grave of Muss Drover. Muss had been a good man, she knew this of him, regardless of how his life had ended, and so the pebbles would offer protection. Mingled among the pebbles was her chain of rosary beads and the fin bone of a haddock, its sleek edges keen against her fingertips. It, too, would protect her against all evil.

She shifted her eyes toward the sky to notice the stars brightening and turning hazy, as though seeming to amass and lower. Down by the harbour, deep-blue searchlights had been switched on, illuminating a clot of thousands and thousands of crisscrossed red lines aimed in a zillion different directions. Miss Laracy counted five searchlights, their wide bands of light spanning out above the harbour. In time, the crisscross of red lights seemed to diminish. The stars became even brighter.

She glanced toward the discs atop the headland and along the hill. They were now a brighter electric-green. Uneasily, she shifted her eyes toward the harbour. The red lines of light had disappeared even more. They were thinning by the moment, the red streaks vanishing until pure black spaces could be discerned between them, from earth to sky. And from high above those black spaces a flash of amber descended at once, like a meteor trail plummeting toward Port de Grave, where it hit and entered a house without damaging it.

Miss Laracy squinted and craned her neck, peering higher. The effect was dizzying. Another streak of amber came shooting from above. It was difficult to be certain from the height of its descent, but she suspected it was aimed directly at her. She waited breathlessly, pinned to the spot, as the amber sped toward her, coming perilously near the ground and entering a house beside the water. The house of Muss Drover, Miss Laracy observed. Expecting the trail of amber to remain in the house as the previous one had in the house in Port de Grave, Miss Laracy redirected her vision toward the sky, only to have her eyes drawn back to Muss' house. The amber light now fled from the house, shot to the fish plant, then took off again, over the harbour and out to sea. A third streak of amber made its way to Port de Grave, hit a house and was extinguished.

A voice sounded over a loudspeaker down by the shoreline. Miss Laracy darted her eyes toward the discs and saw their brightness dimming. The crisscross of red lights began multiplying fiercely again. Then the blue spotlights were shut off and everything was night again. It was calm except for a sound like loud, pounding waves. A violent spray of white foam rose from the base of the headland, arcing into the air. There was no wind. What was driving the waves, Miss Laracy wondered. She watched for another fierce wave, but it did not arrive. She peered toward the sky. No more flashes of amber. Dat's right queer, she told herself, as she turned toward the lilac trees to venture forth and have a sniff. In fright, she stumbled to a stop, gasping, "Mudder o' Mercy!"

A little girl was standing there beneath the branches of the tree, her body vaguely defined in the spill of amber from the lamp Miss Laracy had set on the step.

"Hello," said the girl.

"Ye gave me a bit of a start, young'un. Wha' ye be up ta at dis hour?"

"Nothing. I'm just dead, that's all. The usual."

The lamplight brightened as a moth was incinerated. It had found its way inside the glass orb and to the heart of the flame.

"Are ye a friendly spirit?"

"I don't know. Do I look like I am?"

"'Av ye been touched by love in yer place where ye dwell now?"

The little girl simply stared. Another moth made the flame dance, the shadows inclining the child's expression. Was she smiling, or frowning? Miss Laracy wondered.

"I don't know."

"Is yer mudder or fadder in yer world?" Miss Laracy asked, her hands in the front pockets of her dress.

"Yes, my father is."

"Has he held ye and uttered whisperances of love?"

"No."

"Den ye be an unsettled spirit. Ye be a spirit of wanton destruction." Miss Laracy raised two pebbles from her pocket and held them high, clicking them over each other. In her other hand, she clutched the fin bone of the haddock and stabbed it in the air toward the girl.

"You're funny," laughed the girl, dissolving without further word.

What had been a smile soon turned to a forlorn expression as the child's face faded, this new countenance troubling Miss Laracy's heart in a particularly woeful manner, for a spirit was sad for a reason, and that reason was doubtlessly the fault of the living.

⁂

Joseph's eyes were dredged so deep into the blackness through the window that he barely perceived the sound beside him. At first, it resembled an extremely faraway ting or tinkle. Glass against glass. An audible glimmer of light. While his ears focused on the sound, and his eyes were drawn back from the blackness, he determined that the sound was not glass against glass at all, but the high melodic chirping of what he thought might be a minuscule flying creature. He could not envision what the sound was meant to convey. There was something at the root of the sound. It called to him, beckoned him back through solemnity.

Before he realized what he was doing, he had turned his head to see a woman seated on a chair. The woman appeared to be incandescent in the darkness, her lips were moving, and from between them came the sound Joseph had been hearing. At once, he managed to grasp that both sounds and words were pouring from her. The woman's honeyed voice rose and fell in a mesmerizing, spiralling manner. She was watching Joseph while she made the sounds, and her eyes, eyes that he recognized but were different from what he recalled, stared into him as though he were something more than what he thought. Then she turned toward the little girl in the bed.

Joseph believed that the woman might be connected to him. The woman was beautiful beyond belief; her voice and features implied she was dear to him, yet unlike the one he considered dear to him. His wife. No, this woman could not be his wife. She was singing and she was different, of a purity that made the woman essentially original and unknown to him, yet somehow understood.

⁓◑

A soft lullaby drifted out the doors of the ICU:

> *"When I was but a little girl 'bout two weeks, one day old,*
> *To show my value to the world, a-walking I did go,*
> *I dug my heels up in the sky, I let my head hang down,*
> *I travelled 'bout ten thousand miles, not one foot touched the ground …"*

Singing to Robin, Kim felt steadied by the song's tranquil sentiments. She gently pressed her hand against her daughter's pretty face, cupping the soft cheek. There is nothing as beautiful as the face of a sleeping child, she marvelled. Words rousing in her heart, she sang:

> *"Once I had a wee black dog, a nice wee dog was he,*
> *Around the world in half a day this wee dog carried me;*
> *His legs were eighteen lanyards high and his ears were twelve feet wide,*
> *Around the world in half a day on this wee dog I did ride."*

Kim had never sung that song aloud before, although she was fairly certain she had hummed it at various points in her life, yet now, without effort, she recalled it as if it were conveyed by the voice of her grand-mother. Nanny Neary had sung the song to Kim when she was a child wrapped in a comforter, cuddled against wrinkled skin and swayed to sleep in a rocking chair beside the crackling fire.

Finishing the lullaby, Kim thought: sweet clean sleep of childhood, where has it gone? With no pause for further reflection, she began another song: "In Dublin's Fair City." As a child, she had believed the song was titled: "In Goblin's Fair City.""In Dublin's fair city, where the girls are so pretty ..." she sang, and then another, "Oh, Danny boy, the pipes, the pipes are calling ..." They were all old Irish ballads that had not come to mind in decades, yet, surprisingly, were not far removed from her intellect. The ballads prompted memories of her grandmother, which soon inspired recollections of her mother. Yes, her mother had sung Kim those songs as well.

When she was done reciting the final lyrics of "Danny Boy," she noted the silence in the room, disturbed only by the chirping of the monitors. She soon continued with: "Silent night, holy night, all is calm, all is bright. Round yon virgin ..." While singing, she gazed toward the window to see Joseph lying in his bed and, beyond him, the ghostly reflection of herself and Robin in the black glass, the coloured lights from the machinery blinking and streaming. She focused on Joseph, on the whites of his eyes, and a fresh shimmering that caught the light there. Tears.

"Slee-eep in heavvvvvenly peace."

Joseph stared at her without blinking. In the silence, Kim regarded Robin, studied the length of her and saw on her fingers a stain that she took to be marker, but was actually iodine. A few days ago Robin had drawn a picture of Kim and Joseph together, holding hands. Robin had brought it straight to Kim and said: "See. It's the future." Heartbroken, Kim had wordlessly taken it and placed it in her purse. She had no idea what to do with it. Perhaps she should bring it into work with her, she thought, pin it up on the bulletin board in her university office, or give it to Joseph. In the end, she decided that she simply wanted to carry it around with her. It was in her purse, over there on the chair. She checked Joseph and then went to her purse, opened it and found the drawing neatly folded and tucked along the inner side pocket.

"Did you see this?" she asked uncertainly, unfolding the drawing to show Joseph.

Joseph studied Robin's rendering, then moved his eyes to Kim's face. He seemed to behold her with new reverence. "Sing," he said.

"Why?" she asked. Why should she sing for him? She had been singing for Robin.

"Because ... it's beautiful." A feeble smile struggled on Joseph's lips. "Am I smiling?"

"Yes." The way he had asked made her chuckle sadly. "Yes, you're smiling."

"Sing."

Had Joseph never heard those songs before, she wondered. Her expression was softened as she felt an intimacy that had been denied her and Joseph in recent months. She turned her eyes back to her daughter's sleeping face.

Robin's lips stirred, shaping a word without sound.

Hope swelled in Kim's heart.

"Sing," said Joseph again, giving voice to Robin's unspoken word.

~◐

Lieutenant-Commander French departed the beach with Able Seaman Nesbitt on his heels. He leaped into the driver's seat of the open jeep and engaged the engine. He had witnessed the peculiar streaks of amber in the sky, but as he pointed them out, his subordinates tried to catch sight of them and could not. He felt asinine.

"Nesbitt," he called, impatiently, just as the able seaman clambered into the passenger seat.

They drove through the darkness in silence.

"The refractors seemed functional, sir."

French said nothing, his jaw grinding tighter. He heard a voice coming through his headset: "Lieutenant-Commander French?"

"Go ahead."

"We have an offshore disturbance at 47N 51W, sir."

"Copy." He cursed himself. Here it was. It was happening and he could do nothing to stop it.

French screeched to a halt in front of the community hall, paced past the saluting soldier who held open the door, and headed toward the communications room at the very back of the hall. Nesbitt increased his stride to follow close by French's side.

As French entered the makeshift room, a soldier turned his head in recognition then pointed at the computer screen. "Disturbance at 47N 51W, sir."

"What's that, about one hundred kilometres out?"

"One hundred and three, sir."

"What sort of force?"

"It's hard to say, sir. It's swirling. A water dervish."

"Can we get a sonar feed?"

"No choppers presently in the area, sir."

"This is French," he said, turning away and striding off. "I need a chopper at 47N 51W." French brushed against Nesbitt, who was struggling to keep up, then entered his office. He snatched up his phone, punched a series of digits, reached for his waist to shut off his wireless remote, then shifted the black stem of his microphone away to make room for the receiver. "French here, sir. We have a suspected tsunami developing offshore: 47N 51W." He waited, stared at Able Seaman Nesbitt in the doorway, then swept his arm though the air. Covering the receiver, he said: "Get out and shut the door." Nesbitt spun around and the door was briskly closed. "No. No seismic activity, not yet ... The recent developments in the community, they mirror those that preceded the Burin tidal wave. No, sir." He gave a slight shake of his head. "No seismic activity yet. Regardless, I believe an evacuation order should be issued ... I'm aware of that, sir. This whole coast. I understand the enormity of the undertaking ... I can't explain beyond ... I know, yes, I understand. But when we hear the bang ... yes, if ... if we ... once the seismic activity occurs, we have three or four hours to clear the coast. The loss of civilians will be unprecedented. If we start now ... if we ... Yes, sir. I ... All I can say is that I believe it's linked to the breathing disorder. I'm basing this on information gleaned from previous nautical disasters, sir."

Here he paused and braced himself, hesitant to let go of what he was about to convey. "Seventy years ago, in Burin, there was an outbreak of what the residents at the time thought to be tuberculosis or diphtheria. The progression of the disease seemed to coincide with the widespread introduction of electricity and, perhaps, the radio in the community. For reasons we can't quite fathom, electromagnetic fields are affecting the breathing of the Bareneed residents. It might be mass hypersensitivity brought on by earlier contamination. I'm not certain, but somehow, I don't know how yet, all of this incites a massive electrical disturbance which then causes a tidal wave … I'm not certain why here, sir. There was another factor I didn't mention. In Burin, before the tidal wave, there was a drastic drop in the volume of marine life offshore, and there were bodies in the sea, similar to here." Lieutenant-Commander French shut his eyes. "I understand this is all conjecture, yes, I understand … But … No, sir. Yes, I'll keep you updated. Yes, sir … Yes, sir … . Yes."

French carefully hung up the receiver. He snorted in disgust and shook his head, violently rubbed his face with both hands, feeling like a fool for not only believing such nonsense but verbalizing it to his commanding officer. No doubt he was through. His eyes searched his desk, lit upon his package of cigarettes. Opening it, he found that it was empty. He would be discharged, certified insane, transferred to a private asylum. Booted out because of what he could not stop himself from seeing, from believing. Cursing, he crumpled the cigarette package and hurled it toward his door. If he'd had a gun handy, he would have gladly shot himself in the head.

-❦)

Thompson raised a hand from his lab coat pocket and jabbed the button for up.

In the elevator, he was reminded of a cartoon he had read years ago in a doctor's journal. Two doctors were leaving their offices at the end of the day. The first doctor said to the second: "I only guessed five times today." To which the second responded: "That's great! I guessed seven times." Thompson often thought of this cartoon at moments when he found himself exceptionally tired. How many times had he guessed? Wasn't this whole day one big guess?

Thompson had just gone out into the night to check on Agatha, who was curled up in the back seat of his vehicle. He had not disturbed her. He had then taken the path around to the front of the brick building and stared across the road, beyond the square houses and the newer suburban bungalows, to the water that led to Bareneed. He studied the back of the massive headland and the far end of Bareneed toward the east, the section that was not enclosed by the sheltering harbour. It seemed quiet over there. The lights were still out, yet a few spots of faint lamplight and candle flames glowed in the blackness. He recalled last night, the time he had spent in Wilf Murray's house, the fine meal, the conversation, the refreshing balm of being with people who were as healthy as horses. The children playing and running around everywhere. Why were they well? Why had they been spared? A car passed on the road, and Thompson could see a man in profile driving, paying attention to the road. Coming from where, Thompson had wondered. A bar? His lover's house? Work? Port de Grave, like all the other communities in the area, was still unaffected by whatever had gripped Bareneed.

Watching the car moving past and thinking about the man's purpose for travelling, Thompson had thought again of Agnes. The poor creature was all alone in his vehicle. He should drop her back home where she would be comfortable. He could lay out plenty of food and water and leave the toilet bowl up as well, just in case. In consideration of his feline, he also always left the kitchen tap dripping just a touch. It was dehydration that killed animals, and people too, before hunger. You could go a long time without food, but water was an absolute necessity.

After checking for messages on his cellphone and finding nothing urgent, Thompson had ventured back inside and headed for the doctors' lounge. The television was on, displaying a dark view of what he assumed to be Bareneed. Two of the four doctors present had glanced up at him as he entered.

"What's the news?" he had asked, eyeing the two vending machines. He could go for a chocolate bar. Both machines were empty, stripped bare. No sandwiches, no chocolate bars, no potato chips, no chewing gum.

"The news is no news," said one young female doctor with glasses and a long ponytail. She was facing the television screen, her hands behind her head, fingers webbed. "They're not searching the water any more. The helicopters are gone. Reports say they all headed offshore. One of the reporters intercepted a phone call that said something was happening out in the water. More good news, no doubt." The young doctor had turned to look at Dr. Thompson as if he might have some suggestion to make, but Thompson knew nothing.

"Your prognosis?" she had prodded.

"Maybe it's all over," he'd guessed.

"Knock on wood," said the female doctor, wrapping the wooden armrest of her chair with her knuckles.

Now, on the sixth floor, the hospital corridor was quiet; the dimmed lights from the patients' rooms extended a soothing calm. Dr. Thompson sat in a chair at the nurses' station, slipped on his reading glasses and began checking through the charts. He wrote the names of the patients with the breathing disorder on a blank sheet of paper. When he had collected all of the eighty-nine names, he took out his PocketPC and checked Lieutenant-Commander French's e-mail message containing the names of the victims fished from the waters in Bareneed. He compared the two lists. A young intern, on the late shift, passed Thompson on white cushion-soled shoes and gave a sympathetic smile.

"You ever go home?" the intern asked.

"Home?" said Thompson. "What's that?" He gazed up from his lists. "Ah, you'll find out soon enough."

The intern snickered before wandering into the supply room. How quickly the body and mind adapt, thought Thompson. The intern wasn't even wearing a mask any more, assuming that the breathing dysfunction was not caused by a virus, eliminating the possibility of an extended incubation period. Intuition. Life in a hospital was life in another world entirely and whatever happened in here was authentic. Blood-and-guts real. All of this crisis, he thought, and not a single drop of blood spilled.

Thompson returned to his lists. He circled Donna Drover's birth name: Wells. Then he circled Thomas Wells on the list of drowning victims.

He circled Darry Pottle's name, then skimmed the other list with his finger until he found Aubrey Pottle's name. Circled it. He continued until most of the names were matched. Puzzled, he went over the names again, wondering why there might be a relation between the drowned and those with the breathing disorder. Donna Drover was still in a coma. He had visited Darry Pottle earlier and Darry had muttered the same word that Donna had: "water." Yet when Thompson returned with ice chips for Darry, the young man had not wanted a drink. He had slowly reached for the cup of ice chips and dumped them over his own face. Then he'd shut his eyes, feeling them melt, his lips pursing, relaxing, pursing as if nursing.

Thompson stood from his chair, stretched and yawned briefly. The connection was far from ordinary. He stared down the quiet corridor, doors on either side, and thought of checking on Darry. As he walked toward Darry's room, he was conscious of the sound of his soft footsteps above the beepings of machinery. If only there was one empty bed for him to nap in, as he used to do. The sight of an empty hospital bed at night always infused his spirit with serenity. A white room with the lights switched off, the raised white bed with perfectly fitted white sheets. Not a wrinkle. He would sleep in pure bliss. But there were no vacant beds now.

As he continued to the end of the corridor, he paused in the doorway of Darry's room. He watched the patients in the six occupied beds. Three men and three women. They were all motionless, sleeping. Men and women. No children. He wondered what exactly it was he was beginning to believe.

What were the differences between adults and children, he asked himself. Size, for one. Children are smaller, although Thompson suspected that size had little to do with it. Younger ones don't have as extensive a vocabulary. They play more. They don't have jobs. No jobs. They see things differently.

They see things differently. How? Less corrupted. No, too obvious. They see and say what's on their minds. They're honest. Purer. Why? They accept everything as truth. Why? Their imaginations are wide open, with fewer borders, fewer rules. Their minds are more open. Why? Because they haven't learned to not believe yet. Why? Because they can imagine anything and see it as real.

-⟊-

Watchfully carrying a wide square piece of plywood in both hands, Claudia crept her way through her dark front yard. Her footsteps were measured and her breath was held in check to ensure that the slat remained perfectly level. On the board was arranged the exact miniature creation of Bareneed that she had fashioned from pottery clay dug, sifted and mixed in her own backyard. With painstaking agility, she ascended the tree-lined higher road. It took her a full fifteen minutes to reach the church, its black roof brushed by moonlight. After turning toward Codger's Lane and a night view of the ocean, she inched alongside the patient atmosphere of the graveyard, then began her gradual descent until reaching the path into the woods. Claudia was forced to walk stooped over to prevent the branches from upturning her fabrication.

A man tipped over. It was Doug Blackwood. He had been leaning over his fence, out in his front yard with his items of folk art behind him. And so Claudia paused to set him right. A few of the houses had shifted locations and she replaced them in the spaces where they had originally been erected. The trees were moulded together in solid deep-green clumps and so were the most stable.

When Claudia arrived at the clearing, the ground turned perilously uneven. She could not watch the ground; she had to keep her eyes on the tiny community to make certain not a single object toppled over. She slowed her pace even more as she approached the cliff and was soon at its distinct edge. Sound came up to meet her, carried on the fresh smell of the sea. The water was frothing and hissing far below. She was near enough the edge to peer down and behold the whiteness splayed upon the rocks.

Wordlessly, she held out the board, barely listing it from one side to the other, as though it were afloat, cut free of land and adrift on the sea. In slow increments, and with hands that had begun trembling, she leaned the board forward on a steeper incline. A miniature horse tipped over, and then a cow. Two men and a woman stiffly fell on their sides, unaware as they slid without struggle toward the brink.

With a throaty scream, Claudia tilted the front lip of the slat toward the water. The houses slipped along with the white fences and cars and pickup trucks. The first house to plummet over the edge was Doug Blackwood's — his was closest to the water — then went the houses along the lower road, followed by the trees in the gap that spanned the space between the lower road and the higher road. The Critch house was the second last to go; then, finally, Claudia's. Her scream crescendoed as she watched it drop, the shrill sound carrying across the water to where it might possibly be heard by the residents of Port de Grave. The items were so small and insignificant that they failed to produce a sound or impression upon the featureless black water that loomed in reverse, flat and depthless, like an unmarked chasm.

In time, the board was empty, save for a fine layer of dust from the clay. Claudia stopped screaming and her hands steadied. She raised the board near her chapped lips and blew, sending a grey cloud of dust billowing into the air.

TUESDAY

Doug Blackwood felt ill at ease in hospitals. He had been up all night, shifting and nodding off in one of those God-forsaken hospital chairs in the corridor outside the ICU. Joseph and Kim were waiting in there with Robin. That room was only so big. The night nurse had asked Doug if he was Robin's grandfather and he had laughed and said: "No, I'm her fairy godmother," which had got him nowhere except banished. Regardless, he waited in the corridor. It was a free country, wasn't it? He could wait wherever he wanted as long as he was out of everyone's way.

Doug had tried to catch a few winks, arms folded across his chest, his head nodding forward, and he had managed to drift off to the spot where he'd seen that mermaid in the water, but then he'd either been awoken by the arse of his pants sticking to the Christly old vinyl seat or by someone passing in front of him, a nurse on squeaky sneakers, the breeze of her passing reaching him, tickling his nose. He wanted to stay asleep longer, if only to get closer to the mermaid, to ask her a few questions and take his time feasting his eyes upon her.

His unease was multiplied by his lack of sleep, yet he mustered the inner strength that would help him abide his fate. Hospitals were fake places that stank of medicine and perilous hope. He avoided them at all costs, going so far as to speed up his car whenever he drove past one. And now his great-niece was stuck in the stink-trap, hooked up to machinery and watched over by fellers who thought they knew what they were doing. Hadn't he read somewhere that doctors had no idea how ninety-five percent of the body worked? What in Christ's name were they doing stumbling around a big white place like this, pretending they were holy men who could cure you with voodoo?

Doug rose from his chair, needing a walk to work the tightness out of his back and shoulders. The gift shop was just down the corridor and around the corner from the ICU. He headed there, intending to buy Robin a toy to keep her company. He wished he had a piece of wood with him. Maybe they had a piece of wood he could buy, or a plain factory-made toy that he could carve into something else, a whale maybe. Robin would love whales. What child wouldn't? He had planned to take her out in his boat, just she, he and Bramble cruising along, watching the whales feeding on the millions of caplin that journey all the way from Ireland to spawn on the beaches. Well, if Robin couldn't sail out to see a whale, then he'd carve one for her, just to make do with in the meantime.

Doug checked the pocket of his green work pants, dug past his ring of keys and discovered that he had his whittling knife on hand.

Rounding the corner, he came upon the gift shop. Beyond that, farther down another corridor, a soldier was guarding the door to the emergency area. Another friggin' soldier! Doug entered the gift shop, pausing by the newspaper rack to peek at the front page of the *Telegram*. The big headline at the top read: EPIDEMIC RULED OUT IN BARENEED. Interest piqued, he scanned a few lines and was surprised to learn about what had been going on around him. So many bodies in the harbour. People not being able to breathe in the hospital. All news to him. He'd seen nothing of it and had heard nothing of it from those who helped search for Robin. He thought of Robin and wondered if she had the breathing disease. As far as he could tell from the article, there was no cure. His heart grew sodden and he stopped reading.

Wandering around the shop, he poked at the cheap trinkets. A few people were reading glossy magazines with pictures of smiling women plastered on the covers. He wondered what could be of such interest in those magazines. They were everywhere these days and they were the worst sort of fakery. Fat women trying to be thin all their lives. What a money-making racket! Why couldn't they just stay fat and get on with it. He was fond of plump women, always had been. Emily had been nice and plump, until the cancer took her, stripped away every scrap of her flesh. Is that what women wanted? To look like they were terminal?

He found the toys near a far corner; mostly, they were stuffed animals.

Nothing made of wood. The idea of not having any wooden toys fuelled his ire. He huffed as if the exclusion was a personal affront and paced up to the elderly female clerk standing behind the counter in her blue smock.

"You got any wooden toys here?" he demanded, his hands pressed firmly into the counter as he leaned over it.

"Just what's down there, sir," the clerk indicated in a worried tone. She mildly nodded toward the far corner, then lowered her glance to the small black and white television that was propped up on the counter.

"There's nothing there 'cept a bunch of stuffed cartoons."

"Well then, sir, I'm sorry," she indicated, eyes glued on the moving pictures.

Doug glanced at the images. They were of a landscape, with houses and ocean in the distance. He noticed the words "Bareneed Live" in tiny white letters at the bottom of the screen.

"For Christ's sake, can you haul your friggin' eyes off the television when there's real life going on?"

The clerk took a moment to wrest her attention from the screen.

"Where could a feller get himself a piece of wood 'round here?"

The clerk's droopy eyelids blinked. "A piece of wood?"

"Yeah, for whittlin'."

"Maybe down in the basement. I believe there's a carpenter on staff. Maybe —"

"Where's that?"

"Bottom floor, sir."

Doug Blackwood stared, impressed by the way the woman's lipstick was gobbed in the cracks of her lips. There was even a bit on one of her front teeth. He read the patch on her smock: VOLUNTEER. He cracked a smile.

"Good stuff, missus." He winked. "Thanks fer yer assistance."

The clerk nodded defencelessly and aimed her eyes at the screen.

Out in the corridor, Doug noticed a bunch of people coming and going like it was a shopping mall. The guard was no longer stationed at the door to Emergency. Everyone was allowed to roam freely again, he guessed. Just like that. He found the elevators around a bend in another corridor. There was a woman waiting there with the button for "up" pushed. He gave her a wink and tilt of his head and she smiled at him. She was a fine-looking woman of fifty-five or so. He pressed the "down" button, gave her a big smile, removed his baseball cap and smoothed his hair before fitting the cap back on again. The elevator arrived just as he was about to pass comment on the nasty bit of business going on in Bareneed. He stepped in, gave the woman a wave, and hit the button for the basement. Elevators gave him the creeps. They were unnatural, moving people around through long holes. A big grave going up and down, up and down. Just as well to be in a coffin with cables. The doors shut and he felt his stomach rising. He'd rather be travelling up in one of those contraptions than sinking. Up was better than down. He should've used the stairs, if there was any way of finding them in the bloody maze of the place. Who built these friggin' buildings anyway? Rats trying to get back at humans?

The elevator dinged and the doors slid open on the bottom floor. At once, the stench slighted him. The space before him was calm and empty. He stepped off, on level tile ground, and read the sign. The arrow for maintenance pointed the same way as the arrow for mortuary.

"Good Christ!" Doug grimaced, shook his head, straightened the beak of his baseball cap, and headed down the corridor. Passing the morgue, he had to stop himself from peering through the small windows in the double doors.

"Heebie-jeebies," he said, shuddering, then making a louder noise with his lips.

Unfortunately, there was no one in the maintenance room at the end of the corridor. He tried the metal knob; no give. The stink was too much. "Turn your guts," he muttered, sticking out his tongue in a gesture of gagging. He watched the wall as he walked, his eyes skimming a continuous strip of pine trim, one-by-three, running horizontally halfway up the wall. No doubt the wood was nailed there to give the place a warm homey feel. Again, a shudder rattled him.

Nearing the morgue on his way back, he caught sight of a shorter piece of pine bridging a gap between two longer strips. It was nailed in place with two finishing nails, but not nailed well. A shabby job. He took out his knife, folded it open, and easily pried the wood loose. He got his fingers under it and tugged it free of the wall, his eyes darting up the corridor. No one to catch him at his sculduggery.

I'll be damned if I'm going in that steel box again, he told himself. There was a stairwell somewhere ahead. He'd noticed it on the way down the corridor. The old red EXIT sign. Glancing back, he spied the missing gap in the wood. He hurried away and through the stairwell doors, just as he heard the morgue door opening.

He gripped the rail and swiftly took the stairs to the main floor, glancing over his shoulder for ghouls. No one following him. Street level. He popped open the door and took a deep breath. Fresh air. What a lip-smacking treat. Someone had recently mowed the grass surrounding the hospital and the air was cool and green-sweet. It was morning, a beautiful day. Who'd have ever thought such a thing possible?

Doug spotted a bench made of wooden slats, over toward the main entrance. He could've broken one of them slats off to use, better wood. It was hardwood, but not as thick as the pine he had, which was soft as butter. It'd dent if you so much as looked at it the wrong way. With a grunt, he sat on the bench and fished out his knife, folded it open. A passing woman glanced suspiciously at him, her eyes on the knife as she kept moving. She wasn't from around here, Doug assumed, by the way she was dressed. Must be from St. John's or the mainland, here to snatch a souvenir of the tragedy. "Scared of her own shadow." He raised the knife in her direction and grinned, calling out, "'Twas what a knife was made for." The woman hurried her pace and he chuckled. He shook his head as he began smoothly carving away at the wood, curled pieces of pine dropping near his feet. "Not a friggin' clue," he muttered under his breath.

In a matter of minutes, the sloped graceful figure of a whale began to take shape from the chunk of pine in Doug's hand. The wood grew warmer as it was turned again and again, a sliver removed here, an arcing stroke there, until the whale had absorbed the temperature of Doug's body and had taken form.

~๑

Throughout the night, Kim had remained awake in the ICU, seated between the two beds, singing all the ballads she remembered for both Joseph and Robin while watching Joseph drift in and out of sleep. With the respirator tube in his throat, he, too, was like a child to her now, a child who must be delivered.

As the sun shone its first shadowed light over Port de Grave, Kim was humming "When Irish Eyes Are Smiling." The window steadily revealed a picture-perfect view across the glistening bay. Enthralled by the pristine beauty, she sat in perfect silence. Then she rose to use the washroom. Doing so, she caught sight of herself in the mirror. *Wretched*, she thought. At first she avoided her reflection, but then, after flushing the toilet, she brushed her fingers through her hair. Because her lips were pale and unbecoming and her eyes absent of shadow and liner, her face seemed a fatigued impression of itself. She considered applying makeup from her purse but then dismissed the idea. What did it matter how she looked in a hospital? What she needed was a shower and a change of clothes. She pulled a paper cup from the dispenser and drank water. It tasted fresher than the water in St. John's. She sniffed it, wondering if the hospital screened it through a treatment facility. Back home, there was the odour of chlorine whenever she raised a glass of water to her lips. She had grown up believing that water had a distinct odour and had even questioned teachers in school when they instructed her that water was odourless and tasteless. She was convinced it had a smell. She knew it did. As it turned out, the smell was chemical. Not natural at all, not truly a part of the water.

When Kim stepped out of the bathroom, she saw Joseph sitting up in his bed, staring worriedly at Robin. So perfectly still was Joseph seated, it appeared as though he had been in this position all along. She wondered if he would ever move again.

"You look like you just crawled out of an alley," she said, trying to lighten the mood.

Joseph's hair was a mess and there was a three-day growth of whiskers along his jawline and above his upper lip. The respirator tube lay on the bed beside him. He had pulled it from his throat. Still he did not move.

"Joseph?"

He fidgeted when Kim stepped nearer. Then he bravely looked at her, his eyes bloodshot and wary.

"Is there a change?" he asked raspily. He coughed and swallowed, then touched his throat.

Kim regarded Robin. God, what she wouldn't do to have her daughter sit up on her own. Sit up and recognize her. She longed to feel the small girl arms and small girl body hugging her. "I don't know."

"Is it the breathing thing?" Again, he coughed.

"No, they don't think it's that," Kim replied, moving toward the bathroom. She filled a cup with water and brought it to Joseph.

He took a sip from the cup and laid it aside. "Thanks."

"It's her heart. They say it was weakened by heat loss. Hypothermia."

Joseph braced his hands against the mattress and carefully slid himself forward, his bare feet touching the tile. He took a step toward Robin's bed, hesitated, then managed another step. Reaching down, he carefully slid his palm under Robin's hand while watching the IV needle taped to the back of it. Kim, too, studied the needle. It was punishingly big, not made for such a little hand.

The sight brought tears to Kim's eyes. Her emotions were so raw she felt she might burst into tears if her heart was tugged once again. She recalled that Joseph had been talking in his sleep, mumbling something about faces underwater and air bubbles. Now he stood, coherent and functional, at the side of Robin's bed.

"I could use a coffee," Kim said.

"I'll go." Shifting to turn, his legs wobbled. He paused and stared down at his bare feet. "Where are my shoes?"

"There." Kim pointed to the locker by the washroom. Joseph approached the locker and opened it, lifted out both shoes. They were dirty from his tramping through the woods. "Are you okay?"

"Yes." He shook his head.

"You sure?" Kim watched Joseph confusedly attempt to lace up his shoes. He coiled one lace around his index finger, then, as if coming to his senses, straightened the lace and tied both ends together in a proper bow.

Done with his shoes, Joseph stood, facing her. Again, he remained perfectly motionless, his awe-filled eyes alighting on each of her features. Kim felt she dare not move for fear of disturbing the moment. Joseph then looked at Robin. The injured way he was watching her made Kim yearn to be near him. She thought she might take hold of his hand and squeeze it, but she still could not find it in herself to physically reach out to him.

"What happened?" he whispered.

Kim's fingertips rose to wipe a tear from the corner of Joseph's eye. The tear clung to her fingertips which she rubbed together until her skin had absorbed the wetness. She had never seen Joseph cry before and the sight stabbed a hole in her heart, stripped her of what little strength remained.

"I don't know," he said, as though answering himself, a film of wetness coating his words.

At once, Kim hugged him. "I love you," she burst out, her cheek against his shoulder, massive need flooding out of control. Honesty for once.

Seemingly stunned by the force of Kim's embrace, Joseph stood with arms hanging by his sides.

Kim thought she heard him whisper in disbelief: "This is …" His hands rose and tentatively touched her back. "Real," he said, hands pressing firmly into her, arms holding, hugging tighter.

"Oh, God," he sobbed against her hair. "This is real."

~⟋⟍~

Lieutenant-Commander French had dozed behind his desk, dreaming of amber flashes descending toward a vast plain of blue. Upon touching the surface, the trails continued streaming deeper, radiating blue of a lighter and lighter tint, until the water itself shimmered amber. Each time he awoke, he had to snatch hold of his bearings, wondering where he might be: in a makeshift office, the helicopter screensaver on his computer screen strobing near his face. Activity beyond his office was practically nil. He could hear the low voice of the communications officer keeping an eye on the disturbance offshore. The voice was either coming from the back of the community centre or from his earpiece, the volume of which he had turned down. He wasn't certain and he didn't care.

Again, he dozed into trails of amber. This time he was staring up, watching the amber fall directly at him, like fireworks, so nearby that the cracklings of light dazzled his eyes. I must be floating, he told himself, sensing that the fire was upon him and then passing him, through his body. No, entering his body. His mouth was wide open, and through that gape of a hole the trails of amber were filling him. Was it his mouth that was open, or his entire face? Or was he actually of a mercurial nature, shifting like water, the ocean itself? He started awake, his feet kicking out under his desk, booming the wood. There was more activity beyond his doorway. Lights had been switched on.

He sat up straight and rubbed both hands over his face. For a few moments, he wondered if he had actually seen those flashes of amber in the night, or had he merely been dreaming? Had there even been a disturbance offshore, or had he dreamed that as well?

If there was anything he felt compelled to trust, it was his own senses. But that had been before he arrived in Bareneed. Now, despite his staunch belief in the actual, in coherent and logical explanations as gathered through his duties and campaigns, he could not shake the memory of those trails of amber descending toward the ground and entering houses. What added weight to the memory were the additional episodes of fantasy he had experienced since entering Bareneed. The albino shark, for example. Of course, others had seen that creature as well, yet it had still appeared out of the blue. The fishing of centuries-old bodies from the water. Was this all some sort of mass hallucination brought on by a drug slipped into the water supply, the work of some group of crazed anarchists? French's eyes alighted on the water cooler beyond his office door.

Most of those who had gathered on the shore last night seemed not to have noticed the amber trails like French had. He had also observed Able Seaman Nesbitt watching the sky as if following the trails. Nesbitt had become nervous when French had taken an interest in him.

French gave some thought to calling Nesbitt into his office. He considered the implications of such a meeting. What would he have to say? How would he open the conversation. After careful deliberation and devoting a few minutes to inquiring about the disturbance offshore, which remained suspiciously stable, he resolved the line of questioning best suited for the occasion and said: "This is Lieutenant-Commander French. Contact Able Seaman Nesbitt and have him see me at central."

French skimmed through the doctors' reports from the suspected outbreak of tuberculosis and diphtheria that had preceded the tidal wave in
Burin. Dr. Kearney, the physician at the scene, had noted that this particular outbreak was not consistent with the exact symptoms of tuberculosis
or diphtheria. There was little coughing and no fever, but there had been
sore throat, weight loss and sweating. Those symptoms, of course, could
have been caused by inactivity as a result of the breathing disorder. Dr.
Kearney had noted that the illness might be a new strain of either one of
these diseases and had expressed his concerns in his report.

When the knock came at his door, French automatically called "Enter,"
and glanced up to see Able Seaman Nesbitt alertly stood in the open doorway. The seaman met French's eyes and quickly glanced away. "Sir."

"Shut the door and have a seat." French indicated the chair in front of
his desk. He reached to his waist and switched off his remote.

"Are you comfortable, Nesbitt?"

Now seated, Nesbitt answered, "Yes," yet he seemed pained. He sucked
in his bottom lip, grimaced.

"Mind if I smoke?"

"No, sir."

French offered Nesbitt a cigarette, which the young man accepted.
French then leaned forward to offer him a light. Nesbitt held the cigarette
in an awkward manner, clamped between two fingertips, and sucked in
the smoke, smothering a cough, then nodding. "Good ... cigarette, sir.
I thought I might take up smoking. Thought it just earlier, sir."

French lit up, puffed and reclined in his chair, and studied Nesbitt
with a calmness befitting his position. "You recall when we tested the
refractors last night?"

"Yes, sir, on the beach. I was present." Nesbitt took another draw, this
one deeper. He exhaled conscientiously, without coughing, his lips pursed.

French took another draw, mulling over the words he was about to
speak, setting them in precise order. "You remember when the spotlights
were switched on and we illuminated the microwaves and gamma rays?"

Nesbitt nodded, winced, shut his eyes. Smoke escaped his mouth.

He then jutted forward to edgily brush the ash along the corner of the brass ashtray. "Yes, sir. I was there, sir."

"Shortly thereafter we switched on the refractors, and spaces of sky and ground were cleared. Our headsets went dead, if you recall."

"Yes, sir. I recall that very much. Silence. Not in the head any more. Voices, I mean."

French kept his eyes steadied on Nesbitt. "Do you see these books and documents on my desk, Nesbitt?" He firmly pressed a palm against the book on nautical disasters.

"Yes, sir. I do. I can honestly say that."

"They're about sea disasters, sea monsters, outbreaks of mystery illnesses throughout the years. Outbreaks. Breakouts. I've read a lot about this sort of thing lately."

If it was possible for Nesbitt to pale any further, he did so. Perhaps the cigarette was making him ill.

"These are subjects that don't usually hold any interest with me."

"I imagine so, sir."

"Do they for you?"

"No, sir," Nesbitt barked loudly. "No, sir." He went rigid in his chair and French thought he might bolt to his feet and salute.

"The bizarre occurrences in this town are the doing of what? Any idea?"

Nesbitt stared at French, his eyes widening. He took a draw and held in the smoke, seeming about to burst in anticipation. His eyes grew even wider and his pimpled forehead glazed with sweat, then the words exploded from him in a gush of smoke: "Spirits, sir. Spirits. That's what's doing it, sir. If I may speak openly."

"Spirits."

"Yes, sir."

"How so?"

"Permission to stub this out, sir?" Nesbitt held up his cigarette, the tip erected toward the ceiling.

"Of course."

"In your ashtray, sir?"

"Yes, go ahead."

Nesbitt made a great deal out of crushing the life from the cigarette while licking his lips. Then he sat upright in his chair, his eyes rimmed red.

"Go on," French encouraged.

Nesbitt touched his chin, squeezed it and rubbed it with uncommon vigour. "I don't want to be crazy, sir."

"Me neither, Nesbitt."

"I enjoy being here."

"On Earth?"

"Yes, sir. I mean, no, sir." Nesbitt corrected himself with a troubled expression. "The navy, sir. I don't want to be crazy."

"I'm not saying that you are. In fact, if you are, then everyone within a twenty-kilometre radius is grappling with insanity."

"It's not craziness, seeing things."

French said not a word. He wanted to further console Nesbitt, to express his understanding, to declare that he, too, had seen the trails of amber in the sky, that he had witnessed the monsters in the sea, but to do so would level him, set him up for failure, sink him beneath his station. Instead, he offered this: "From what I've read, from one of the theories proposed, these sort of attacks of outrageous fancy happen when a people's identity is threatened. Vast leaps and bounds of imagination and invention take place. Fishers of men. You see those words written up on the board out there?"

"Yes, sir. Every day."

"Fishers of men no more. It's not only about having your lifestyle threatened, it's about losing your place, your sense of self, if you will. A civilization that has been occupied or overthrown by an invading force has seen their storytelling capabilities peak to the point where visions are commonly recorded. Visions are manifested as a sort of coping mechanism. It's been documented over the centuries. The Jews and Jesus, the creation of the Bible. The undefeatable strength of the slaves, the stories of their roots that wouldn't die, but grew and grew until equality was manifested. The missionaries praying to destroy the Indian gods, but they could not. The Indians rose brighter, their feathers became more colourful, their dances more soulful. Visions. Are you following me, Nesbitt?"

"Yes, sir."

"The people react against the invading culture or the loss of identity. A mass hypnosis kicks in, one that everybody believes because they have to, in order to survive. Mentally, I mean. Survive beyond what has been taken away from them."

Able Seaman Nesbitt sat and stared, stunned beyond belief.

"When the refractors were switched on," French continued, "what did you see?"

Nesbitt flinched. "Nothing, sir."

"Are you certain?"

"Nothing." The young seaman's eyes shifted while he appeared to wrestle with his thoughts. Then something connected inside him and he was jolted as though punched by an invisible fist. "Not you," he said, with a look of brightening wonder followed by a faint hopeful smile of camaraderie. "You, sir?"

Concerned that he might have given away too much of himself, French remained silent and hardened his expression. This ever-so-subtle rebuke wiped the smile clean off Nesbitt's face.

"Tell me what you saw," French said flatly. "I know that you saw something."

Nesbitt jerked his head sideways as if warning himself against what he might say. He shifted in his seat, then shifted the other way. "You know what I saw, don't you, sir?" he asked pleadingly.

"I saw you watching something in the sky, following something."

"But did you see. For yourself, sir?"

French inspected Nesbitt's crazed eyes. He studied the way the seaman's hands were rubbing the armrests of the chair, the way he constantly opened and shut his lips, making tiny sounds. Observing the condition that Nesbitt was in, French resolved there was only one responsible admission to make: "No, Nesbitt. I didn't see anything out of the ordinary." And with those words, he lowered his eyes to study the speculative documents before him. "Try to get a grip on yourself, Nesbitt. Dismissed."

⁊⁊

Gradually, as colour drained from the room, images failed to thoroughly form in Rayna's head. When she tried drawing to mind a person or thing, the intent would vanish before her brain could fabricate whatever it was she had begun to recollect. She had no thoughts of the future. Nothing. At first she had experienced fits of terror and subsequent panic. Yet, as the condition became more intense, her unrest, rather than increasing, actually ebbed; she could not recall what it was she had been fearing in the first place. She was at peace, far away from her body, and, even, it seemed, her mind.

Then a man had sat down by her side, a peculiar-looking man with a narrow head and a tuft of hair on top, and crooked teeth behind a pointed grin. Rayna could make no sense out of the man's face. She only realized its features as he spoke. With words, his eyes became filled in, defined from a progression of wavering ripples. Yet more words and his chin was patterned. In this way, Rayna began catching glimmers of colours, not so much in the manner she had grown accustomed to, but colours flashing from the man's lips, filling in and contouring objects around him. Recollection had come to her, and there had been rushes of terror and panic once again until she began to recognize who the talking man was and what he was saying. Words assembled thoughts and then images.

"Dere were a mermaid widt long copper hair. Oh, she were a right pretty t'ing. She made me giggle widt glee each time I clapped me eyes upon her. And narry a stitch of clothing did she wear." The man's cheeks flushed and his eyes dipped toward the floor. "Twere da finest kind of wicked."

Tommy, said a voice in Rayna's head. *That might be the man's name. Tommy.*

"Den, furder out, dere were da giant squid off da point of Port de Grave." The man raised his arms and wiggled his fingers fiercely. "Tentacles like mighty fat worms poking out t'rew da surface of da water, reaching ta snatch at me boat. Da squid were a violent beast, but da whale. Oh, now dat were anudder story. Da whale would come along as sweet and meek as any a creature and da squid would run fer cover. Zoom. Gone ta da deeps. Da whale, it spoke ta me, watching with its big round eye from under da ocean surface in a way dat made me t'ink I knew da creature from before."

Rayna saw him fully now. His name was definitely Tommy. She began to remember. They were friends. Good friends. Tommy Quilty. He had helped her many times in the future. No, in the past. It was the past. Before now. Before this moment. That was the past.

"Centuries o' dust," Tommy told Rayna.

She wondered what that meant. By the look of Tommy, he didn't seem to know either. The words had just spread out of him.

"Dat whale confessed ta knowing me t'rew centuries o' dust. Dat's what dat old lovely whale said ta me. It —" He paused to look toward the doorway. A woman in white had entered the room.

"There's no visitor allowed here," she had huffed, starting in with her saucy nurse lip.

Rayna felt sudden fear for Tommy. He appeared to grow horribly ill.

"Come on, out now." The nurse shooed him from his chair.

But as he rose to leave, Tommy Quilty appeared stricken. He plopped back in the chair beside Rayna and struggled to breathe. Rayna noticed that the gasping for breath was not the same as what she had experienced, if memory served her well. It was not so much a shortness of breath, but a releasing from within, a slackening of muscles. Tommy acted as though he were having trouble pulling in air, whereas she had simply had to remember to breathe or it would not happen on its own.

The nurse had pressed the button by Rayna's bed and then had worriedly escorted Tommy out of the room.

"We'll get you to a bed," she said, her tone changed, now filled with concern and sweetness.

Rayna had later learned from the nurse that Tommy was admitted and put in a recently vacated bed on a ward down the hall. Room 611.

She saw all of this in her mind as if it had happened moments ago when, in fact, hours had passed since its occurrence. There was no need for her to be in the hospital any longer. She was not scared for her health, physical or mental. She was feeling herself once more, and needed only to get away from all these sick people before she became sick again. Every person on her ward, including herself, was hooked up to a respirator. She didn't need to be, and the tube was hurting her throat. It was sore as hell. Plus her head was splitting with pain. Nicotine withdrawal, she thought. A cigarette would set things right. Maybe they would give her a nicotine pill or gum or patch or needle. She thought of buzzing for the nurse, but a better notion, fleeing the hospital, struck her. If she left, she could buy her own pack of smokes. Smoke three or four at a time. Get the nicotine into her quick-like.

Raising her right hand, she watched her fingers. Jittery. They reached for the tube in her mouth and gripped it, her wedding ring clicking against the tubing, a hollow sound that she felt in her throat. The vibration. She squeezed tighter and carefully tugged on the tube, felt it come free of her throat, inching up, making her want to vomit. With watery eyes searching the ceiling, she waited, holding still, as her breath continued on its own. She licked her lips, smiling briefly. Her mouth was mulchy, dry, disgusting. She sat up in bed and stared across at a woman lying there with the respirator pumping air into her lungs. It was Bonnie Turnbull from Bareneed. They had never been friends. Bonnie was a gossip, spreading lies about Rayna when they were in high school together, that she had slept with one of the other girl's boyfriends. How long ago was that? More than ten years now. Lies.

Rayna shifted her legs out over the edge of the mattress and slid down onto the cool linoleum. Even though she had been in bed for only a day her muscles were unsteady. She took her time stepping across to Bonnie. When she reached the side of the bed, she raised the sleeve of her blue hospital gown to shield her mouth, breathing into the fabric, feeling it grow warm. The last time she had seen Bonnie was in a therapy group for victims of domestic violence. Bonnie had attended one meeting but then had never shown up again.

Now, Bonnie was sleeping. The small swing-arm television was switched on above the bed. Rayna watched a blonde-haired woman in a red skirt and jacket talking into the camera. At the bottom of the screen were the words: "Bareneed Live." There was no sound. Rayna pressed the power button, shutting it off, then swung it to the side. Bonnie's eyes weakly opened and watched her, giving no sign of recognition. She simply stared at Rayna, her eyes black as wet stones.

"Hi," Rayna whispered from behind the fabric. She noticed a bruise beneath Bonnie's left eye. It was yellow and green and speckled with purple. "What're ya at?"

Bonnie made a garbled sound behind the tube. Her eyes sluggishly shifted toward Rayna's bed and then regarded Rayna again.

"I had it too," Rayna said, smiling without a care in the world. "Now, I can breathe, no sweat." Drawing a deep breath, she lowered her arm away from her mouth and held her hands out at her sides. "On my own. It just happens. I got better."

Bonnie's eyes darkened beyond black as Rayna leaned down, no longer concerned about catching a virus, knowing deep down that it was not like that, no longer fearing it.

"It goes away," she whispered kindly. "Like you can think it away."

Bonnie's eyes shut as though she would not permit herself to hear.

"I'm going looking for Tommy Quilty." She took notice of Bonnie's left arm; a bruise by her wrist and another toward her elbow. "Take it easy, all right." Rayna headed for the doorway. Poking her head out into the corridor, she saw two nurses far up at their station. She ducked back in, waited a few tense seconds, then checked again. The nurses weren't looking her way. She scooted out, the linoleum chilly on her bare feet, and headed across the way and down three doors. Hurrying into room 611, she faced six beds, none with a curtain drawn, and all occupied by men, four of them watching the swing-arm televisions. She heard the humming as her eyes searched out and found Tommy toward the far corner, by the window.

At once, she went to watch over him. His eyes were closed and he seemed to be smiling while he hummed with great energy. Rayna reached to touch his cheek, but hesitated and gave his shoulder a shake instead. His eyes opened wide. He was looking right at her and his smile grew with good cheer, exposing two rows of crooked gapped teeth. He nodded with open devotion, obviously delighted to see her in fine health again. He edged up on his elbows.

"How ya doing?" she asked, her throat raw from the respirator tube.

Tommy shrugged. He reached up and tried to pull the tube from his mouth. Rayna helped him gently ease it free. As soon at it was dislodged, he said, "I were only pretending, sure. Ye knew dat, right?" He chuckled wheezily and set his fingers to his lips as though caught at a silly prank.

Rayna chuckled, too, and her eyes sheened with joy. "I can breathe right normal."

Tommy nodded. "Ye are a sight fer sore eyes, me lovely Rayna." He grabbed hold of her hand and held it firmly in both of his, warmly rubbed it with his thumbs, shook it up and down, then brought it to his cheek.

"We should get out of here, Tommy," she said, checking over her shoulder to see the same saucy nurse stepping into the room. Sighting Rayna, she immediately strode toward her.

"You shouldn't be out of bed, missus," the nurse said in a tone of distress and accusation while eyeing Rayna's blue hospital gown.

"I'm the finest kind."

"You can breathe okay?" the nurse asked with a shocked intake of breath.

"Yes."

"You sure?"

"Yes." To demonstrate, Rayna drew huge deep breaths through her nostrils, then let the air out through her opened mouth. "Perfect as anything, sure."

The nurse watched with suspicion, until she could no longer suppress a smile. "That's wonderful," she said, "but you better get back in bed till the doctor examines you." With this, she turned and hurried out of the room.

Rayna faced Tommy, bit her bottom lip and raised her eyebrows. She smiled brightly, giggling. "I'm in the worst sort of trouble." And Tommy giggled along with her.

As their outburst of mirth subsided, Rayna caught the nurse's voice talking with another nurse farther down the hall. One of them said: "They told us to call the army station if anyone got better."

"Oh no!" Rayna playfully gasped. "Come on. We better bust out of here."

"No greater trute," said Tommy, grinning to the high heavens.

⁂

The blue sky floated above Robin, a blue mirroring the exact shade of sea. There was no division between air and water as the wooden boat, in the figure of a hollow whale, gently rocked.

"You see how much fun it is?" Jessica asked from her seat toward the bow. Her hands loosely held the slat beneath her and her face was filled with only a bit of the ugly colour that had been spread all over it before. She was beginning to seem almost pretty.

Robin shrugged and watched Jessica gazing around with a look of fascination and wonder. "You can see everything," Jessica stated.

"It's all just blue," Robin said flatly, unimpressed.

"No," Jessica protested. "No, it's not. It's everything. You're just not here yet. Not all the way here."

A stream of amber light whooshed by overhead, chased by two more gushing streams.

"They're gathering," Jessica said, staring up, then gazing back beyond her shoulder. She raised her arm to point toward the plain of limitless blue. "Out there."

"Who?"

"The ones who've been cut off by the people on land."

"What people?"

"Their relatives. When the line's broken, they gather out, far from shore. They move toward the place where the centre is. There's one near every place where people settle, down in the bottom of the sea, a hole where everything came from, where they all came from once. Where water came from too."

Robin stared, not understanding Jessica's words.

"You're okay. Your people are still connected. They believe in you. One long unbroken line. They can still imagine who they are. They *know* who they are."

Another amber streak whooshed by overhead. Robin felt like ducking but she didn't.

"The ones that're cut off make the water worse; they make waves and storms, make the clouds black. They're tumbling and swirling in the waves and storms. It's their anger and love. That's not too bad, but when enough of them are cut off, when enough of them gather, they can crack open the hole in the bottom to stop the ones on land who can no longer see themselves." She leaned over the side of the boat and watched down into the water. "Everything's beneath the surface, far down."

Robin leaned on the edge of the boat, her hands braced to the side. She tried to see more, yet only saw blue. "It's blue."

"When you let go, you'll see. You're still stuck to your body. That's why you can't see all the way. Let go of your body. Your father's gone now. He's not by your side. You can drift easier. Away. Pretend you're closing your eyes, but keep them open."

Robin shut her eyes.

"No, don't close them. Just pretend."

Robin opened her eyes and stared. Jessica was smiling, even prettier than before, the ugly colour almost gone completely.

"That's better. Now, close them again."

Robin stared. Again, she shut her eyes without moving her eyelids, and saw that Jessica was unbelievably beautiful: her skin was smooth and her orange hair was like silk.

"You see? Look." Jessica nodded toward the rim of the boat.

Robin leaned and watched the water. She could see blue, and then flashes of yellow and green and red. The swirling shape of something becoming distinct.

"Okay," said Jessica. "Now, keep closing them, and you'll get deeper and deeper. You'll see what's really there, beneath the lying surface."

⌀

The world looked normal enough, gleaming with morning clarity as Joseph drove along the road that led out of Port de Grave. Houses, lawns, pickup trucks, the ocean to his left, Bareneed far across the bay. He passed a convenience store, saw a man and his daughter entering the building. Joseph's hands grew unsteady on the wheel. Everything was normal enough, except for Robin.

Kim had been worried about Joseph's condition, but had also needed her overnight bag from the Critch house. She required a change of clothes and her other essentials. Joseph had assured her that he was fit enough to travel. When he had left the ICU, after being checked and released by a doctor, one of the nurses had mentioned that things seemed to be settling in Bareneed. There were no more bodies, no more new patients with the breathing disorder. Everything had stabilized. If this was so, then Joseph hoped that as things reverted to normal Robin would become normal too.

Of all the places he could've picked for a vacation, he'd chosen the one that would be struck by an unheard-of catastrophe. Was it somehow his fault? Had he brought this upon himself and his loved ones? He felt like a character in one of those tragic novels that Kim was always reading. How could such an abundance of bad luck befall a single person? Robin, his own daughter. He shook his head as the crystalline sparkle of fear spanned beneath his skin, chilling him. His entire life would be changed by this. What would he do without Robin? What if Robin did not get better? He could not even begin to imagine the extent of his remorse. He did not want to, and turned his thoughts away from the possibility. Only hope, he told himself. Just hope.

On the desolate stretch of Shearstown Line, he passed two army jeeps heading fast in the opposite direction. Another army vehicle, this one a canvas-covered truck, zoomed passed. Seated soldiers with passive faces could be seen through the open back. They must be coming from Bareneed. They were not needed there any longer; the emergency was over.

Shortly after taking the turnoff for Bareneed, Joseph was surprised to find that the field where the media had been stationed was deserted. Where once there were crowds of people and numerous vehicles, now only litter and garbage remained. Up ahead, the first series of roadblocks was disassembled. The third barricade, once erected twenty feet before the community hall, was gone. In its place, two soldiers stood casually watching cars pass by. Joseph slowed his car, but they made no motion for him to stop. He passed the post office and the community hall, where an army jeep and van were parked. A yellow media van was pulled into a driveway alongside one of the old bay houses. There were people out on the front lawn being interviewed by a blonde-haired woman in a red skirt. A small crowd stood in the background, having spilled out of the house where they were gathered.

Joseph's eyes skimmed the harbour as he took the higher road toward the Critch house. No helicopters. No sound that he could detect. He rolled down his window and listened. Heavy waves sprayed upon the shore. A storm was on its way. There was no wind to speak of, but thick black clouds were banked off in the distance. He watched the road, then glanced back at the harbour as a purple whale broke the surface, hanging in the air for a second before descending. A massive shower of white turned silver in the air. The silver flashes rose higher, darkened from silver to brown, then flew off in a uniform pattern, tilting toward the east as they glided out to sea.

Had a flock of birds flown in behind the spray when Joseph hadn't noticed? Or had they manifested themselves from the water? Either possibility was highly believable at this point.

A red spiked tail, as long as a cargo ship, rose atop the water to skim the surface as a creature swam, concealed, out of sight, deeper in the sea. What sort of mad fantasy book was in his mind? Contrary to what people seemed to suspect, everything was not reverting to normal. Joseph eased the brake on and stopped the car in the middle of the road. The water in the harbour was churning, twisting and swelling like the black water he had experienced during foul weather while on patrol out at sea. But the water remained blue, and there was a perfectly blue sky above.

A horn tooted behind him. Joseph checked his rearview. Another media crew, in a white van, was looking to get through. He accelerated and rose higher, passing the solar house, then swerving dangerously into the Critch driveway. Climbing from his car, he watched a brown-haired woman in the van's passenger seat roll down her window and call to him: "Did you just get here?"

Joseph ignored her and continued toward the front door.

"Can we get your reaction on this?"

He stopped in his tracks, turned. "Reaction to what?" he called hotly.

"What's happening here." The woman threw open her door and leaped from the van. She was wearing a white skirt and a white jacket over a bright yellow blouse. The driver had already jumped out and was steadying a camera on his shoulder, anxiously aiming it toward Joseph.

"And what's that?" Joseph asked.

"Mic," the woman said, snatching the microphone from the camera-man. She stammered and stuttered and trod closer to Joseph, "I ... what is ... The sickness."

"*You* are the sickness." With this, he opened the door, stepped inside, and shut the door behind him, barring the woman. He stood still, waiting for his nerves to calm. The house was quiet. Joseph listened, detecting not a sound within the walls. He was hoping to hear the van drive on outside, but there was no indication of it doing so. He faced a strange house in which he realized he was achingly alone. The idea of staying there by him-self tripled his uneasiness. The door to the parlour was shut. He glanced farther up the hallway. The kitchen door was also shut. He gripped the bannister and raced upstairs. As he gathered Kim's bag from the guest room, his eyes lingered on the empty bed where Kim had been sleeping, the sheets and homemade checkered quilt tossed aside. He thought of climbing in and being with Kim in this way, sensing her lingering presence in the sheets, but the fabric would no longer be warmed by her body.

His mind flashed on last night. Uncle Doug, the old woman, Kim, himself. They had all been in this room and they had been safe. Everyone had been in their place. They had been safe, but he had not. What had hap-pened to him? Robin had not been with them, and the trouble that had befallen her was the result of negligence. He should have been there for her instead of existing in whatever chemical world he was inhabiting. How many pills had he taken? He had no idea. He should be there now, in the hospital. What the hell was he doing in this strange place picking up clothes? Were clothes really that important? He felt his thoughts slip out from under him and feared a recurrence of his previous condition.

Out in the hallway, he glanced across into Robin's room, saw the unmade bed. Robin. She hadn't made her bed. How had she fallen into the water? It was not like her to go out alone into the night. She never did that.

As usual, there were sheets of paper on her bed. Drawings. Blue and red colours. Urged on by the pictures, Joseph stepped nearer and stared down at the three sheets, one covered by the other. The blue was the harbour and the massive headland that framed it on the far side. The red was the tail of

a sea creature skimming the surface. With mounting interest, Joseph
picked up the paper and examined the drawing. The perspective was identical to his view of the harbour when he had driven up the higher road only
a short while ago. No more than five minutes had elapsed. The second
drawing was of a purple whale. Again, his perspective. Rather than unnerve
him, this discovery eased his unrest. The third and final rendering was of
a man standing back-on with his head bowed and his hands raised to a wall
of blackness. The man resembled Joseph and, with his hands held in that
position, he seemed to be halting the blackness from progressing any farther.
Beneath the drawing there was the symbol Robin often drew, the green
and blue and brown orb with the swirling orange-red centre. Joseph often
thought that the drawing was of the sun because there were orange-red
rays, wavering lines, emanating from the orb. However, unlike the sun,
these lines were emitting from the orange-red centre, not from the surface
as was the case with drawings of the sun.

   Noise from downstairs, someone entering the house, entering by the
front door. Light footsteps. Could it be the media woman? Was she capable of being that bold? Of course she was. They were vultures, after all.
They'd risk going anywhere to pick a strip of flesh from stricken bones.

   Joseph held his breath and made not a single movement, save for the
blinking of his eyes. Careful footsteps shifted toward the back of the
house to check the kitchen; he heard the gentle rattle of the brass knob
being gripped, the door squeaking open. He would have to wait until the
woman left. Wouldn't she be calling out? Seeking him? Being obnoxious.
And wouldn't she have the cameraman with her? Yes, she most certainly
would. Without video, what would be the point of intruding upon his life?
If she ventured upstairs, he would hide. He was uncertain what she was
capable of. His eyes darted toward Robin's closet. He laid down the drawings and tiptoed toward it as he heard footsteps on the creaking stairs. His
hand reached for the glass doorknob. He had never looked in the closet
before. What might be in there? Emptiness? Shabby things smelling of
mothballs? The drowned dead with their open expressions, waiting to spill
from the watery enclosure? He twisted the prismatic knob and carefully

eased the door toward him. The hinges squeaked. The footsteps paused
on the stairs. Joseph's heart beat fiercely.

⊸🜋

Miss Laracy had shut and locked the parlour door in the Critch house to preserve her peace and was presently sitting upright on the chesterfield, sleeping
like the dead. There was no waking her. Snapshots of bodies flitted through
her mind; the faces were of the dead she had beheld in the fish plant. Groups
of individuals stood in distinct columns, each face in each row resembling
the one behind it. Only the hairstyles and clothes varied. Definite strings of
people who, if not related, bore an uncanny resemblance to one another.

An image of Uriah rose in her mind. She tried forcing her eyes open and
the lids dissolved in a fluid upward motion. Uriah was seated across from
her in the parlour. He was sporting a lovely expression, jovial, sly yet meaning well. At first, his lips were shut, but as he continued watching her his
smile widened to a grin in appreciation of his fiancé and their shared circumstance. Beholding Uriah, Miss Laracy felt his energy transferring itself
to her, sensed the smile raising her own lips. Uriah was charming and handsome beyond belief — a generous man who would gladly do anything for
anyone who requested a favour. His hair was neatly groomed and he was sitting back in the chair, his hands on the armrests. Comfortable. With eyes
still fixed on her and gleaming with good cheer, he leaned slightly forward.

"Are ye at peace?" Miss Laracy asked.

The glimmer of amusement faded from Uriah's eyes, then the smile
steadily wilted. His body became shrouded in a blood-red pulse that
clarified to streams of thin red lines, a multitude of them piercing and
leaving his body. He held out his hands, fragmented by blank spaces while
his face dissolved into particles; his nose became a stumpy white fish as it
separated, his eyes two throbs of jellyfish, his top lip a succulent sea
cucumber, his bottom lip a moray eel.

Tears of wonder and spectacular loss sprang to Miss Laracy's eyes,
spilling hotly down her cheeks. Uriah was at a distance now, not in sight,
but deeply within her. He had withdrawn from the surface.

Once more, Miss Laracy tried opening her eyes and found that she was already awake, or at least seemingly so. Why hadn't she seen Uriah in the fish plant? Why couldn't she go there now and gaze into his face as she had the others? Where were his people? None of them had been there.

Suddenly, she understood what it was that had been troubling her about the bodies in the fish plant. She understood why she had not discovered her Uriah lying flat upon one of the filleting tables, why he had not washed ashore. Uriah's parents were long gone and he had fathered not a single child. His lineage had stopped dead with his passing.

Doug Blackwood had avoided the hospital long enough. He had wandered away from the brick building, crossed the street and trodden down a well-travelled grassy path between two houses that led to the shore. Pausing to take a deep inhale of the salt air, he then stepped over the beach rocks, approached the water, and set the tiny whale on the surface to see if it would float. It bobbed and turned in a peculiar circle, then proceeded to soak up water. Waterlogged, it sunk pitifully, until it rested in the murky silt. Doug shot an accusatory glance back toward the hospital.

"Expect as much of wood taken from a place like that? Deadwood, it be." He glanced around and spied a piece of driftwood washed up on shore. The small and large beach rocks were unsteady beneath his shoes as he manoeuvred toward the gnarled piece of salt-bleached driftwood and bent down, raised it in both his hands and grinned in profound appreciation. It was more than two feet long and half a foot thick. He carried the driftwood away from the water and settled on one of the great rocks by a bank of wave-worn earth. With the driftwood in his lap, he commenced whittling. "This'll be a proper whale," he muttered, nodding with resolve. "Wood from the sea. Guaranteed to float."

When he was done, he used both hands to raise the carved whale up to the sky and, against the blue, gave it a good steady inspection. He made it swim up and down as if bouncing on waves. Satisfied, he stood and revisited the water's edge. Gentle waves lapped the shore, wetting the bottom edges of his shoes. Paying the water no mind, he bent down and set the whale on the sparkling surface. He stood and watched it float out, as though heading for the open sea, then revolve in a slow wide arc and faithfully float back to him.

"Finest kind," he exclaimed, winking to himself while crouching down to scoop the whale from the water. He gave it three solid shakes to expel the droplets clinging to its bottom, and headed for the hospital.

In the main lobby, he couldn't help but curse "My Christ!" and turn his nose up at the antiseptic stench. The soldiers were no longer guarding the doorways. He could choose to enter whichever passageway he liked.

On hurried feet, and with the whale tucked under one arm, he made it to the ICU. He huffed down the corridor, the bright white lights burning his eyes, until he arrived at the double doors where a sign told him to ring the buzzer. He stabbed the buzzer while trying to catch his breath. When admitted by a harried nurse, a nurse he had never set eyes on before, Doug lied and told her he was Robin's grandfather.

"Wait here," the nurse said with an urgency that shot a shaft of icy fright through Doug's heart. The nurse rushed off and, a few moments later, a doctor appeared.

"You're the girl's grandfather?"

"Yes." Doug shifted the whale from one arm to the other.

"I'm sorry." The doctor's eyes dipped distractedly to the whale then back to Doug's face.

"Sorry?"

"She went into cardiac arrest."

"What?" Doug yelped.

"Cardiac —"

"What?" he shouted. "Where's the girl's mother?"

"She's with the girl."

"The father too?"

"I'm sorry. I don't believe I know."

⌁

"Joseph?"

Who would know my name? Joseph wondered, the question further tensing his nerves. As if to find a means of escape, he stared searchingly into the closet. There was shelving along the bottom on which sat old shoes, pale-coloured hat boxes of varying shapes, and bulky folded blankets. The smell of mothballs rose to him, an odour he had not encountered since exploring his grandmother's house as a boy. It would be impossible for him to squeeze into the closet and shut the door. He heard the voice speak his name again, a troubled wondering voice now directly behind him: "Joseph."

Heart hammering, he snapped around to see Claudia standing there in a cream-coloured gown with flared sleeves and intricate turns and coils of copper embroidery along the front. On her feet, were matching slippers with similar embroidery. Her copper hair was swirled and pinned up, soft strands dangling by her cheeks, highlighting her pale slender neck.

"Is it okay?" she asked.

"What?" His fingers seemed empty, lighter, and he noticed that he had dropped Kim's overnight bag. "Okay what?"

"To enter your house. I've left mine. Each house is a separate world, you know. We never live in just one."

Joseph glanced anxiously into the closet. "I was looking ..."

"There's an inordinate amount of old things that we can never seem to let go of. Antiques. Museum pieces. Stillborns."

Joseph agreed with a grimace and stared at Claudia, her pale face, her pink lips, her hands peacefully joined in front of her rounded belly. With the exception of her belly, she was thinner than he remembered, her expressive eyes seemingly larger as if her face was drawing in on itself, sinking deeper to her core.

"You okay?" he asked.

Without the slightest effort, she was two steps nearer. "You know," she said, "I've often thought of throwing myself into the sea. Instead, I cast everyone else in. I thought that might make me well, if we were all there together, in the same boat, so the speak." She gave a light, curious laugh. "One thing I forgot: I neglected to sculpt a figure of myself." Closer still, her breath against Joseph's lips, her languid tongue shifting the words around, her hand near his hand but not yet touching. "It's through my eyes that I see. I see everything so much clearer because I'm removed, nothing but an observer, an onlooker. Isn't that sad?" With this, her cool fingertips found the back of his hand.

"Robin's in the hospital," Joseph blurted out," and …" His voice trailed off as he furtively backed away, checked toward the window. A tree's sturdy branches were intertwined just beyond the glass. Claudia was scaring the hell out of him. Yet her choice of words and otherworldly composure were pure seduction that he found himself incapable of resisting. A ghostly danger that excites. The possibility of stiffening demise. But how could he begin again with Kim and Robin if he allowed himself to enter Claudia? Lose himself in Claudia, or in Kim. Bury himself. To get away, he might leap out the window, snatch hold of a tree branch, hang there, wait forever if need be, for rescue.

"Is Robin okay?" Claudia stole another deliberate step toward him. Again, she fingered his hand. The scent of overwatered flowers, decay, rotted leaves underfoot was adrift in the air.

Joseph shook his head. Talking about Robin with Claudia further sullied Joseph's heart, tripled the guilt. The woman had no right speaking his daughter's name. Not when Robin was ill like this. No right.

"Is she living?"

"Yes." Joseph insisted. "Yes, she is." He shuffled to move past Claudia, yet feared she might snatch hold of him. Her skin was so white. Her long fingers began curling and uncurling above her belly, like roots divining an underground spring. He couldn't help but stare there. A child floating within Claudia. Whose child? Suddenly, there were ripples of movement beneath the fabric.

"Come downstairs. I'll prepare a pot of rosehips tea." She gave him a blossoming smile that calmed his centre. Then she made away from him.

Joseph barely heard her descending the stairs. He bent for Kim's bag and left the room. Standing at the top of the stairway, he hesitated until hearing Claudia fussing with dishes in the kitchen. He then took a deep steady breath and silently trod down the stairs. In the first-floor hallway, he noticed that the parlour door was shut. He took a searching look back toward the kitchen.

"I should be at the hospital," he called. He faced the muteness of the house, waiting expectantly, but there was no reply. "Claudia? I'll see you later. Okay?"

No sound. No voice.

With each curious step down the enclosing hallway, he became more aware of the kettle hissing. The tiny sketches hanging on the walls to either side of him were of peaceful ocean scenes, sunsets blazing across calm water, and he was reminded of Robin's drawing, the green and brown and blue orb with the orangy red centre. A sun inside an Earth.

Crossing the kitchen threshold, he found Claudia preparing two mugs, her back to him. The sight of her, the feminine gestures that she exacted with such fluidity, calm and reassurance filled him with a purely adolescent longing. Love so easy. Longing so acute. The past unmarred by the commerce of a marriage.

"I should …" he said.

Claudia turned to look at him and her eyes were merciful. There was a naturalness to her that seemed mistaken before. Joseph had barely seen her smile, yet when Claudia had mentioned Robin's plight her mood had relaxed.

"We've risen from the same wave, Joseph," Claudia explained.

"Wave?"

Claudia's fingers reached for his, loosened them from the strap of Kim's overnight bag, which landed softly on the floor. She then entwined her fingers with his, the coolness of her skin soon generating a warmth that made his hand seem not to be his at all, but something newly alive. He watched his fingers, then peered into Claudia's eyes to see that she was concentrating on him. Stepping nearer, she pressed the side of her head to his chest.

"Everything will be fine," she professed as the kettle began to whistle. "I'm in your house now."

~⦿~

Miss Laracy sat in stunned contemplation of where she might be. While her gaze moved around the room, brief utterances of no particular meaning escaped her. She was in a parlour, not her own, of this she was most certain. The furniture was familiar yet of no fitting arrangement. Not her

house. The Critch house. And was Uriah here? With a devotee's anxious-
ness, she considered the barred door. Had he come back to her?

The lingering qualities of the dream, if that was what it had been,
goaded her with hope. She studied the empty chair across from her. What
to do now? Where to go? Her dream had been heartening; it had spoken
to her of lineage. It had been consoling to be among the dead. It was not
the empty flesh that gave her solace but the hovering spirits. She wondered what spell needed to be undone to deliver them, set them free to
seek out and reenter their living loved ones? What was driving them to
cling to bodies that were of no further use to them?

Groaning, Miss Laracy pushed herself up off the parlour sofa. "Me old
bones," she protested. It would be a brief walk to the fish plant, mostly
downhill and requiring little effort. Regardless, she thought of telephoning
that nice young police officer to give her a ride in his automobile again.
Finding that she could not recall his name, she gave her head a miserable
shake and shuffled toward the parlour door, unlocking and opening it.
The front door was directly to her right. She went for it without giving the
house another moment of consideration.

Out in the yard, she paused for a leisurely look at the garden; the purple
pansies were doing just fine. "Yer all grand," she said to them. The lobelia
was spreading and the red rose bush was practically in full bloom. Bending
down, she brushed her palm over the luscious satiny petals, shivering in
delight at the sensation. She thought of the more flimsy wild pink roses
that flourished behind her own house. In a matter of six or seven weeks,
they would be blooming and the raspberries that grew in union with the
roses would be ripe for picking. She'd make her jams in early September.
Raspberry. Blueberry. Patridgeberry. Bakeapple.

On the flagstone path, she paused at the edge of the asphalt to look
down toward Atkinson's wharf across the lower road. The plywood walls
that had been erected all along the beach to prevent people from entering
the area were torn down and remained in disorder. Beyond the rubble,
a pink dolphin leaped high into the sky, diving back down with a splash
that sent water sparkling into the sky. Miss Laracy chuckled and continued

on her way, crossing the street and descending the higher road. If her dream was correct, if it was instructing her as she assumed it was, then something had changed at the fish plant. She had divined this in her vision. The glorious trails of amber she had witnessed last night must have conveyed particles of inspiration and enlightenment. Halfway down the road, a military vehicle pulled up from behind her, and the soldier in the passenger seat asked if she needed assistance.

"Nar, I'm jus' out fer a stroll, lover." She casually pointed ahead of herself. "Goin' ta da plant ta 'av a gander at da bodies."

"That's a restricted area, ma'm."

"Restricted?" She stopped dead in her tracks and huffed indignantly. "Restricted?" Glancing from one soldier to the other, she could not believe her ears. She gave a loud raucous laugh. "Sure, I'm over eighteen years o' age. I'm t'irty-nine, if ye must know da God-honest trute."

The driver chuckled, but the passenger didn't seem to catch the joke.

Miss Laracy grinned, her pink gums wetly sheening. "I'm s'posed ta identify da dead. I been doin' so fer ye fellers already da once."

The passenger door swung open and the serious soldier leaped out. "Please," he said, indicating his seat. He caught her hand in a mannerly fashion and helped her up into the vehicle, then slammed the door and nodded. The jeep drove on toward the fish plant.

"Where ye from?" Miss Laracy asked the soldier at the wheel. He didn't seem to hear her; instead, he was talking to himself.

"Cripes, ya listenin' or wha'?" She poked him in the ribs with her finger and the soldier gave a sharp cry. "Yer a hignorant feller."

"Sorry, m'am. I was just talking to headquarters about your arrival."

Miss Laracy squinted at him. "Talkin' ta headquarters? Sure yer as nutty as two fruitcakes put tagedder."

"Your name's Eileen Laracy, is that correct?"

Miss Laracy grinned. "I'm dat famous, eh?"

"I was talking to headquarters. They identified you." He pointed his thumb at his wireless microphone.

"Talkin' ta outer space 's more like it, talkin' ta a bunch o' Martians."

Again, the soldier chuckled and Miss Laracy warmed to him. She liked a man with a healthy sense of humour despite the circumstances. It was humour that saved many a soul in peril. Nothing worse than a sad sack to clutter up your mood with grief and woe.

"I were asking where ye hailed frum."

"Peterborough."

"Dat's in Ontario," Miss Laracy avowed.

"Yes, ma'm."

"I were always da best kind widt maps." She jabbed at the side of her head. "I'm as sharp as a tack, ye know. All me life I were praised fer me keen wits."

The jeep swerved to pull up in front of the fish plant. The driver briskly departed his seat and helped Miss Laracy down. Making certain he had a firm grip on her arm, he carefully guided her toward the main doors.

Inside, Miss Laracy saw that something was awry as she gazed over-head. The spirits were still lingering, yet there were two gaps, each above a body. Those spirits were missing. Miss Laracy exclaimed aloud, and in a fit of enchantment she hurriedly shuffled toward the bodies. The driver trailed after her, his boots clicking on the concrete floor. Clicking like all those computer keyboards down toward the back.

Once upon the first spiritless body, she examined it and made the sign of the cross, fingertips swiftly to her forehead, heart, right shoulder, left shoulder. It was Rayna Prouse's husband, Gregory. The second body belonged to Rayna's great-grandfather, Gordon Vatcher. Fearing that some-thing unfortunate had happened to Rayna, Miss Laracy crossed herself again and offered up a prayer to Saint Anthony, patron saint of lost souls.

-◊-

Two soldiers arrived within minutes of the nurse's call and escorted Rayna from Tommy's room.

"Please follow us," ordered the shorter of the two soldiers.

"Where to?"

"There's no need to get changed," insisted the taller soldier. "We're staying in the building."

"Oh."

They boarded the elevator and descended to the basement where, upon arriving, the soldiers directed Rayna left. They travelled down a corridor for more than a hundred feet until reaching, at the very end, a rust-coloured door with a radiation symbol beneath large red letters that spelled WARNING. A security-code box was mounted on the wall. The shorter soldier pressed a series of digits and the door clicked opened. Moving inside, Rayna found herself in a narrow cinder-block room with a caged fluorescent light overhead and yet another door directly in front of her. The shorter soldier knocked, while the taller soldier turned to make certain the first door shut fully on its spring.

The inner door was opened by a thin dark-skinned man in a lab coat. A security tag was pinned to his top pocket but the print was too small to make out his name. Behind him, there was another rust-coloured door.

"Rayna Prouse?"

"Yeah?"

"I'm Dr. Basha." He gave a welcoming nod. "I've been asked by Lieutenant-Commander French to examine you."

"I'm fine."

"As it seems. Yet we're generally concerned with what's beyond the obvious, particularly in this case."

"What?"

"It's what's inside."

Rayna glanced at the tall soldier, whose eyes were searching the floor.

"Just beyond this door, there's an examination room. A few moments of your time, please. It's extremely important."

"To who?"

"Perhaps the health of the others." Dr. Basha turned to open the door. He glanced back at her and tipped his head in encouragement. "This way, please."

The tall soldier stepped ahead, as did the shorter one, and Rayna was caught up in the progression. In the next room, there were two doors, one directly ahead and another to their right. Dr. Basha opened the door to the right to reveal an examination table and a series of shelves on which medical supplies were arranged. Rayna looked skeptically at Basha, who smiled hopefully and tipped his head again. He gestured toward the table.

"Please, have a seat."

Rayna reluctantly moved beside the table and touched it with her fingers. She noticed a distinct mechanical hum in the room. When she turned again, the soldiers were gone and the door was shut. Only the doctor remained standing there.

"Please."

Rayna sat back on the table, watched the doctor. "My breathing's fine," she insisted as if to counter anything the doctor might say.

"We know that," confirmed Basha. "It's not the breathing now. It's up here." With this, he pressed his fingertips against both temples. "Do you know who you are?"

Rayna burst out with a mocking laugh. "Yeah. Rayna Prouse."

"No, not your name. I mean *really* who?"

⁓∅

"It's been so long," Claudia whispered, searching Joseph's eyes as she carefully set her hands to his cheeks. He was much like Reg, this quiet man with a beard who genuinely wanted to help her. Reg had once been a gentle man. "So long since I've felt connected to anyone." She pressed her belly against him, tipped her face nearer, dizzied by the spell of proximity and resistance. Her eyelids fluttered shut and her head gently swam from side to side. When her lips met Joseph's, the moistness further conveyed the attraction, her hands in his hair, then down along his back, holding on as though the act were magnetic. She trembled fiercely as their kissing grew more deliberate, until Claudia, opening her eyes, stepped back and dauntlessly reached for the bottom edge of her gown, easing it up to her knees.

"Reg," she said with a groan, her jaw cracking, her eyes so dry it pained to move them. "If you're to drown, it's to be in me."

The man stood without movement, watching her with an unfathomable expression. Claudia permitted him no time to decide whether he might be living or dead. She surged toward him, kissing with urgency, pressing her belly hard against his groin. He was hers. She would take him. She would kill him if that's what he wanted. She would do it all for Reg, because he was still her husband and there was love there for him, wasn't there? Wasn't there love for him? Yes, she assured herself, wanting to weep openly, but no tears would rise. There was love for Jessica, too. Yes. Claudia was the one left behind. The one living mistake. This was the way back to them, through this man. She focused on him. His hair had lightened and his eyes were somehow different. He was fairer now.

"You're my husband," she said, nodding.

But the man, the man she hoped might be Reg, shook his head and was no longer himself. It was not Reg, but Joseph. Claudia's face registered awe. Frantic and dismayed, she kissed the man more fiercely, biting him, biting his lips. Moaning in spurts, she tried forcing her body through his. He must be inside me first, she told herself, to kill every life-giving surge from him.

"You're a dead man," she whispered. Her eyes shut as hands slid down her back, fingers stumbling over the round ivory buttons. The pleasure of simply being held was so immense that Claudia felt the clench of a sob buckling in her chest.

"Reg," she moaned, "Reg, Reg …" She felt his fingers stop at the sound of his name. There was resistance as his body inclined away.

"No!" Claudia said, desperate hands on his face. "Don't …" She saw that he was regarding her with eyes that were once so familiar and warm, but now stared with a look that questioned her very existence.

"I'm sorry," he said, gazing beyond her.

This man. Who was he?

Vision blurred with thick sluggish impossible tears that seemed dredged and strained from her blood, for that must be the only liquid circulating in her now, she turned to check over her shoulder. There were two small forms. Two girls standing side by side and holding hands. Jessica and Robin.

Claudia shook her head. "No, this place is fine, please," she pleaded. "Please stay."

"I can't … I have to go. This is …" The man edged away, his hands leaving her completely so that her body was appallingly alone and only itself again. He was trying to be someone else as he backed toward the kitchen door. "I have to see my daughter …" He faltered on the word "daughter," his expression implying that he might have harmed her with that word.

Claudia followed a few steps after him before stopping. "Our daughter," she screamed.

The man had no sooner turned for the hallway when she rushed toward the drawers, threw one open and then another, manically searching. He would not leave her again. This man. He would not die unless it was by her hand. If the guilt that she suffered perpetually was to be hers, then it should be of her doing. She found the handle. She found the blade and raised it to her eyes to see Jessica's reflection flash back at her.

~∅~

Uncle Doug had received news that pained his heart miserably. The little girl, his great-niece Robin, had passed away.

The nurse quietly led him into the room at the ICU to see Kim bent over the bed, weeping and hugging the lifeless child. A tall young doctor stood across from Kim. He appeared stricken, wordless, vacant.

Doug had no idea what to do with himself. He remained on the threshold and watched the terrible sight of Kim clutching desperately at her daughter, rocking the small body back and forth, the slim arms dangling, hugging as if her fierce love might revive the child. He felt his chest heave and a sob rasped loose. He shifted the whale carving from one arm to the other. It was all so useless. What should he do with the carving? It had been created for Robin and now she was no longer with them and never would be.

The carving grew heavier in his hands, its weight seemingly increasing. Doug considered laying the whale on the bed, but the sight of his intentions, his tribute, would cause even greater grief. Kim had not yet looked at him. She was stroking Robin's hair, kissing her forehead, hugging her, trying to bring the child even nearer, gathered through her chest and into her heart. He slipped the burdensome whale behind his back, hoping he would not lose his grip on it, hoping no one would catch sight of it. What good could it possibly do now? The death of a child.

-◐)

No words passed between Rayna and the soldier at the wheel as the jeep sped to the makeshift military headquarters in Bareneed's community centre. The soldier had introduced himself as Able Seaman Nesbitt. He was young and a bit nervous as if trying to find words, but nothing came. He was different from the other two soldiers who had escorted her from the basement back to her room to get changed, then taken her down again to the jeep. This soldier was more like a normal person. He wasn't so hard and perfect. And he even had a bunch of pimples on his forehead, like a teenager. It made him look sweet.

Dr. Basha had asked Rayna a lot of questions about her past, about memories and people she knew. He had also asked her phone number, her licence plate number, birthdate, shoe size. He compared her answers to the words printed on several sheets of paper held in his hands.

When the doctor was finished ticking off answers, Rayna had asked: "Did I pass?"

"If passing constitutes answering the question 'are you yourself' in the affirmative, then, without doubt, you've accomplished the task."

Whatever the hell that meant! She assumed it was a "yes."

Arriving at the community centre, Rayna was immediately led alongside the two big doors for the fire trucks and toward the main entrance. Nesbitt was moving quickly, but Rayna slowed to a baffled standstill when she noticed activity in the harbour. There was something mottled green, about the length of a ship, but curving like a snake, floating on the water. Around it, huge blue fish, the exact colour of the water, leaped over the snakelike form and splashed down on either side. Rayna shot a surprised glance at Nesbitt. She laughed outright. "Wicked!" she exclaimed. "This is right wicked. It's like a movie or somethin'."

Nesbitt smiled nervously but his eyes were sad. He opened the door for her and tilted his head, as if trying not to let his eyes catch sight of the harbour.

"What's going on?" she asked, glancing at the water. "Look at that!"

Nesbitt shrugged. "Everyone's seeing it now."

"That stuff?"

"Yeah. I saw it for a long time," he confessed. "Now everyone's seeing it."

"Like Tommy."

"What?" Nesbitt peeked at her eyes, then watched the ground again.

"Like Tommy said: you're safe if you see."

"I don't understand. Safe?"

"Nothing." She took another look toward the water, but the snakelike creature had disappeared. Staring for a while, she waited to see if it would resurface. It didn't, so, at the urging of Able Seaman Nesbitt, she stepped into the community centre. She had been in this building on countless occasions over the years, for birthday parties, card games and holiday dances. Now the inside was nothing like it had been at those times. Four small rooms had been built along the far wall.

"This one," said Nesbitt, pointing ahead.

When they arrived at the office doorway, Nesbitt said: "Lieutenant-Commander French, sir?"

The man behind the desk looked up from a list he had been checking. A thick book of Atlantic fish species sat open on his desk along with several nautical maps. "Yes."

"This is the recovered patient from the hospital," said Able Seaman Nesbitt.

"Who else but Rayna Prouse." French stood and extended his hand, which Rayna shook. He seemed genuinely happy to see her.

"Hi." She liked his handshake. It was strong and his eyes were the most beautiful blue. Plus he was handsome in a rough stony sort of way.

"It's so nice to meet you," he said, watching her face. "And to know that you're feeling better. Breathing okay?"

Rayna shrugged. "I suppose. Ask that Frankenstein doctor in the basement." She noticed several books stacked on a chair in the corner: *20th Century Nautical Disasters; Atlantic Tidal Waves; Pervasive Culture: Allegiance with Electromagnetic Fields; Electromagnetic Hypersensitivity.*

French motioned toward the empty chair directly in front of his desk. "Please, have a seat."

Able Seaman Nesbitt saluted and backed away.

"Can I get you a coffee or anything?" French asked, his voice almost drowned out by a helicopter overhead.

Rayna shook her head. She waited for the helicopter to gain some distance, then said: "No, I'm okay." She gave him a smile that came out all wrong, snarky. She just wanted to go home and sleep. She hadn't had much sleep. And she didn't like uniforms. Cops or army guys. She didn't like the way her mind felt, like she was already half-dreaming.

"Seems so," French said, studying her in a way that made her feel like he knew more than he was letting on. She didn't like that either. It meant something was going on that she didn't know about. She could really use a drink right about now. And a cigarette.

French raised a pack of cigarettes from his desk and offered her one. The sight of them almost made her burst into tears. Someone who actually smoked!

"Can you smoke in here?" she asked, pinching the cigarette and sliding it from the package.

"Who's going to stop you?" He leaned across his desk to offer a light from a fancy lighter.

"You're the boss then," said Rayna, taking a deep drag, relishing it. She even moaned a little, "God, that's good."

French lit up and they both sat wordlessly, French in composed wonder, Rayna in nicotine delight, both of them watching each other while filling the office with a haze of blue smoke.

<hr />

"Oh God, oh God," Kim would not lift her hands from her daughter for fear that either she or Robin would be carried away. Robin was still warm, so warm. How could she not be alive? She was warm. A wave of excruciating grief swamped Kim's body. It trembled in fits and starts. Her arms grew weak, as though overworked, and she released hold. She stood quaking to fully regard Robin, the length of the body that further crippled her. She barely heard the voice; her hands were holding the sides of her head and partially covering her ears. Muteness throbbed through her.

"Mrs. Blackwood?" It was the doctor. He was about to ask her something, something about her daughter, something about taking her daughter away. She shook her head and bent to hug Robin again.

"Mrs. Blackwood?"

Through her sobbing, she detected another voice. A man's voice she barely knew. Firm hands were on her. "No …" She turned in desperation and fear to see the tear-blurred image of Uncle Doug.

"Look," he said, eyes toward the glass that gave a view out over the main room of the ICU. "Look," he said, smiling. Smiling!

"No." She pawed at her eyes. "What?"

"The monitor."

Kim turned her startled gaze toward the heart monitor.

"We've got a heartbeat," the doctor called, and a nurse immediately rushed into the room and to the other side of the bed to inject Robin. Her lips were now moving, whispering weakly.

"What?" Kim was coaxed back from the bed by the doctor. "She said something." Kim pulled away from the doctor and pressed her ear to Robin's lips to hear: "Daddy's coming." She was guided back again by the doctor and nurse. Robin's eyes remained shut and her lips were still.

"We have to work," the doctor said. "You need to leave. Please, a few minutes."

Uncle Doug steered Kim away, toward the doorway, where she stopped to anxiously regard the scene.

"Is she alive?" she asked, still in disbelief, while the doctor and nurse laboured around her daughter.

"I believe so," said Uncle Doug.

"She said something." Kim wiped both palms beneath her eyes and smiled. "She said 'Daddy's coming.' Did you hear her?"

"No."

"You didn't hear her?"

Another nurse squeezed by them. At once, she shifted the spare chair from the foot of Robin's bed, back toward the wall. On the chair, there sat a carved wooden whale which wobbled back and forth.

"Come on," said the nurse, returning to lead Kim and Uncle Doug outside the ICU. "We need to clear the way."

Kim leaned against the wall, fretting again. Waiting was the worst sort of torment. How long had Robin been dead before she came back? It seemed like hours, but it must have been only five or ten minutes since the doctor had pronounced her dead. Kim had heard of people who had died and returned to life. Occasionally there was brain damage. Had Robin been dead that long? She searched up the corridor, watched Uncle Doug pacing.

"Where's Joseph?" she asked him, as if Uncle Doug, Joseph's flesh and blood, would be the one most attuned to his whereabouts. "He left a while ago," she told herself, remembering. "He's been gone a while, hasn't he?"

Uncle Doug shrugged. "I don't know. Maybe I should have a look for him?"

"Robin said he's coming." After a few moments of silence, Kim said: "Yes. He went to get things for me." She glanced at her watch and briefly touched the rim as though attempting to determine the time. A nurse passed by and Kim glanced hopefully toward her, only to see the back of the nurse's head. No word was spoken.

"About an hour ago," she said to Doug. "How far is it to Bareneed?"

"Fifteen minutes each way." The idea of Joseph not being present obviously aggravated Uncle Doug. He didn't try very hard to hide it. "I'll go and see," he volunteered.

Kim watched Uncle Doug head down the corridor, then turned toward the doors to the ICU. When would they come? When would they tell her what was happening? Christ!

↤⊙

Here were the man's wife and daughter needing him and where was he?

"I'll try the phone," Doug muttered to himself. "Might be up and working. Where's the friggin' phones?" Out in the lobby, he caught sight of Sergeant Chase speaking with a doctor and waved him over.

"How's the little girl?" Chase asked right away.

"I don't know. She was … heart stopped. But it started up again. We're hoping." He raised his crossed fingers and patted Chase on the shoulder.

"Yes, let's hope." Chase searched Doug's face as if wondering what the man might need. "What can I do?"

"I need a ride," Doug said.

"Where?"

"Bareneed."

"Nice place for a vacation, I hear."

"No laughing matter."

"I'm not laughing. These lines here." He touched the corners of his eyes. "Worry lines."

In the car, the two men buckled up and headed out.

"Where in the name of Jehosepha is that nephew of mine?"

"Maybe he's been stopped at the roadblocks," Chase suggested. "Detained. He was acting … out of the ordinary."

Doug scoffed at the idea.

The radio made a squelching noise and Chase raised it from the console. He glanced at Doug before saying: "Sergeant Chase."

"We've got a call from a Miss Laracy for you, transferred through the fish plant in Bareneed."

"Copy."

"Patching it through."

"What the hell does that woman want now?" Doug grumbled, watching Chase's hand on the radio.

"'Lo?"

"Hello."

"Dis be Sergeant Chase?"

"Yes."

"Dis be Eileen Laracy. Ye remembers me? Da right gorgeous woman ye met up at da Critch house."

Doug spitefully shook his head, folded his arms across his chest.

"Yes, you're unforgettable." Smiling, Chase reached the head of the Port de Grave road and waited at the intersection for a long fuel truck to pass. Doug pointed in the right direction, just in case the Mountie didn't know the way. Chase took a left onto Shearstown Line.

"Well, I'll tell ye dis bit o' news dat'll straighten yer whiskers, if ye had any. Da bodies be missin' a few spirits."

"How'd you mean?

"I'm widt da bodies in da fish plant now."

"Yes?"

"I knows a good lot o' 'em. Dey seems ta be all frum Bareneed."

"Yes, I remember."

"I 'ad a scarce bit 'o rest 'n I got ta t'inkin'. I were gunna tell dem army b'ys, but I don't trust dem buggers as far as I could t'row 'em. Dey're a stubborn bunch, dose lot. Right stiff 'n wooden 'n 'artless."

Doug tried not to listen. Fidgeting in his seat, he watched the landscape. No time for such foolishness such a spirits and the like.

"Tell them what?"

"Da bodies seems ta all belong ta people widt da sickness."

"They're in the hospital."

"No, not dem. Da ones related ta da sick. Were like da dead be comin' back ta da stricken."

"They must *all* be related, though. It's a small community."

"Fer da love 'n honour o' Christ, no. Listen up 'n don't be daft. Get dis t'rew yer noggin. Dey be specific ta da sick. I saw da list o' sick."

Doug scowled at Sergeant Chase. How much more of this would the Mountie take?

Chase paused, then pressed the radio button: "What about the missing spirits?"

"Yays. Dere be two spirits gone a'missin'."

"Gimme that." Doug Blackwood snatched the radio from Chase's hand. "What the hell are you talking about woman? Spirits!"

There was the sound of cackling laughter from the other end. "Doug Blackwood, ye old crotchety frigger."

"What're you doing wasting the Mountie's time with such claptrap?"

"Shut yer gob, ye old fool, 'n put da Mountie back on."

Chase raised his hand and patiently took hold of the radio. "This is me again."

Doug didn't like the way Chase was watching him. He stared out his window, gave his head a dejected shake and muttered a plea for sanity.

"Da two missin' spirits belongs ta Rayna Prouse."

"Two spirits."

"Yays. Two from 'er dead. 'Er 'usband 'n 'er gran'fadder."

"And Rayna Prouse is one of the sick, correct?"

"Yays, she be on da list."

"I'm on my way to Bareneed now. I'll check into it."

"Finest kind, I'll see ye at da fish plant. 'Tis a date, lover."

"You're on."

Doug gave Chase a censuring glare and was doubly vexed to see the mountie smiling.

⟿

Flesh, Claudia was thinking. *Flesh. Fish. Flesh. The currents. To swim in the currents.* She admired the sleekness of the thin filleting knife. It was like a finger pointing the way. Turning, she saw Reg and let out a shriek, her knife hand involuntarily jutting forward. Reg's eyes were filled with dark gleamings. In each hand, he held a fish. The sound of her scream had drawn the man, Joseph, back to the room. He stood in the doorway with the overnight bag dangling from one hand.

"What?" he asked.

Claudia pointed to her husband, who raised the fish high and squeezed them. From one shot a flow of fluorescent amber eggs, from the other a jet stream of milky-white sperm. The rivers collided in mid-air to shape a diminutive person, a child. Jessica with rounded eyes and lips that pulsed open then shut, pulsed open, as if sucking for air. The child turned away completely, her back to Claudia as Reg grinned and nodded, raising the fish, one at a time, to slide them expertly down his throat. Then, stepping forward and reaching for her hand, he took the long thin filleting blade. His grin widened as he turned the blade on himself and set the point against his own belly.

"What happened?" Joseph asked, his eyes on Claudia's hand.

Claudia pointed to Reg. Her cheeks reddened with fright while Reg unbuttoned his shirt and parted the fabric, revealing his hairy white belly. He carefully crafted a tiny incision vertically above his navel, drawing the blade up until the slit was three inches long and delicately parted, revealing the salmon-pink flesh. No blood appeared, only a clear fluid trickling free, staining his already soaked trousers. As the fluid ebbed, there was a flash of silver and the tapered head of a fish poked loose. Reg nodded at Claudia as if in agreement. The fish head wiggled and pried itself loose, its body halfway out as it snapped back and forth, rested, snapped back and forth to further deliver itself. Finally, the weight of its bending body was tipped by gravity and it slid fully out, dropped like lead onto the floor. More fish swam out of Reg, spilling liberally until the kitchen floor was a thick mass of writhing scales, and Joseph was approaching her, his hand extended.

"Let me take that," he said.

A shudder stiffened Claudia's spine. Shutting her eyes, she stumbled and slammed against the counter, sliding sideways. Reg rushed for her and grabbed her in his arms. She saw his face close to hers. She knew him. She did know him. A glint of light caught her right eye and she shifted her focus to see her arm hanging at Reg's side, the knife handle in her fist, the blade tip pointed toward him.

"Reg," she said.

"No," replied the voice. "It's Joseph."

"I don't care," she muttered, "who dies."

"Can you sit? I'll get you some water."

"No." She weakly raised the hand that held the knife. "No, no water," she pleaded, then thrust the blade down into flesh. Fish. Flesh.

-⟨⟩-

A group of boys and girls were gathered in a field, playing a game of ring-around-the-rosie. When they were finished the game, they crouched in the long grass, batted the blades down and began rearranging objects on the ground. Stones. The children stacked the stones into houses or, moving on their knees, pushed them through the grass, pretending they were cars. "This is my house," said one little girl. "This's my car," said one little boy, making the sound of an engine with his lips while he crashed his car into the little girl's house. "No cars allowed," said the little girl. "They'll just run us over." "Yeah," agreed another girl. The daylight above them flickered and they all peered toward the sky. There came a metallic warbly chirping as the sun itself seemed to swirl and fade out. The children stood in cold dimness, not knowing what to do. The metallic warbly chirping continued.

Thompson woke, disturbed by how the dream sound had followed him into the waking world and was now somewhere in his house. Agatha leaped out of the armchair, where she often napped, and stretched with the graceful agility that only a cat was capable of. Thompson watched her dumbly, his brain not yet fully connected to waking. Daylight flooded through his living room window. He realized he had fallen asleep on the couch.

"That's my cell." Shoving himself up to a sitting position, he was instantly and thoroughly agitated. He wiped at his face and yawned, the panging in his ankle coming alive. He remembered the silver cane he had taken from the hospital and discovered it on the floor next to the coffee table. Leaning for the handle, he gripped it and used the cane for support while manoeuvring toward the kitchen. His cellphone was where he had left it on the counter. He raised it, saw the number calling, someone from the hospital, pressed the "talk" button, and said hello.

"Sleeping?" It was Basha.

"No, not now."

"You might like to know that Rayna Prouse is breathing on her own."

"No!" Thompson said, flabbergasted, then heartened by the words. Smiling, he straightened slightly, taking some of the weight off his cane. Good news, for once.

"Yes. And she completed the Personality Recognition Test with flying colours. Let's hope the others follow suit."

"Yes, definitely." Again, he yawned. Too little sleep. Plus he was hungry. "Sorry."

"Forgiven."

"I'll be down soon."

"Toodle-ooh."

Thompson shut the cell. He felt a million times better, if only slightly rested, and the news further fortified him. Perhaps this was the end of the tragedy.

Agatha was crunching her food in the corner. Thompson rested the cane against the counter and hobbled to the fridge to lift out an opened can. He bent near the cat's dish and scooped out soft food on top of the hard.

"There's a treat, Agatha." He rubbed the sleek black fur on the cat's back. "Rayna Prouse is better, girl. That's cause for celebration. Eat up."

Agatha meowed a few times as though engaged in elaborate conversation, then went back to her food. The sight of her eating compounded Thompson's hunger. Again, he yanked open the fridge door, this time bringing out a bottle of pickled artichoke hearts. Just what he wanted. He gathered a fork and went fishing in the bottle. Vinegar. Oil. Soft pulpy leaves that were of such a subtle flavour, minus the vinegar and the oil, that they were practically tasteless. Almost bland, like bakeapple berries or caviar. You had to have extra-sensitive taste buds to appreciate the elusive flavours.

Done with his meal, he swabbed the oil from his chin with a paper towel.

"You coming or staying?"

Agatha gave one short meow.

"All right then, I'll see you soon."

Leaving his house, Thompson was startled to face the brilliance of the afternoon sun. Lately, the sun seemed highly out of order. He recalled his dream of the children and the darkness in which they stood. Merely a dream. Who could ever know what it meant?

Climbing into his vehicle, he found the heat suffocating. He tossed his cane on the passenger seat and left the driver's door open for a moment, while he rolled down the window. He then engaged the engine, shut the door, and glanced at his book on the passenger seat. *The Watery End.* Agatha had been lying on it. Her black hairs were everywhere. His eyes felt itchy and he rubbed them, wondering where his allergy pills were. He checked his pockets. He hadn't taken any of his pills today. No matter. He'd survive. Regarding the book again, he studied the drowned body on the cover, face down in the pool of water. His thoughts skimmed over the plot. Would he ever get the chance to read more, to determine the cir-cumstances that led to the man's demise?

There was no need to go back into the house for his pills. He could get some from the hospital. There were samples kicking around everywhere. Glancing in the rearview, he shifted into reverse. A bread delivery truck passed, then he backed out.

At the hospital, when he arrived at Rayna Prouse's room, he discovered that her bed was empty. No one was in the bathroom either. She couldn't have been discharged. She was his patient and he had not signed her out. Had she left of her own accord? A definite possibility, considering her strong will. At the nurses' station, he was told that Rayna had been taken out from under his care and placed in the custody of Lieutenant-Commander French. Hotly, Thompson read over the faxed document that the nurse handed him. It was signed by the medical chief of the hospital.

"Soldiers took her away," the nurse cautiously explained, eyeing his cane.

At once, Thompson snatched up the telephone receiver and called French's number. He demanded that Rayna be returned to the hospital.

"That's not a possibility," French informed him.

From the finality in French's tone, Thompson suspected that pressing the issue would be pointless.

"I understand your concern, doctor," said French. "I'm not trying to undermine your authority, but this is a matter of the utmost importance to public health and safety. Of course, you realize this." French paused, no doubt awaiting a reply from Thompson. The doctor knew that if he opened his mouth at this point the wrong words would charge out. French continued, "Why don't you join us at the community hall? Ms. Prouse is here, as we speak."

"I'll be right there," said Thompson.

Speeding back out of Port de Grave, he passed Hickey's Auto Repair and Wanda's Convenience, the old and new houses with their spectacular views of Bareneed across the water. Children ran or played in a few of the yards. Cars cruised in the opposite direction, sun glinting off chrome. It was just another sunny summer day, despite his annoyance. He muttered an oath under his breath.

Nearing the end of the road, Thompson noticed the stop sign fast approaching and realized just how quickly he was travelling. His heartbeat increased while he quickly slowed, stopped, waited a few moments to collect himself, then turned onto Shearstown Line. He wondered what day of the week it might be. Was it Tuesday? How were his patients doing now that his office was shut down? He couldn't keep his practice closed much longer. His patients. Rayna was better. What had made her better?

He reached the turnoff for Bareneed and veered left. Mercer's Field was deserted. Farther down the main road, he was intrigued to find all the roadblocks taken down. No need to present his credentials.

Bringing his four-wheel drive to an abrupt halt in front of the community centre, he snatched the handle, but then paused. God, he was all fired up again. His blood was pounding in his head. He took a deep breath to calm himself. There was no point rushing in there and causing a commotion, making a fool out of himself. How would that look in a military headquarters where everyone went about their business in a professional and orderly fashion? He took a few more deep steady breaths and then opened the door. He stepped out with an air of decorum, and reached back in for his cane.

Up ahead, a rumbling noise made him gaze toward the harbour. Waves were crashing against shore, pounding the headland across the harbour, the reverberation much like the sound of a dynamite blast. As his line of vision swept toward the distant fish plant, he wondered how many bodies had been retrieved. The last he'd heard, corpses had stopped floating to the surface.

The sky was blue above Bareneed, yet toward the horizon thick dark grey clouds were amassing. In the air Thompson could smell the electrical scent of a forthcoming storm. He heard a splintering of wood and swiftly turned his head toward the half-circle of the community wharf. A dory had been tossed up onto the deck of a larger vessel. It rested there on its side, the bow sticking out over the railing.

Toward the headland, two swordfish leaped from the sea and thrust their heads downward, slicing each other in half. The four halves dropped away and pounded into the water, where the surface began bubbling with frenzied activity.

Delirium? Fever dream? Nightmare? Thompson suspected for a moment that he had not actually risen from his couch back home. He tried forcing open his eyes. They were already open. He tugged at the hairs on the back of his hand. It hurt. He was awake. A surge of fear flooded his stomach and lit every nerve. They were in mortal danger. What else could the graphic presence of the fantastic insinuate? Without the constraints of reality, there could only be chaos and dread. Harm. Annihilation.

He gazed at the community hall. A red building, unchanged; a single soldier stationed outside, staring straight ahead, not even seeing him. Thompson glanced back at the harbour. Three seagulls drifted over the water, watching down at the peculiar action beneath the surface. They sailed lower, surveying the possible feast, and were swallowed out of the sky by three immense flying orange fish. In unison, the three flying fish plunged beneath the surface, leaving the sky vacant.

Transfixed, Thompson sensed horror solidifying in his dry throat. He sucked together what little saliva remained in his mouth and fought hard to swallow. He thought he might choke. Panicky, he continued with his efforts until, mercifully, his throat finally relaxed and his frog-like gulp was audible. Anxious to pull away from whatever it was he was seeing, he limped nearer the community hall.

The soldier moved aside and opened the door for him, making not the slightest mention of the fantasy play that existed no more than twenty yards away. Was it only he who saw the spectacles, he wondered. Or was it all an unworldly secret, not to be spoken of, for fear of tempting it toward validation?

꧁

A sound like knocking from the direction of the front door. Joseph's eyes strained to gaze up from the floor upon which he was lying. He thought he might have fainted. Claudia was standing over him. Her hair had come loose and was hanging like a blaze around her face. Her sunken eyes watched him with a look of wonder. She was of a singular monstrous beauty inconceivable in this world. In her fist, she held the blade that had punched three holes in Joseph's side. Yet the blade was clean; not a pearl of blood stained its glimmer.

"When a man and a woman find each other," she whispered, gazing directly down at him, "they're from a comparable wave of energy. They recognize the exact candle flicker in their hearts and souls. They often resemble each other. Drawn together because their energy merely desires itself. Love at first sight."

The knocking grew louder, compelling Joseph to slide toward the door, despite the horrific pain that contracted every muscle in his body and drew rivers of sweat from him.

"Don't move." Claudia pressed the sole of her cream-coloured slipper against his side, making him flinch with inflated pain. His eyes jammed shut. "Stay still."

Behind his lids, Joseph imagined Kim trying to enter the house. Was the door bolted? Whoever was there would soon be at the back door. Gasping, he opened his eyes, shifted them to the rear porch. From above, Claudia descended in supplication to kneel hard on his chest. Her hands along the back of his neck, her fingers caressing there, her delicate breath blowing as if to cool him, dispel his heat.

"Their energy's perverted by particles from another man or woman. The energy no longer melds when it enters." Her fingers crept around front, tip-toeing like spiders' legs. "Conflict, clashing, contamination, and the energy in the man or woman must destroy the other in order to fully pull away. Attraction to repulsion."

Claudia's fingers tip-toed farther along his throat, then paused, remaining inactive, until spreading, and seizing hold.

Joseph's finger clutched at Claudia's, yet her fingertips pried steadfastly into his windpipe, her nails biting into his flesh like claws. He croaked and rasped while struggling to slide away. The pain drained everything out of him. Strength. Ability. Reason.

Through gritted teeth, Claudia growled: "Flux of desire. Misdirection of will. The hole that must be filled."

Joseph laboured to swallow. Impossible. He tried breathing. A scraping, gurgling noise sounded instead. The muscles in his throat were thick and aching sharply, a million pinpoints steadily pricking him. His face flushed as the pressure mounted behind his eyes. Flailing his arms, he continued working to slide away while powerlessly reaching up to grab a fist of flesh or hair. Everything out of reach. Everything numb. The grip on his throat remained constant. Rasping and croaking, he found it utterly impossible to breathe. He was further panicked by how rapidly his trembling limbs turned weightless. This would be the end of him. Life strangled out. He was losing himself, fading. The snarling beast above him, its coppery hair blazing brighter, lowered its teeth to his face to bite, and quickened with life.

～๑)

Lieutenant-Commander French respectfully cleared the books from the spare chair and set it in front of his desk, beside Rayna's chair, for Dr. Thompson. French gave Rayna a cursory glance and remained standing while Dr. Thompson made himself comfortable. Then, sitting, French picked up a pencil and held it horizontally between his fingers and thumbs. "Dr. Thompson here is concerned for your health."

"No need for that," said Rayna, shrugging at Thompson.

French transferred his attention to Thompson. "As I've already told Ms. Prouse, the reason she's here is because she's the first to recover from whatever syndrome this town seems to be suffering from." He stood from his chair and regarded a map of Newfoundland pinned to the wall. He then studied Rayna for a moment before asking: "Are you a fisher person?"

"Was."

"Yes, was." He laid his pencil in the centre furrow of the opened book on his desk and glanced toward the door of his office. Able Seaman Nesbitt had appeared there. Dr. Thompson scooted his chair to the side to allow French to pass.

"Sir, the refractors on the south side will be operational at twenty-three hundred hours. This appears to be one hundred percent at this point."

"Thank you, Nesbitt." French watched Nesbitt salute and turn away, walk off toward the two other remaining seamen, Crocker and O'Toole. No doubt they suspected that turmoil was inescapable, and that they might be in its direct path. Failing to securing an evacuation order, French had sent all non-essential seamen away and retained only the minimum number of required personnel. The seamen knew perfectly well what was happening in the harbour and from this they could easily surmise a ferocious change was forthcoming. Despite the fact that activity offshore had stabilized, the situation could only be mounting — not easing, but merely switching form.

Crocker and O'Toole had been the first to pull the dead from the harbour. They were aware of what rested beneath the surface of the ocean. Their boat had been capsized several times, until it was unsafe to return to the water and the remaining bodies were fed upon by whatever lurked beneath. The creatures. On the word "creatures" French's thoughts were confounded by the ludicrous nature of this new reality. A new reality had intruded, one that could not be a part of *their* reality. It had to be disabled in order to return the world to normal. He gripped the frame of the doorway and held it for a brief moment. He watched the seamen outside the office glance away, and stare down the length of the community hall to where the tables and chairs were stacked. French shut the door, then sat behind his desk and collected his thoughts. "Do you have any idea why you can breathe freely now?"

"No."

"No idea?"

"No."

"Did anything happen out of the ordinary?"

"Like what?"

"A shock, a fright?"

Rayna shook her head.

"Did you come in contact with any substance that might be foreign to you? A smell? A sound?"

"They asked me all that in the hospital."

"Right." French stared at the thick volume on Atlantic fish, then glanced at Thompson. "Could've been anything, right?" He paused, but no one was willing to add to the speculation.

Rayna shifted in her seat. Her eyes were weary. Perhaps she was in need of another cigarette. "Did anything change in you, a release or breaking of fever, a series of thoughts?"

"I don't know."

"When did you feel better?

"In the hospital."

"Yes, but when exactly? What was around you?"

"After I was talking to Tommy."

"Tommy?"

"Tommy Quilty."

French reached for his waist and switched to channel five. He glanced at his computer screen and said: "Tommy Quilty." Several listings flashed in order of birthdate. He stated "Bareneed," and the information appeared, with a colour photograph from the man's driver's licence.

"Who's Tommy Quilty?" French asked, drawing his eyes from the screen and switching back to channel one, which was presently quiet.

"A friend. Good friend."

"And what did this Tommy Quilty do?"

―◌―

When the soldiers arrived to take Rayna away, Tommy had put the tube back in his mouth and fallen on his pillow as if dead to the world. The soldiers had no idea about Tommy yet. It would be a little while before that happened. Best to get out of the hospital before they set their hands on him. He could see much in the future, but could not envision his own fate, only the fate of others, excluding instances relating to him. With this peripheral view of the coming days and years, he feared the future more than most and was often in a state of distress trying to determine how the forthcoming events might be connected to him.

He hoped that Rayna would come to no harm. The windows in his room, at the back of the hospital, gave a view of evergreens rolling up over a hill. It was while watching trees, water or sky that Tommy caught flashes of things yet to be. These visions were mostly specific, a single image or action, and Tommy could not often see the full context. He might picture Rayna preparing a sandwich, walking down a road or speaking a sentence. Sure enough, the army had taken her, but they just wanted to know why she was better. Tommy had watched the sweeping blur of her aura as Rayna was escorted out the doorway. Her light was back with her. This had lifted Tommy's spirits, gifting him with the determination to continue his work.

It was important for him to leave, but it was equally important for him to stay in the hospital and talk with his friends. Each of the five men in the room with him was lying in the fog of his own disbelief. Only scant and sporadic pulses of light swayed off them. There was Fred Winter, Paddy Wells, Zack Keen, George Corbett and George Newell. They were all from Bareneed and they needed his help. If they continued to slip away, they would be misplaced forever, erase themselves like a blank tape. Fred Winter was in the worst condition of the bunch. He had practically no idea who or what he was. The near-absolute scarcity of his bodily light attested to this fact.

Tommy probably had just enough time to try to save Fred, but after Fred, he had to hurry on his way. The soldiers would take him and he would never wriggle free to do what he had to do. This was how he saw it, though he knew it might not be the truth.

Sliding off the hospital mattress, he visited the side of Fred Winter's bed. Respectfully, he sat on the chair and watched old Fred. Fred wouldn't look at Tommy. His eyes were shut and the machine was making him breathe.

Reaching forward, Tommy used the butt of his palm to nudge Fred's shoulder. No reaction. Tommy leaned forward and whispered: "Fred, ye got ta listen up, me old trout." Tommy checked Fred's shut eyes like a physician testing for signs of life. He then leaned his lips nearer to Fred's ear and spoke about how Fred's father, Gabe, while a mere boy of twelve years old, had rescued a man at sea. Gabe, while sailing with his father, had been the one to catch sight of the capsized boat near dusk and had given out a cry that echoed over the water. Gabe and his father had sailed close to pull the man from the water and wrap him in blankets and revive him with their warmth, rubbing his face and hands with their hands and breathing their warm air into his mouth until the water trapped in the man's lungs bubbled and spurted out and the man was again breathing. They had returned the man to shore and delivered him to his distressed family, who were waiting on the very edge of the wharf in an agony of near hopelessness.

Tommy whispered: "Yer grandmudder, Sarah, were a kindhearted wondrous woman. She knitted all da mitten, cap and sweater fer da Coles family who could afford not ta be buying such articles, nor could dey even afford da wool to put stock in such undertakings. And yer grandmudder, a woman small in stature, as ye might recall, and with one hand twisted fiercely with rheumatism, would accept narry a stain of gratitude in kind. She would hear none of it, wave it off widt her crippled hand and chuckle that it were her will to do such t'ings in da name of heavenly fellowship."

Tommy had hushed as Fred's eyelids flickered. Soon, they flickered more steadily and gradually opened. Fred stared at the ceiling while Tommy continued with his recitations. They drew the colour to Fred's skin and gave him new heat.

As Tommy went on talking, a thin streak of rippling blue wavered through Fred's black eyes, then another streak, this one green and luscious, followed by a sprinkle of brown, floating as though tossed into the air. Blue eyes, green eyes, brown. The lines continued being carefully stroked, painting a picture of houses at a shoreline, the sky, green grass and the earth, the blue stretching as far out as the eye could see, the horizon so distant and immense that not even the imagination was capable of grasping, and holding steady to, its sprawling mass.

⁓◌

Kim sat in the waiting area outside the ICU, her head in her hands. Next to her, there was a middle-aged man with an older woman. Kim did not want to see them or hear them. They were silent and still, exactly like her. No one dared exchange a word or move a muscle. The sense of blind enclosure was the only feeling she could manage. Her own hands over her face and the darkness. If only she could plug her ears at the same time, block out every sight and sound that might deepen her despair.

The surgeon, Dr. O'Shea, had informed her it was necessary to operate at once. Robin had gone into cardiac arrest for the second time and it was essential to implant electrodes that would stimulate Robin's heart without having to resort to the continued trauma of the defibrillator.

"She's too young to keep zapping like that," the surgeon had said after first giving the medical name for the condition. Kim had never heard of it, until now. Assuming that the name meant nothing to Kim, the surgeon had added: "It's not connected to the breathing disorder."

How would you know? she had wanted to demand of him. How could he be so calm amid all this tragedy? How could he?

Please, help, she was now saying to herself. *Please, please, please, help,* but she knew not whose help she was beckoning. Where was Joseph? The bastard. Where had he gone? Not here. Not here. *God, please, help my little girl.*

Footsteps neared and Kim looked up to watch a nurse pass under the honed clarity of fluorescent lights. The nurse gave her a kind smile, a smile that was swabbed with rubbing alcohol. Kim wanted to rush to her feet and punch the nurse, the same nurse who had assured Kim that word concerning her daughter would get to her at once. Kim felt so removed; she did not belong in this place. It was not where any of them belonged. How long had it been since she last asked about her daughter? She was hesitant, almost afraid to inquire yet again. She took a deep breath and stood, went to the nurses' station outside the ICU and waited there, holding the counter. The nurse behind the ledge told Kim that they were still operating.

"How much longer?" Kim asked, her voice quavering.

"I'm sorry. I don't know. But we'll let you know the minute we hear anything. We will. Is there anything we can get you?"

Kim shook her head.

"If you need anything, just ask."

⁓✤⁓

After catching a glimpse of the scene through the kitchen window, Sergeant Chase immediately unholstered his revolver and, finding the back door locked, kicked it in. The wooden-slat door burst to splinters. Doug Blackwood was somewhere behind him, so he held back a rigid arm which instructed Doug to remain where he was. Chase charged into the porch, gun levelled at the shaggy black dog biting at the unmoving form of Joseph Blackwood, its paws on his chest, its claws trying to dig.

Chase fired a shot that barely missed the dog. Startled by the explosion, and without so much as glancing back, the dog bolted down the hallway toward the front of the house. Chase heard a noise behind him and spun around to level the revolver at Doug, who flinched back while crossing his hands protectively around his upper body.

"Jesus, Mary and Joseph," Doug sputtered. "What in the name of Christ are you doing?"

Chase lowered the gun, pressed the button on the radio clipped to his pocket. "I've got a man wounded at the Critch house in Bareneed. I need an ambulance." He then spoke to Doug, who was bent near Joseph. "Do you know CPR?" But Doug was already administering mouth-to-mouth. Through the kitchen window, Chase saw the black dog race past a young girl with orange hair who was standing on the front step of the solar house. The dog entered the house and the girl stared toward Chase as though the dog had been sent there on a mission and was now returned to her. She then entered after it, shutting the door behind her. Chase wondered how the dog had made it out through the front door of the Critch house. It had been shut on his arrival. Locked. He checked to see that Joseph Blackwood was coming round from unconsciousness.

Between breaths, Doug said, accusingly: "Your daughter's in hospital getting worse," another breath, "and you're wrestling with a mongrel," another breath as he huffed in disgust. "You're the most sorry excuse for a man I ever clapped eyes on."

Chase spun for the back door, his heavy boots thundering against the wooden flooring, and took off in pursuit of the black dog.

~◊~

"He didn't do anything," Rayna said, feeling as if she should defend Tommy. What would these people do with Tommy? What would they blame him for? "He was just talking."

"What was he talking about?"

"I don't know. Stuff, you know."

"What stuff?" The guy in charge, French, leaned back in his chair, folded his arms. He watched Rayna and then the doctor.

"I don't know, stuff."

Sighing, French shut the book of fish species and slid it to the edge of his desk. A book of electrical storms was open beneath the one he had just set aside. His fingers skimmed over the grey and black photo of a storm at sea, jagged fingers of lightning touching down, connecting, travelling underwater. "What exactly were you talking about?"

"Stories, I guess."

"About what?"

"Fishing."

"Catching fish, storms, tall tales, what?"

"I don't know." Rayna's eyes pained her. She felt dizzy, thirsty, hungry. Tired, so tired. She wanted to go home. Go to sleep in her own bed. Soft pillows. "Tall tales like Tommy always likes to tell."

"And you felt better after?"

"Yes."

"Why?"

"How should I know?"

"Think. Why?"

"I *don't* know. You tell me why."

Dr. Thompson stood from his chair. The sudden action startled Rayna.

"That's enough," he said. "Ms. Prouse needs rest. Why don't you —"

"She doesn't need rest. I can tell," French raised his voice. "Sit, doctor, or leave. Now."

The two men stared each other down.

Reluctantly, Thompson sat.

"Rayna, there are no such things as tall tales. They're nothing but a slipping of the brain's grasp on the physical world" French unfolded his arms and set his elbows on the desk, used his hands to gesture while he continued:"The imagination isn't real. It's an abstraction. People invent tall tales to make the teller seem heroic or adventurous or larger than life … Don't believe it. Life isn't as large as that."

"What do you mean?" Rayna felt confused. She waited and listened to the silence around her. She really needed a cigarette. She would suck it to the butt in one drag. She eyed the package on French's desk. Her shoulders ached and throbbed with wanting. A headache was pressing hard at both sides of her head.

"Why would you believe such nonsense?" French insisted. "These things are invented to make a boring insignificant life seem interesting. Myths. Mythology. We're simple slabs of meat. Flesh and bone, that's it. There's nothing inside. When we die, we vanish." He snapped his fingers. "Like that. Gone."

In a daze, Rayna stared at French's fingertips. None of it made any sense. Why was he telling her this? She pulled her eyes away to look at Dr. Thompson. She wanted him to help her, but the doctor merely watched her with a powerless expression. Her breath came heavy through her nostrils as if she had been punched in the lower stomach. Opening her mouth to snatch a breath, she found that she was feeling ill again, grey around the edges.

Dr. Thompson watched her with new interest that soon turned to shock."What're you doing?" he demanded of French.

"Making her sick." French reached for his waist and turned a button. "There's a Tommy Quilty in the hospital. Find him and call me once you've located him. Hold him there. I'm sending his file." He tapped three buttons on his keyboard.

"No," Rayna said, her lungs empty. Sweat prickled out on her scalp. She sat straighter in her seat, her hands reaching out."Oh, no." Suddenly, she was grossly frightened. She hated this feeling. Her mind was fading, taking all her thoughts with it, leaving her in a mist of grey.

French had his eyes locked on hers. He knew what was happening, what he was doing. The bastard knew. Then he started talking, "Rayna? Listen to me, I was lying. Tommy speaks the truth. All the truth. It all exists. Everything. It's all out there now. Out in the sea, waiting. You can go and look. It's all coming to life. You can believe what I say as truly as you believe Tommy. I've seen these things, too. I've seen them all. They exist."

Rayna wanted to believe him. She stared at his face. Was he lying now?

"It's the truth," French assured her, reaching across his desk to touch where her fingers had gripped hold of the edge. His caress was warm and caring. "The absolute truth. Do you believe me, Rayna?"

"Yes," said Rayna, her breath smoothly gliding back to her, melding to instinct. "I do." And with these words of conviction, her mind steadied from a ghostly waver to clarity.

⁓⁂

Someone was beating at Claudia's door. Was it the police officer, Reg or Joseph? She had charged into the safety of her house and bolted the lock. Panting for breath and with the filleting knife still in hand, she dashed toward the wooden stairway and raced up, stood at the top landing. She pawed a strand of hair away from her parched lips and turned, ran first into her bedroom, then out to her studio. Frantically, she searched the room, for what? A way out. Would she kill whoever was at her door, if he should come in? She had already killed Reg. No, Joseph. Why? What had she accomplished? What had she done? What?

Pacing toward the window, she had difficulty swallowing, her throat so dry that she felt not a stain of fluid remained in her. She could throw herself through the frame of the picture window, crash through the shifting scenes she had watched for years. Death would be the most penetrating escape. All perfectly unreal now, her life. Or was she already dead? Had she finally managed to perish of dehydration, and been sucked into the bizarre world of the deceased or near-deceased?

She noticed the knife gripped in her small fist and took it in both hands, aiming its tip toward the studio doorway. She needed someone to run to, someone to be comforted by. The sound of the downstairs door being forced open startled her body into spasm. Her eyes searched every-where for possible entry. A man stomped around the living room, then he was on the stairs, big boots coming fast. Around her, the pottery houses on her work table fired to life in succession, flames flickering as a match held by a phantom hand passed from one to the other.

The police officer stood in Claudia's studio doorway, a man in a uni-form, his revolver levelled at her, then slowly lowered — as though he was awed by realization — until the gun hung at the end of his limp arm.

Claudia stumbled back against the wall. Sobbing, she took a hesitant horrified glance down at the knife, seeing it as though for the first time, the shimmering blade reflecting in her childlike eyes. She pressed the tip against her lower stomach, unable to help herself, mimicking Reg's actions of earlier. The cut. The slit, allowing life to stream out and be free.

"Little girl," the officer called in a voice so loud it jerked Claudia's hands; the tip of the blade nipped past the fabric of her dress. Staring wide-eyed and cold with intrigue, she pressed the tip deeper through the cloth of her dress into her bloated stomach, the quiet whispering, almost scraping sound, of her flesh being cut as the steel entered her. She felt so numb and rootless. Her breathing was rapid and deep, her pulse fast and weak. A contraction gripped her left leg, then her right, shoved at her lower back until her hips ached.

"Please, put down the knife, sweetie." The officer made an awkward for-ward movement, his actions arrested as Claudia raised the knife in both hands and held it in the air, the blade shaking violently while she growled and gritted her teeth. The officer froze, his eyes fixed on the slit she had made in herself. She glanced down, yet saw not a spot of blood.

Claudia carefully, lithely, fitted the tip back into the dry hole she had made and tightened the muscles in her arms as she thrust it in deeper. Her spine flinched and her face tilted back as if struck by a gush of wavering heat. Shutting her eyes, she slowly withdrew the blade and was surprised to feel a cool trickle flow over her fingers. Curious, she opened her eyes. The police officer was near her. She raised the knife toward him and he backed away. Looking down, she saw a well of the finest sand spilling from the gash, coursing into a tidy mound on the floor.

"I thought I was filled with fishes," Claudia whispered girlishly, her eyelids heavy as the sand continued collecting on the floor, widening and rising to a higher peak. "But I'm dry." Moment by moment, her belly grew less distended. Mystified, she ran her hands through the flow, then inquisitively dabbed her fingers around the slit's delicate edges.

When every grain had escaped her, she collapsed into the pile of sand, specks sticking to her lips. The entire house shook from the impact, the vibration knocking over three pottery houses and several bottles of glaze. Lit candles ignited the glazes which spread like gasoline, rushing over the edge of the table and along the wooden floor in a dividing line between her and the officer.

Claudia witnessed the officer attempt to rush across that line but flinch back. He bound toward a wicker chair that had burst into flames, but, again, was thwarted by the quick billow of flames that leaped at him, creating a translucent wall. She heard her hair sizzling and was aware of the uncommon scent that accompanied it.

The officer grabbed a shawl from the back of her work chair in an attempt to smother the stretching fire conveyed on glazes, but the shawl was soon singed and ablaze. He kicked at the flames and cupped a hand over his mouth, coughing. Smoke drifted across the room. It was white and it was deep grey. The officer slapped furiously at his pant leg, hopping back toward the bedroom doorway.

Through the waver of heat, the officer appeared to be indefinite, aqueous, his edges vacillating. Claudia watched him calling on his radio, shouting warbling words about fire. Then he was gone, flickering out of her vision. Where had he gone and for what purpose? She could not tell. Her eyes were so dry, clouded by smoke, void of moisture to such an extent that they could no longer budge. The room around her had evaporated, yet she felt as serene as glass. The swirling fire brought to mind the red-hot coils in her kilns, fiery ovens in which she baked her once malleable clay to make it hard, fixed and posed in an immutable position. If there was any water in the clay, if it had not dried sufficiently, it would explode into bits while being fired. Claudia considered the water within the walls, water being heated by sun and glass and pumped through the house-shaped configuration of pipes as needed.

The heat from the fire, intruding upon her skull, was of such an intensity that her tongue felt thick and pulpy, like a half-chewed piece of steak. Shifting her tongue around in her mouth, she felt, by probing with the tip, that her teeth were loose. She tried opening her eyes, but the lids were gone.

She decided that, yes, it was unreal. What else could it have been but a dream that had forced her to exist in a dangerous world where the climate changed and the people who became such an integral part of her were arbitrarily ripped away?

With her dry skin off, with every drop of moisture finally drained from her, she felt there was a possibility she might be safe, that she might remain constant, fixed as she was now in this artful and enduring pose.

~◊)

Chase descended the stairs two at a time, his hand barely skimming the bannister. Racing around the living room, eyes sweeping over every article, he was frightened as he searched for the siren-red or orange of a fire extinguisher. Nothing in sight. His only thought: the little girl upstairs is burning. There were tears in his eyes.

He ran to the kitchen and spun open the taps. They failed to yield water. Frantically, he searched under the sink, grabbing at pipes to determine if the shut-off valves were closed down, but there were no such devices cut between the two lengths of copper pipe. He tried yanking the pipes free. He shook them violently but they would not break. He then scanned the space for a receptacle to carry water. No bucket. Standing from where he was squat, he threw open the cupboards above the counter. Glasses, plates, and small bowls. He snatched a few bowls in one hand and hurried back into the living room, noticing, through the large front window, a flash of the ocean, an immensity of water tauntingly out of reach. He hurried into the bathroom to his right, tossed the bowls into the white porcelain sink and spun open both taps. Not so much as a drop. He tried the bathtub. Nothing. By the time he returned upstairs, a grey haze of smoke was evident toward the top landing. Crouching down to avoid the smoke, he searched the two bedrooms for a fire extinguisher and for the little girl's mother, checked the closet in the room that obviously belonged to the girl. No extinguisher mounted in there. Suddenly, he was struck by a fit of coughing, his lungs filling with smoke. Regardless, he pressed on, searched the other bedroom, obviously the mother's. It was empty. Coughing and ducking lower, he flung open the closet and faced a number of gowns all drawn upon with elaborate scrawls of ink, the sleeves covered in written words. He pawed around for an extinguisher that might be mounted in there. Pressure was increasing in his chest. It was almost impossible to breathe, and by the dull staggering feeling in his head, Chase determined that if he remained where he was for much longer he would run out of oxygen and lose consciousness, never to regain it again. Another fit of coughing as he turned for the hallway and rushed to the studio which was now engulfed in flames. He jolted toward the girl who lay motionless, burning. The vigorous heat, ten times stronger than noon sunlight on his face and hands, punished his body. He edged sideways, crying out in futility, threatening to rush directly into the flames. If he moved fast enough, would he be burned that badly? His tear-filled eyes on the girl, he again jutted forward, but the heat seared his face, fiercely pained his skin. The fire, now eating up the walls, was working its way from a crackle to a roar.

In desperation, Chase raised his radio and, through his spasms of coughing and sobs, shouted for a fire truck. As he did so, he caught the odour of fish frying. It was well past suppertime. His stomach grumbled, then was swamped with a wave of violent revulsion as he realized that what he was smelling was not fish at all, but the sizzling scent of the little girl he was attempting to save.

–◌

Joseph opened his eyes to see his father's face very near his own. His father had aged and his features had thickened. The head was fitted with a red baseball cap, which his father never wore. Through this subdued shift of recognition, Joseph soon became aware that if this was, in fact, his father's face, then his father had changed. And why wouldn't he have? In this place

where he was now, anything might be possible. Or was it the face of someone much like his father? A man he had not known for very long, yet
perhaps for much longer than he suspected. A relative. A long-lost brother.

"What kind of fool are you?" his father demanded. "The worst kind,
that's what sort." He glared at Joseph and shook his head in spiteful astonishment. "I never saw the likes of it in all my life. Never. Get up, ya lazy
bastard. Get up and go to your sick daughter." The man straightened
from his crouching position to tower over Joseph. "Those cuts are nothing.
Get up." The man was not his father. He had an accent that was particular to a bay community. His father had no such accent, even though he
had come from the same community. Two men as mirrors of each other,
yet fundamentally different. The man was his father's brother.

Daughter, Joseph thought in a fit of alarm. Robin. The fright chilled
beneath his flesh. He braced his hands against the wooden floor and
attempted to give a push. As he did so, pain split down his side; the muscles in his throat and at the back of his neck seemed capable of slicing
straight through him. His head thudded back to the floor. He winced and
grimaced. There was the sound of a siren in the near distance, coming
closer as if to his house.

"Who the hell let that mad dog in here? You're not bleeding. It's
nothing. Flesh wounds, that's all. I've seen worse on a boat at sea. Grown
men wouldn't even be bothered by it. Sliced open and vomiting from the
pain, they'd keep fishing till the day was done, paying no mind to the gape
of their injury."

Joseph rolled onto his side. He could barely swallow. He struggled
with the effort for several seconds before accomplishing the task. His
hand reached for the leg of a chair, then higher, for the seat. Uncle Doug
remained standing above him, berating him.

"You got legs or what? They work? Get up." Doug leaned down, extending his hand, which Joseph took. Doing so, Joseph was whisked to his feet
with such vigour that his brain seemed to spin in his skull. He braced a
hand against the tabletop, and shut his eyes, thinking that he might white
out. In his head, he now saw what he had been dreaming while unconscious: an image of one of Robin's drawings, the amber swirl that churned

with heat and streams of radiance which emitted from the core, was burned behind his eyes. He gazed down at his hands. They had been clawed by Claudia. Beside his feet, there was Kim's overnight bag. He bent to take the strap and the sweat popped out on his forehead and scalp. Regardless, he retrieved the bag and held it tight to his chest, hugged it, squeezed it, the smell of Kim rising to him.

"Get your arse in gear." Doug slapped Joseph on the arm and headed off, toward the hallway, giving a call back, "For the love and honour of Christ, get moving."

His thoughts on Robin, Joseph shuffled and flinched after his uncle toward the open front door. Sunlight up ahead. Joseph smelled smoke and, stumbling out into the day, noticed a police cruiser parked along the side of the road near his driveway. With Kim's overnight bag still pressed to his chest, he glanced toward Claudia's house. His car sparked to life before him, the engine revving. A red fire truck was parked in the road. Yellow hose trailed toward the burning house. A wide, steady blast of water gushed forth, drenching the outer walls. Three firemen stood near each other and a police officer stood farther back, motionless, staring at the upper storey. Joseph took a distant painful step toward it.

"Claudia," he muttered, his voice a keen-edged rasp. It hurt to speak. "Is she ... in there?"

His car horn drilled; Uncle Doug was in the driver's seat, waving and gesturing frantically, making emphatic twisted expressions behind the windshield.

Joseph limped toward the car, favouring his wounded side. He held the overnight bag with one arm and dug in his front pocket for his cellphone to call ... who? He felt as though he might white out again, and leaned against the car. Call who? The fire department? No, they were there. The hospital? Yes, to check on Robin. He opened the phone to discover that the battery was dead. The passenger door was flung open by Uncle Doug, who had leaned across the seat and popped the latch.

"Get in and go to your family. Get that gutless look off your face. Is that all you are? A gutless wonder."

Joseph regarded the harbour. By the position of the overhead sun, it must be no more than an hour past noon. The water was black in the harbour, crested grey and white where it boiled and rolled. The pain in his side was almost bearable, as long as he kept his jaw clamped as tight as he was able.

"Joseph," Doug barked and Joseph dropped his cellphone on the grass, stared down at it but thought the pain that would come from bending to retrieve it far outweighed its value. He crumpled into the car and sat with the overnight bag propped on his lap. He had to rest a moment before shutting the door with a sigh and letting his head fall back against the seat. He was sweating excessively again. Hot and cold at once, his clothes soaked. Sealed inside with his uncle, who shifted the gear stick into reverse and raced backward, straightened, then thrust forward, bucking Joseph back and forth.

With his mind wavering toward hallucination, Joseph stole a look at the fire truck through Doug's window as they passed. The firemen spraying water on the house. Water from the sea. Black water that stained the front as though painting it with charcoal.

"Let's hope no one's in there," Doug muttered, eyes on the house.

"Is Robin okay?" Joseph asked.

"She had an operation on her heart. Much as you'd know."

"What? What do you mean?"

"I mean she had an operation."

"Is it over?"

"I don't know any of it."

"Is Claudia —"

"Who?"

"Claudia. In there."

Doug glanced at Joseph's throat. "That dog made a mess of ya."

"Dog?" Joseph craned his neck toward the burning house, receding on the hill behind them. It hurt to strain so much. Was his uncle referring to Claudia as a dog?

"Someone should find that dog and shoot it."

Joseph could gather no sense from Doug's statement or the new information about Robin. What had been wrong with her heart? He couldn't bear to think about Robin in distress.

The car reached the bottom of the higher road, the harbour directly across the way.

"My eyes are deceiving me of late," said Doug, regarding the water before driving on, heading east along the lower road.

"Dog?" Joseph repeated, numbly.

"Maybe the mongrel has a grudge against fisheries officers."

They drove in silence. Joseph tried to piece things together.

"I don't think she knew what I was," Joseph said.

Doug laughed. "The dog?"

"What I am, yes."

"And what's that?" asked Uncle Doug, callused hands firm on the steering wheel.

"A fisheries officer."

"Is that what you are?"

"Yes."

"Is that what you are or is that what you do? It's harder to change what you are than it is to change what you do."

"Aren't they the same thing?"

Doug snatched a look at Joseph, his eyes hard with reproach and scrutiny, before his features slackened and the tiniest hint of a smile became evident. "Now, there's the first few words of wisdom I heard outta you. There might be hope for yer maggoty self yet."

※

The ambulance was of no use and so it was sent away. The charred diminished body would have to be photographed and studied before it could be transported to the morgue. The coroner, Dr. Basha, would be required to pay a visit. Chase imagined the zipped-up black bag; watching the weight of it being lifted by the paramedics always sickened him. Garbage to be taken away. When the ambulance disappeared down the higher road, Chase was left standing in the front yard of the burned solar house. The top floor had yet to cave in and perhaps would not. Several of the walls were scorched through completely, revealing a complex framework of large copper pipes that ran the entire width, length and height of the house. Even though the fire had been contained, water continued to pour from the hose.

Unlike his experience at most crime scenes, he was left alone, except for the volunteer firemen who most likely were facing this sort of tragedy for the first time. A burned little girl. They were ordinary men, fathers and sons who worked as government clerks, carpenters, heavy machine oper-ators and at other trades, and who regarded him with wonder and speculation for having been in the fire, for having seen. They were all silent. No one spoke a word. Chase had no true colleagues here. They were busy elsewhere, containing the unrest in other communities. He stood in the front yard with the sun behind him and rubbed his nose. He assumed his nostrils were coated with soot, his skin as well.

The percussive sound of helicopter blades toward the south hills drew his attention. They were assembling another row of giant dishes that mirrored the row across on the north ridges. At first, he thought they might be communication discs for the navy, but the sturdy abundance of their numbers now implied some sort of secret arsenal.

He glanced back at the solar house. Empty. Black. Its windows melted or shattered. He had been inside no more than twenty minutes ago. He had been there with a living child who had taken her own life, had gutted herself in the most disturbing manner.

Now, he was outside and the girl, a girl with reasons he could never begin to comprehend, was dead and burned beyond recognition. Burned black. A girl once so pale and seemingly as delicate as a curl of fine paper. It was the desolate scene before him, its senselessness, that made him think of his wife, her mind as black and fragile as ash, yet her face perfect, the eyes through which she watched perfect and beautiful as well. He could blow a breath into her ear that might crumble her thoughts to powder. No, her mind itself might be fragile yet there was nothing brittle about her thoughts. He sus-pected they were actually pitch and dense beyond known measure. If her thoughts were burned, then the burn had made them heavier, had added bulk as opposed to destroying molecules. A burn that compounded dead weight.

Again, he searched the harbour, his eyes lingering on the fish plant. He remembered the old woman, Miss Laracy. He was supposed to meet her there. Backing away, toward his vehicle, he thought he should offer some sign of departure to the three firemen, but he could not seem to speak. One of them, a short man with glasses and a thick black moustache, noticed that Chase was leaving and simply raised his yellow-gloved hand in a gesture that was part tribute and part fellowship.

Miss Laracy could not bear the chill in the fish plant. In no time, it seemed to infiltrate the marrow of her bones. It had been like that when she worked there years ago. It would take hours sitting before the crackling fire to reclaim warmth once her shift was done. Presently, she stepped outside the fish plant to catch a breath of warm afternoon air. That brisk air in the plant pained her lungs. She stood away from the corrugated-tin building, watching the smoke pouring from the queer-looking house up on the higher road.

"Mother of mercy," she said sadly. There was a fire truck up there. *Da black dog*, Miss Laracy told herself as she heard an automobile pull up on the gravel lot. Turning, she was heartened to see the handsome police officer behind the windshield.

"Da news be widt 'im," she said aloud, and walked directly toward the vehicle. "Where were ye? Yer as slow as cold molasses."

Sergeant Chase said nothing as he climbed out of his police car and shut the door. He never even gave her a smile, simply stared at the ground while he tugged up his heavy black belt. Miss Laracy took a whiff of him, then studied the black marks of soot on his hands and face, the trails of tears.

Miss Laracy pointed toward the hill. "Were dere a tragedy?"

Chase watched Miss Laracy's face and she felt his eyes seeking something in her.

"Da artist?"

"No," he said.

"'Twas da black dog. Someone were marked fer deat'."

Chase cast his eyes toward the hill. Miss Laracy, too, watched that way. The smoke was so thick and deeply grey that its shade leaned more toward black. She stepped near the officer and licked her thumb, reached to rub soot from his chin.

"Wha' part did ye play in it?"

Chase shook his head, glanced at her hand which she lowered. He wiped a sleeve across his nose then walked toward the fish plant. "Nothing," he said, his flat tone insinuating guilt.

Miss Laracy trailed after him, desiring further news of the grave circumstance.

When they were back inside the building, Miss Laracy gasped, her step faltering. Three more broken and tattered spirits had vanished. She shuffled toward the first body and bent near, staring straight into the man's face, closely studying the lips and cheeks, the youthful slant of the chin.

"Dat's Fred Winter's son, Edgar." She shuffled ahead, pausing beside an older man dressed in the fashion of the 1700s. "Don't know 'im, but 'is spirit's buggered off too." She hastened on, pausing by a body farther toward the back of the plant, closer to the wall of computers where only two people now worked. "Looks like a Winter ta me. One o' Fred's people. Could be t'ree of 'em all belongs ta 'im."

"Where's Fred Winter?" Chase asked.

"In da hospital. Dat's wha' I suspects."

"Like the others."

"Yays, but I suspects 'e be gettin' bedder. Ye could figure dat dese spirits show demselves in times o' peril ta dere lineage. Dey be a right mess aft' endurin' da wires. Dat's wha' I t'inks in me shrivelled ol' brain."

―◑―

Chase raised his radio from his top pocket and contacted dispatch. He requested that his call be transferred to a land line and patched through to the hospital in Port de Grave. He spoke with the head nurse on duty on the sixth floor and inquired about Fred Winter. He was told that Mr. Winter's condition appeared to be improving, just as Rayna Prouse's had. "That's two now," the nurse said with relief.

Chase gazed out over the dead of Bareneed, seeing nothing of the spirits the old woman spoke of, only dead bodies, more dead bodies than he had ever seen assembled in one place. Photographs of the drowned. The files on his computer came to mind. If he looked closely at these real people, no doubt they might be familiar, might resemble some of those in his "My Pictures" folder. Trying hard not to stare, to spook himself, he regarded Miss Laracy.

"Who should we tell?" he asked her. "Who's there to tell?"

Miss Laracy shrugged. "Narry a difference who ye tell, me lover. Da damage be already done. As me fadder used ta profess: Dere's nuttin' more refreshin' den da feelin' dat yer doomed." With this, she winked and gave a bountiful grin, her pink gums glistening like a newborn babe's.

―◦◦―

With the strap of Kim's overnight bag wound around his hand, Joseph headed for the hospital entrance, leaving Uncle Doug behind to find a parking space. Inside, he ducked into a bathroom, shut the door and laid the bag on the toilet seat. His shirt was torn and bloody. Fortunately, the receptionist at the main desk, too absorbed in her own busy troubles, had not bothered eyeing him when he entered.

As he faced the bathroom mirror, he was startled by the reflection of the bearded man he had once seen in his bedroom window. Joseph did not recognize himself. His face was scratched and dirty, and bore a thick growth of beard and moustache. He resembled a wilderness wild man. He brought his fingers to the cuts along his throat and remembered Claudia's grip, her fingernails, her teeth. Why had she tried to kill him? And where had she disappeared? Had she been in the burning house?

Twisting on the taps, he flicked his finger in the water until it ran warm, then cupped his hands and splashed his face. There were no paper towels, only a hot-air dryer, so he raised the tail of his shirt and scrubbed at spots of dirt until they were gone. The shirt stuck to his wounds as he began removing it. When he gave it a tug, it hurt less than expected. He balled up the shirt, tossed it in the garbage, then examined his wounds. The removal of the shirt had torn off bits of clotted scab but there was no bleeding. Flinching, he dabbed the cuts with his fingers, wondering how deeply he had been injured. There was no way of telling. In the bag, he found an oversize pale-blue T-shirt that Kim sometimes wore to bed. He pulled it over his head, catching the lovely, heart-melting scent of his wife, then zipped shut the bag and limped from the washroom.

Joseph followed the arrows to the ICU until, taking a turn in the corridor, he was halted by the sight of Kim seated on a padded hospital chair toward the far end, her eyes fixed on the tile floor. She raised her head at the sound of Joseph's careful footsteps and watched him limping toward her. As he neared, Kim's expression grew curious, then worried as though she might ask a question. Under the brilliant fluorescent lights, Joseph could plainly see that she had been crying; her eyes were bloodshot, her nose pink, her lips swollen. She stared at him, without shifting a muscle.

"How's Robin?" he asked, coughing lightly to excuse the hoarseness of his throat. He laid the overnight bag on the seat beside Kim.

"They're operating now, on her heart." Kim sobbed into the crumpled tissue in her hand. The sob was cut short as though it had simply ended, run to a numb stop. Despite the terrible uncertainty of the situation, Joseph was vaguely relieved to see his wife in this condition. He felt deeply bonded to her by empathy and love. He knew better than to ask too many questions. He simply offered silent comfort.

A doctor was paged over the intercom. Joseph frowned, uncertain of how close he might permit himself to get to Kim. He hadn't seen her like this since they'd lost the baby, and the recollection thinned him.

Kim was usually so strong, capable, unfaltering in the face of indecision. A heroine out of one of her novels. Was this what was meant for her: calamity and affliction, all of her children perishing? Was this what she secretly pined for? To be the stricken woman of yesteryear? The intelligent yet forsaken one whose gloomy observances were golden?

The worry and sleepless hours had actually altered Kim's appearance. Her eyes caught on something along Joseph's throat, and she was concerned for a moment and then angry again. Fingernail or teeth marks.

Sighing, Joseph shifted the bag over and sat beside her, placed a palm on her shoulder. Kim leaned away and raised a hand to him, holding it in the air, holding it steady. The hand said: Enough. He painfully took notice that on her other hand, the one holding the tissue, her wedding ring was missing.

"Where is she?"

Kim wiped at her nose and tipped her head toward the doors to the ICU.

"Is she okay?"

His wife gave a brisk shake of her head.

"Kim?"

"I don't know," she sobbed loudly. Attempting to straighten the crumpled tissue with both hands, she then gave up, balled it tightly in her fist and pressed it to her lips. "I can't believe it."

"Believe what?"

"Any of this." She turned her sorrowful eyes on him. "This. Robin. You. What's happening in there. I can't believe any of it."

Another announcement sounded from the intercom. Joseph reached out and brought his hand to rest on Kim's. With this touch, a surge of emotion welled up inside him. Kim studied his hand and it became obvious, by the doubt and wonder in her eyes, that she was entirely uncertain of what he meant to her.

~⦿~

Lieutenant-Commander French regarded Dr. Thompson, who stood against the wall, patiently awaiting instruction. The doctor had a vague grimace on his face, no doubt due to his arthritic knees and the injury to his ankle. French then looked at the old woman now seated in the chair Thompson had previously occupied. The police officer, Sergeant Chase, the Metis who was six-foot-six if he was an inch, had delivered Miss Laracy to French's office. Miss Laracy had told them all what she knew about the spirits. The information was sinking in. Hence the silence.

Chase towered behind Rayna with his arms loosely folded against his chest. French joined his hands atop his desk and frowned at the absurdity of what he knew: that every single person in the room might be drowned in a matter of hours. This was what his intuition told him, what he saw in his mind. His intuition was never wrong. It was the reason why he was the lieutenant-commander. How would he present the information to the doctor, the female civilian, the police officer and the old woman? Which version would ensure they acted the way he wished? Which version was needed to preserve, and further dignify, his authority?

"I'm going to be forthright with you all," he said, thinking: *honesty.*

Thompson nodded. Miss Laracy tapped both feet in succession against the floor as though a tune was running through her head. Sergeant Chase remained still while Rayna merely stared and nibbled the corner of her lip.

"Situations similar to this one appear to have already existed throughout history." For some reason, he could not take his eyes off Miss Laracy, the way she was watching him, her generous, good-humoured smile. She nodded and winked.

"When?"

French glanced at Thompson, the reasonable man, the man of science, a man very much like himself. "Over the continents, but more specifically on this island. Close to seventy years ago, when electricity was first introduced to the Burin area. Again, more specifically, when radio was introduced. There were records of the same disorder as the one troubling the people here. Couldn't breathe, no other symptoms. The fish stocks had dwindled. And there were sightings of sea creatures never seen before. Several fishermen kept journals detailing the fantastic sightings."

"Burin," Thompson pondered under his breath. He picked at his beard while engaged in deep thought, drawing information from memory. "Seventy years ago." The doctor grew unfocused, yet his eyes remained on French. "Wasn't there a tidal wave around that time?"

French gave no reply. He switched his gaze from Thompson to Miss Laracy. The room was silent again as everyone turned the information over in their minds.

"Wait a minute," Thompson burst out with a mirthful laugh. "You can't be saying that this disorder precipitates a tidal wave."

"Jesus!" Rayna straightened in her seat, struck by shock instead of humour.

"No." French raised his palms to them. "No, not necessarily."

Miss Laracy laughed, glanced toward the ceiling. "'Lectricity," she muttered. She then cast her eyes toward the west wall, as if able to view the harbour beyond it. "Yays b'ys, da spirits be angry. Da water rear up 'n carry da charge." She looked to Sergeant Chase for encouragement, but he did not say a word.

"We suspect it has something to do with electromagnetic fields. A mass of energy has gathered out at sea. It seems to have emanated from here."

"Spirits," Miss Laracy said, grinning and nodding, smacking her gums together and licking her lips in certainty. "I saw 'em comin' down frum da sky when ye put dose big machines ta use. Da spirits can't get at dere loved ones 'cause o' dere sickness. Why's dat?"

"They can't breathe," Thompson speculated. "Do they breathe the spirits in?"

"Naw," said Miss Laracy, waving her hand dismissively at him. "Dey can't see da spirits. Dat's wha' 'tis."

"The patients don't know who they are," Thompson explained. "Or what they are. It's like they're fading. Disappearing. Amnesia. They can't see themselves."

French listened patiently, but he would not put forth his own beliefs. Instead, he offered a fabrication: "We suspect the energy has something to do with the micro and gamma rays. We're going to see if we can shut the energy down. This area is a major crossing point for telecommunication signals, signals that are invisible but potent. Maybe those electromagnetic fields are gathering here and bouncing off the hills. The fields are in the air, heading out to sea and causing some sort of disturbance. We've shut the power off, but that doesn't seem to do much. The electromagnetic waves are flowing from everywhere beyond here. Billions and billions of microwaves and gamma rays that link the world. We've set up refractors on the hills." French glanced around, wondering if the others took stock in his explanation.

"'Lectricity cuts da spirits ta shreds," Miss Laracy added. She fished her handkerchief from up the sleeve of her dress and gave her nose a healthy blow, then poked at each nostril. "But why does da spirits return now ta da bodies in da fish plant? Wha' be dey comin' here fer? Has sumtin' ta do widt da loss o' breat'."

"Nonsense," French said with unaccustomed spite.

Miss Laracy glared at him for some time, her fingertip circling a small spiral on his desk that curled bigger and bigger. When she spoke again, it was in a tone of conviction: "Ye knows better den dat. Yer foolin' not a soul udder den yerself widt such lies, Frenchie b'y."

⌐◑

Claudia and Jessica appeared vaguely see-through and phantom-like on the boat slat before Robin. They were holding each other, hugging as they became more substantial. Claudia opened her mouth to speak, but she had not yet found her voice. It seemed far away, as though it was drifting from down a wide tunnel in which she was moving, a dot at the end of the end. Jessica's arms were wrapped around her mom's waist, and radiance swelled from them, further solidifying Claudia's presence.

Robin was amazed at how much they looked like each other.

Then there was an alarming thud against the bottom of the boat, directly beneath Robin's feet.

"That's just Dad," said Jessica. "He's coming up because Mom's here now." Releasing hold of her mother, she peered over the side of the boat, as did Robin. "Come on, Dad."

A wavering face materialized near the surface, grew larger and less unsteady, then surged up from the water with a splash of transparent droplets. Big hands rose to grip the side of the whale-shaped boat, which failed to sway even slightly. Reg hoisted himself aboard, dry as a bone, to settle by Jessica's side. At once, he grinned and hugged her. Claudia leaned forward in front of Jessica to accept the kiss her husband offered.

"Oh," said Clauda. "This is so wonderful."

"We're all better," Jessica said to Robin, "now that we're free of gravity."

The three family members sat smiling across from Robin, each with an arm around the shoulders of the other. The boat gently bobbed on blue.

Jessica said: "Now that your father's not dead, you might not be let go."

"My father?" Robin asked, her voice even smaller now.

"He's back."

Robin stirred in the boat. "Was he dead?" Her voice was a peep, going out.

"My mother strangled him."

"I didn't mean to," said Claudia, fondly smiling at her daughter. "You know that." She mussed up Jessica's hair. "Silly."

"You thought that's what we wanted," Jessica told her mom. "Me and Dad. You didn't see us right because you were still in the world. You see only what you want when you're still in the world. You put words in our mouths. You invent us the way it might explain things, make things easier to understand." Jessica shifted to face Robin again.

Robin noticed that her friend's eyes were blue and then brown and then green …

"The living always do that," Jessica continued. "They change us. They make believe that we're there when we're not. We can't get back to land."

Robin smiled at Jessica. It was nice to see her with her parents. They sat there, as still as a family snapshot in which everyone was so very happy. "I really want to see my mom and dad," she said, but her voice was practically silent, as if only she was aware of what she was saying. Or had she merely thought it?

"You should just wait for them here," Claudia suggested, nodding encouragingly, "and save the burden of a lifetime."

"You have to get better," Jessica put in.

"How?" The question was a hollow sound, a numb pulse in her head.

"You can't do it. Your mother and father have to do it for you."

"How?"

"If they can forget everything else, and just love you. When they're together like that, their energy multiplies and they can draw you out of the sea. Your energy came from them. Their energy, from the energy of their own parents, made you. When they put their energy together again, they can draw you back."

"I want them to do that." Suddenly, Robin felt completely deaf, yet continued hearing the voices of the others. "I want to leave here."

"Don't you feel okay?" asked Claudia.

"You'll feel okay, soon," said Reg, winking.

Robin shook her head. She had almost had enough. "I feel weird." Only her lips were moving.

"We're just energy waiting to be drawn to someone," Jessica explained, "We always have to cling to someone to be formed."

Tommy collected his sketch pad from the table beside the hospital bed, waved goodbye to Fred Winter, and fled the room. No nurses in sight. At the end of the corridor, he found the red and white exit sign, and took the stairs, in the hollow-sounding stairwell, down to the metal door that popped open out on the parking lot. Fresh air.

Although he desperately desired to help the others, he feared that the soldiers were coming for him, and — more importantly — he feared what the immediate future held. Never had his thoughts been flooded with such gloom; a wall of wet blackness climbed behind his eyes as he watched out over the cars and the trees and houses. He had a clumsy yearning to draw, but could not see a single thing in that part of his mind. Not a single shape or movement could be made out.

Nervously, he hurried across the parking lot, weaving between cars, thinking of what he might do. He could wait for someone to come out of the hospital, someone he might know who would drive him to Bareneed. But that would take too long. No, a car wasn't any good. He wanted to see Rayna right now. There was only one other route. Hastening toward the edge of the parking lot and onto the side of the road, he paused, stared toward Bareneed, then checked both ways before crossing the road. A narrow worn trail led between two houses to the shore. He had travelled down it many times before to eat a sandwich and watch the water when taking a break from visiting with the sick.

The sun was low on the water and there was a small dory tied up at a rickety old beach wharf made of salvaged boards and skinned tree limbs.

The dory itself seemed seaworthy. He picked up a heavy beach rock and jumped in the boat, steadied himself, set his sketchpad on the seat beside him, and placed the grey beach rock on top to prevent the pad from blowing away. He leaned to gather the line from where it was tied to a post and cast off with Bareneed in his sights. The engine started on first flick. In a fit of nerves, he glanced back to see if he might be caught. No one was coming out of the houses close to shore. He aimed the bow toward the headland. It wasn't that far, but seemed a greater stretch as he traveled, the land appearing to stay the exact same distance from him, no matter how fast he turned the throttle.

Finally, the illusion broke and Tommy knew he must be getting closer. Although the ocean was calm, as he neared Bareneed the boat began to toss, and the sea noisily lapped the sides of the craft.

Farther on, the sea turned even rougher. The water swelled greyish-green with whitecaps everywhere, hissing and sizzling. Foaming at the mouth, Tommy thought. There was a thump against the bottom of the boat, and Tommy looked to see that the rock had shifted off his sketch pad and fallen. He picked up the pad and held it to his chest. Ten feet beyond the bow of his boat, a skull-like head with shoved-in thick cheekbones rose from the sea with great veils of water gushing from it. Another monstrous face soon followed, towering nearer to him than the first. Both heads were seemingly attached to the same scaly neck and both were wearing tarnished gold crowns.

Tommy had drawn the creature before, so he had been expecting it and was not too fearful. Instead, he was amazed. He knew there were more heads, and soon a third one emerged from the water to stretch directly above him, its eyes watching down, its great mouth mute. At the sight of this, and guessing at the size of the body beneath the water, which would be directly beneath his boat, Tommy gripped the engine handle with trembling hand to steer back toward Port de Grave in hopes of avoiding collision. The boat veered slightly, but was soon snatched off its course, quickly drawn sideways toward Bareneed, and hauled fast through the water. It rose, as if on its own accord, out of the ocean to float into the air.

Zooming along, Tommy gazed down at the hull resting on the back of the creature before he found himself suddenly catapulted forward, tumbling head over heels. Sailing heavily through the air, while desperately squeezing his notepad to his chest and clamping his eyes shut, he began dropping while muttering: "Mudder o' God, Mudder o' God, Mudder o' God …" until he struck the frigid water before he expected he would. At once, his breath froze as he sank in a thrashing of water and white foam. A mass of air bubbles crowded around him.

In his descent, he forced his eyes open, and caught sight of the distant water-blurred heads. None of them showed any interest in him. He counted six while holding his breath, his cheeks puffed out, the salt water trying to push up his nostrils and flow into his lungs. Where was the seventh head? Kicking his legs to spin around, he found the seventh facing him directly, watching him with black eyes, its pointed crown gleaming dully. In terror, Tommy kicked away, only now fathoming the fullness of the huge creature as it swam beneath him. The hydra resembled a serpent with a spiny ridge along its body and cumbersome paddling rear feet with claws like a bird's. Twenty feet down its broad back, toward its curved tail, sat three rimmed spots, ovals resembling giant eyes that blinked. The seven heads, now sensing Tommy's presence, all pivoted to regard him.

Tommy thought: "Dere's no sense tryin' ta chop off any of its heads, even if I had a sword handy, 'cause two'll only grow back in da stead of da cleaved one." He had read that bit of information in a book somewhere. It was his last series of imaginings before the hydra began to smear in movement, colours bleeding, as though the creature might be dissolving. Its shape and texture lost dimension. Seeping, it pooled away from itself and was soon nothing but a sepia-coloured spill surrounding Tommy, who had just ran out of breath and, clutching his ink-leaking notepad, made an urgent scramble upward for air. How far above, he despairingly asked himself. How high over his head was the surface?

TUESDAY NIGHT

Darkness.

Lieutenant-Commander French, after leading all of those gathered in his office to the shore across the road, now stood beside the first of the three large EF-7 spotlights calibrated for the detection of gamma rays, microwaves and background radiation. The remaining two were positioned farther up the beach. When switched on, the spotlights would detect microwaves from cellular telephones, microwave ovens and base-station masts, nuclear and ionizing radiation from X-rays and alpha and beta contamination, electromagnetic radiation from electrical appliances, electricity pylons, power lines, building wiring and transformers.

French glanced at his watch: 22:17. Despite the low hum of the gas-powered generators, he could still hear the wet flapping of fish tails newly washed onto the beach, joining the dead ones of all shapes and sizes and the billions of caplin eggs mingled with and stuck to the sand and rocks. Every now and then the wind would carry the stench of rotting fish and eggs to him, an odour so appalling that he felt his mouth pool with saliva, the bile rise in his throat, and his eyes water, yet he would not wipe the tears away. The breeze blew them dry. Regardless, if he were here for any other reason, and if he had a gas mask handy, he would wander down to the shoreline and study the species of fish, generally uncommon to this region. He could make out the reds and blues and silvers shimmering iridescently by the tungsten lights that had been set up at their post. He could also see the back of Rayna Prouse, who was staring expectantly out to sea. The wind was picking up, blowing in from the restless water.

"Smells like human flesh," Sergeant Chase commented, then fell silent. He shifted his eyes toward the houses on the hill — the solar house with no sign of smoke; and the Critch house, seemingly invisible in the night.

French knew that Chase was wondering if the burned girl had been taken away. He knew the police officer was thinking of his wife and his need for her. When would he go home? Why would he go home? Chase was imagining the once-beautiful girl in the house, and how anyone could have the stomach to examine her. No doubt, someone would be obliged to.

"Nar human flesh, 'tis jus' fish," said Miss Laracy to Dr. Thompson, who glanced around as though trying to determine what he might be doing there, what he might expect.

They were all out of their element.

French glanced at the fish plant, its windows lit by generators, its white paint discernible. Inside, the dead were laid out. What did they have to do with any of this? He raised his binoculars and aimed them toward the south hills. Blasts of eratic bluish-white light flashed against the dark hills. His men finishing up their welding. The sky melded with land. An endless succession of black. Lowering the binoculars, French spoke into the wireless microphone, "Lieutenant-Commander French. Time estimation?"

A voice in his headset, ten times clearer than tone carried through a telephone line, clearer than the highest-fidelity stereo system, a voice seemingly tapped directly in his brain, replied, "Ten minutes, sir."

"Conditions at sea?"

"Coast Guard reports the same whirling dervish in sector seven."

French turned toward Dr. Thompson, finding comfort in the doctor's presence. Someone to save them all, should the world suddenly blind them.

"You know," he said to Thompson. "I'm trying to believe this is an electrical disturbance."

"Isn't it?"

"Your guess is as good as mine."

"I'm a physician. I just tinker with the body."

"The body is electrical."

To this, Thompson gave no reply.

"You mentioned people in the hospital seemed lifeless, without the will to live. Something of the human spirit destroyed?"

"Yes, but why?"

French kept his expression unchanged. "I don't know." Raising his binoculars, he sighted the bluish-white flecks blinking in the distance like tiny signals. He heard Thompson and Miss Laracy chatting about possible eventualities.

Miss Laracy spoke up: "'Tis about da spirits, I tell ye. Yer all as stunned as me arse ta be deaf ta da trute." She raised a fist and waved it at both men. "'Tis about da spirits being shut out by all da crap in da air. I knows it. Ye let dem loose 'n ye'll see. Frenchie, ye got da sight, fer Christ's sake use it."

Thompson shifted on his feet, cleared his throat.

French lowered his binoculars. The expression with which he had chosen to counter the accusation was one of pity. He watched the old woman as though sympathetic to her archaic beliefs, but in his heart he abhorred them. He thought: *Whatever cost to return life to order. No price is too high to end this.*

Miss Laracy had fixed her eyes on French but not another word was uttered between them. There was a sound offshore, the cry of a faraway voice, the lament lingering in the air. They all stared out to the black sea.

The voice wired into French's head spoke again: "Refractors ready, sir."

"Activate the refractors, north and south side." He then addressed Able Seaman Nesbitt, "Switch on the EF-7s. Anticipate communication downtime."

The three spotlights were switched on by the three remaining soldiers, and blue lights swept up into the air, illuminating the chaotic crisscross of red lines as an impassable red wall, fully extending from ground to sky. On both hills surrounding the community, the giant discs glowed green. As the range of their brilliance increased, the clot of red lines were aimed in all directions, bouncing off people, hills, headlands, the road, the land, the water, to shoot skyward. Then they gradually dissipated so that narrow black spaces could be discerned between the lines. Within thirty seconds, the red lines had waned completely and there was only night and the electrical hum from the spotlights.

"Switch off the EF-7s," French shouted. The command was called from Nesbitt to the second soldier, who passed the order to the third.

The three sweeping blue lights were switched off and French watched the sky. All heads followed his lead, turning their eyes skyward. The stars, in their pristine clarity, pulsed brighter and, seemingly unable to endure their own expanding radiance, disintegrated. Amber particles of light sifted free, gathering, but not dimishing the light of the stars. The stars were not crumbling at all. The renegade light was much lower, nearer to Earth.

"A reading on the sky," French muttered into his wireless microphone. He suspected that there was a massive energy output.

No voice responded. Communication interruption; he had forgotten. There was no voice in his head, not even static. He felt entirely alone.

Swirling waves of amber light expanded in descent, hovering in the sky above Bareneed. Like gusts of amber snow, the light sprinkled lower to the beach, forming vague faces of countless ages and expressions that intently peered at the watchers, as though seeking recognition and camaraderie. The light lingered only momentarily before streaming toward the houses of Bareneed, entering through walls and windows and shut doorways. The light flickered within, glimmering off glass panes and casting out brighter strobes as the sparkles streaked before mirrors.

In a brief moment, the search was over. Exiting the walls, the amber streams gusted off, toward the east, toward the sea.

The voice in French's head said: "Increased electrical activity reported in sector seven. It's triple the output. Hurricane force disturbances in the water, but no wind. Lightning observed, sir. The sea seems to be ... dividing." Yet the voice was not broadcast from his headset. He simply heard it as an affirmation of what he anticipated, what he knew, what he *saw*.

French regarded Thompson, then Chase, each one ignorant of what was happening beyond the shore upon which they stood. Miss Laracy, seeming to be wise to something, laughed and winked and hummed a tune while anxiously rubbing her palms together.

The voice in French's head: "We have seismic activity. An energy force seems to be entering the divided sea. Activity at two on the Richter ... The energy's diving deep. Sonar indicates the seismic activity is generated by an energy mass hammering the ocean floor."

French shot a look toward the glowing green discs on the hills. Was it too late? Was it enough? How much power could be unleashed before the entire world might be destroyed? He raised his arm and fired a blue flare into the sky, the predetermined signal to shut down the refractors. He dropped the flare gun, raised his binoculars with one hand, and watched the hills. His free hand was extended before him as if testing the particles of air. The voice in his head, his voice or another's, came again: "The refractors are deflecting the microwaves and gamma rays out to sea. They're causing a disturbance." Another voice corrected the first: "No, it's the spirits. They couldn't find their loved ones."

The discs on the hills dimmed. The starlight faded.

French lowered his binoculars, muttered: "The energy punches the hole."

The voice wired into French's head. It was a different voice, most definitely not his own: "We're up to seven, sir."

French flashed a glance at Dr. Thompson, then at Sergeant Chase. He regarded Miss Laracy, who had abandoned her merriment and was now staring down at the beach rocks gently clicking off each other. Hard and cold as the water rolled. The wind blew a harsher stench to him. The clicking sound gained in momentum and volume, surrounding them from all directions, up and down the beach. French checked the ground as the rocks shifted beneath his feet, the ground rumbling as beach rocks slid and bounced over his boots. He stumbled as the reverberation unsteadied his footing. He grabbed for Miss Laracy's arm, but she had fallen over.

Farther up the beach, a crash sounded with the explosion of glass. One of the spotlights had toppled onto the beach.

The rumble subsided as Dr. Thompson helped Miss Laracy to her feet.

"You okay?" Thompson asked.

"Bit of a spill, dat's all," replied Miss Laracy, anxiously brushing herself off. "No harm done. Finest kind."

The voice in French's head said: "Number three EF-7 went over, sir."

"Are you injured?"

"No, sir. Heading for your position."

The group stood silent, listening to the waves lapping the shore with new vigour. From high above came the sound of a screech. It could have been a seagull or a crow; either one would have been peculiar this evening. One by one the heads tilted to gaze up. Other bird cries gathered above as the sounds of wings flapping ruffled the air. Birds awakening to the darkness. Another distressed cry from offshore, this one human.

"Who's out there?" French whispered. No more than forty feet away, he noticed a flash of glistening wings cascading upward as a wall of wet birds took to flight from beneath the ocean surface. The sea was awash with frantic activity as schools of exotic fish broke the surface and threw themselves onto shore.

In an astonishing flurry of feathers and wings, a violent ruffling of sound like a solid wall before the watchers, the birds swooped down to scoop up the fish until not a single one remained. A voice in French's head announced: "We have a tsunami, sir."

⌒

The overhead fluorescent lights flickered spasmodically, imbuing the hospital corridor with an unearthly quality that suited its general ambiance.

With both hands, Kim clutched the foam edge of her seat. *Hold on*, she told herself. *Hold tight*. Her eyes shifted from the doors of the ICU to Joseph, beside her. His face fell into shadows, then was lit again.

"Did you feel that?" she asked.

"What?" he countered.

Lights came on full, as though too bright, while Kim and Joseph squinted toward the ceiling. The lights flickered once more. Kim took hold of Joseph's hand at the exact instant they went out completely.

"Joseph!"

A few moments later, dim emergency lights gleamed on toward the far ends of the corridor.

"That's it," said Joseph, bolting to his feet. "Let's go." He pulled Kim up and hurried toward the doors of the ICU, jabbing the buzzer frantically. When the nurse answered, Joseph brushed past her and deeper into the unit where another nurse was anxiously scurrying around, flicking switches, pressing buttons, checking monitors and respirators.

"Where's Robin?" Joseph demanded.

"I don't know," Kim answered, although she knew his question was not directed at her. She searched the glass where her daughter had been, seeing a bald old man in one bed, an elderly woman in another. In the next room there was a dark-haired man in his forties, and a child, a child she would know anywhere, a child who shot her heart with pain and tightness and a charge of protective love.

"There," she said, pointing, leading Joseph.

They both entered the inner room and hurried to Robin's bed. A nurse followed after them and began to protest, "She just came down from OR." She waved them back, "You have to wait —" but Joseph turned on her and shouted "Shut up," with such vigour that the nurse relented and skulked back, returned to her duties.

"Robin?" said Joseph, clutching his daughter's hand.

Robin's face was passive, not a stir of expression. A white gauze bandage was taped to her chest, above her heart.

"Robin," whispered Kim.

"Sweetheart," said Joseph. He touched the vague traces of Robin's drawing on her own arm, the swirl and the monster face and the man and woman in the boat. He ran his finger over the design. "I love you," he said, tears wetting his eyes and lashes while he bent lower, nearer. "I love you, sweetheart."

Watching her husband, Kim thought: *What happened to you, Joseph? What happened to you?*

"Robin?" said Joseph. "Can you hear me, Robin?"

Kim took hold of Robin's other hand and joined with Joseph: "Robin?"

"Robin? This is Daddy."

"Robin, sweetheart? This is Mommy."

"Robin."

"Robin."

⁕

Lieutenant-Commander French spoke into his wireless microphone: "We have a tsunami travelling at fifty-five knots, heading for the northeast side of Newfoundland. We have approximately thirty minutes to evacuate the area. Send in all available ground and air transport. All ground and air transport. Copy?"

Able Seaman Nesbitt and Able Seaman O'Toole held a map flat on the beach. The third able seaman, Crocker, stood by Miss Laracy, who was speaking to him about the cook-ups she used to have in the fall of each year when she'd go blueberry picking with her parents.

"Areas from Heart's Content and southeast to Conception Harbour must be evacuated. We require air transport at the hospital in Port de Grave and Our Lady Nursing Home. Inform the patients that they are being transferred for their safety. Do not enlighten them as to the pressing nature of our predicament. Not at this time. Verify other medical locations and begin evacuation immediately. Copy?"

"Should I make a call for a chopper, sir?" Nesbitt asked.

French, as if coming to his senses, stared at Nesbitt. He then gazed at the people who stood in wait with him in the dim light. "We're low priority, except for Miss Laracy and Ms. Prouse." He glanced toward the shoreline. Rayna Prouse was staring out to sea. What was she searching for? She had been in that exact position for quite some time. "We'll take ground transportation to the hospital as soon as all civilians have been moved from the community."

"Forgive me, sir, but we only have thirty minutes. With such short time and the suspected size of the tsunami, shouldn't we be leaving now?"

French studied Nesbitt's eyes. They were anxious. Not the eyes of a navy man, but of a young civilian with a life and loved ones. French checked the other two recruits. They, too, were young men with lives ahead of them. "There are people here. Go and get them out. You know the occupied houses from your patrols. The Murray house. The Cutland house. The Greening house. Do a quick sight-canvass of the other houses. Around the loop."

The three seamen saluted and Able Seaman Nesbitt watched French. "Permission to stay and ensure the safety of the lieutenant-commander, sir."

"Denied. Take the jeeps and search the area. When you locate civilians, instruct them to board their cars and head southwest to Salmonaire. If necessary, inform them about the tsunami. Insist that they *must* leave." He turned his attention to the fish plant. Three sets of headlights were pulling away, forming a tight line as they quickly headed around the arc of the harbour and then sped west. He realized that his microphone was open to all channels. Had he willed it that way, he wondered.

Offshore, a massive crashing sound boomed out over the water. All heads turned. White foam hung frozen in the air. The foam remained suspended for a count of seconds, before returning to the sea. It appeared as if something immense had fallen into the water. A single wave had smashed into the headland, rocking it, beating a chunk away. The foam sizzled loudly as it pattered down onto the black boiling water.

"Should we call for a transport truck, sir?" Nesbitt asked.

"No time. They were called back to main base by senior officers."

"When we notify the civilians in the community, will we return for you, sir?"

"Yes. Get moving."

"Thank you, sir." Nesbitt saluted and hurried off, with O'Toole and Crocker, into the darkness at the perimeter.

Miss Laracy stared at French. She was tight-lipped and eyed him with sombre suspicion.

"Wha's dis zumami all about?" she challenged.

French considered his choice of words: "Big wave."

"Aww," she murmured, her glance cast longingly toward the sea. She grinned. "Surf's up."

"My wife's in Port de Grave," Chase announced, tipping his head toward the distant lights on the outstretch of land across the bay.

"Does she have anyone with her?" asked French.

"No. She's not well."

"Right. You should get to her. Take Dr. Thompson, Ms. Prouse and Miss Laracy with you to the hospital for evacuation."

"Sure." Chase turned to Thompson, but Thompson said: "I'll wait here in case anyone needs medical attention." The doctor then addressed French. "We'll get air transport, won't we?"

French nodded. "Soon."

"Just as well to wait here as over there." Thompson stared across the water at the scattering of lights as Rayna left the shoreline to quietly join them.

Sergeant Chase extended his hand to Miss Laracy, but she pulled away.

"G'way widt ye. I've no intention o' leavin' me 'ome." She opened her arms to Chase, who stepped into her embrace. "Ohh, give us da biggest hug o' yer life." She squeezed him and moaned in adoration, then patted and rubbed his back. "Da spirits finally spoke up," she said in a hushed voice. "'Tis right lovely."

"All right, she can wait with us," French agreed.

"I'll stay with Miss Laracy," Rayna announced, taking hold of the old woman's hand, her eyes distractedly searching toward the water as if she had heard something barely out of range.

Chase surveyed the group, then backed away, farther and farther, until he melded with the blackness.

"You should be off, too," French said to Thompson. "Might only be so much room in transport."

"I don't know that I want to leave." Thompson gave a sad-eyed smile and raised his eyebrows. "This is just too intriguing."

"Don't be foolish. You have a vehicle, right? Make use of it."

"Physician heal thyself."

Thompson's comment brought an uncustomary smile to French's lips. "Exactly." The doctor frowned in thought. "I've got a cabin in Horsechops." He then addressed Miss Laracy. "I can take you there until —"

"I'm nar goin' anywheres udder den where me feet're planted. I never left dis community all me natural life 'n I sure as Christ ain't leavin' now 'cause o' a wee splash o' water."

"It's more than a splash —"

"Piss on da wave. Wha's it gunna do ta me? Get me a little wet. I'll hang meself out ta dry 'n be none da worse fer it."

Thompson glanced at French, who nodded and flicked his eyes toward Miss Laracy, indicating that he would attend to her safety.

"If anyone requires medical attention, they'll be airlifted out." French said this by way of reassuring Thompson. "You should go. We don't need any cripples around here."

"Don't you know you can't use that word any more?" Thompson examined the naval officer's face then extended his hand. French firmly shook it.

"Good luck," said the doctor.

"God's speed," French remarked.

"How fast is that?" Thompson asked.

"Nar very fast, me love," interjected Miss Laracy, who held her hand out to the doctor. Thompson shook the old woman's hand and set his free palm on her shoulder.

"Take care of yourself."

"Dat I will do, doc."

Thompson turned away, his steps slightly stiff, his cane bottom unsteadily slipping between spaces in the rocks. When Thompson reached the small embankment that led up to the road, French called out: "Need a hand?" to which Thompson waved an arm in dismissal and struggled up on his own. Soon, the doctor was swallowed up by the inky night. A few moments later, there came the sound of an engine being engaged. Headlights stretched far up the road.

Miss Laracy had turned her interest toward the shore to see Rayna near the water again. She bent, poking at the newly beached colourful fish with a driftwood stick. The old woman turned toward French, took a deep breath of the fishy air, then said: "Bet ye could do widt a nice cup o' tea 'n a raisin bun?"

French chuckled. How much time did they really have before it was all over? Again, he heard the sound of pebbles shifting underfoot, someone walking on the beach. He turned to see a man, dripping wet, stepping into the light from the emergency lamps.

"Tommy Quilty," screeched Miss Laracy, blessing herself. "Saints preserve us."

Rayna shrieked with glee and hurried to Tommy. Flinging her arms around him, she kissed his lips with such abundant joy that Tommy stammered and blushed fiercely.

"I knew ye were here," Tommy said to Rayna, holding up his sopping wet sketch pad.

Grinning, Miss Laracy proclaimed: "Well, buddy, yer a sight fer sore eyes."

-⁂-

The jeep raced toward the lit windows of Wilf Murray's house. Arriving there, O'Toole waited at the wheel, Crocker in the back seat, while Nesbitt dashed inside to inform the gathered people that an evacuation order had been issued. A few of the hearty souls present guffawed and others roared with laughter to such an extreme that dishes rattled in the cupboards. None of them would leave their homes and community. As one fine old fellow put in: "We won't be having no strangers telling us where we might be off to."

Nesbitt, seeing how many children were present at Wilf Murray's, became further unnerved and, feeling an urgent need to protect the young ones, revealed the nature of the impending tragedy. This only brought on further laughter, although a few women and younger men seemed concerned, casting brief glances at one another.

"I'm pleading with you," Nesbitt finally cried out in desperation, which brought the house to utter silence.

"Leave me home!" griped Wilf Murray. "Come hell or high water."

All eyes, presently on Wilf, now shifted to Nesbitt, who reached for his waist and shut off his remote. "Please. I know that it's coming and I know that you'll all be drowned. You will."

With this, Wilf Murray stared somberly at Nesbitt. "P'raps he has an eye cast in da future," said Wilf. A few people tittered and loosely shook their heads, but the rest remained attentive.

"You have to leave," insisted Nesbitt, gazing down at his boots and the worn floorboards beneath them. "This house will be struck by the wave."

Wilf Murray straightened the bill of his baseball cap. He set a palm to the back of his cap and pushed it tighter to his head. He contemplated Nesbitt with bright clear blue eyes and then, as though intuiting fact, he nodded vaguely.

"Listen ta da young feller," said Wilf. "Let's be gone."

On Wilf's word, there was an immediate scraping of chairs and murmurs of conversation that eventually grew louder as women gathered up the children, and people departed. Outside, car engines were engaged. Stepping from the house, Nesbitt saw a handful of people briefly lingering to chat in the front yard before boarding their vehicles.

Mr. and Mrs. Murray were the last to leave. Nesbitt watched Wilf take hold of his wife's hand to steady her while she stepped out.

"Got to drop a few pounds," she said with a huff.

A lamp was still burning down the hallway.

"You might want to extinguish that," cautioned Nesbitt, pointing toward the doorway.

"Always leave a light burning," Wilf Murray professed, and winked at Nesbitt.

After determining that all the people gathered at Wilf Murray's could be accommodated in the available vehicles, Nesbitt, O'Toole and Crocker continued on to Bren Cutland's. Fiddle and accordion music was pouring through the open front door. Again, Nesbitt spoke with conviction and heartfelt fervour to those gathered, and the house, though not without resistance, was eventually evacuated.

The third and final house belonged to Honey Greening. Unlike the two previous houses, the windows here were not ablaze with light from candles, kerosene or battery-powered lamps. Only one pane, at the side yard of the house, held a faint candle gleam. The dark front door, on which the scarlet paint was peeling, was shut when Nesbitt knocked. No reply arrived to answer him. He tried the cool tarnished brass knob and found that it turned. Pressing the door slightly open, he called out a tentative "Hello?" Again, no reply.

With mounting apprehension, he stepped inside and guardedly advanced down the hallway. Up ahead, at his left, there was an open doorway through which faint candle gleams flickered. He listened, but whatever sound there might have been prior to his entering had suddenly hushed. Nearing the doorway, he turned to see, gathered there in the squat kitchen and under the dim glow of two candle gleams, five people gazing at him in dreary silence as he leaned near the threshold. Four were seated around the table. The other, perhaps a child, was crouched in the corner. Gloomy expectant looks were trained on Nesbitt, stopping him dead in his tracks, for he realized, with a frightening chill that coursed wildly through his body, that these five souls already knew of what was fast approaching.

The eldest of the group, a woman with straw-like grey hair and a grey rumpled face made shadowy by the candle gleam, stared undaunted at Nesbitt. She would be the first to speak.

"We were telling stories," the woman confessed in a voice so scratchy it brought to mind the lash of a violent winter wind. The others huddled nearer and nodded in hungry communal agreement. A few gripped the edges of their seats and shifted them farther ahead. One of the gathered, a young man with an oblong head, savagely crooked teeth and one turned eye, grunted emphatically and pawed at his nose twice.

The small person standing in the corner, at first mistaken for a child by Nesbitt, was revealed to be a man; his limbs were twisted in tangles and his face was an almost featureless lump. He began to sing in a growling, mucous-plugged voice:

Oh, I've seen storms I tell ye when t'ings looked rather blue
But somehow I were lucky and always 'av got through,
Now I'll not brag, however, and won't say much but den
I'm not much easier frightened den most of other men.

'Twas one drear night I speak of we were off da shore a way,
I never shalt forget it in all me mortal days,
'Twas in da dim, dark watches I felt a chillin' dread,
It bowled me down as if I'd heard one calling from da dead.

Den on da deck dere clambered all silent one by one,
A dozen drippin' sailors, just wait 'til I 'av done,
Right on da deck dey clambered yet not a voice we heard,
Dey moved about together 'n never spoke a word.

Dere faces pale and sea-wet shone ghostly t'rew da night,
Each took his place as freely as if he had a right,
And dey all worked da vessel, da land being just in sight,
Or rather I should say, sir, the lighthouse tower's light.

And den dose clamberin' sailors moved to da rail again,
And vanished in da deep below ere sun could shine on dem,
I know not any reason in trute why dey should come,
And navigate da vessel till just in sight of home.

It were da same poor fellows, I pray God rest dere souls,
Dat our old craft ran under one night near George's shoals,
So now ye have me story, 'twas just the way I say,
And I've believed in spirits since dat time … anyway.

Nesbitt stood frozen on the spot as the small man shuffled and crept his way to join the others around the table. At once, the old woman rose from her chair without sound or evidence of intended movement and drifted toward the mantel above the kitchen stove where one of the two candle gleams flickered. Leaning her face toward it, a face on which many of its deep furrows were smoothed in the full golden light so that her countenance now appeared fresh and youthful, she opened her mouth, sucking in air, and the flame vanished, leaving her expression in a void of blackness.

The single remaining candle sat in the centre of the table where the old woman joined the other four. United in reverence and gripping each other's hands, they stared forebodingly into the flame.

"Wwwe wwwere," stammered the young man with the oblong head, "tuh-tuh-ttelling stories." He proudly grinned a mouthful of blackened teeth at Nesbitt while the woman at the young man's right, a large-boned woman with copper hair and a gluttonous leer, huddled the young man's head to her bosom and stroked his thin hair protectively.

"Hush, hush," said the big woman to the young man. "We are nearing the end of the yarn. Able Seaman Nesbitt has found us now."

Ripples of shivers coursed through Nesbitt's body, though he dare not ask how the woman might know his name.

Soon, in the gentle calm, the men and women returned to gazing into the flame with expressions of mysterious supplication. At once, the five of them opened their mouths and sucked in air, and the single candle gleam broke into five bits that were equally distributed among the lot. They closed their mouths and all light was vanquished.

The last thing Nesbitt saw was the small man pressing back into the corner, two flesh-clotted eyes trained on him. Nesbitt, standing in blind darkness, felt his heart beating fiercely as he expected hands or claws to be upon him at any moment. Nesbitt backed away from the room and stumbled out into the yard, where he leaped into the jeep.

"Are they leaving?" asked O'Toole, checking toward the open door. "You're white as a ghost."

"No one there." Nesbitt shook his head. "Drive," he said.

"You going to shut that door?" Crocker piped up from the back seat.

"Drive. Just drive," he said, staring straight ahead.

On the lower road, cars and pickups were heading west, toward Shearstown Line and, no doubt, the highway beyond. The three seamen searched the loop for light and signs of life, but found neither.

Certain that their search had been comprehensive, they circled back for Lieutenant-Commander French. But when the jeep pulled up at the post on the beach, not a single soul was there. The shoreline was deserted, save for the generators, tungstens and EF-7s. Beyond the military equipment, colourful fish glowed beneath the light of a huge moon that had broken free of the black clouds to loom above the headland. The fish flapped desperately on the shore before being clamped between the beaks of fierce, swooping birds and whisked into the air.

Nesbitt switched on his remote. "All houses in the Bareneed loop cleared, sir."

"Nesbitt, we have left the beach and are accompanying Tommy Quilty to his bus. Copy?"

"Yes, sir."

"His vehicle will be used to evacuate residents farther west along the main road toward the highway."

"Copy, sir. Yes, sir. Copy that."

"You will proceed west, toward the highway at full speed. Copy?"

"Copy, sir. Yes, sir. Copy."

Tommy had been a bus driver for the school board until he was dismissed for giving the children huge hugs. It wasn't his fault. He'd see them in their tiny coats and caps, with their innocent eyes and their clumsy steps up the bus stairs and he'd want to kiss them all because they were so adorable and gleaming yellow. He'd grab them and hug them and know that they were the sweetest things that ever walked the face of the Earth by the way their energy purified his. The school board said they had no choice but to let Tommy go. There already had been complaints from parents who feared Tommy Quilty, feared for his mental competency. The woman at the school board told Tommy, over the telephone, that his sort of behaviour might have been tolerated years ago, but not now. Not in this day and age. No one was permitted to touch anyone else without the express consent of the touchee.

"Nar even in friendship nor in joy?" Tommy had asked, to which the reply from the school board authority had been a severe and dead-ugly: "No."

That had been five years ago. The bus sat idle for a year before Tommy was commissioned by the church to carry residents to bingo and card games. When the bus wasn't in use, he parked it in his backyard, checking it each day to make certain that the mice and squirrels who made homes of the abandoned buses did not inhabit the usable bus as well.

Tommy felt strange sitting in the bus now, at night, especially as his clothes were sopping wet, heavy and sticking to his skin, bugging him. He felt peculiar to be switching on the headlights with a navy officer, who pretty much kept his thoughts to himself, sitting in the seat behind him. Night usually meant Tommy was off to pick up people for the games. Now, the bus was being used to save people from a danger he could not understand yet felt to be complete and forthcoming. His soaking notepad lay on the seat across from the navy fellow. All of his drawings had been drowned. The pages were stuck together and the ink and paints ran into one solid colour without definition.

Tommy tried the engine. It whined a few times before turning over and roaring.

"Let's go," Lieutenant-Commander French called above the noise.

Tommy thought of Miss Laracy as he checked the rearview then wiggled the long vibrating gear stick. She had refused to join them, claiming she wanted no part of Port de Grave or the hospital. Instead, she sought solace in her home. There was no time to argue, the commander had said. Rayna had decided to stay with Miss Laracy, to keep the old woman company until French returned with the helicopter.

The big engine revved louder as tears streamed down Tommy's cheeks. He feared desperately for his friends, plus his soaked clothes were sticking to his skin, pressing against him in a tormenting manner. If only he could take them off and put on nice dry ones. He pulled down the wide driveway alongside his house, passing close to his van. Out on the road, he turned and, once straightened and on his way, shifted the long stick into second. More heavy roaring as they hit a pothole and bounced in their seats.

"I'll send a chopper for Rayna Prouse and Miss Laracy," French announced, as though intuiting the source of Tommy's sadness. "We have to check for residents in their houses. It's important."

Tommy pawed at his eyes so he might see where he was going. He felt that, at this point, there weren't any people left along the road, but he gave no word to the navy fellow, not wanting to interfere. Again, he smeared away his warm tears, thinking that if he could talk with the sick in Port de Grave, if he could make them well, then nothing bad would happen after all. Everything that was happening, all the creatures and the returning of the dead in the sea were brought to light by the people who could not breathe. In his drawings, he could see that they had lost something. It had broken away, in a flourish of colours, and returned to the water, to its original place of creation. Now, it had to go back to them.

"Whatever's happening here is all about energy," said the navy fellow as the bus rocked over another pothole.

Tommy was not sure if the navy fellow was talking to him or using his microphone to talk to people miles away.

"There's energy in those spirits and it's amassed." He leaned forward to try and see Tommy's face as if what Tommy thought might be important. "The Coast Guard reports a wall of amber light behind the tsunami, tidal wave. Maybe it's the same energy we saw leave here." The navy fellow was quick to correct himself. "Some saw leave here. Did you see it leave here?"

"Yays."

"Maybe it's the energy of the dead in the fish plant. I don't know. Do you?"

Tommy shrugged. He hit a big dip in the road and it gave him a funny feeling in his stomach. It reminded him of when he used to drive the children on the school bus. He smiled a little at the thought of how he would speed up whenever he neared those big dips, just to hear the children scream with glee. He'd always laugh along with them.

"Miss Laracy told me that you were taken by fairies when you were a baby. Is that correct?"

"'Twas true, sir."

"And you have second sight?"

"Yays."

"That force behind the wave could be the spirits of the dead. Couldn't it?"

Again, Tommy merely shrugged, distracted, then he said, in a low uncertain voice: "I suspects dere's a crack at da bottom of da sea where dey go ta return ta da swirlin' dervish."

"What?"

"Da swirlin' dervish at da centre."

"What's that?"

"Beneat' da water."

"What is?"

Tommy glanced back at his soaked notepad. He sucked on his bottom lip and remained silent. If only he could show the navy fellow his drawings. The ones that detailed the crack in the ocean bed and the amber entering to rejoin the swirl at the centre. The navy fellow might understand then.

"What's beneath the water?"

Tommy peeked in the rearview to see the man watching him for an answer.

"Everytin'," replied Tommy.

The navy fellow stared at Tommy, then glanced at the side of the road. "Pull over. I'll check this house."

Tommy did as instructed, his hands trembling on the steering wheel. He nodded, even though he knew it was a waste of time and, by stopping and stopping again, they were saving no one and assuring nothing, other than their own demise.

⁓◊

Doug Blackwood skimmed the flashlight beam over the swept-clean floor of his barn, glad to see that there were no codfish present this time. No visions of ghosts, no mermaids waiting to blow him a heartfelt kiss. His mind appeared almost back to normal. He knew exactly where the generator was and went straight for it.

Because his land was on a high point along Codger's Lane and his house faced the water, he was able to see a good portion of the community. He also had an unobstructed view across the inlet to Port de Grave. From his vantage point, he had watched the army jeep racing around the community, stopping at Wilf Murray's, then at Bren Cutland's before making a final stop at Honey Greening's. Shortly thereafter, Doug had witnessed a mass exodus, everyone racing away like a bunch of lunatic crybabies. When the army jeep had slowed outside his place, he had switched off his flashlight, hushed Bramble and stood quiet as a church mouse, waiting for them to pass. Those soldiers were nothing but a frigging nuisance. Good riddance to them, now that they were gone. Peace and quiet at last.

With Bramble sitting patiently in wait, Doug set up the generator on the grass beside the barn. When he made use of any labour-saving machine, he never failed to hear his father's dismissive words about such contraptions: "Sure, dere'll be nuttin' left o' a man if he puts fait' in dose doo-hickeys. Not a muscle left on 'im. He'll be as t'in 'n as small as a louse in years ta come." His father had shunned any invention that made life easier, releasing the longest litany of curses Doug had ever heard when he first clapped eyes on an electric can opener. "Lard, jumpin', jiminy, rip-roarin', thunderin', Christ Almighty!" his father had exclaimed "Dun't anyone 'av a clue 'ow ta use dere hands any more? Pushin' buttons like a bunch o' foolish magicians tryin' ta trick demselves outta healthy labour."

Doug checked the tank for gasoline and found it full and ready, just as expected. He would have it no other way. In fact, he recalled exactly when he had last topped up the generator. It was three weeks ago. He had lain in bed at night wondering what was bothering him and realized that the generator was not full. That day, he had used it to power his log splitter, and had cleaved and stacked his firewood in orderly fashion to dry over the summer. Done with his chore, he had carelessly forgotten to refill the tank. The thought nagged at him so ceaselessly that he was forced to rise in the middle of the night and top up the tank from the red plastic container in the barn.

Doug pulled the cord and took joy in its smooth humming. "First yank," he proudly told Bramble.

The 1,500-watt spotlight was inside the barn. Doug brought it out, plugged it into the generator and switched it on. "Cripes," he griped. "Brighter than I thought." The light was electric-white and blindingly brilliant. Bramble rose from sitting, stared up at the light, then backed away and sat again.

Doug reentered the barn to gather a can of paint and the new paintbrush he had bought specifically for this task. Stepping outside, he noticed several giant fluttering shadows on the side of the barn, and paused. Bramble's long white snout was pointed in that direction, her eyes intensely studying the flickering shadows. She whined as the shadows pulsed and strobed. Moths beating themselves off the light.

Doug bent and opened the paint can lid with the edge of his screwdriver, carefully laid the lid aside, and dipped in the brush tip. This was quality paint. Thick and rich. None of that cheap stuff that peeled off in a year. He stroked the paint on one dry slat and marvelled at how smoothly it covered the wood. It'll be good as new, he assured himself. No one could ever accuse him of being lazy. That was for sure. With pride, he nodded fiercely to himself and continued stroking on the fresh paint.

"How's it looking, Bramble?"

The dog continued watching the flickering shadows multiply in numbers, then whined again, casting her eyes toward sea.

"What's the matter, girl?" Doug asked as the silhouettes of insects thickened, drawn by the tens of thousands to the intense throb of light. Soon, every glint was blocked by a swell of black shudders, and — in the place of brilliance — a wall of shadows wavered portentously, engulfing the side of the barn.

-๑๐

When the bus arrived at the hospital, after passing an endless string of cars racing in the opposite direction, the anticipated time of impact stood at fifteen minutes. The seven houses French and Tommy had visited along the road out of Bareneed contained no civilians. Two transport choppers, a Labrador and a Sikorsky, were loading female patients at the edge of the hospital parking lot. The noise of the chopper rotors smothered all sound in French's headset. There was a sense of urgency in the patients' progression, yet no sense of panic. Moving in a systematic fashion, they appeared merely perplexed.

"Have the patients with the breathing disorder been transported yet?"

No reply. French listened, waited, pressed his earpiece tighter to his ear. Tommy stood beside the bus, studying the sick, in their slippers and pyjamas or nightgowns, as they filed toward the choppers. Some wheeled IV stands beside them, others carried magazines or books. One pale young woman wore headphones and clutched a portable music machine to her belly. At the entrance of the parking lot, which intersected with the main road, two soldiers were directing the progression of cars awaiting exit.

"Who is out there? This is Lieutenant-Commander French."

Watching the line, Tommy became agitated. He shuffled around in a wide, then tighter and tighter, circle before veering off toward the hospital.

French followed on Tommy's heels, hearing the faint voice: "No, sir. Patients with the breathing disorder occupy the sixth floor. We're presently at the fifth."

"Copy." He swerved around a string of ambulances, doors open, loading patients, and neared the emergency doors. "What about the women?"

Silence. He entered the hospital behind Tommy, who hurried through the empty waiting room, his shoes sloshing and his clothes still dripping while he held his soaken pulpy sketch pad to his chest.

"I repeat, what about the women?"

They rode the elevator to the sixth floor and, stepping off, Tommy pointed ahead to a room at the end of the corridor. He kept his arm raised as his pace quickened while French increased his trot to a jog to keep up. They passed a number of people being led by soldiers and a row of occupied beds pushed to one side of the corridor. A tight squeeze to get by. As Tommy and French sped on, a matronly, flustered nurse gave them an anxious look.

"Not certain if the women have been transported, sir. There's a misunderstanding."

"Copy. What're you doing?" French called out to Tommy, who ignored the question and ducked into a room.

Immediately, Tommy found his place at one of the bedsides and watched over the man lying there. He began to talk earnestly to the man. French dragged a chair toward the centre of the room and called to Tommy, patting the seat. "Here's where you need to be, isn't it?"

Puzzled, Tommy watched French, then grinned his pointed grin and hastened toward the chair. He climbed up, hugging his soggy sketch book. Becoming more serious, he cleared his throat and watched from bed to bed, then spoke woodenly, as though acting in a play: "I were once out in me boat widt a fine blue sky above me, narry a forecast fer any swells. I were sitting dere widt a line overboard, jigging fer cod." He gave a brief encouraging smile as the pleasant memory appeared to fully visit him. During the pause in Tommy's tale, two heads listlessly turned toward him.

A few moments later, Tommy's smile faded and he stared worriedly down at his grey sneakers. "Den a blackness come over me. A shadow like sumtin' blockin' da warmt' from da sun. But dere were narry a cloud ta be seen. I heard da rushin' like a river in spring 'n I look over me shoulder ta see da sea rearin' up on da horizon. High as a mountain, t'was, 'n she were comin' upon me. I were starin' at she, 'n starin'. I'd never seen nuttin' like she before. I were sittin' in me boat 'n I could narry stand. From dat far away, she were like a force, pinnin' me ta me seat. 'Twere beyond me ta budge a muscle." By this time, the other four men in the beds had stirred, and turned their faces to intently watch Tommy. "I knew it were all over fer me. I watched da blackness comin' fast as anytin', roarin' closer, 'n den …" Tommy caught his breath as all eyes remained fixed on him "… it weren't dere no more. She were gone, b'ys. Gone …" Tommy's voice trailed off. The room was still, silent, save for the rising and ebbing hush of respirators. "I don't know where I were even … Was I upon da sea at all or were it just me imagination tryin' ta spook da cripes outta me?"

A few men grumbled or coughed, trying to speak up with the respirator tubes in their mouths; others nodded weakly. All eyes were fixed on Tommy as he stood upon his chair, his clothes dripping a whiff of seawater onto the floor, the puddle trickling in all directions to reach the metal bed legs. The men's eyes brightened as the scent found them. Moments later, four streams of amber shot through the windows, one entering the head of each man.

A voice in French's head said: "Tsunami losing momentum, sir. Energy output reduced to 20,000 KP. Wave slowed to forty-seven knots. Impact delayed by approximately ten minutes."

"Copy," he said, then asked Tommy: "Where else?"

Tommy leaped down off the chair and grinned emphatically, giving the men around him a stiff thumbs-up. He then led French into the room across the hall where some of the women had been confined, but the beds were deserted. Crisp sheets. Fluffed pillows.

"What happened to the patients?" French demanded of the matronly nurse who had arrived to inquire of their purpose.

"The army carted them away," she guardedly replied, taken aback by the quickness of French's tone. "Women went first. A while ago."

"Where're the rest of the men with the breathing disorder?"

"All along this corridor." The nurse leaned, indicating the row of doors. "We're prepping them for travel. No visitors now."

French tipped his head at Tommy, who entered the next room. Again, Tommy took his position up on a chair and wove another tale, one that seemed particular to the needs of the men in that room. And, again, in time, the men came back to themselves.

From his post in the doorway, French studied an old man in the bed nearest him. He noticed how the man was peering at Tommy, the old man's lips quivering, his fingertips twitching on the sheets. The blackness of his pupils, like two pools of black ink with a tiny spot of reflected light in each, consumed the man's eyes. A jerk of his head and his eyes appeared to brighten, the black retracting. Two pale blue irises. French looked toward the window: a trail of amber noiselessly gushed through the pane and entered the man's mouth.

The voice in French's headset reported, "Energy output 15,000 KP; thirty-nine knots. Impact delayed by another ten minutes. Point of impact now approximated at twenty-three, forty-seven, sir."

The old man gave a faint, glimmering smile, then shut his eyes with a nod of windswept affection.

"The sickness," French whispered in dismay, "is creating the wave. The spirits."

"Couldn't copy, sir."

Dumbly, French searched around and noticed that Tommy was absent. He paced out into the corridor and checked the next room, finding Tommy loftily propped up on a chair, now using his hands for dramatic effect while waving his ruined notepad around, reciting his tall tales with newfound bravado.

⌇

"If ye be a'scared, den ye be safe down 'ere." Miss Laracy hung the kerosene lamp from a nail on one of the support beams and stared into its warm, endearing light. The rafters, low as they were, forced Rayna to stoop for fear of striking her head, but Miss Laracy, standing at her full height, had no such worries. "If dat wave ventures fort', da water won't seep t'rough dose floorboards." She pointed overhead to reassure Rayna. "Dey're as t'ick as bricks and sealed with gum in da cracks. Dis house were built like a boat, by me fadder who were a boat builder. 'Tis made ta float. 'Twere floated ta dis very spot many year ago." Miss Laracy turned her eyes to a steamer trunk that sat beside a shelf full of bottled preserves, pickles, jams and jellys, on the worn clay floor.

"I'd rather wait for the helicopter. Upstairs. I can see then —"

"Give dat one a shove outta da way," Miss Laracy instructed Rayna.

"This trunk?"

"Yays, dat very one."

As Rayna bent and struggled to shove the blue, brass-strapped steamer trunk aside, Miss Laracy's eyes curiously scanned the beams overhead, listening. *Rescue*, she thought. *Truly a word fer fools.* She returned her attention to Rayna, who had budged the trunk a mere ten inches.

"'Tis 'eavy, no doubt. I used ta be down 'ere ta such an extent dat me fadder barred me frum visitin' da cellar." She gazed around, gratified to soak up the feeling of clay-cool enclosure and comfort. "Me fadder shoved dat steamer in place so I cudn't get ta wha' lays be'ind it. Da object o' me affection."

Grunting, Rayna gave another heave and a gap was opened up, revealing a polished wooden chest. "God, that's heavy," said Rayna, straightening and blowing out breath.

"Dat's me 'ope chest in dere," Miss Laracy revealed. "It be made outta rosewood by me fadder as well. Rosewood be a beauteous sort of wood. Rich 'n smood widt dramatic grains. Dat's what Uriah said o' it. He 'eard as much frum me fadder." Inclining toward it, she lovingly ran her hand over the top, stroking it twice, before carefully lifting the lid.

Inside, men's garments were stored. A navy-blue sweater, a number of handkerchiefs, and pairs of grey or brown trousers. All neatly folded. Miss Laracy slid a handkerchief into the flat of her palm, the embroidered corners limply hanging over the edge of her hand.

"I stitched dese 'kerchiefs fer Uriah." She raised the treasure so Rayna could see the fine details.

"Nice," said Rayna. She was distracted, her hands bunching together and unbunching. She twitched and watched the ceiling. "Was that — I heard a rumbling …"

"Ye needn't be worried yet," Miss Laracy guaranteed her. "Dere's no mortal danger will come ta ye dis evenin'." She laid the handkerchief to rest and nimbly lifted the navy-blue woollen sweater. Doing so, she let out a soft loving gasp. In a reverie of remembered pleasure, she brought the thick sweater to her nose and shut her eyes, sniffing the wool that contained the resin from her hands and the still-lingering scent of her tragically lost lover.

"Uriah's mudder bequeathed Uriah's clothes ta me, as I were 'is intended."

A noise was now evident overhead, a faint reverberation that carried through the wooden frame of the house. Immediately, Rayna wandered toward the stairs and paused there, waiting and holding out her hand.

Miss Laracy paid Rayna little mind. She took another sniff of the sweater and shut her eyes, holding the breath in, savouring it, her head swimming dizzily with rapture.

"We should go."

Coming back to herself, Miss Laracy opened her bewildered eyes and slowly exhaled the cherished breath. She then neatly folded the sweater, set it back in its exact place and patted it securely.

"That's the chopper," said Rayna, wiggling her fingers and edging up a few stairs toward the dark house above. "Come on, let's go."

"Nar ta worry." Miss Laracy shut the chest lid. Again, she slid her hand over the polished wood, cleaning the dust away. "Uriah," she whispered, staring a moment at the grains of wood, before reaching high to take down the lamp. In a wash of melancholy, she joined Rayna, who grabbed her hand and guided her up the steep, narrow stairs.

Miss Laracy glanced back into the darkening basement that grew blacker with their ascent and departure. "Wha's yer hurry," she muttered to Rayna.

Then again, in a voice so despondent and deeply unto itself it was barely audible: "Wha's yer hurry … ta be lured away?"

~◊~

Agatha had eaten all of her food and the water dish was dry. When Dr. Thompson hurriedly entered the kitchen, his cane bottom squeaking off linoleum, and shone the flashlight on the sorry state of affairs, he apologized profusely to Agatha. She meowed and her eyes glowed at him in reflection. He scooped up the chubby cat. At once, she pressed against him in pure fits of pleasure. Thompson directed the flashlight beam into the open bathroom door to find the toilet seat up.

"You've had your water then."

On his way back to the front door, preparing to flee with Agatha in one arm, Thompson was caught by a thought and halted himself. He spun to gaze around his living room and swept the flashlight beam over the still, almost ghostly, articles. Then he studied his watch.

"A few minutes yet," he mumbled. He paced to the kitchen, out into the back porch then down over the basement stairs, careful not to trip over the length of his cane. Reaching the wine cellar, he wondered aloud: "What to take?" He found a brim sack on the floor, dropped his cane, and, with one hand gripping the flashlight, perched Agatha on his shoulder. What were his favoured bottles? How could he possibly choose? He shone the flashlight on the labels, all so elegantly and austerely designed. Pure refinement. PORT, CABERNET, MERLOT, BORDEAUX and BRANDY.

Agatha purred close to his ear while he concentrated on his efforts, meticulously laying glass against glass until his actions sped up and he was filling the sack with the swiftness of a looter. Done, he gathered the material of the sack in one hand and hoisted it, groaning while he slung it over his shoulder. The cane would have to stay where he had dropped it. It was the cane or the sack. He shone the flashlight ahead of himself and limped for the stairs, bottles clinking at his back, feeling as if he were pillaging a stranger's house.

Upstairs, in the refrigerator, there were three types of cheese: brie, harvarti with dill, and his salty blood-pressure accelerating favourite, feta.

He found his Russian caviar and a box of fine wheat-and-sesame crackers he had purchased just last week in a specialty shop in St. John's. If he was to be holed up in a cabin on Horsechops, he would require nourishment. He filled a plastic bag with edibles and dropped it in the sack.

"No, down off my head, Agatha," said Thompson, heaving the sack over his shoulder again and hobbling out into the driveway where his four-wheel drive was idling with its headlights blazing.

Once in the vehicle, with Agatha seated comfortably in the passenger seat, Thompson said: "Oh, Agatha, oh, my darling little pussy, what a feast we will have. What a dining extravaganza." He spun his head toward the back seat, where the sack had been secured in a seat belt, and took a solid sniff of the air. With a moan, he shifted the gearshift in reverse and glanced at the clock on his dashboard.

"How far up the road do we need to get ourselves," he wondered, licking his lips in anticipation, "before we can stop for a picnic under the stars?"

Miss Laracy watched, through the parted lace curtains, the flustered lit-up image of Rayna out in the yard, staring up at the helicopter's searchlight and shielding her face at the same time. The light grew brighter as it neared and began its gradual descent. Rayna's image throbbed whiter, glowing, until there was little definition left to her.

"It's the helicopter," Rayna shouted toward the front door, not knowing that Miss Laracy was peeking out.

The chopper set down in the middle of the road, and the spotlight swept toward Miss Laracy's window, brightly illuminating her through the glass so that she noticed her hand up to the curtain, the loose skin and the blue veins, the green sleeve of her housedress. Squinting, she backed away from the harsh pool of light. She turned up her nose, "Tryin' ta blind me widt yer voodoo." Then came a booming in the walls. The front door was flung wide open, allowing the sound of the rotors and whirring engine to fully invade the house.

Hearing the noise, Miss Laracy scurried toward the couch, where she sat and grabbed up her knitting. As Rayna entered the room, Miss Laracy shouted, "Shut dat friggin' door. Da rackets goin' ta bust me eardrums."

"Come on," Rayna called, out of breath.

Miss Laracy paid Rayna no mind. She pearled and stitched, then held up the white scarf to examine its length.

"You got to come now."

Miss Laracy continued ignoring the intrusion as the house grew noiser and shook on its foundation. When Miss Laracy raised her eyes again, Rayna was gone and Lieutenant-Commander French stood in her place. A fine, neat uniform and a beret to the rescue. That man meant business.

"Ye returned widt yer machinery," she called, battling the noise. Waving him nearer, she patted the cushion beside her and said: "Come in, me son. Come on in 'n get settled. Time fer a nice cup o' tea 'n a raisin bun? I'll put da kettle on."

French gravely shook his head. "No time."

Miss Laracy grinned and laughed, her gums sheening in the stretching sweep of the spotlight. "Now, dere's always time, skipper." Again, the spotlight caught her. "Tell dem buggers ta turn off dat light. I'm poisoned by da sight o' it. In dat wicked glare, I must look like sumtin' da cat dragged in."

"You look fine."

"Why, t'ank ye."

"We have to leave now. Otherwise, I can't guarantee your safety."

"Where's Rayna hid herself to?"

French tilted his head toward the front of the house. "In the chopper," he replied, without the slightest hint of impatience. He was all solid rock. Practical. A man's man, as they used to say.

"Where ye from anyway, buddy? I never asked."

"Burin."

Miss Laracy pearled and stitched, her knitting needles clicking. "Likely story. Yer no Newfoundlander." She peeked at him for reaction.

"It's no story." French allowed his eyes to roam for an instant. "Nice old house."

"It's me home."

"Come on, it's time to go." He gave a firm nod and glanced toward the window.

"Ah," she griped. "Narry interested."

"We've got about five minutes."

Miss Laracy shrugged. "Ye've got 'bout five minutes. I've got 'bout ten."

"Come on out into the yard and have a look. Just the yard." French stepped nearer and offered his hand. Miss Laracy stared at it, the big fingers, the rough skin. He wasn't living a cushy life. He used those hands plenty. She found her fingers reaching toward his and allowed herself to be drawn to her feet. At the speed of ascent, she gave a girlish giggle, then reached down with her free hand to grab up the photo album that rested on the coffee table. She felt a gush of pride at being led by the navy fellow. He was an officer and all, a man who could battle against insurmountable odds and step through the fire without a hair out of place. Not only that, he had his wits about him too. He had to have brains to be an officer. They entered the front yard, faced the noise and wind. Her and her man.

Letting go of French's hand, Miss Laracy pressed the photo album to her bosom with both palms as if to protect it from the elements.

The chopper remained parked in the middle of the road. Tommy and Rayna were in it, among a crowd of faces unfamiliar to Miss Laracy. Regardless, she waved amicably to them and they impatiently waved back, imploring her to come, cupping their hands around their mouths and calling.

French's steady eyes gazed toward the harbour. Miss Laracy looked there too. Blackness. No outline of land, only a vague inky shimmering. French pointed. "The land was there before I went into your house, now it's gone. You get what I mean?" He clasped hold of Miss Laracy's arm and began urging her ahead, but she pulled away and whacked him soundly in the chest with the photo album.

"Bugger off," she said. "I'm not gettin' in dat piece o' junk t'ingamajig."

French checked back toward the chopper. Sighing, he regarded Miss Laracy and, without warning, scooped her up in his arms and bolted toward the road.

"I can't leave you here," he said loudly.

"Den stay widt me 'n get soaked t'rough yer clothes," she muttered, fiercely kicking her legs. In the throes of activity, the photograph album slipped from her grip and dropped to the grass.

French said in a stricter voice: "Distance?"

"Wha'? Me photo album." She reached out, wiggling her fingers, but the opened pages were far away now.

"How soon?"

"'ow soon what?" Miss Laracy was still in his arms as he boarded the hollow of the chopper. Immediately, it began lifting off, giving her a sickening feeling in her gut.

"Ye made me drop me photograph album, ye rascal." She smacked at him with her palms and then with her small closed fists. "Set me upright, be a friggin' gentleman. Ye got da class o' a beggar."

French relented and stood Miss Laracy on her feet. She huffed and straightened her dress, then, casting a glance at the ground, leaped out before the machine was too far from the earth.

Steadying herself, she hurried to the spot where the photograph album lay open on the lawn. She snatched it up and hugged it soothingly.

There were shouts and calls to her as the helicopter hovered three feet above the road.

"Ye g'wan," she said with a swat of her hand. "Yer world's narry fit fer me."

-◊-

Chase set his keys beside the potted plant on the stand near the door, unhooked his belt and hung it on one of the wooden pegs, then stood for a moment to appreciate the feel of his home, the sensation of entering and resting, of blocking out the world, of safety and enclosure. The house was quiet, seemingly unoccupied. Bending to unlace his boots, he felt that each of his actions was somehow contrived, as though he was too aware, far too aware, of his movements. Yawning, he poked his head into the living room. Empty. In the corner, the television set was blank.

Chase took a breath, the smell of ash still lingering in his nostrils. He wandered down the dim hallway, past the little country-house night light gleaming faintly where it was plugged in above the heater. The carpet was soft beneath his socks and there was an enduring scent of Theresa in the air: part lotion, part medication. He passed his office door, stuck his head in to fully realize the whirring sound of the fan in his computer, the screensaver bouncing around the contained box in colourful waves. He thought of the photographs of murder victims he had saved in the folders on his hard drive. The victims' faces would no longer be turned away, facing the earth or twisted to the side, but would be watching him directly.

Crossing the office threshold, he sat at his desk and slid the mouse a few inches to the right, brought the screen to life. He clicked through the series of windows until he dug out the folder labelled "Stabbed," then clicked to open it, revealing rows of jpegs. Each was a picture of a murder victim who had been killed by blade. The pictures captured the indecency of each death, the specifics, the details, there for all eyes to study. The pictures stretched from a time when crime scene photographs had first been taken, up until present day. From black blood and white skin to vivid sloshes of colour.

Chase selected all items and clicked the "delete" option. Are you sure you want to delete these 143 items? Yes. Next, he opened the folder labelled "Shot" and deleted every person. "Bludgeoned," "Strangled," "Suicide," "Drowned"... All of them erased from his memory, then purged from the recycle bin. He remembered the little girl in the burning solar house. He remembered the ancient dead in the fish plant. Who was more real?

Standing, he clicked off his computer without shutting it down according to procedure. He moved toward the bedroom doorway, where he paused to watch over the full image of the bed. Theresa was sleeping beneath the covers. She might be dreaming of nothing, drugged into a void, or she might be dreaming horrible dreams, dreams with such obscene and violent images that she refused to repeat the specifics to Chase. He studied his wife. All of his words of reassurance and support had meant nothing to her. All of his love equalled zero. Theresa was in the grip of an illness that excluded him. Her mind was trapped in a darkness that he had lived and brought home to her. His work. His life's work was little more than a terminal fascination with death. His labour of death.

Stepping deeper into the still room, he approached Theresa's side of the bed and noticed the bottle of pills on the night table. He reached down for the bottle and closed his hand around it. He returned to the hallway and entered the bathroom, halted by his own reflection sliding by beside him. He turned to face the mirror. He needed a shave. He was haggard, seemingly old before his time. His uniform required laundering. It was dirty, stained. All of this was so unlike him.

I have done my duty, he told himself. *I have done my duty and I have neither failed nor succeeded. I have kept my small part of the world somewhere between good and evil. Haven't I? I have done my duty.*

Uncapping the bottle, he leaned toward the toilet and tilted the container, watching the tiny white pills tumble from the lip and drop into the toilet water. The pills floated there. He had expected them to dissolve but they were harder than he suspected, more resilient than his will. He flushed the toilet and watched as they were sucked down into the transparent swirl.

At the sink, he washed his hands then cupped his palms with cold water and splashed his face again and again. He raised a white towel from the rack behind him and dried his skin, expecting to see black stains on the cloth, but there was nothing. The material remained perfectly white.

Back in the bedroom, he did not bother undressing. He simply lay atop the blankets and sheets in his uniform, and held Theresa, cuddled in to her covered form and pressed his lips against the exposed skin at the nape of her warm neck. She did not stir. The only sound was that of her deep, even breathing.

At this moment, at this most desperate point in time, he held her tighter, hugged her fiercely, adored her more than he had ever thought possible, for there was no future left for either of them and this negation charged him with love.

-∾

Robin had begun smiling, although her eyes remained shut, her skin pallid.

"Robin?" Kim whispered, bending near and caressing the hair along her daughter's forehead. "Darling? It's Mommy. Robin?"

Robin's smile widened as Joseph took notice. He was still holding his daughter's hand. Glancing at Kim, his hopeful eyes caught sight of something over her shoulder. He stared in wonder. Kim turned to see pure darkness beyond the window.

A nurse hurried into the room. "We have to wheel her out now. The medevac helicopter's waiting." A few minutes ago, the same nurse had informed everyone in the room that Kim and Robin must leave at once, ahead of Joseph, but Kim had refused. They were evacuating the area for fear of a further outbreak of the breathing disorder.

"Now?" Kim asked.

"We have a minute," the nurse said hastily, then sprinted out of the room as Joseph stepped away from the bed. He went to the window and stood entirely still.

"Joseph?"

Her husband looked back at her and his face was pale and blank. From where she stood, she could see out the window to sea. The black wall of night seemed to glisten for a moment. Black fluidity. Then the shimmer grew brighter, catching vague reflections of moonlight.

"What's that?" Kim asked, pacing toward Joseph.

"I don't know."

Kim pressed close to the glass, her reflection, like Joseph's, vague and staring back at her, yet not substantial enough to impede her view of what lay beyond. A wall of water had stormed ashore from the east, blocking all light from the sky. It loomed over the road as it advanced, forcing Kim to step back as the liquid darkness swept by, barely washing the windows of the hospital, the outer regions like a giant aquarium that had suddenly been filled. As she gasped, her reflection trembled and the glass shuddered with noise.

Stumbling away, Kim raced toward Robin to protect her, to bend over her, to hold her. "No, no ..." She hugged tightly, her daughter's cheek against her cheek. She kissed Robin's skin, then tried lifting her from the bed, but the machinery connected to her body would not allow distance. Kim held her daughter in both her arms, a foot above the bed.

"It's passing," said Joseph while the glass shuddered more fiercely. He raised his hands to the pane and stared out. "I think it's passing by."

"Mommy?" came a girl's voice near Kim's ear.

"Robin!" Kim saw that Robin's eyes were open, watching her.

"Hi, Mommy."

"Robin. Oh sweetie?" Kim lowered her daughter's body back onto the bed.

"Daddy?"

"Yes, Daddy's here. Over there."

Robin's eyes languidly shifted toward the window where Joseph stood, head bowed, hands pressed against the glass, as though keeping the blackness at bay.

⁓◊

French's body was a tangle of buckling urges. Struggling to keep himself from leaping out of the chopper and grabbing Miss Laracy, he braced his hands against the steel of the doorway with Tommy and Rayna to either side of him. One of his boots was held over the edge, hesitantly in the air. There was nothing beneath it. He had to pull it back. Frantically, he searched around the chopper for a harness, shoving people aside. Finding it, he slung it over his head and beneath his arm, then yanked the tether to the required length. If he jumped, the tether would pull him back once he had hold of Miss Laracy.

A voice in his headset said: "There's no time, sir." French shot a look toward the pilot, who was eyeing him, shaking his head, pointing his thumb at the ground. "You'll pull us down, sir."

French surveyed the faces around him. They were watching Miss Laracy, no doubt willing her nearer or farther away.

"Go," a young man shouted at the pilot. A plump woman tried grabbing the pilot's shoulder but he leaned away.

Through the chopper windshield, the black wall could be seen no more than one hundred feet ahead. Two women screamed at the sight of it, while the young man shoved the plump woman aside and tried reaching for the pilot himself.

French cursed and gritted his teeth, fighting to keep order. He wanted to shout, *Lower the chopper. Lower it now.* But he could not. The others would die as the wave swept in, knocking the chopper out of the sky like a toy and drowning them all.

The chopper's spotlight shifted unevenly over the yard where Miss Laracy stood, facing out to sea with her photograph album clutched to her chest. Her face was tilted back as if she might be admiring the mist from a sweet summer's rain.

Port de Grave had either disappeared or was blocked from sight. The wave was now entering the harbour, about to collide with the headland.

"Awaiting orders, sir," said the pilot's strained voice in French's head.

French checked the windshield. The wave was no more than sixty feet away. He looked down to the ground, braced his hands harder against the steel doorway frame, was about to jump.

"Sir? Orders, sir."

"Higher," French finally burst out, although he meant "lower," the command paining every nerve and muscle in his body. Lower, lower, lower.

All eyes, most of them squinting with fear, were fixed on Miss Laracy as the chopper rose above her, twenty feet, twenty-five …

The old woman had dropped her photo album and thrown open her arms, holding them wide in a gesture of embracing welcome. Above the panicky shouts from within the chopper, French caught the hint of a melody, a few strings of stray words: "… girl on shore … tear will shed … who lies on da ocean bed …"

"Higher," he shouted, then bit into his tongue, bit into it as if to chew it off, as the wall of black water surged into Miss Laracy, not knocking her over, but simply causing her to vanish. Flooding the space directly beneath the chopper, the water rose higher until it lapped at the hull. There was more screaming as the occupants clutched at one another and scrambled back against the far wall.

"Higher," French roared, tasting blood in his mouth, and the others joined in, chanting: "Higher, higher …"

-⟋⟍-

Tommy covered his ears with his hands. Rayna held tightly to his chest, forcing her weight back against him. Tears were blurring the colours that Tommy saw beneath him in the close water, the colours that had been clinging to Miss Laracy and now glowed and spread through the sea, leaking like pigment until they twinkled amber and shot toward the east.

The black water rose as quickly as the chopper, spilling into the floor as the occupants hopelessly kicked at it, desperately trying to drive it out. As the water flooded in, the rotor engine whined under the strain. Soon, the chopper was floating, a mechanical creature stuck and bobbing, wanting to leap into the air. The occupants continued kicking and pressing harder against the far wall as the chopper rode in the current of the wave, about to sink, trying to rise, its engine whirring and grinding as water sloshed around the interior until Tommy smelled smoke and thought there might be fire.

The painful noise of the engine mounted, louder, shriller. The craft shook violently, metal grinding as though it might rip in two, until, with a bucking jerk, it commenced tilting on its side, the open door dipping deeper into the sea.

Everyone shouted and screamed as if with one terrified voice. Tommy seized hold of Rayna, fearing, like the others, that the chopper was going under as it tipped on a greater incline, kicked and bucked, the rotor seeming to jar and slow before the craft jumped sideways, struggling to rise from whatever gripped it, then yanked free, rose higher, spilling the gushing water from the compartment and forcing the occupants to clutch at the strapping, their feet dangling toward the door, as the chopper lifted off on a seemingly impossible angle.

Tommy burst out laughing as the chopper ascended, the water chasing after it, rushing higher, again prodding the bottom of the craft, until the hull was only a foot above the black water. All eyes watched down through the opening as the water level created a wider gap on its own, shrinking and shrinking, until distant trees on the hill toward the west were once again revealed and the water commenced drawing back, eventually retracting fully to where it belonged.

Lips were kissing Tommy's cheek. They belonged to Rayna. He blushed and chuckled while keeping his eyes on the ground to make certain it was all over. There were no creatures in the harbour now, only the dark violence of the sea itself in its plainest form. And there was Bareneed, changed and yet the same, the peaks of its dark houses arranged around the bay, the white boats remaining largely untouched.

High above it all, Tommy, Rayna, Lieutenant-Commander French and the others stared down in wonder, watching the gleaming land and houses reappear beneath full moonlight. The beaming shades of the animals in the forests. Blues and greens and browns. The trees, washed clean, now aglow with majestic colours.

Even in the darkness, Tommy could tell the trees by their colours, the faint pink of the maples, the golden yellow of the evergreens, and the brightest pink of all radiating from the fragrant flowers of the burgeoning lilac trees.

EPILOGUE

As told by Robin Harvey (née Blackwood) to her grandchildren: Jordan, Katherine, and Emma Sarah

The fish plant, and the remembered or unknown dead who had occupied it, had been washed out to sea by the unearthly force of the tidal wave. The following day, the sea was a calm, even blue in the mollifying morning sun. The tidal wave had uprooted trees and fences, ripped houses from their foundations, spun them on various angles and set them down in unfamiliar locations. The tidal wave had flipped cars onto their sides or upside-down and pulverized old unstable barns to splinters.

Contrary to expectations, not one boat had been lost or upturned, and fish were discovered overflowing in the holds of every sea vessel. Fish were also sighted inland, tail-flapping in trees and in fields, in backyards and inside houses. The fish were of various species, yet each one was identifiable. They had managed to find their ways into cupboards, beds and toilet bowls.

Following the tidal wave, those afflicted with the breathing disorder had fully recovered, as if the coming water had somehow absolved them of their ills. As the adults returned, children flocked to their parents, welcoming them home with open arms. No one knew for certain what had caused the illness and what had taken it away.

The first order of business was providing shelter for all the returning Bareneed residents. Houses were desperately in need of repairs. Electrical crews worked around the clock to restore electricity and thus return life in the community to normal. It was a tall order. Power lines had been torn from their poles, tangled and hauled out to sea, with a great number of poles snapping off and trailing after the wires like twigs.

The residents of Bareneed settled in and existed by candlelight, oil and kerosene lamp. Generators were donated by one large manufacturer, yet the machines remained largely unused. Members of the community cooked on wood stoves, or on open fires circled with beach rocks in their back-yards. The glow of orange flames on the faces at night heartened ardent fellowship as the people gathered and exchanged stories of the current disaster and disasters that had preceded this one.

It took two and a half months before the missing power poles were replaced and the power lines restrung.

On the seventy-seventh day following the coming of the tidal wave, the electricity was switched back on. The media covered the event as a follow-up to the story they had labelled: "Great Big Wave."

The residents of Bareneed had grown so accustomed to functioning under the warm glow of lamplight that they stared at the pristine sterile quality of the electric lights in awe. Some shed tears, for reasons they could not explain. Some welcomed the light, praising its ease, while others felt as if a fundamental serenity had been faithlessly conquered.

"'Twas a terribly strange beauty," one old-timer commented before flicking off the master switch on his power panel for good.

In the days to come, many in Bareneed switched off their lights and reverted to lamplight and wood stove. Stories were told of hardships overcome while children sat around and listened in wide-eyed wonder. The residents of Bareneed returned to the sea as the fish were gradually replenished. In time, every last person reverted to lamplight and wood stove, and a special sitting of council was convened to order the removal of the new power lines and poles from the community.

Deep into the night, the community remained in darkness, lit only by starlight, moonlight, and, from the houses of the residents, the candle gleams of spirits wandering up and down the stairs, once again safely sheltered at home.

And, for generations to come, grandmothers and grandfathers sat their grandchildren upon their knees and told the story of the time when there was an absence of spirits. They told the story of how the creatures that once dwelt solely in the darkest depths of the sea rose to show themselves. They told the story of the time that the people of Bareneed forgot how to breathe, until they came to recognize who they truly were and, through the turmoil of calamity, reclaimed their lives as their blessed own.

ACKNOWLEDGMENTS

I would like to extend a special thank you to the Writer in Residence Program at Memorial University in St. John's, Newfoundland. During my term at Memorial, I was able to rewrite, and conclude research on, this book. Also, thank you to Janet Power for helping to determine the novel's tone and direction. As with most of my books, bits and pieces of the stories contained within were stolen from my parents. Without them and their tales, this would have been an entirely different novel.